Hundreds of
reflecting the m
from the shadow
back only by the will of the antlered thing before her—
neither man nor beast, but something far older.

"You are mine, Hweilan. You were always mine."

FOR WHAT SHE WANTS

"What is the one thing you desire most?"

"Vengeance," she said without thinking.

"Truth at last. But know this: The Master is not one to bargain. You do not make demands of the Master of the Hunt. Obey him, or do not. There is no middle ground."

AND FOR WHAT SHE MUST BECOME

"She's trying to make me into a beast," said Hweilan. She'd been raised in a household of knights, to whom honor was more precious than life. To them, battle was an art, could even be a sacred act of devotion. To Ashiin, killing seemed a primal instinct, a need, no different than hunger or fear. To Ashiin, being a killer was not a matter of doing, but being, and Hweilan feared that she could never become that.

"She is not." Gleed turned away from the iron cauldron he had been stirring. "A beast cannot be made, stupid girl. A beast is woken. No. Ashiin is not making you into a beast. She is trying to beat the scared, spoiled little girl out of you so that when the beast does come—and it will; it will—a little of the woman might survive."

CHOSEN OF NENDAWEN

Book I
The Fall of Highwatch

Book II
Hand of the Hunter

Book III
Cry of the Ghost Wolf
December 2011

ALSO BY MARK SEHESTEDT

THE WIZARDS

Frostfell

Slavers stole her son and she would sacrifice everything to get him back. In the uncaring, frozen north, will it be enough?

THE CITADELS

Sentinelspire

With the powers of an archdruid at hand, the mad master of the fortress of Sentinelspire will bring death to more than just his enemies—he will call down doom on all of Faerûn.

MARK SEHESTEDT

FORGOTTEN REALMS

Chosen of Nendawen, Book II

HAND OF THE HUNTER

Chosen of Nendawen, Book II
Hand of the Hunter

©2010 Wizards of the Coast LLC

All characters in this book are fictitious. Any resemblance to actual persons, living or dead, is purely coincidental.

This book is protected under the copyright laws of the United States of America. Any reproduction or unauthorized use of the material or artwork contained herein is prohibited without the express written permission of Wizards of the Coast LLC.

Published by Wizards of the Coast LLC. FORGOTTEN REALMS, DUNGEONS & DRAGONS, WIZARDS OF THE COAST, and their respective logos are trademarks of Wizards of the Coast LLC in the U.S.A. and other countries.

All Wizards of the Coast characters, and the distinctive likenesses thereof are property of Wizards of the Coast LLC.

Printed in the U.S.A.

The sale of this book without its cover has not been authorized by the publisher. If you purchased this book without a cover, you should be aware that neither the author nor the publisher has received payment for this "stripped book."

Cover art by: Jaime Jones
Map by Robert Lazzaretti
First Printing: December 2010

9 8 7 6 5 4 3 2 1

ISBN: 978-0-7869-5627-2
ISBN: 978-0-7869-5812-2 (e-book)
620-24746000-001-EN

U.S., CANADA,	EUROPEAN HEADQUARTERS
ASIA, PACIFIC, & LATIN AMERICA	Hasbro UK Ltd
Wizards of the Coast LLC	Caswell Way
P.O. Box 707	Newport, Gwent NP9 0YH
Renton, WA 98057-0707	GREAT BRITAIN
+1-800-324-6496	Save this address for your records.

Visit our web site at www.wizards.com

Acknowledgments

Thanks to Ed Greenwood, for creating such a vast world for the rest of us to play in.

Special thanks to the Cocktail Slippers for streaming their albums on their Myspace page. During many late nights of writing, you were my soundtrack. If the royalty checks are kind, I will buy the albums. Promise. And if I ever save Brooke Shields from drowning, you will be the band playing my birthday party!

And extra special thanks to Erin Evans for being such a great editor, equal parts encouragement and threatening the breaking of fingers. Several of the really cool ideas in the story were Erin's ideas, and I'll never tell which are which.

PART ONE

THE GIANTSPIRES

CHAPTER ONE

Toril
The Giantspires

NIGHT CAME QUICKLY TO THE MOUNTAINS, AND Darric wanted their camp secured by dark. They chose a small valley—little more than a wide spot in the path, really—but it had a swath of trees hugging a cliff wall that would provide shelter from the wind and help to hide the light from their fires. Midsummer though it was, they were in the mountains west of Narfell, and a bone-chilling cold settled in with the dark. After picketing the horses near the cliff wall, those men not on watch huddled in their blankets close to the fires.

Darric sat by the fire and tried to rub the soreness out of his legs. For two days they'd been on mountain trails too treacherous for riding, so every man walked, leading his mount. They'd already had to put down one horse because of a broken leg. A sad loss, but it had added to their meat stores.

Darric rubbed his knuckles into a knot that had taken up residence a few inches above his right ankle. All this . . . all this for one girl. He had railed at his father, citing friendship and honor and justice for the fallen of Highwatch. But really, this was all about a girl he hadn't seen in years. And yet in all those years since, not a day had gone by he hadn't thought of her.

"The scouts are back, my lord."

The words brought Darric out of his reverie. His mind had been wandering. Not good. Not in their current situation. If they were to have any chance of getting out of this alive, they all had to stay sharp.

Valsun stood before him, helmet in his hand. In his early fifties, he was the oldest in their company—the only tried and true man that Darric had managed to talk into defying Duke Vittamar and coming with Darric to Narfell. Valsun was one of the finest knights in Vittamar's service. But looking at him in the dim firelight, his tabard dirty and worn from days of hard travel, he looked much as the rest of them: a vagabond. The bits of mail peeking from under his cloak and the sword riding his hip hinted at the veteran warrior he was.

"They've found something?" said Darric.

Valsun shrugged, then spat into the dust. "I'm not sure, my lord. The Nar demands to talk to you and no other."

"Ah, well," Darric said as he pulled his boot on. "Feet were getting cold anyway."

They walked to the edge of the camp, just at the barest edge of the firelight, to where their scouts waited under the watchful eyes of two men—one a sellsword Darric had hired on their last day in Damara. The other was Darric's adopted brother Mandan—easily the biggest man in their company.

Just shy of seven feet and with a frame that made the most hardened blacksmith look soft as new butter, Mandan probably weighed more than both the scouts put together. He dressed in the armor, tabard, and cloak of a Damaran knight. At home, he usually kept himself clean shaven, but they had been on the road many days, and unlike the others who looked a few days past scraggly, Mandan's beard was already full. His eyes, a brown so light that they were almost yellow, shone out from under thick brows, and they had the odd tendency to reflect the firelight, which unnerved many of the newcomers to their company. While most of the men carried a sword or spear, cradled in Mandan's arms was an iron-banded club thick as a man's arm. At tournaments, Darric had seen other knights mock Mandan and his club. But their mouths closed when they saw him shattering broadswords.

Neither scout seemed particularly bothered by the Damarans' mistrustful gazes. On one side of the path crouched Gyul, elbows on knees. No mistaking him for a human. His leathery skin had an orange cast. His eyes, which seldom opened more than a lazy squint, were yellow, and sharp canines thrust out of his bottom lip. He spoke broken Common, and fluent Damaran and Nar, but in this part of the world that wasn't all that unusual for a hobgoblin.

His companion stood beside him, leaning on his spear. Urdun. The man had the features of a Nar—dark skin, straight black hair that hung down his back, and a slight cant to the eyes that showed West was giving way to East. But in dress he looked more hobgoblin than human—a combination of coarse leather, fur, and metal. How an outcast Nar and a hobgoblin who claimed to be Razor Heart clan came to be such steadfast companions . . . well, Darric knew there was surely a story there. But he had more pressing concerns.

"What have you found?" Darric asked them.

The hobgoblin and Nar exchanged a glance. "Me and Gyul go no farther," said Urdun.

"What?"

"We agreed to take you through the mountains by other paths than the Gap," said Urdun. He pointed to the two peaks before them—one high and sharp, the other no less sharp but half the height of its companion. "Through that pass. Turn south, and you will be a hard day's ride from Nar-sek Qu'istrade."

"Then why—?"

"To go any closer to Nar sek Qu'istrade"—the man grabbed some sort of relic made of bone that hung from his neck, kissed it, and finished—"is to risk your soul. Things now haunt Highwatch that mortals dare not challenge. It is a cursed place. Go if you wish, but you go without Gyul and me. We have fulfilled our bargain."

With that, Gyul stood, and the two of them started walking back westward through the line of men and horses.

"Stop!" said Valsun. "I *command* both of you—"

"No," said Darric. "Let them go."

Mandan tore his gaze off the retreating scouts and glared at Darric. "Are you mad?"

"They fulfilled their bargain. We're here. We need them no longer."

"We don't *need* them?" said Mandan. "How are we supposed to get home?"

"There are scouts in Narfell." Darric forced a confidence into his voice he did not feel. "And if not, we know the way now, eh?"

Darric clapped Mandan on the back, and they headed back to the fire. But he saw the look Mandan and Valsun exchanged.

• • ◉ • •

"What do you think he meant?" said Valsun later. "About Highwatch being cursed?"

Valsun, Mandan, and the wizard were the only three who shared Darric's fire. The wizard, a youngish westerner named Hureleth, was not Damaran, and he spoke the language with a heavy accent. Darric had found him in Merkurn, just one step ahead of the hangman's noose. Hureleth had been only too happy to join up with them. Valsun didn't trust him. And truth be told, Darric didn't either. But he had to admit that without him they never would have escaped the last raid two days back.

Hureleth snorted into his cup. "Do not worry yourself about such things. Nar are barbarians and far too . . . what is the word? Supple stitches?"

"Superstitious," said Valsun.

"Yes, thank you," said Hureleth. "Superstitious. As for this Nar's hobblegob friend . . ."

"Hobgoblin," said Mandan.

"Hobgoblin, yes. Well, Highwatch knights terrified them for years. Nothing new is there."

"Vandalar and his knights rule Highwatch no more," Valsun told him, though he watched Darric as he spoke.

"*If* the rumors are true," said Darric.

The wizard chuckled into his cup, then said, "When one man says a thing"—he shrugged—"truth? lie? Who knows? When many people say a thing, it is a rumor. But when *every* people say a thing, bet your gold there."

• • ⊚ • •

Sleep was only a few breaths away from Darric when the horses began to whicker, stamp, and pull at their pickets. Darric stood and threw off his blankets, as did Mandan, his massive club in one hand. Valsun sat up a moment later.

"What is it?"

"The horses," said Darric. "Something's spooked them. Wake that damned wizard." He unbuckled his cloak and let it fall to the ground. Midnight cold bit into him, but his sword arm was free.

Others had begun stirring as well. The campfires were still flickering, and by their light Darric saw one of the men, sword in hand, moving off to check on their mounts.

"De-*sist*!"

Darric turned to see the wizard slap at Valsun's boot, which was nudging his ribs.

"Here," said Mandan, "like this." With one hand he grabbed the wizard's ankle, blankets and all, and lifted, dangling the wizard upside down a good foot or more off the ground.

"Smoking Hells!" Hureleth shrieked as he tried to untangle himself from his blanket and cloak. "Unhand me!"

Mandan set the wizard's head and shoulders gently on the ground, then dropped the rest. "He's awake now."

"Awake and bruised!" said Hureleth. "What is the meaning of—?"

"Quiet," said Darric. "Something's spooked the horses."

The wizard sat up, still clutching his blankets around him. "We are less than a day from the steppe. Probably just wolves."

Mandan lifted his head and inhaled deeply through his nose. "No," he said. "It isn't."

From the edge of the trees where the sentries kept watch came a cry—a scream that ended all too abruptly.

"Ah," said Hureleth. "Perhaps not wolves then."

Darric never saw the arrow before it hit him. A sound of air ripping, then something slammed into his chest. He wore two layers of clothing under his mail, and a tabard and coat on top of it all. The arrow bounced away, but it struck with enough force to knock him back a step.

The wizard stood, reached inside his vest, and when he removed his hand, the orb he held was alight with inner fire. Hureleth thrust his free hand forward. At a word, light churned from his fingers and formed a transparent red wall, slightly curved, in front of them. Three arrows struck it in quick succession, one of them shattering in a cloud of sparks. Two arrows flew over their heads from behind as their own archers returned a volley.

"Fools!" Valsun shouted. "Save your arrows till you see your targets!"

"Allow me," said the wizard. He thrust forth his hand holding the orb and spoke another incantation. Sparks flew out of the orb, spun around the wizard's arm, then shot outward, passing through his shield with a popping hiss like water thrown on hot iron. They struck a tree several yards away, and every branch and needle erupted in flame. It lit their campsite and the canyon for a hundred yards in every direction.

"Idiot," said Mandan. "You've just lit a beacon for anyone within ten miles!"

But Darric didn't think the wizard had even heard. By the light of the burning tree their attackers were clearly visible—long-haired men dressed in skins and leathers, spears and swords in hand. Hureleth laughed as shards of white light, nail-thin but each as long as a knight's lance, shot from the pulsing orb in his fist. When one struck a man, he went down screaming, clothes and skin giving off thick smoke.

After the first few went down, the others realized the danger and took cover behind the trees. A few farther back loosed arrows, but none could penetrate the wizard's shield.

The screaming of men and horses had become such a constant that Darric put them in the back of his mind to concentrate on the attack. And so when the first horse ran past them, his first thought was that the men behind them had organized a charge.

"Stop!" he called out. The trees were too thick to make a mounted charge effective. Then he noticed that the horse was riderless. Turning, he saw that their mounts had broken their picket line and were fleeing in every direction. The horses seemed frightened of the wizard's shield and gave it a wide berth, but Darric saw one of his men run down.

"Let them go!" Valsun shouted, then quieter so only Darric could hear, "No help for it now."

"Back to the trees," said the wizard, though he kept his gaze fixed on the fight. "Shield will not be lasting much longer."

Together the four of them backed toward the cover of the nearest trees. Hureleth held the shield, but even Darric, who had no knowledge of magic, could see its light dimming, and the last arrow to strike it stuck there a moment before falling to the ground.

Darric turned. The light from the wizard's spells and the burning tree painted dark shadows against the cliff. A flash of light as Hureleth cast another shard from his palm, and in the sudden white-brightness Darric saw it—

A large object falling down the cliff face. Something heavy crashed through the branches of the brush nearest the cliff, and Darric felt his chest tighten. If their attackers had gained the height, they could hurl rocks down on Darric and his company.

"Beware above!" he shouted. "They—"

But his breath caught in his throat. Whatever had fallen from the height and struck with bone-breaking force was standing up. It rose in the shadow cast by a tree, and Darric could see only the outline of its shape—man-sized, but hunched over and swaying as if it was having trouble keeping its feet.

One of Darric's men had been hiding behind the tree. The man charged, blade held high. The two shapes merged. Darric squinted, trying to make out what was hap—

A strong hand grabbed the collar of Darric's coat and pulled him to the ground behind a tree.

"Watch out, my lord!" came Valsun's voice. "Wizard's shield is gone. He—"

A shriek cut off his words. Men had been screaming since the attack began—taunting the attackers, calling those wounded in the initial attack or by the horses, shouting words of encouragement to Hureleth. This drowned out all that.

As a child, Darric had been playing in the courtyard outside the kitchens when one of the dogs tripped a maid carrying a pot of boiling water. She'd pitched forward, spilling the boiling water all over the dog and down the back of the head cook. The shriek of the cook and the dog was one of the few sounds that had been forever seared into Darric's brain. He'd been no more than four at the time, and for months after he'd woken from a nightmare with that sound echoing down the corridors of the crumbling dream. It embodied everything that surprise and utter, complete, mind-numbing agony ought to sound like. Without a doubt, it had been the most awful sound he'd ever heard. Until now.

Valsun had been holding Darric down, covering his lord with his own body. But he turned away at the sound, and Darric sat up. Together they watched one of their men bound past them, shrieking as he ran.

Make him stop! Darric's mind screamed, and he'd half-opened his mouth to give the words voice when he saw why the man was screaming.

The man's right arm was gone from the elbow down. Blood pulsed from it like a fountain spout, and by the bits of ragged cloth, skin, and muscle Darric saw—in that brief instant, no matter how hard he tried, he could not look away—he knew that no blade had taken the man's arm. It had been torn off.

The horror of that had just sunk in when their campsite was lit by another flash from the wizard's spell. In the harsh white light Darric saw the man's face—or what was left of it. One eye, white and round as the waxed winter moon, stared out from a mass of blood, ravaged skin, and here and there—oh, gods, yes it was true—the ivory glow of bone. His other eye was gone, as was most of his scalp.

"What could have—?" Valsun managed, then they both saw it coming at them.

The thing had the semblance of a man. A Damaran even. It wore the uniform and mail of a Damaran knight, though the cloth was torn and soiled. Its hair was cropped short, like a knight's. But the eyes . . .

Darric could find nothing human in them. Just a blackness, empty but somehow still alive. It was not the empty of nothingness. More like the void of hunger, of want, of lust. A fire lurked in the very center of those twin black orbs, and Darric knew instinctively that it was not a reflection. Something hot and hungry burned behind those eyes. Some famine that would stop at nothing to feast.

"Behind us!" Darric called, and pushed himself to his feet. Valsun tried to pull him back down, but Darric shrugged him off and called, "Wizard, behind us, damn you! Now! *Now!*"

From some part of his mind that still held on to reason, Darric heard the wizard laugh—actually *laugh!*—and then the attackers were among them, steel and spears striking at Darric's company. Swinging his club in a wide arc, Mandan shattered two spears and one skull—and after that none would come near him. The rest of the Damarans struck back when they could, for most had not yet seen the horror that walked among them.

Another flash, and a spear of light shot over Darric's right shoulder—he actually felt the heat of its passing, even through all the layers of his clothes—then it struck the thing advancing on them. The bolt struck it square in the chest. Clothes and flesh and bone burned away like parchment in fire, but still the thing came on, its eyes fixed on Darric.

Three more steps . . .

Darric brought his blade around. A clumsy blow. One Valsun would have berated him for. No grace. No thought for counterstrike. No balance. Just raw force behind sharp steel. Darric knew if he missed he'd find himself flat on his back, staring at the sky.

His sword hit the thing where its shoulder met its neck. A bit of skin and soft flesh covering a thick net of muscle over bone. Darric's blade cut through them all, sending a shock up both his arms, even rattling his teeth.

His eyes locked on the thing's face, saw the lips peel back. Not in pain. It was pure, gleeful malice. Even with a yard of steel lodged in its neck, its left fist shot out, striking Darric's double-handed grip on the sword. It felt like a smith's hammer hitting him, breaking Darric's grip. Darric fell forward, rolling into his foe.

It was like hitting a wall. And then Darric was in the thing's grip, being pulled upward. The thing's eyes narrowed to slits, which made their inner fire seem all the more intense. Its hands were iron strong. They squeezed Darric's arms into his ribs and kept squeezing. Darric screamed and kicked at its shins and knees, then drove his knee into the crotch. His captor didn't even flinch.

The thing gave Darric a quick shake, back and forth just once, but with enough force that Darric's teeth clamped shut over his tongue, and he tasted blood. He stopped struggling and looked up, afraid that one more shake like that would break his neck.

The thing opened its mouth and inhaled, taking in a deep draft of air, tasting it. A shiver passed through the thing's entire body—so strong that Darric felt it in his bones, so sudden and fierce that the thing's skin actually rippled. It was like watching a cocoon in the final moments before the moth tore through.

The thing looked down at the yard of steel imbedded in its shoulder. Not with pain or concern. Just an odd sort of curiosity. It released Darric's left shoulder and grabbed its neck.

"Be still, little mouse," it said, and again the fetid breath washed over Darric, so strong that it made his eyes water. "Be still or I snap your neck. It's better . . . so much better if you're still alive for me."

Still alive? Darric's mind seized at the words. For what?

The thing released his other arm and used the free hand to wrench the sword out of its shoulder. Darric hard the snap of steel working its way through shattered bone, and heard the sucking sound of the skin and muscle clinging to the sword, but there was no surge of blood when the weapon broke free. It was as if no heart beat in the thing's chest. It was only then that Darric's mind seized on the obvious—

Call for help, you fool! But he could hear the clash of steel on steel, and from somewhere that seemed all too far away the sound of Valsun shouting, "Help him! Damn you! Help—!" And then more steel and screams.

The thing lowered Darric until his knees rested on the ground, then it planted the point of Darric's own sword against his cheek.

"Scream," it said.

"No," Darric said through clenched teeth. With the grip crushing just under his jaw, it was all he could manage. His mind came up with a dozen defiant curses, but he didn't have the breath for one of them.

"How will you scream, I wonder," said the thing, "if I cut you here—and here?" It ran the edge of the blade down

Darric's cheek, first one side, then the other, just hard enough to break the skin. "If I unhinge your jaw, are you strong enough to scream while I eat your tongue? Or will you swoon like a tavern drunkard?"

Darric renewed his punches and kicks, aiming for every vulnerable spot he'd been trained to strike.

"Ahhh . . ." The thing twitched, blinked, and again Darric was struck with the image of something trying to break out of a cocoon. "I can feel your heart beating. So fast. Hammering. You are scared, yes?" Its eyes opened wide, glistening black eyes with hearts of fire, and looked down at Darric. "Good. Fear makes the blood run fast. Makes—"

Darric was looking right at the thing when the arrow hit it. A perfect strike, missing the top of Darric's head by less than a foot, then hitting the soft flesh between the thing's throat and chest, going in deep. The sheer force made the thing stumble back a step, but it didn't fall or loosen its grip on Darric's neck. Just stood there looking down at the black shaft of the arrow. The beginning of a snarl twisted the thing's lips.

But then a crack of green fire sparked along the black shaft of the arrow. No, Darric saw. Not a crack. The light expanded, like flame running along oil, and Darric could see that the fire traced a pattern of intricate runes all along the shaft.

"No!" The thing's eyes widened and it let Darric go. He hit the ground and forced air through his throat.

"No! No! No-no-no! N-n-no! N-n-n-n-n—!"

Darric heard genuine panic in the thing's voice. It grabbed the arrow with both hands. Close as he was, Darric heard the flesh *hiss* as if he'd grasped a branding iron fresh out of the coals.

The thing shrieked. It was a cry beyond sound, bypassing Darric's ears and raking down his spine like jagged fingernails on slate. It was beyond human, beyond anything he could have imagined.

The red embers in the thing's gaze died, and green fire shot from its eyes and mouth. Fumes poured out of its nose and ears—black and heavy, falling over its shoulders and down its face, a thick miasma. The shriek died, fading away like a final echo. With it, all strength left the thing's body, and it fell to the ground like the dead flesh it was.

Later, looking back at that moment, Darric felt sure what happened next lasted no more than a moment. Certainly no longer than the time it took for the body to hit the ground. But time seemed to stretch, every detail clear in Darric's sight, every sound distinct. The Nar stood dumbstruck. More than a few jaws dropped, and every eye, round and wide, fixed on the lifeless corpse that only moments ago had been their feared leader.

But the stillness broke. Someone out of Darric's sight cried out an order in Nar. Darric's command of the language was limited at best, but he caught one word clearly—"Kill!"

Three Nar, blades in hand, ran for him.

Darric pushed himself up and scrambled for his sword. But the thing's death grip was locked around the hilt and he couldn't pry the fingers loose. Cursing, Darric reached for the dagger at his belt.

He was halfway to his feet when he felt the wind of the arrow's flight. He heard it pass overhead like an angry wasp, and there was a *crack* as the arrow struck the nearest Nar. The man flew backward, his arms thrust before him, and hit the ground a good six feet away from where he'd left his feet.

His nearest companion stopped in his tracks. He crouched, causing the arrow to hit him in the head. The man's head went back with such force that Darric heard the neck snap, and the entire body flipped backward. When the torso hit the ground, the feet were still in the air.

Through the dust Darric found himself staring at the man. The arrow had gone all the way through so that a good six inches of the shaft protruded out of the back of the man's skull. What kind of bow—?

The Nar evidently had the same thought, for they scattered in every direction, forsaking the fight. Within moments, it was over.

Wide-eyed, panting, his heart still hammering, Darric looked around. Mandan was several paces away, club still raised, looking back at him. Valsun was a ways behind him, standing over two dead Nar. As near as Darric could tell, none of the blood on Valsun was his own. Just beyond him was one of the sellswords Darric had hired. He thought the man's name was Jaden, but he couldn't be sure. Darric suspected the man might be more cutpurse than sellsword, but he fought well.

The rest of the Damarans and hired blades lay unmoving. Hureleth lay closest to Darric. His body sprouted two arrows, and it looked as if someone had given him several good blows with a sword, just to be sure. His open wounds steamed in the cold night air.

For several moments, the survivors just looked at one another, the only sounds that of their labored breathing and the fire consuming the tree. For his part, Darric was almost overwhelmed by two conflicting feelings—horror and disgust at what had just happened, and heartfelt gratitude that he and his two dearest comrades were still standing.

"There!" Valsun pointed with his sword.

Something in the darkness moved.

A shape emerged from the shadows and into the flickering orange light cast by the burning tree. The figure stepped with such grace that its footsteps made not a sound. Darric could tell by the body's curves that it was a woman. She held a bow that was almost as tall as she was. She wore dark, fitted clothes that seemed to drink in the darkness, but her face . . .

There was no face. Darric instinctively tried to gasp, but it came out more of a strangled choke. No face!

Two bright eyes, wide with a feral glee, stared out from a face of bone. But as the woman stepped fully into the light,

Darric saw that, horrible as it was, the mask was just that—a mask made from the skull of some animal. Not old and ivory white. Still fresh and slick, so that the firelight wavering off it made it seem almost the color of fresh blood, and the eyes looking out from the deep sockets watched them with something very close to . . .

He knew not what. But Darric shivered.

From the distant dark came an agonized scream. Darric looked nervously in the direction, and the other men did the same as they sat up.

"Don't mind them," said the woman. "It's just Uncle taking care of any lingerers."

"Uncle?" said Darric. "Who is Uncle? And *who are you?*"

The woman looked at Darric and said, "My name is Hweilan."

Darric's jaw dropped.

He heard Valsun gasp.

Mandan gaped at her and said, "Shar's sullied shit."

Jaden looked at them all in turn, then said, "What in the smoking Hells is going on?"

The woman picked up one of the larger rocks that the Damarans had used as a campfire ring, then she walked over to the dead man with the arrow through his head and kneeled beside him. Without looking at any of them she said, "Do I know you?"

Darric said, "My name is Darric."

Mandan said, "He came to find you."

At the same time Valsun cried, "What are you doing?"

The woman brought the rock down sharply on the dead man's skull. It didn't crack so much as *crunch*.

"Holy gods," said Jaden, then turned on his hands and knees and was violently sick.

Hweilan smashed the dead man's skull twice more then tossed the rock aside.

"What are you doing?" said Mandan, more curious than horrified.

"Retrieving my arrow," she said. "Can't cut through bone, so I have to break it out. A good arrow is hard to make, so I'd much rather break a dead man's skull than my arrow."

She pulled the arrow out of the broken wreck of the dead Nar's head and proceeded to clean it on his clothes. Once satisfied, she slid it back into the quiver on her back, then walked over to the corpse holding her arrow in his chest. She looked down, and Darric heard her murmur, "Damn. Going to ruin the fletching."

She kneeled, turned the corpse on its side and grasped the haft of the arrow where it was protruding from the Nar's back. Holding it in a firm grip, she twisted and pulled, dragging the fletching through the chest cavity. It emerged bloody and featherless.

"I don't know anyone named Darric," she said as she used the dead man's clothes to clean the arrow.

"If you are Hweilan of Highwatch," Darric said, "daughter of Ardan and Merah, granddaughter of Vandalar, High Warden, then you do know me."

She looked at him. When he'd first seen those eyes, he'd seen a feral glee in them. There was no glee now. Just pure ferocity. More like an animal's eyes than a woman's. Darric could not look away. His mouth opened and shut once, then again, but he could not think of a thing to say.

"Tell me how you know those names," she said.

Silence held them for a long time, the only sound that of the fire.

Mandan spoke up at last, "Forgive my brother's lack of eloquence. He is indeed Darric, heir of Duke Vittamar of Soravia, and he has come—"

"We heard of Highwatch." Darric found his voice at last. He gave Valsun and Mandan a sharp look, hoping they saw it and divined its meaning. "That it had fallen. To Nar. No one believed it, of course. But when our messenger hawks did not return . . . we came to find the truth for ourselves, and offer what aid we could."

Mandan smirked and said, "*He* came to find *you*."

"Be silent, Brother!"

Hweilan looked at Mandan. And Darric saw it—her nostrils widened as she scented the air, and then her eyes narrowed ever so slightly. She studied Mandan a moment, then looked back at Darric. He could see her considering, and he thought—

She knows. I don't know how, but she knows. I'd bet my inheritance on it.

"Brother?" she said at last and looked at Darric.

Mandan tensed and raised his club. A moment later, Darric saw why.

The wolf padded out of the darkness, silent as a ghost. In the dim torchlight, Darric could not tell if it was white or a very pale gray, but he was quite certain that the dark wetness staining its muzzle almost up to its eyes was blood.

"Beware!" said Mandan. He ran forward, grabbed Hweilan, and tried to pull her behind him.

Instead, the woman twisted in his grasp, used Mandan's own weight and momentum against him, and the much-bigger man found himself flat on his back, looking up at the woman and the wolf, who stood calmly beside her, licking the blood from his muzzle.

"Darric of Soravia," said the woman, and she looked around at the others, "and company, meet Uncle."

Darric could take no more, so he said, "Hweilan, what in the Hells happened to you?"

PART TWO

THE FEYWILD

CHAPTER TWO

"OH, NO."

The small figure scrambled and slid down the slope. The dark did not bother him, and the thick canopy of the forest held back the worst of the rain. But the runoff flowing down the hill made footing treacherous and swelled the already swift valley stream well past its banks.

The body lay half in the stream—her legs on the bank, her hips and everything above them all the way in the water. The current undulated her hair, and her left hand bobbed and waved in the current. At least she was on her back, her face just out of the water. That was some small mercy. But her eyes . . .

Her eyes were open to the storm. Sightless. Water dripping off the branches rained down on her, some of it right into her empty gaze, and she didn't blink. Didn't even flinch.

"Dead," he said as he dropped his staff in the mud and jumped into the water. "Still the bells and sod the Hells. Oh, gods she's dead and he'll kill-me-kill-me-kill-me."

He dropped to his knees, lifted her head out of the water, and cradled it in his lap. She was shivering.

All breath left him in one long hiss. Alive! She was alive!

He patted her cheek, softly at first, then once with a hard smack. Nothing. He shook her. "Hey! Hey, girl!"

Lightning flickered overhead, but only nail-thin shafts of light made it through the thick canopy of trees. Thunder washed over the valley, shaking the stones in the river. The rain, an endless rattle on the leaves, became a torrent, a roar. The swell of the river quickened. She'd be underwater soon.

He scrambled out of the stream. The girl was wearing fur-lined boots, suitable for a much colder place than this. Braided leather laces bound them up to her knees. He worked his fingers under the laces, planted both feet in the ground, and pulled. She moved, perhaps an inch. Then two more. A relieved smile creased his face.

Then both his feet skidded out from under him and he went down, mud and water slipping into his clothes.

He sat up, spat water and grit, and let loose with a long litany of curses.

Water was coming right off the hillside into the stream, and his fall had opened a nice little rivulet so that water was flowing over the girl. He leaped back into the stream and lifted her head out of the water. She made a choking noise then coughed. He looked at her, saw her eyes blink once—knew that in the darkness there was no way she could see a damned thing—and had time to say, "Are y—?"

The girl screamed and surged upward—

• • ◉ • •

The horror had not passed. But it had retreated. No longer ripping and tearing through her mind, it had pulled back to—

Watch. Watch and wait. For now.

She fought to get back to light and breath and sound. But the darkness would not let her. More than the absence of light. This darkness had weight. Presence. And worst of all, a will.

". . . he'll kill-me-kill-me-kill . . ."

A small voice. Not weak, but far away, as if she lay at the bottom of a well, listening to voices far above.

"Hey! Hey, girl!"

Something broke through the darkness. Not pain exactly. A jarring sensation. It seemed that she lay still, but the world shifted around her.

Cold. A wet cold was the first sensation to break through. Water, flooding in, choking her. She drew in breath to scream, and the water poured down her throat.

All her senses snapped back, and the darkness disintegrated like the bursting of a bubble.

• • ◉ • •

Night. Dark, yes, but not that other presence that had tried to consume her. This darkness held no weight. An incessant roar filled the air. Rain. Storm. And all around her—washing over her—water, water, and more water. All the world had become a cold, lightless wet.

But a little of the darkness before her had a solidness to it. Then it spoke.

"Are y—?"

Instinctively, she screamed and lashed out. Her arm came around, and the back of one fist connected with flesh and bone. The figure fell back and the river swallowed it.

She ran. Her clothes were sodden, heavy, and they pulled at her. Her boot slipped in the mud, she went down in a splash, then came up again. She made it perhaps half-a-dozen steps, but then her boots sank into the muck. Momentum carried her upper half forward, and when her hands thrust out to break her fall, they too sank up to her wrists. She pulled, but the ground pulled back, yanking her until she was up to her elbows in mud.

She screamed, and only then did she realize she could see. Green light lit the wood around her. Where—?

The ground heaved, encasing her up to her chest, lifting her, and turning her around. For a moment, she thought she'd been caught in a mudslide brought on by the storm, but then she saw the figure standing at the water's edge.

Only a little over half her height had he been standing upright, he was made smaller still by his hunched posture. His right hand held a staff longer than he was tall. It twinkled with tiny lights in a hundred shades of green—sparks cast by dozens upon dozens of tiny amulets, coins, bits of chain, and random scraps of metal that tinkled with even the slightest movement. He held his other hand beside his face, and she could see his fingers working in intricate patterns. More light shone from there. Patterns—runes, most sharp edged—decorated his skin, and each of them blazed with an emerald fire.

She screamed.

The mud encasing her surged forward in a wave, then stopped and settled so that she was only a few feet from the small person.

"Be silent," he said.

The mud pressed on her. She couldn't move her arms, and the weight of it made breathing an effort.

"My name is Gleed," said the figure. "I just saved your life. The Master has sent you to me. Your name is Meyla. It means 'little girl' in my mother's tongue, for that is what you are—an ignorant little girl—until I say differently. Until you *prove* differently. Understand, Meyla?"

Rain and grit was streaming into her eyes, but she could not wipe them away.

"My name . . . is Hweilan."

His eyes widened and he took in a sharp breath. She had never seen a creature like this before. Small as a five-year-old child and scrawny as an old man. But even a fool could see he was shocked. Stunned.

"What did you say?" he said.

"My name"—she fought to get enough breath into her lungs—"Huh-Hweilan!"

He blinked twice, and the fingers of his left hand stopped their intricate motions. The lights decorating his skin and staff dimmed, but they did not go out. She felt the mud around her loosen, and a great deal of it sloughed off into the river, washing over the little creature's feet. Then his eyes narrowed, part suspicion and part curiosity.

"What do you remember?"

• • ⊛ • •

The Hunter's eyes blazed. Two green forge fires that gave no heat. A thousand howls filled the night. Raucous cries rained down from the boughs overhead.

Hweilan looked up.

Hundreds of ravens looked down on her, their black eyes reflecting the moonlight. Yellow wolves' eyes watched her from the shadows under the trees. Waiting and hungry, held back only by the will of the antlered thing before her—neither man nor beast, but something far older.

You are mine, Hweilan. You were always mine.

He took off his mask.

She screamed. And then he was inside her.

It was inside her. That presence, that mind, ripping through her essence. She'd once seen a wolf pack ripping into the carcass of a swiftstag, the strongest members of the pack barking and growling and snapping to get at the soft undersides. They beat back the others with tooth and claw, then set to their meal. Now and then a wolf's entire head disappeared into the carcass to get at the choicest bits.

That image flashed through her thoughts as the Hunter's mind tore through hers. Biting and clawing and consuming her. Chewing through every memory, every want and desire, every hidden hope, every secret shame, then going deeper still to—

He bit down.

And something bit back.

Something hidden. Something that had been sleeping for . . . forever—at least in terms of her own life.

But it was awake now. Awake and raging.

The Hunter bit down upon it, and that thing—that other—blazed.

Like a wolf who had bitten into its prey, anticipating soft flesh, only to find blazing molten steel in its mouth, the Hunter screamed, more a shriek of spirit than sound.

The world shattered.

Her mind snapped, like a rope holding too much weight, and she fell.

The horror had not passed. But it retreated. No longer ripping and tearing through her mind, it had pulled back to—

• • ◉ • •

"What do you remember?"

Gleed lashed out with his staff, and the thick knob of it struck her across the forehead. "Answer me, Meyla."

She blinked through tears, which fell down her cheeks and mixed with the rain. "My name is Hweilan."

"So you say. What do you remember? And *how* do you remember it?"

The lights on his staff and skin blazed again, and the wet earth holding her constricted. She could feel her muscles being squeezed around her bones. The mud pulled her closer to him, so that his face was only inches from her own. In the light cast by the runes she could see that one of his eyes was a milky blur. His hot breath wafted against her face. It had an oddly bitter, spicy scent, like a very strong exotic tea.

"Now, girl," he said, "you are going to tell me everything."

"H-h-he . . . *killed* him." It all came out in a burst. "Th-that . . . that thing k-killed Lendri. Ripped . . . ripped his heart right out of his chest. Oh . . . holy gods!"

Hweilan vomited. There was little in her stomach, but bile surged up her throat and out. Gleed barely managed to step away in time.

"Mad as a half-drowned songbird," he muttered. "Best get you inside, eh? Then you can tell me everything. You *will* tell me everything."

He turned away, and the mud holding her collapsed with a splash. She found herself laying face first on the ground, one foot dragging in the river.

She squeezed her eyes shut and let her head fall into the mud. "Please go away."

Something tapped the back of her skull.

"Hey!"

Gleed stood before her, green light still spilling off his staff and upraised hand. "You're going to be difficult, aren't you?"

He nudged her with his staff again, and something about it made her suddenly angry. She slapped it away and glared up at him. "I'm not going anywhere until you tell me who you are and where I am and how I got here."

"Have it your way," he said, then broke off into a low incantation.

Hweilan tried to ignore his voice. But then she heard something else: a wet, raspy slithering. She looked up. The nearby foliage—vines, branches, leaves, even roots dripping black mud—twisted and turned, forming a vaguely manlike shape. No head or eyes, but it had two massive arms. Too late she realized they were reaching for her.

The branches and vines entangled her and lifted her up.

She yelled and kicked and thrashed. But the branches only pulled tighter, pinning her arms to her sides and wrapping her legs together, snug as a shroud.

"Struggle all you like," said Gleed. "But I do wish you'd stop the screaming. It might draw attention we don't want. There are far crueler things in these woods than me."

Hweilan screamed louder.

Gleed shrugged, then turned and walked away. Just when the rain and shadows were about to swallow the last of his light, he gestured over his shoulder, and the mass of vines and branches holding Hweilan shambled after him.

• • ⊛ • •

The storm passed. Hweilan had stopped screaming—her throat had gone too raw. When she felt the thing carrying her stop, she opened her eyes. The forest ended at the shore of a lake, its flat black surface sparkled here and there with moonlight breaking through silver-limned gashes in the clouds.

In the midst of the lake stood the most decrepit tower Hweilan had ever seen—and she'd grown up in a land dotted with old ruins. Not much taller than a healthy spruce, the tower stood on an island only slightly larger than the base of the building. The tower looked as if it were only being held together by the moss and vines entangling it. Ravens roosted along the crumbling upper turrets, and dozens of bats fluttered over the water, feasting on insects.

The lake was fed by a waterfall that fell over a small ridge a stone's throw to their left. The sound of it made Hweilan shudder. The Nar word for waterfall was *kuhunde*, which meant "mountain laughter." In Narfell, the snow in the mountains only melted enough to form waterfalls in the height of the hottest summers. To the Nar, the sound of the falls sounded like the mountains laughing for joy at the rare warmth. But this waterfall, coming out of the dark woods to feed the stream that ringed the tower, held no laughter. It sounded more like the growl of some ill-tempered beast, warning her to stay away.

Gleed led them along the shore until they came to a small spit of land that pointed to the tower like a slightly hooked finger. He stood at the water's edge, raised his staff, and muttered an incantation that Hweilan could barely hear over the fluttering of the bats. The water rippled, and a bridge emerged. Parts of it were made from old flagstones held up by the roots of sunken trees, but great lengths of the bridge were formed of the roots themselves, raw bedrock, or soaked waterweeds that squished under Gleed's shoes as he led the way.

As the vine-thing carried Hweilan over the bridge, she heard something else. The whole structure of the tower rattled and tinkled in the breeze. Hanging from every available vine branch, twig, and shoot were hundreds of bells—some large as helmets, others smaller than thimbles. And amongst the bells were bits of chain, chimes, and coins of every shape and size. As they were out of the woods, the moonlight seemed very bright, and by its light Hweilan saw that some of the coins were old and black with tarnish, while others seemed newly minted.

Gleed saw her staring. He gestured around with his staff. "Nasty things haunt these woods. Lots of nasty things. There's power in gold, silver, and iron. Especially iron. These talismans keep all but the nastiest away when I'm not home."

"Demons," Hweilan rasped, and winced at the pain in her throat.

"Eh?" said Gleed. A few bats fluttered around him. He shooed them away with his staff.

Hweilan was no scholar. But she had seen the mad, hungry thing looking out from her Uncle Soran's eyes—and later from Kadrigul's. Nothing could stop them. Not arrows and blades, or even the earth-shattering power of Kunin Gatar's magic. Everything Hweilan, her friends, and her enemies had thrown at the thing had done no good. It just kept coming. Relentless. Until it had faced Nendawen. Only then had it truly faltered. And the scream that had seemed to stab needles into her bones when Nendawen had destroyed it . . . she could think of no other explanation.

She looked up at the metal-encrusted tower. "Will your talismans keep out demons?"

"No demons here," said Gleed. "This isn't the Abyss, though you may think otherwise in the coming days."

The vine-thing bore Hweilan through a door and down low hallways cut through the black stone of the lakebed. As Gleed led them downward, torches sputtered to life in his wake, flickering blue-green flames that popped and hissed but gave no smoke. Shiny green beetles scuttled out of the light and sought refuge in the cracks between the bricks. Silver spiders—small bodies, with long legs that looked sharp as needles—scuttled out of the shadows and sat in their webs or hung from tiny threads and watched them.

They passed other doors, all shut tight, runes and arcane symbols etched or burned along every board. Beyond, one passage was so utterly black that Hweilan couldn't see anything. But she could hear water dripping inside, and the smell that emanated out of the dark was so utterly rank that Hweilan's jaws locked and her throat constricted.

Not far beyond that, the passageway ended at an archway that filled most of the wall. A few stairs led down to a stout wooden door.

Gleed turned. "Your escort can go no farther. Time to walk."

He snapped his fingers, and the life humming through her bonds burst and seeped away. To Hweilan it felt like an arrow piercing a full wineskin—an instant of collapse, then the contents soaked into the ground and were gone.

Hweilan found herself on the passage floor in a mass of vines, wet roots, and mud.

"Get up and follow me," said Gleed.

Hweilan pushed herself up on legs that felt hollow and brittle. How long since she'd had a good meal? She couldn't remember. Her stomach felt small and shriveled, and her hands trembled as she tore away the vines and slipped out of the roots. When all but a few clinging tendrils lay in a pile at her feet, Gleed turned and started down the stairs.

Seeing him in the torchlight was the first really good look she'd had at him. Hobgoblins and worse filled the mountains west of her home, and she'd seen them a few times—prisoners brought in for questioning or bandits for judgment. They had been larger and much haler-looking than this shriveled old creature, but if he wasn't a goblin, he was certainly close kin to them.

Hweilan made her decision between one breath and the next. She turned and ran, going back the way they had come. Weak and hungry as she was, she knew that little creature stood no chance of catching her—if she could get out of the range of whatever dark arts he had at his command.

Behind, she heard him curse, but she kept going, past the room of dripping rankness and the dozen doorways, around the bend and up the stairs into moonlight.

Her foot was on the topmost stair when she saw him. She stopped so suddenly that she almost fell.

Lendri stood naked at the water's edge, one hand hanging limply at his side, the other grasping at the ruin of his chest, trying to hold in the heart that still beat there. He fell to his knees.

"All dead," he said. "Your family, Scith . . . me." His voice took on the timbre of a snarl. There had always been something of the beast in Lendri. But this was rabid. "All dead. Because of you. Because you—"

Hweilan heard the cawing of ravens.

Wolves in the distance.

And then the darkness took her.

• • ◉ • •

She could hear a crackle and the low hum of coals breathing and she felt herself surrounded in the warmth of blankets soft as rabbit fur. A rich earthy aroma filled her head, and her ears caught the soft clink and scrape of a spoon stirred inside a kettle. She lay there, for one brief moment thinking she was home again, spring on the wane, and any moment one of the handmaidens would come through her bedroom door, telling her if she didn't get up and wash soon, she'd have no time for breakfast before today's lessons.

But then she opened her eyes.

A fire burned in a stone hearth, a black iron kettle set over the flames, and Gleed hunched over it, sipping from a silver spoon.

"Awake at last, eh?" he said, and turned to her.

He no longer wore the thick cloak and hood in which she'd first seen him in the woods. His feet and arms were bare, and he wore clothes of simply cut brown canvas, a long vest closed by a belt rope, the ends of which dangled to his knees. A dozen or more necklaces hung around his neck—fine chains, braided leather, and others no more than fraying thread. Hanging from every one were tiny jewels, bits of bone, black feathers, and medallions—some round and gleaming like silver coins, others that looked to have been crafted from iron nails twisted into intricate shapes.

Seeing his ruddy, leathery skin, the too-wide mouth, tiny nose framed by huge, round eyes—one orange the other milky and blind—and the pointed, erect ears, and there was no longer any doubt.

"You're a goblin," she said.

He smirked. "Oh, you *are* a bright one."

She looked around, her eyes skittish as a bird who has returned to her nest to find a viper coiled around her eggs. She lay in a nest of pillows, blankets, and rugs. Beyond was a chamber—so low-ceilinged that she would knock her head on the cobwebbed rafters if she stood to her full height. A bed and low table took up one wall. No chairs—the table was low enough that one obviously sat on the floor. Other than the doorway and hearth, every bit of spare wall space was filled with shelves holding tomes, scrolls, the reconstructed skeletons of small animals, and dozens and dozens of bottles of colored glass, wood, and clay. Not a single window. It looked more like the room of an eccentric old scholar than a wrinkled old goblin.

"Why am I here?" said Hweilan. Her eyes seemed drawn to the kettle bubbling over the fire, and she remembered every story about goblins she'd ever heard.

Gleed chuckled. "You're far too big to fit into my pot—and I stopped eating girls a long time ago."

She couldn't tell if he was serious or not. He used the spoon to pull the kettle from its hook and set it away from the fire to cool.

"Usually I have a whole speech prepared," he said. " 'My name is Gleed. The Master has sent you to me.' Then I give them a demeaning name to keep them in their place. But you, little girl, you seem to have broken the pattern." He made a sound that was part laugh and part cough. "I've been teaching your kind since before your grandmother's grandmother caught her man. But in all my years, you are the first to come to me knowing who you are. Before, my charges came with their memories wiped clean—their hearts new iron, ready to be honed according to the Master's will. But you . . . you know who you are . . . Hweilan. How can this be?"

"I don't know," she rasped.

Gleed's eyes narrowed and he watched her, obviously disbelieving. "Tell me what you remember," he said.

She tried to swallow. Her throat felt rough as baked boot leather—from her screaming earlier. And how long since she had last taken a drink?

"Water," she said.

Gleed shambled off, then returned with a silver goblet that looked very large in his hands. His other hand crumbled something and sprinkled it into the contents of the goblet, then he handed it to her.

She took it and stared at the pinkish contents. "What—?"

"No poison," he said. "If I wanted you dead, I'd have left you in the creek to drown. Just a bit of wine and water with a few special herbs. They'll soothe your throat and settle your stomach so that you don't wretch all over my floor after you eat."

She took a tentative sip. Both wine and herbs were very bitter, but the concoction seemed more water than anything. She drank it all in three swallows, each hurting a bit less than the last.

Gleed retrieved his staff from the nearest shelf and leaned on it. He fixed her with his one good eye.

"Where is Menduarthis?" she asked.

"Who?"

"He . . . he helped me escape from . . . that thing."

The old goblin chucked. "Well then, I'd say he did a poor job of it. I do not know this Menduarthis or what might have happened to him."

"He was hurt." He might have been more than hurt. Might be dead. The last Hweilan had seen of him, he'd been lying senseless on the ground, bleeding profusely from his head.

"I've told you I know nothing of him, girl. Now, speak. Tell me of Hweilan and how she came to be here."

She gave him no intimate details. Nothing of her childhood or family. Just "Creel killed my family" and then picking up where she'd met Lendri in the foothills. Gleed grinned as she told of Kunin Gatar and how she, Lendri, and Menduarthis had escaped. Her breath caught as she came to Lendri's death—not so much at seeing him killed as at the memory of his ghost in the moonlight outside. She told how the thing that had killed Lendri had been about to kill her.

"And then *he* appeared," she said, her eyes closed, her breath scarcely above a whisper. A figure, taller than any man Hweilan had ever seen. Moonlight glinted off pale scars that ribboned his muscled frame. His left hand dripped blood. In his right he gripped a spear, its black head barbed and cruel. Antlers sprouted from his skull.

"The Master," said Gleed, and in his voice Hweilan heard . . . not reverence. Ecstasy. The voice of a drunk long denied his drink who is suddenly given a priceless vintage.

"The . . . Master?" she said.

"Nendawen to those mortals who knew him best," he said. "Master of the Hunt, lord of this realm. He saved you, yes?"

Eyes still squeezed shut, Hweilan nodded.

She heard Gleed chuckle. But there was no humor in it. It was the laugh of a little boy dangling a mouse over the cat.

"He . . . *filled* you, yes? Spirit and mind. Heart and soul. The Master sifted you, scraped you, *immersed* you in his holy will."

She didn't know about that. Remembering it, she thought it had seemed more of a violation than a blessing. She certainly hadn't been willing. She'd heard priests speak of communion with the divine, comparing it with the passion of a lover. Hweilan had never been with a man, so she had no comparison in that regard. But what Nendawen had done to her mind had not been the ecstasy of lovers. More like consumption—the terror a deer might feel when it knows it will still be alive when the wolves start to feed.

Gleed kept talking. "You are the first whom the Master has left with any knowledge of who they are. Why? I do not know, but it is not for me to question his will. The Master has chosen you to be his Hand, little girl, but you are raw, unshaped . . . unworthy. To serve the Master, to *honor* the Master, you will be honed into the perfect weapon."

The first whom the Master has left with any knowledge of who they are . . . Hweilan wasn't so sure about that. The Master had seemed determined to do something to her—wipe her memories perhaps—until he had come upon something inside her. Something that fought back.

But she didn't tell this to Gleed. Instead she seized on the last thing he'd said, about being *honed*.

"By you?" she said.

Gleed scowled and his voice came out barely above a whisper. "Don't underestimate me, girl. I could turn you to ash with a word. But to speak the whole truth: You will have three teachers, of which I will be one. I will teach you, yes. Teach you Making. But before you can Make, first you must Know. You will be given the Lore."

"Lore?"

Gleed ignored her question. "I will feed you—can't have you dying on me—and then we should see to your wounds. Whatever you've been doing these past days, you've gotten yourself covered in cuts and scrapes.

"Tomorrow you will meet Kesh Naan, and it will be most dangerous if she smells blood on you. Kesh Naan will give you the Lore, and then you will return to me—if you survive. So listen to me very carefully."

CHAPTER THREE

"Your brother is dead." said Argalath.

Jatara shrieked. The two Nar holding her flinched and strengthened their holds on her arms. They'd forced her to her knees. She could feel the tendons in her shoulders stretching. The blood running from her mouth and nostrils was staining the rug that took up most of Argalath's bedchamber. The rug was ruined. At least it would give the Nar something in which they could wrap the two dead men on the floor behind them.

"Release her."

Argalath's voice. Strained with weariness, but no fear. Both guards looked up in shock. Jatara followed their gaze.

Argalath sat in the room's one chair. Here, in the privacy of his bedchamber, he'd removed the robes and wore loose trousers and a sleeveless undershirt. The mottled blue of his spellscar covered every inch of exposed pale skin, from the tips of his fingers to the top of his hairless head. Behind him stood a tall, imposing figure, the fine Damaran clothes covering a frame of hard muscle and sinew. Guric. Or what had once been Guric. The body no longer breathed, the heart lay still in his chest, and the hunger lurking in his black eyes had not been born in this world. The remains of the table Jatara had shattered in her attempt to murder her lord lay strewn on the floor before Argalath. Had Guric not been there, she would have succeeded, and there would be more than two corpses cooling in the room.

Argalath spoke again. "I said release her."

The man holding her right arm kicked the bloody knife away. It clattered against the far wall, then both men released her arms and stepped back.

Jatara collapsed. Sobs shook her, and the sound of her weeping drowned out the crackle of flames in the hearth.

Squinting against the glare from the fire, Argalath looked down on her, shook his head, and said, "I am sorry."

From the corner of her one remaining eye, Jatara could see the Nar just behind her and to her left. He'd stepped back. But not enough.

"You're . . . *sorry*?"

Her arm snapped out and she snatched the knife from the Nar's belt. He lunged backward—sure that in the next moment he'd feel his own steel spilling his guts on the rug.

But Jatara leaped for Argalath.

He didn't move, but from behind him Guric did, stepping around his master and crouching to meet her.

Jatara knew her business. This monster had thwarted her once. She didn't need to kill Guric. Just get past him.

She landed and kept low, spinning prone and aiming one boot at Guric's knee. Bone shattered.

Guric didn't cry out in pain. Didn't even wince. But he did topple as his leg collapsed under him.

Jatara was on the move again before he even hit the floor.

Guric's hand shot out to grasp her, but she twisted away. Another three steps. She raised the knife and lunged.

Argalath's spellscar glowed.

The center of Jatara's chest constricted, and agony shot outward from it, locking her limbs in a tight spasm. She crumpled to the floor. Her head bounced off the rug so close to Argalath's foot that she could have counted the stitches lining the sole of his boot. She had no idea if she still held the knife; she couldn't feel her hands. Couldn't feel anything except the pain radiating out from her chest. She tried to draw breath, but that only made blackness close in around the edges of her vision.

"You know better, Jatara." Argalath's voice, seeming faint and far away. "Now stop this foolishness. I did not kill Kadrigul."

The pain left her as swiftly as it had come. But with it went the last of her strength and the will to fight. All she had left was the hollowness inside. She couldn't even muster the strength to cry.

"Help her up," said Argalath. "Put her on the bed."

The Nar obeyed, laying her atop the thick fur coverlets. Guric was sitting up and staring at the lower half of his leg, which bent outward.

"Your brother is dead, Jatara," said Argalath. "And even if your grief makes you think otherwise, I am indeed sorry. I loved him as you did." His gaze flicked away, and for a moment the barest hint of a smile bent his lips. "Well, perhaps not exactly as you did, but I loved him nonetheless. I did not kill him. But I know who did. We will discuss it here, now, and then never again. You know me. You know my word. Do you understand?"

He leaned forward in his chair, his chin resting on his clasped fingertips. He stared at Jatara, where she still lay strengthless on the bed. The flames in the hearth were burning low, and the room was more shadow than light. She could not see Argalath's eyes. Just two wells of darkness. But she could feel his gaze on her. Her heartbeat still felt stiff and strained, as if it had just been thawed and was straining to its work. Her limbs were tingling, and she couldn't stop the shivering in her body.

Jatara made a sound of assent. Her mouth was bone dry and she didn't yet trust herself to speak.

"Very well," said Argalath. "Your brother died in my service. You and he have both faced death in my service more times than I can remember. You did so with honor. Without complaint. With eagerness even. Why do you now blame me?"

Tears welled in Jatara's eye. Her brother, the only one in the world she truly loved, was dead, and she hadn't even been there. Wolves and ravens would eat his corpse.

"You sent him," she said, forcing the words out through a throat that still seemed narrow as a pipe stem. "With that . . . monster."

Argalath sat silent a moment, as if waiting for her to continue. When she didn't, he said, "That *monster* as you call it did not kill your brother. He was, in fact, the best protection I could have sent with Kadrigul."

"You could have sent me."

"Then you, too, would be dead."

Had the knife been within reach, had she been able to muster the strength to move, she would have tried to kill him again. The damned, cursed fool. Didn't he know she'd rather *be* dead than have to live without Kadrigul?

"But," Argalath continued, and she heard a strange note in his voice, "here you do speak—speak truly—of my mistake, and I beg your forgiveness, Jatara."

Nothing he could have said could have shocked her more. She'd heard him ask forgiveness from others before—those whom he served or who stood in higher station than him. But never to one who served him. And never with such sincerity.

"I thought we were going after one scared girl. I thought I was sending *more* than enough to do the job—swatting a fly with a smith's hammer. But it seems that our little fly found unexpected aid. I swear to you that had I known the baazuled was not up to the task, I would never have sent your brother with so few."

"Baazuled?" said Jatara. She'd never heard the word, though the flavor of it reminded her of the incantations Argalath used in his most secret rites.

Argalath motioned to Guric, who still sat in the floor. "Our new friends. You see the flaw?"

Jatara shook her head.

Argalath stood, so quickly that the chair toppled behind him. Jatara flinched, and she realized that her heart was beating so hard she could hear the blood pulsing in her head. The sudden movement sent a breath of air through the room that made the fire flare, painting him in a hellish light.

"Masks," said Argalath, in a tone like a street prophet about to explain sin to the unworthy.

The two surviving Nar exchanged nervous glances. The one from whom Jatara had snatched the knife looked at it longingly where it still lay on the floor.

"We all wear them," Argalath continued. He spread both his arms. "These mortal bodies are nothing but masks—the image we present to the world, hiding the true life within. And when we die, that life . . . departs. Such a waste. Leaving the body an empty shell. But"—and Argalath pointed down at Guric— "that shell can be filled by those who know the ancient ways, the secret arts of our ancestors. Is it not so, Jatara?"

She tried to swallow, but her mouth held no moisture. *Our ancestors?* Argalath claimed that his mother had been of the Nar, but his father of her people, the Frost Folk. Which ancestors did he mean? The shamans of her people had many secret arts, but she had never heard of anything like these baazuled until Argalath.

Argalath turned, extended one hand, and his chair leaped up, its back slapping into his open palm. The two Nar each made the sign to ward off evil spirits, and she could hear one of them muttering a prayer. She could see his breath. The temperature in the room had dropped suddenly. The air had taken on a still, almost brittle state, making every sound sharp and clear, and it was then she realized what had just happened.

She'd long known of Argalath's ability granted by his spellscar. He could move things with his mind—small things only, but his cunning had learned to put it to great effect.

Moving anything larger than a flagon of wine pained and weakened him. But he'd discovered that there were veins and organs inside the human body far smaller than a flagon. A slight squeeze applied to the right area could kill. The wounded pounding of her own heart reminded her of that.

But the entire chair—a heavy thing of solid oak and iron—had jumped off the floor into his waiting hand. And Argalath's spellscar had not so much as flickered.

Argalath sat down again and motioned to Guric. "He hoped that his beloved wife would return to fill her shell. It was not to be. Not even the gods themselves can force the unwilling dead to return. Instead, something came from . . . elsewhere."

"Demons," Jatara rasped. She had heard stories of demons and devils called forth to serve practitioners of the dark arts. Some managed to break free of their would-be masters and possess them—or worse. That Argalath managed to maintain control over such spirits proved how powerful he really was.

Argalath laughed. "Call them what you like. But that is not what we must discuss, Jatara. What we must *settle*. Once and for all. Look at our friend there. You shattered his leg. Even the strongest living warrior would be weeping in agony at such an injury. But there he sits, calm as you please, awaiting my command. And yet . . . something out there managed to best one of them. For as formidable as our baazuled are, they are not invulnerable. Can you guess it, Jatara? The weakness?"

Jatara looked down at Guric. He—no, *it*—just sat there. But she had seen what these baazuled could do. That Guric wasn't howling in pain over his shattered leg was impressive enough. But she'd seen them heal wounds that would have been lethal—heal before her eyes, after feeding.

"The mask," said Argalath. "The body. In this case—the corpse. A dead shell. Powerful as the spirit is, even it cannot overcome this. It is not a weakness of the physical. No. It is a weakness of the . . . *elemental*." Even though he was sitting in shadow, Jatara caught a flash of white and knew he was smiling. "The baazuled are beings of vast power—far beyond we pitiful mortals. But this world is not theirs, and though they can use our empty shells, it is not unlike a Nar warrior trying to ride a dead horse—forced to move the limbs himself, fill the lungs with air, *force* it to gallop. How much better, how much *stronger* is a living warrior upon a living horse? But what if warrior and mount could be one? One living, breathing, thinking . . ."

Words seemed to fail him at last, and he looked at Jatara. He took a deep breath, and when he next spoke, his tone was that of the Argalath she knew—soft spoken, almost weary, but always as if he knew something she didn't.

"Your brother died in my service. That debt must be paid. To strike one of my servants is to strike me. To strike me is to strike the one I serve. Is it not so?"

Jatara said nothing.

"So, the question you must now ask yourself is whether you will mind your place, and bring vengeance to those who killed your brother. Or whether you will blame me. You can't have both."

Jatara forced herself to sit up on the bed. It made the room spin around her and her stomach clenched, but she managed. She still felt hollow inside. Completely drained. Stripped of all will to live. But the rage was gone.

"You said my brother died in your service. I thought we were taking Highwatch, and then . . . whatever we please. But what you're doing . . . goes beyond that. Yes?"

"Oh, yes," said Argalath, and again she saw the dim flash of his teeth in the darkness. "My plans extend far beyond this hovel. Are you ready to . . ." He paused, and seemed to search for the right words, then said, "Expand your vision?"

"Will it bring vengeance to whoever killed my brother?"

"Oh, yes. That I swear to you."

"To strike one of your servants is to strike you. To strike you is to strike the one you serve. Your words."

A moment's silence, then, "Yes."

And so Jatara asked the one question she had never asked—had never dared, and never much cared, because to her it did not matter. It mattered now.

"Whom do you serve?"

CHAPTER FOUR

The shivering dragged Hweilan back to consciousness. When she heard the loud rattling, she gasped and sat up, fearing some huge insect was scuttling near her face, then realized it was only the chattering of her own teeth.

She opened her eyes.

Gleed, the tower, the lake . . .

Gone. She was alone in the pathless forest. She remembered Gleed yammering on, feeding her some stew that was surprisingly good, then more of the herbed water. One moment she'd been listening to him extol the wonders of the Master, the next . . .

"That little toad put something in the drink," she said to herself.

She looked down and saw that she was dressed only in a strange sort of cloak. More like a knee-length blanket with a hole in the middle for her head. Compared to frigid Narfell, the air seemed balmy, but it was still cool enough that her breath steamed, and the thought of the old goblin taking her clothes gave her a sick feeling in her stomach.

She sat in a bed of old leaves, made sodden from last night's rain, surrounded by the roots of a massive oak. At least she thought it was an oak. The leaves were the right shape, but just one of them was larger than both her outstretched hands.

And though the bark was the right texture—even encrusted in lichen as an old oak ought to be—the color was just a wisp lighter than black.

Hweilan had grown up in a land nestled between mountains and steppe, where most of the moisture fell as snow and clung as ice for six months out of the year. What few woods there were clung to the foothills and mountain valleys—mostly pine and spruce, trees that could survive the harsh cold. The forest she'd seen in the realms of Kunin Gatar had been dense. But nothing like what surrounded her.

Nothing but trees and brush in every direction. Trunks and branches turned and twisted, almost as if they'd been dancing and had frozen in place at the sight of the strange girl blinking at them. Never had she seen such monsters as these trees. Some of the leaves were big as shields. The sky lay hid beneath the ceiling of the leaves, and Hweilan could only guess at the trees' height. A hundred feet? More? No way to know. They might climb all the way to tickle the moon for all she could tell.

But the faces . . .

As a child enjoying Narfell's brief summers, she had often lain in the tall grass of the steppe and seen shapes in the clouds or the profile of a face on some crag. But the knots and holes in the trees around her . . .

The trunks had knots that looked much too much like eyes, and they seemed to watch her. A broken branch looked very much like a nose. And the cracked and split bark in the trunks stretched like mouths. Some seemed almost sad, or frozen in a scream. But far too many held a malicious glee.

Hweilan stood. She had no idea where she was, had no idea what time of day it was—the wood seemed caught in a perpetual twilight; enough light to see, but plenty of shadows in which anything could be hiding. She knew she wanted to be anywhere but there.

Leaves rustled far overhead as the upper boughs caught a slight breeze, but down below the air was still. She could hear the chirps of birds, but they stayed hidden in the upper branches. There was no sound of the waterfall. She was obviously far away from Gleed's tower but had no memory of how she'd come here. What had that little beast put in her drink?

Hweilan started walking. She had no idea where she was or where she was going, so she simply went down the slope. Other than her bath and bed, Hweilan had never gone shoeless in her life. To do so in Narfell would be folly. But here, the floor of wet leaves was soft and easy on her feet. Still, it was cool, and even after walking briskly for what seemed a mile or more, she couldn't stop shivering.

Once, she thought she heard singing in the distance—childlike voices, though raucous. But when she stopped and held her breath to listen, there was only the sound of the breeze in the highest boughs. Down here, the air was deathly still. Black moths and dark blue butterflies flitted around her now and then, and once a dragonfly shot past her so fast that her first thought was that someone had loosed an arrow at her.

Which brought Gleed's words from the night before fresh to her mind.

There are far crueler things in these woods than me.

Almost as if summoned by the thought, she heard something approaching from her right, crashing through the brush.

Hweilan stopped and held her breath. A few of the black moths fluttered around. But nothing more. She looked for a weapon. Nothing. Not even a sizeable rock or broken branch.

Then she saw it—a flash of red. A fox bounded out of the brush, its back almost arrow straight as it ran. It saw her, stopped, then bounded off again, disappearing as quickly as it had come.

Hweilan let out a breath she hadn't realized she'd been holding. Her heart beat so fiercely that she could feel her face pulsing like the skin of a drum.

"Only a fox." It came out a whisper, but still seemed very loud in the silence of the forest.

Hweilan kept going, following the lee of the hill. It was getting steeper the farther she went, and the light dimmer.

The trees grew even larger, and some of their roots broke out of the ground, forming arches under which she walked. Spiderwebs draped the low branches, and although the few spiders she saw were no bigger than her smallest fingernail, still she walked around the webs rather than through them.

The hill was getting steep enough that Hweilan was beginning to slip and had to lean against one hand as she walked. But she could hear the rush of water again and thought she might be getting close to the lake and Gleed's tower.

Ahead of her a particularly massive root broke out of the side of the hill and arched over her path before seeking ground again. Sitting atop it, watching her, was the fox. Its golden eyes seemed very bright in the gloom.

Hweilan's feet slipped out from under her. She went down and caught hold of a sapling before she slid down the hill. Lying there in the cold, wet leaves, she looked up and saw that the fox was gone.

In its place atop the gnarled root, a woman crouched. Like Hweilan, the woman's feet were bare, but she was dressed in an array of stitched skins and leathers. She had the look of an elf—lean, angular build, a face of sharp angles, canted eyes, and ears that topped in sharp tips. Crouched as she was, her hair, thick as a pelt, hung past her shins, and in the gloom of the wood it seemed just a shade above black. Her skin was even darker than Scith's, and black designs—whorls, waves, and vinelike twists sprouting thorns—decorated her hands, bare arms, and face. Seeing someone, if not human, then at least more familiar than Gleed, almost put Hweilan at ease. But then she saw that the woman's eyes were a golden yellow, very bright in the gloom, and split by vertical pupils. And her toes and fingers ended in claws. A dark, wet something ran out of the corner of the woman's mouth—*that can't be blood,* Hweilan thought—and then the woman licked it away.

Gleed's words sprang to her mind—*Tomorrow you will meet Kesh Naan. Kesh Naan will give you the Lore.*

Hweilan swallowed, took a deep breath, and said, "A-are you K-Kesh Naan?"

The woman canted her head to one side, expressing something between curiosity and amusement. " 'A-are you K-Kesh Naan?' " she said, in perfect imitation of Hweilan's own voice. She licked her lips again, as if tasting the words, then shook her head, left shoulder to right shoulder, very slowly, and said, "No."

"Who are you?" said Hweilan.

The woman's lips peeled back, revealing sharp, yellow-white teeth.

Hweilan almost screamed, but her breath caught in her throat. She pushed herself carefully to her feet.

The woman jumped down, landed a few feet in front of Hweilan, then slowly stood and said, "I am . . ." She paused, as if searching for the word, then finished, ". . . *hungry*."

Hweilan turned and ran.

She made it perhaps five or six strides, then a weight hit her square in the back and two arms wrapped around her—one around her neck, the other under her arm. Claws bit through the cloak and into her skin.

Hweilan fell, the full weight of the woman coming down atop her, knocking all the breath from her body. But they kept moving. The slope was steep and they slid, gaining speed, crashing through bushes, over roots, breaking through young saplings and bouncing off bigger ones.

A snarl, and then Hweilan felt sharp teeth sink into her shoulder. She screamed, and an instant later they slammed into the trunk of a tree. The rough bark scraped a swath of skin off Hweilan's arm, then they were moving again.

Hitting the tree had weakened the woman's grip around Hweilan. The next broke it altogether. But it also knocked all the air out of Hweilan, and she thought she felt a rib crack.

She kept going down the hill, the world tumbling around her, branches and rocks scraping and gouging her skin.

Hweilan could hear the other woman crashing just behind her, but all she could see was a blur of green and brown as the world shot past.

And then there was nothing. No grasping arms. No roots scraping her back or trees slamming into her ribs. Just open air washing past her. She had time to take in an agonized breath as she went over the cliff.

Hitting the water felt like slamming through a wall. But this wall had a current. Hweilan scraped along a rocky bottom that tore away the cloak she'd been wearing. Panic seized her. Hweilan had just enough rational thought left to clench her jaw shut. Terror pushed her to scream, but she knew that if she did the river would fill her lungs and she would die down in the cold gloom.

Hweilan pushed off the riverbed. Her head broke the surface just as the river crashed down a steep slope over boulders in a series of rapids. She had only an instant to take a breath, then she went under again.

This time she tumbled. She lost the light, had no idea which way was up, and could no longer see the bottom. Hweilan clenched her jaw shut, fighting the reflex to breathe.

I'm dying, she thought. A moment of panic, so fierce it shut out all other thought, then a strange sort of peace settled over her. The pain in her chest was beyond agony, and her head felt as if it were about to burst. She knew that no matter how hard she tried, she wouldn't be able to hold her breath much longer.

Then her foot scraped along the bottom.

Her body reacted instinctively, and when she pushed, half her body shot out of the water, and she filled her lungs with sweet air.

She had never learned to swim. In Narfell, the only water were the shallow streams that thawed in summer. At Highwatch, the deepest water she'd ever seen was her bathtub. But the river wasn't deep—not much above her head. Hweilan sank, pushed off the bottom to breach the surface, took a breath, sank, pushed off the bottom, breached, took a breath... again and again and again.

The initial panic subsided, but she knew she couldn't keep this up. Already her limbs were aching, and she knew all it would take was one cramp to put her under the water forever.

On her next breach, she took a look around. She was in the middle of the river, and the shores on either side were at least fifty feet away—and both were sheer rock walls, slick and mossy. Upstream and behind her was only the river—no sign of the woman that had attacked her. Downstream...

Panic seized her again at what she saw.

Nothingness.

A hundred yards or so, and the river just ended in a mist. She'd grown up in mountains. She knew what that meant. She was headed for a waterfall. It might only be a few feet, or it might be a thousand. No way to tell from her vantage.

She went down again—and this time she went deep. Her feet could not find the bottom. The constant roar of the river deepened, strengthened, filling her so that her entire body *thrummed* with it—and by that she knew the fall before her was no slope of a few feet. She was about to go over a cliff.

Hweilan scrambled and kicked and thrashed, desperate to find the bottom. Nothing. Only water, flowing faster and faster by the moment. Her lungs, wanting air, began to ache. She gave up trying to find the bottom and began to try to claw and thrash her way to the surface. But for every foot she gained, the current pushed her down another two.

Hweilan clamped her jaw shut, but her body betrayed her. Try as she might, pure instinct took over, and she inhaled, filling her lungs with water.

The water's roar became an explosion. For a moment she felt herself going down and down, water above crushing her, and then...

• • ◉ • •

Hweilan sat up and retched so hard that her ears popped. Water and bile poured out her mouth and both nostrils, splattering the ground in front of her. She took in a ragged breath, then retched some more. Again and again, until she fell over on her side, her eyes closed, panting like a dog.

Never had she felt so wretched. Every fiber and pore of her body, inside and out, pulsed with pain. But she was alive, and every ragged breath filled her body with air. She lay there a long time, listening to her own hammering heart and labored breathing. Before, up on the hill, she'd been shivering from the cold. But suddenly, she was shaking so hard that she could feel her flesh bruising against the rocks. But she couldn't muster the strength to move.

After the fall, after drowning . . .

She didn't know. Had no idea how she'd come here. Come . . . where?

Hweilan opened her eyes. She lay on a bed of stones—gravel really, though each one was round and smooth as river stones. Lifting her head, she saw that a black pool lapped the shore just beyond her toes.

Hweilan rolled over onto her stomach, forced herself to her hands and knees, then fell into another coughing fit that tinged the world red. When she was able to breathe again, she raised her head and looked through the wet lanks of her hair.

The red tinge hadn't been just brought on by her coughing. She was in a cavern. Stalactites large as temple columns hung from the ceiling above. Some had melded with similar columns springing from the floor and formed pillars of rock that glistened in the red light. Roots poked out from the ceiling, some twisting around the stalactites in thick braids. Long strings of lichen and spiderwebs dangled between the stone like thin curtains. They waved back and forth slowly, almost as if the cave were breathing.

Hweilan looked around, searching for the source of the light. It wasn't red like fire or late sunset, but it completely filled the far side of the cavern away from the pool. She could find no direct source. Even the columns of stone cast no shadow. It was almost as if the rock itself glowed.

Hweilan pushed herself to her feet. Her legs felt hollow and brittle. Looking down, she saw that under her right breast a swath of skin wider than her palms had been raked away, and blood oozed down flesh that was already turning an angry purple. She could feel more blood running down her shoulder from where the woman had bitten her, and the rest of her naked body was a latticework of shallow scratches and deeper cuts, oozing blood.

From somewhere in the distant dark beyond the water, she thought she heard a voice. She almost caught the words. Just enough to stoke the memory of what Gleed had told her.

Tomorrow you will meet Kesh Naan, and it will be most dangerous if she smells blood on you.

And here she was, smeared in her own blood and leaking more with every heartbeat.

Hweilan looked around. No one in sight. The cavern had no real walls. The ceiling simply lowered and the floor rose until they met, forming a great domed chamber. But across from her, framed by two of the columns, a cave broke through the rock. The red glow of the cavern did not penetrate there.

She couldn't bring herself to brave the water again, and there didn't seem to be any other way to go. She took a step forward.

And then she heard singing.

At first she thought it was just a trick of her mind, but when she stopped and listened, she heard it even clearer. A woman's voice, coming from the darkness of the cave. There were words in the music, but in no tongue she'd ever heard before. Still, something in the cadence and melody reminded her of the songs her mother had sung to her when she was small. It called to her and repulsed her at the same time. She imagined that was how a moth must feel at the sight of the candle's flame.

"Wh-who's there?" she called. Hearing the tremor in her voice, Hweilan realized she was shivering again.

"Alet, kweshta."

Hweilan gasped. Those words she knew from her mother. *Come here, dear one* in the tongue of the Vil Adanrath.

The singing had stopped, but the voice called again, "*Alet . . .*" followed by a long string of words that Hweilan could not understand.

Hweilan's skin seemed to tighten around her, and every hair stood on end. There was a tone to the voice now that she didn't trust. No malevolence or threat, but something—

Coaxing.

"*Alet, kweshta. Alet.*"

A woman emerged from the cave. At first, she was nothing more than a pale something amidst the darkness, then she stepped fully into the light of the cavern.

She was tall, elf lithe, her skin pale as old bone, her face ageless. Her nose was little more than a slight bump on her face with two slits of nostrils to either side. Her eyes, both browless, had no whites, but seemed to swirl with a half-dozen colors, like a thin sheen of oil over black water. Silver hair hung past her waist, and she dressed in a gown of what Hweilan first thought was black silk. But as the woman moved, threads of it floated in the air around her, finer than pollen on summer breezes.

"Hweilan, is it?" said the woman. "She who knows her name." The woman's voice held no warmth, but neither was it particularly cold. Simply dryly curious.

"Yes," said Hweilan, and she found herself taking a step back for every step the woman took toward her until her heel touched the edge of the water. She stopped. "Are you . . . Kesh Naan?"

The woman gave a tight smile, revealing no teeth, just a curve of her lips. "And you know my name."

Hweilan didn't understand, so she said, "Gleed sent me."

The woman's smile melted away and she stopped a few paces in front of Hweilan. She watched Hweilan a long time. Hweilan was suddenly very conscious of her nakedness, though she no longer felt cold. On the contrary, the blood suddenly felt very hot under her skin.

Kesh Naan closed her eyes, bent her head back, and took in a deep breath through her open mouth, almost as if she were tasting the air.

It would be most dangerous if she smells blood on you.

Gleed's words. Hweilan looked down and saw the blood streaking her side, running down her hip and leg to mix with the mud.

Kesh Naan lowered her head, and when she opened her eyes, the look in them had changed. She had the gaze of a hungry beast, the leader of the wolf pack who has just caught sight of the straggler in the herd.

Hweilan swallowed and said, "I—"

Kesh Naan struck, a lunge so swift that there was nothing Hweilan could have done had she tried. The pale woman seized her. Kicking and clawing and screaming, Hweilan could not break free, could not even loosen the woman's steel grip. Kesh Naan pulled her in close. A black tongue emerged from between her pale lips, and Hweilan felt the cold flesh slide along the wounds on her shoulder, licking at the blood.

Hweilan screamed.

Kesh Naan held her at arm's length and sighed, like a destitute drunkard enjoying his first taste of a truly fine wine. But then, as Hweilan watched, the look froze on Kesh Naan's face. Her upper lip curled into a snarl, and Kesh Naan threw Hweilan away—so hard that she flew across the cavern, slammed into one of the stone columns, then hit the ground, dirt and grit raining down upon her.

She heard Kesh Naan spitting. "Blood burns and bites—gah!"

Almost paralyzed with fear and confusion, Hweilan managed to look up. Kesh Naan was staring at her—*studying her*—through eyes narrow as the slash of a razor. Very slowly, she wiped her lips with the back of one hand.

"What are you?" Kesh Naan said.

"I . . . I—"

"What *are* you?" Kesh Naan's voice came out more the roar of a beast than that of a woman. Each word brought her a step closer.

"I—"

"What are you, girl?" This last came out a whisper, but she was so close that Hweilan could feel her breath against her cheek.

Hweilan squeezed her eyes shut and tried to crawl away. But she came up against the stone column and could go no farther. She felt the strong hands grab her again, lift her, and when she dared to open her eyes, all was darkness. They were in the cave.

Blind panic seized Hweilan. She knew they were moving, could feel the steady rhythm of Kesh Naan's tread and the slight movement of air against her bare skin. Kesh Naan had a grip like steel chains, and one arm held her chest so tight that it was all she could do to draw shallow breath after shallow breath. The dark was utter and complete. The only sound that of Kesh Naan's heavy breathing and the slap of her feet against the tunnel floor.

Hweilan bucked and thrashed, but Kesh Naan only held her tighter. Hweilan tried to scream, but Kesh Naan's grip was too tight. Every movement made seemed to find the crack in her rib and grind it. She could not gather breath. Lights danced before her eyes.

Just when the play of light and darkness was about to overwhelm her senses, she heard Kesh Naan scream—almost in disgust, she thought—and the crushing grip was gone. Hweilan felt cool air rushing over her naked skin and knew she was again flying through the air.

She landed on one shoulder, then tumbled and slid across gritty stone. For a long while she could do nothing but lay there, desperate for air, each breath sending a lance of agony through her side.

When she opened her eyes, she saw that the lights were still there—but farther away. She was in a huge cavern, far larger than the one from which she'd come. It was devoid of any sun- or starlight, yet it sparkled with a thousand colors. Lying on her back, she watched them. Thousands had been too timid an estimate. By far. Looking up, she saw what were probably millions of tiny lights, all constantly on the move, some on a ceiling that sloped into a deeper darkness where the lights would not go, some scuttling across the walls and floor, and some hanging in midair—a few close enough that had she reached out she could have touched them.

They were tiny spiders, transparent as crystal, their plump bodies pulsing with colors—reds, greens, blues, yellows, silver, gold, and purples of every shade. The lights they cast sparkled off webs strung around the cavern. Terrified as she was, every breath a stab of pain, still Hweilan could not help but feel overwhelmed at the beauty of it all.

As her heart began to slow and her breathing to calm, Hweilan could hear them moving—the susurrus of millions of minuscule legs moving over stone and soil and each other. It sounded like the rustle of a summer breeze on the grass of the high steppe. Soothing. One of the spiders dropped from its web and landed on her shoulder. It felt soft as goosedown.

But then she heard something else. Something scuttling in that impenetrable darkness far above. No, not something. Some things. Her eyes were adjusting to the new light, and she saw that amidst the millions of small spiders, dozens of larger spiders moved. She hadn't seen them at first, because unlike their smaller cousins, they were black as moonless night, visible only because of the other lights reflecting off their hard carapaces.

"K-Kesh Naan?" she tried to call out, but it sounded no more than a whisper. Hweilan swallowed, winced as she gathered a full breath, then tried again, louder. "Kesh Naan?"

The black spiders dropped, a dozen or more striking the ground around her. The smallest of them was big as a cat, and the largest was almost the size of a hound. They turned to face her, the mandibles on their faces *click-click-click*ing together, in a horrible rhythm. Something about the sound seemed on the verge of forming words.

Hweilan forced herself to her feet, but the spiders surrounded her. She didn't dare try to rush between them, and she knew she wasn't strong enough to leap over.

"Kesh Naan!" she screamed. Her side screamed at the movement, but she bit back a scream and forced herself to stay put. "Please. Gleed sent me to you."

A sharp hiss from the nearest and largest spider. Nothing remotely human in it. Hweilan swallowed and decided to try another tactic.

"The Master sent me," she said.

Hweilan held her breath. Silence.

"You must teach me!"

The spiders surged into movement, so quickly that Hweilan screamed. But they weren't coming for her. All of the giant black monsters leaped onto each other, their legs scrambling in a writhing mass, faster and faster until they blurred together into a swirl of blackness. Before her eyes, the blackness took shape.

Kesh Naan stood before her, clothed in the gossamer-fine threads of darkness. "You wish to *Know*, girl?" she said.

Had Kesh Naan moved toward her, Hweilan might have scrambled away. But the woman just stood there, looking at her, the slightest curve of a smile on her lips.

"You desire . . . en-light-en-ment?" She broke the last word into pieces, emphasizing each syllable. "You ask for Lore. *Ahwen* in the sacred speech. Say it."

"*Ahwen.*"

"And why do you desire this?"

Truth be told, Hweilan didn't. The only thing she desired at this moment was to be far away. Even Gleed's dank tower seemed a paradise compared to this nightmare. So she said the only thing she could think of. "Th-the Master sent me. Nendawen."

"Yes," said Kesh Naan. "But why are you here?"

"I . . . I don't know."

Kesh Naan smiled—fully this time, revealing gums pale as her skin and teeth black as onyx. She raised both hands, palm outward. "I smell the lie in that, girl."

"I—"

"Truth now. Has fear so clouded your mind that you forget? Let me help you. What is the one thing you desire most? If you could have only one thing right now, what would that be?"

"Vengeance," she said it without thinking.

"Truth at last. But know this: The Master is not one to bargain. You do not make demands of the Master of the Hunt. Obey him, or do not. There is no middle ground."

"My family—"

"Vengeance will not bring them back. It will not ease your pain."

"Jagun Ghen killed my family!"

"Ah," said Kesh Naan. "Now we come to it. Jagun Ghen killed your family. Do you know why?"

Hweilan could not look away. The woman's eyes . . . depthless. But they held her. Hweilan opened her mouth, but before she could speak—

"The truth now," said Kesh Naan. "Only the truth."

And so she spoke the truth: "I don't know."

"You will," said Kesh Naan. She clapped her hands. Just once, but it filled the air like the crack of a whip.

And the spiders came. Thousands of them. Millions. Dropping from the ceiling and running across the floor, covering Hweilan's skin, crawling into her ears and nose. She rolled and thrashed, crushing hundreds, desperate to shake them off. But for every dozen she managed to smash or shake loose, a hundred more took their place. Their tiny legs did no more than tickle, but their fangs—

They bit, again and again and again. One of them surely would have done no harm, been no more than an irritation. But thousands biting her at once—

Hweilan screamed.

Spiders swarmed into her mouth, biting and biting and biting . . .

Lights exploded in Hweilan's mind. Each tiny bite bringing a spark, every flicker its own unique color, every one trying to swallow all her other senses.

She let them.

CHAPTER FIVE

On the Northern Ice the winter dark lasted for months, and even high summer could not melt the frost. Yet still people managed not only to survive there, but to thrive in their own way. It was a hard land, and the people harder still, but even so, Jatara could remember a time when she'd been allowed to be a little girl. Pampered by the elders. Fed the choicest meats from every hunt. Given the softest, warmest clothes. She'd even had a little doll, made from baby-soft sealskin. In the darkest winter nights when the wind howled over the ice and the elders made sacrifices to keep demons at bay, Jatara had huddled in her blankets near the fire, the doll cradled against her chest, and with her free hand she would stroke the soft sealskin over and over, imagining that she was her mother, and the doll little Jatara. No matter how the wind howled or the priests shrieked their blood rites, that little doll had helped Jatara feel safe. As an adult, when she thought *home,* it was not her clan's faces she saw, not her mother or father, but the scent of a fire, and the feel of that little doll against her palm.

"Home . . ." she said. It came out a croak. Her throat felt raw. The pain jolted her out of her reverie. She held the doll close and stroked it.

But something was wrong. *Felt* wrong. Not the softness of sealskin. She could feel the doll's skin, yes, but it was not seal soft. No. It was rough, torn, and—

Wet.

Warm, yes, but that was quickly fading.

And the smell . . . no. Smell was the wrong word. The *stench* was tangy, coppery, and foul.

Jatara stroked the doll again, grasping for that reassurance of *home,* but the ragged wetness under her palm only drove it farther away.

With a very great effort, Jatara opened her eyes.

And remembered.

Home was far away. Not separated from her by hundreds of miles, but years upon years. She was not a little girl anymore. The doll long gone. Under her hand—

A man's head lay in her lap. It was still loosely attached to the body by a mangled web of skin, flesh, and tendon. His jaw was gone, as were both eyes and an ear.

"What—?" she said.

Then her eyes saw the wet blackness under her nails, and she could feel more of the same in her teeth and gums.

A small part of Jatara—a very small part—screamed at the memory of what she had done. But the scream was very faint, like the final cry of a drowning man. Something else filled her. Immersed her. Like rich dye permeating old cloth.

Jatara laughed at that image. How fitting. The new presence within her was not her, but it filled every pore. She had no word for it.

"How do you feel?"

The voice came from behind her. She recognized it at once. Argalath . . . and something else. Something like her. Like flame is both heat and light, two separate things combined into one vibrant . . . *power.*

Jatara stood, and the corpse fell off her lap onto the blood-soaked grass. The sun was up, but hidden behind a curtain of thick cloud. The wind cut over the steppe, making a sound like a saw through dry wood. It still held the bite of winter, but she didn't flinch. The cold of Narfell was a kiss compared to the land where she'd been born. Swaths of snow still clung in the shadowed places of the hills or in the gullies, but dun-colored grass had broken through on the high ground where they had performed the rites. Where Jatara had been reborn.

She looked down at her hand and bare arm, black up to her elbow in blood and gore. It was like seeing it for the first time.

"I feel . . . *alive*," she said. "More than alive, I feel . . . there are no words."

"I know," said Argalath.

He stood nearby, his robes around him, his deep cowl pulled down so that she could see only his chin. But she heard the pleasure in his voice. And more, she could sense his mood, and his thoughts seemed just beyond her reach, almost as if there was some invisible string between them, vibrating with life, and together they formed a beautiful chord. Jatara was awestruck at the power she felt there, just below the surface. She was amazed that the man's skin didn't vibrate at containing such power.

Over Argalath's shoulder, she could see Vazhad standing atop the next rise, holding the reins of their horses. He was almost a quarter mile away as the crow flies, but even with only her one remaining eye she could count the stitches on the horses' saddles and see the few strands of hair that had come loose from Vazhad's topknot and wafted in the breeze. She could even smell the leather and sweat, and in the lulls of the breeze she thought she could hear Vazhad's heart beating. Something inside her stirred, and an urge struck her. For a moment, she wanted nothing in the world more than to bound over Argalath, use the raw power in her limbs to run over the grass, then seize Vazhad, throw him to the ground, and ever so slowly burrow her finger between his ribs until she could feel his heart thrumming. How he would scream . . . even Vazhad, who never laughed, who never cried out even in battle. He would scream if she did that.

Jatara swallowed and buried the urge.

"It worked," she said, and looked around. Carnage—the remains of the three Creel guards and one horse, the gore and torn earth obliterating all but a few traces of the pact circle Argalath had burned into the grass. She remembered the rite. The words of Argalath's incantation that had seemed so strange to her the previous night had a comfortable, even familiar flavor. She remembered the blade flashing in the firelight, the pain of the cut, and then the *thing* that had come, rising from the pact circle like a lover creeping through her bedroom window. For a moment, the old Jatara had recoiled. Sensing the mind of the other, she had wanted nothing more than to run. But she'd held one thing firm in her mind.

Kadrigul. Her brother. The only thing she had truly loved in the world. In the years since their clan had been slaughtered and they had had only each other to hold in the dark, he had been the one constant in her life. The one remaining bit of him that was more than memory. The memories were dear to her, but Kadrigul was flesh and blood. He was real, and he was hers. And he was dead.

And so she had opened herself to this new power.

"Oh, yes," said Argalath. "It worked. Now you see. Now you understand. Now you *know*."

"Now," she said. "I hunt."

CHAPTER SIX

Lights swallowed Hweilan's senses, her emotions, her . . .

Everything.

She let them. More, she welcomed it. All the fear, all the confusion, all the hurt—burned away by the light, until she was left with only . . .

Hweilan. That essential spark of *her*. Not of wanting or doing or hurting. Just being.

And when she knew that, when she was only awareness, the light became not just a purifying fire, but revelation. Thought became more than the light. Before she had seen the light. Now, she could see *by* the light. And she saw—

A hundred lifetimes of her ancestors. Vil Adanrath. People of the Hunt. She saw through the eyes of her grandmothers and grandfathers, every intimate detail. And she saw with the eyes of gods, beholding all as if from afar. Life for her people was not paradise, but it was good. They lived, they loved, they served their gods, and they died, for hundreds of generations. To survive they hunted, mostly the deer and elk and other herd animals of the high hills and northern snowfields. But there was never any lack. And when the Vil Adanrath died, their bodies returned to the ground, where they fed the grass, which fed the herds, which fed the people. And thus did they live in the Balance of *Dedunan*, of Silvanus the Forest Father, living, loving, killing, dying, being born, world without—

No. Because it did end. With Jagun Ghen.

Burning Hunger. The Destroyer. From the Abyss he came, and for generations we fought him, but he grew stronger, destroying our homeland. We fled. . . .

A voice out of her past. She almost put a name to it, then it too bled into the light, swallowed.

She saw the devastation Jagun Ghen brought. She felt disgust and horror, and even anger and pity at seeing what the Destroyer did to the People. But it had not touched her. Years and generations separated her from all this.

Dedunan intervened, the familiar voice again. *Jagun Ghen was cast from the Hunting Lands, and escaped to Toril.*

But his flame was not extinguished. Only banished.

The voice from the light changed, and this voice she did know. It was the mind that had ripped through her own, that face that almost drove her to madness. Nendawen. Hunter.

In the Hunting Lands, Jagun Ghen almost conquered. Only hundreds of years of blood and sacrifice vanquished him. Here . . .

And she saw Toril, floating in the void amidst the stars.

. . . in this corrupt world beneath its cold stars . . .

And she saw mountains. Ones she knew. The Giantspires, running like a jagged spine between frozen Narfell and the lands of the Damarans.

Here . . . Jagun Ghen could become a god. . . .

• • ◉ • •

"The power you seek," said the old crone, "is not like the Art of southern spell-weavers with their muttering and powders and twaddling fingers."

She leaned in close over the low fire, the orange flames painting her pale skin and paler hair a devilish orange. So deep were the wrinkles in her face that each of them was its own well of shadow, so that her eyes shone out as if from a burning mask.

The man across from her sat in shadow by the wall of the tent. But when he looked up the light of the fire caught in his eyes.

"Sorcerers' spells, the incantations of the strongest wizards I could find, ministrations of priests . . . none could help me, could cure my . . ."

He leaned forward, leaving the shadows behind, revealing the horror of his features. He was bare from the waist up, completely hairless, his skin a mottled patchwork of snow-white and bruised blue, and he squinted against even the dim light of the fire. Spellscarred.

When his sentence remained unfinished, the old woman said, "Affliction?"

"Will this pact cure me?" he said.

The crone closed her eyes and shook her head. "As I told you, the power you seek . . . it is not like the Art. Here, there are no strict laws—give, take; empty, fill; push, pull; act, react. Here, you are not dealing with the forces of nature, or even the intricacies of the Weave. Here, you are wrestling with a *will*, a being of vast power and knowledge beyond our imagining. It is not in its nature to serve another. To bend it to your will—"

"*Will it cure me?*"

Even though her eyes were still closed, she turned away. "Spellplague" she almost spat the word. "If there is a cure, it is beyond any power I have ever known."

The man's face twisted in a rictus of fury, and he took in a rattling breath.

"*However*," the old woman spoke before he could, "the one you seek has power far beyond any I have ever known. Beyond any mortal's. If there is a cure—*if!*—then it lies in the pact. But I give you no assurances. Only hope."

"Then I need only one thing from you—the name."

The old woman opened her eyes and gave a resigned nod. She seemed, for once, at ease, relieved. "You have everything else you need? The words of summoning? The sacrifice? The—?"

"I need only the name."

The old woman hesitated, as if catching something in the man's tone. "I wonder . . . what is your . . . affliction? I have heard that the spellscars grant some great power. Yet you seem desperate to be rid of yours."

"*Some*"—the man's upper lip curled, revealing flawless white teeth—"bear no more than a tangle of blue flesh, easily covered. Look at me." He leaned forward so far that the smoke from the fire wafted over his torso. "Look at me!"

The old woman shied back a moment. Then she cackled and said, "Look at me."

She spread her arms so that the fabric of her robe fell away. Scars riddled both arms, front and back. Her left hand lacked two fingers, and half the thumb was gone from her right. One of the larger scars running from the inside of her elbow to her wrist trembled slightly, as if something were wriggling just beneath the skin.

"The pact . . ." she whispered. "You play with fire, boy, you be ready to burn. And you are playing with something *much* worse than fire now."

"I am not playing, old woman."

"And yet you still haven't answered my question." She lowered her arms and leaned forward so that her nose was only inches from his. "What does your spellscar do?"

He didn't back away. "I want the name."

"Tell me the nature of your spellscar, and I will tell you the name."

The man opened his mouth, then looked askance as if something had occurred to him. The hint of a grin flickered in one corner of his mouth, then he sat back, both hands on his knees. "Tell me the name," he said, "and I'll *show* you."

She watched him through narrow eyes, weighing his words, searching for any sign of deception.

"Very well," she said at last, and she told him the name. "Jagun Ghen. Destroyer. Burning Hunger. The rites you have prepared . . . call Jagun Ghen."

"Thank you," said the man.

The blue patches on his skin flickered with a pale blue light, like the very base of a candle flame. Then they flared, a bright flash.

The smile froze on the old woman's face, her last breath rattled out of her, and she fell forward into the fire, sending up a shower of sparks.

• • ◉ • •

He knew the demands of the pact, and he knew just the place: An open vein leading down into the darkest heart of the world—a cave in the last of the Giantspires' northern foothills. He went alone, for he had no acolytes, no friends. His own people had never truly loved him, but after the Spellplague, they had shunned him, naming him *Kharta Vaaj*, shunned of the gods.

Down and down he went, far beyond even where bats roosted, to where his only companions were spiders and other crawling things that fled from the meager glow of his lamp. There lay a cavern, its center filled with black water, columns of stone everywhere, some thick as old pines, some thin as needles, all damp and slick and smelling of secrets.

He made the circle on the shore of the pool, scratching it into the dust with the burned, jagged end of an antler, then filling the grooves with twice-burned ashes. Muttering the incantation that would prepare his mind, he punctured the center of his left palm with the antler, then mixed the blood with the ashes to make the symbols of power inside the circle's edge.

And here, Hweilan's vision expanded. A part of her remembered a time from another life, long ago and far way. She had stood in a high window of a castle, looking down on a courtyard where her grandfather's warriors gathered. The window glass was thick to keep in the heat and push back the outside cold, and when her mother entered the room from behind her, she cast a distinct reflection in the window, so it seemed as if her ghost walked over the men below. Two scenes, separate, one atop the other, bleeding into one. This was like that.

She saw the hairless, mottled man, etching foul symbols into the dirt with his own blood and ash. But atop that she saw—

The Forest Father intervened. . . .

Jagun Ghen's servants were cast from the Hunting Lands into the Abyss. But their Master fled. The Hunting Lands held no more safety for him, but neither would he suffer the Abyss. And so . . .

Deep within Faerûn, the spellscarred man called upon forces beyond his world, summoning them to his pact circle.

He did this alone, but in those final moments, he remembered the words of his own master, the demonbinder of the tribe—

"The circle, the words of power, the symbols that contain the words and more . . . properly done can open a door to beings beyond this world. But take care, Argalath. Take care. Make the sacrifice. Speak the words *exactly*. Still . . . with an open door into such places, one is not always certain what may come through. Make your circle well. Strengthen your own will. For such is the binding that . . ."

She lost the rest, and with her vision in both worlds, she saw why. Desperate in his flight Jagun Ghen fled to the first open door he found. At his first sight of the demon, the name faltered on the binder's lips, and Jagun Ghen tore his way through the circle, overwhelming the spellscarred man.

But just as Nendawen was not of Faerûn and thus not free to roam as he pleased, Jagun Ghen could not wholly roam unbound. He fled into the one place of safety he could find—the room prepared in Argalath's mind. He took it, making it his own, and over the ensuing years taking more and more of Argalath's mind, fusing it with his own.

He bided his time, searching for the way to break into the prisons of the Abyss where his brothers and servants lay locked away, tormented by their own twisted minds. At long last he found the lore, the key that would unlock their prisons.

And a new vision superimposed itself over these. She saw the moonlight mountaintop, the desecrated shrine, the gathering of acolytes and supplicants, and she recognized some of them. Argalath, Guric, and men of Guric's company whose names she did not know. Several young Nar were there as well—by their shaved heads and scars, she thought they had to be Argalath's acolytes. She saw poor Valia, three years dead, unwrapped from her burial shroud. Guric's soldiers dragged forward a man, bound and gagged. She knew him as well. Soran . . .

That name brought forth the first pang of emotion since she had been reduced to awareness. Love, admiration, respect, but also a hint of fear. No, not fear. But real terror, and horror at something he had done, some—

And she saw Argalath unlock the foul thing's prison, saw the demon enter the dead woman and raise her to an undeath filled with a never-ending hunger.

Here . . . Jagun Ghen could become a god. . . .

And in that state of almost pure awareness, she knew it had begun.

CHAPTER SEVEN

Jatara could feel the party approaching. She'd been trained to hunt since she was nine years old, and she had long since developed a hunter's mindset of being in tune to the world around her, aware of the sounds and silences, the paths of local predators, the scents on the wind. But this was something more. Something new. She could sense them, like an itch on the front of her brain. Given their location and the sheer number approaching, it was most likely hobgoblins.

She knew her own party was outnumbered. She had left Highwatch with ten men and two women. None of them Nar. Even the Creel would not go into the deep mountains without being whipped the entire way, and this was not a task where Jatara could afford to be distracted by her own lackeys. And so Argalath had given her mercenaries—Damaran outlaws mostly, though the women and two of the men claimed to be exiles out of Kront. They had been part of the group of swords hired to help in the taking of Highwatch. Argalath had confided to Jatara that it would not displease him if they did not return.

Including herself, her party numbered thirteen, and Jatara knew she could probably count on at least four of her company to turn cloak if things went bad. As for the eight Damarans . . . well, that would depend entirely on who was coming. But really, it didn't matter. When it came down to it, Jatara could only depend on herself.

Jatara and her company had been following Kadrigul and the girl's trail for almost two days. Jatara could sense both. The trail had led them into the upper foothills of the Giantspires where the woods thickened and they had to ride single file. Jatara took the lead.

She looked around. If the trees grew much thicker, they'd soon be forced to dismount and lead their horses. Not exactly the best place for swordplay. But it also meant that archers would have to come in close, making a true ambush difficult.

They were close. Perhaps watching Jatara and her party right then.

Jatara dismounted and drew her sword from where it hung against her hip.

The next rider nearest her, one of the women from Kront, reined in her own horse and said, "Problem?"

"We're about to have company," said Jatara, and she stepped away from her horse.

"Orders?" called out one of the Damarans. Half of them had dismounted and drawn weapons, but the others remained in their saddles, reins in one hand, weapons in the other. Their mounts whickered and tossed their heads, some of them fighting their reins. The horses could sense those approaching, probably had picked up the scent. It wouldn't be long.

Jatara's horse tried to turn. Seeing the way blocked, it trotted off down the path, and she let it go. She scanned the thick brush on the upper slope. Most of the hobgoblins were coming from that direction. A few were flanking them already, but most would come from uphill.

From up the path where her mount had fled came the scream of a horse. It ended abruptly, cut off.

"Orders?" the Damaran called again, a note of desperation in his voice.

"Try to stay alive," said Jatara. "And stay out of my way."

The slight breeze that had been rattling the branches all morning gusted, and in the same instant Jatara smelled the things coming, she saw the first of them. The smell was a musty animal reek, mingled with the oil of steel and leather. The sight matched. The creature moved with the combination of the graceful stealth of a warrior and the lumbering gait of a bear.

The thing inside Jatara *lurched*. A *thrum* filled her head, and for a moment the world blurred around her. In between one heartbeat and the next, she felt her consciousness slipping. She clenched her jaw and forced it back.

"No!" she said.

"No what?" said the woman near her.

The look Jatara turned on her made the woman gasp and take a step back. For a fleeting moment, Jatara could see the blood pulsing beneath the woman's skin, could hear the beat of her heart and her breath rasping through her constricted throat, could smell the woman's fear. The thing inside Jatara surged, eager, and again Jatara pushed it down.

"Damn and double damn," she heard one of the men say.

More of the things were in sight. Jatara's instinct had been correct. Hobgoblins. Fiercer and more cunning than their smaller cousins. They stopped just past the nearest trees. Man-sized, every one of them walking on two legs, but there the resemblance ended. In the gaps of their tarnished armor, Jatara saw unwashed skin the color of bad ale, and thick hair that bristled more like a beast than a man. Sharp ears stuck out from their helmets, and brown and yellow teeth protruded from their lips. Their narrow eyes had an unhealthy yellow cast. Their armor was simple, unadorned, and crude at best, but the thick blades and short spears they carried looked well made—some of them even new. Jatara had heard rumors for years that Yarin Frostmantle had been supplying the goblins of the Giantspires with weapons in hopes of keeping the lords of Highwatch from gaining too much power. From where she stood, Jatara counted two dozen, but she knew more were keeping under cover.

"What do we do?" one of the men from Kront said, and when Jatara didn't answer, he added, "My lady, what—?"

His horse reared, and he had to fight to keep it from bolting through the line.

"Off the horses," said one of the hobgoblins in Damaran. "Weapons on the ground and you can walk out of here. We just want the horses."

To their credit, every member of her party looked to Jatara.

"Won't ask again," said the hobgoblin.

"My lady?" said the man again, and when she still didn't answer. "Jatara?"

She spared the man a glance then returned her attention to the hobgoblins. It hit her then. The sight was unnerving enough—seeing every wrinkle in their skin, every bit of tarnish in their armor or crack in their leather harnesses. The stench was worse. But then all of a sudden she could *taste* them. And not just the hobgoblins. The men. The women. Even the horses. The taste of them filled her mouth. Her stomach rumbled.

"They'll never let us out alive," said the woman from Kront. "Back the way we came?"

"Jatara?" said the man.

Jatara spat, trying to dislodge the taste, to convince herself that the hunger rumbling in her belly didn't feel so . . . *good*.

"Forget her!" said the same man.

And then it all happened at once. Those of her company still in their saddles turned their horses and kicked them into a gallop. The hobgoblins let out a roar and charged.

Later, Jatara could not remember the specifics of the following moments. She remembered screaming. Especially the screaming of the horses. For some reason, they stuck in her mind more than the screams of her dying companions. In her dreams that night, she could almost hear words in the horses' screams. They conveyed a meaning baser than language. More primal—confusion, excitement, and above all, terror. And because they were more primal, they hit her all the stronger.

The smell was almost overwhelming. The reek of blood. Sweat. Marrow spilling from shattered bone. Bowels loosening in death. The entrails of men and beasts. The cold, oily scent of steel.

The thing inside her overwhelmed all control, taking over, and later Jatara knew that she had killed. Had killed many. Had even struck at one of her own companions in her berserk state of mind. But in the end, just when she might have struck down those coming for her, the presence—

Did not leave. Did not forsake her. It simply . . . let go, the power draining from her, leaving her empty. Her blade, dripping blood, fell from strengthless fingers, and her knees hit the ground beside it. The world hummed. Her vision trembled as if she were seeing the reflection of the world in a pool, and someone had just tossed in a stone.

She heard a shriek, cut off abruptly by the sound of steel through flesh and bone. Jatara could actually *feel* the new warmth in the air. So much life spilled. Wasted, wafting away . . .

She saw the leather boots of the hobgoblin stop before her. Felt the slight tremble of his tread in the ground. Heard the leather-and-iron creak of his armor. Smelled his sweat and the blood dripping from his blade. Heard—

"We really did only want the horses, you stupid bitch."

Then he brought the heavy iron of his blade down into the flesh between her shoulder and neck.

There was no pain. But in the darkness that overwhelmed her, she could still feel that new presence inside her. And it was laughing.

CHAPTER EIGHT

The sound of drums woke Hweilan. Her head felt full to bursting, and she had to force her eyes open. The world was a strange array of gray and green and the shadows between. The first thought that occurred to her was—

Why has the world gone upside down?

And she realized that the world had stayed as it ever had, but she was hanging upside down, and the sound of drums was her own heart, filling her head with blood. Her hands, dangling so that her fingertips brushed the dead-leaf carpet of the forest floor, felt thick and ready to burst.

Hweilan looked up at her feet.

Thick whitish thread encased her legs, hips, and thinned out just over her navel. No, not thread. The small movement of her head set to swaying, just a little, and she felt the stickiness of the stuff over her bare skin. Not thread at all. It was webbing.

That realization brought back the memory of Kesh Naan, the cave, and the spiders. The thousands upon thousands of spiders . . .

Her head fell back. She felt sure her hands and arms and every last inch of her would be a mass of swollen flesh and fang-ravaged skin. But there wasn't so much as a scratch. In fact, every nick and scrape she had suffered over the past days was completely healed, her skin flawless. Except for one: The livid burn scar across her palm, the Dethek runes spelling kan—"death" in the tongue of the Vil Adanrath. But everything else . . . completely healed. How long had she swooned under the spiders' venom? How long had—?

Something moved through the brush of the trees overhead.

She looked up again and saw black shapes moving through the leaves, making their way over the thick branches of the tree from which she hung. More of the large, black spiders. Every one of them was headed straight for her. The sheer number of them made her heartbeat quicken.

She tried to move her legs. The spidersilk encasing her did not loosen in the slightest. She tried to pry at it, but her fingers only stuck to it.

The nearest of the spiders emerged from the leaf-thick branches and she got her first good look.

They were not as large as the ones in the cavern that had joined and become Kesh Naan. But they were still far larger than any spider ought to be. Each spider's abdomen was the size of a dinner plate. Its head—sprouting moist fangs and a dozen glassy eyes—was bigger than her fist. The spiders were not hairy, but black and shiny, a thing completely of chitinous armor.

Hweilan screamed.

"Kesh Naan! Kesh Naan, help!"

She thrashed, and her fingers swept through the leaves under her. The nail of her middle finger hit something hard. She looked down.

A knife lay there, buried in the leaves. She recognized it. A long flat of steel, etched with runes, hilt bound with thin strips of leather. She had first seen it in the snowy foothills of the Giantspires in what seemed another lifetime. It was an elf's knife. Lendri's knife.

A vibration ran through her, ever so slight, no more than a tickle in her bones. She looked up. The nearest of the spiders had reached the point from which began the tangle of web binding her to the tree. Its front two legs sought a grip on the web, found it, and the spider climbed down toward her. More spiders—a dozen at least—were crawling over each other in their eagerness to join the first.

Hweilan shrieked and stretched her hand out for the knife. It was a near thing, the tips of two fingers brushing over the cold steel, then she swung back. She thrashed again, gaining momentum, and on her next try she swung closer. The flat of the blade slid between her fingers, she tightened her grip, pulled, and slapped the handle into her other hand.

The spider passed her feet, her knees, her thighs—probably hoping for a spot of bare skin in which to sink its fangs.

Her fear and revulsion had robbed her of any thought of strategy or finesse. The spider's fangs twitched once, then opened wide to strike. Hweilan attacked. The point of the knife raked through the spider's eyes, and they burst like a bundle of overripe berries. The spider scrambled back so quickly that it lost its grip and fell. Hweilan's second strike batted it away. The feel of its hard carapace and the sharp points of its feet as her forearm struck made bile seep into her throat.

The blinded spider scrambled away, spraying dead leaves in its wake. The others, gathered on the branch overhead, hesitated only a moment before beginning their descent.

Hweilan tried to slice away the webbing by sliding the edge of the knife under the silk. But it was stuck fast to her skin. Given hours of careful work, she knew she could probably manage to slice away enough to free herself. But she had moments at best.

The spiders came down. The webbing vibrated like a harp string, and she could feel their claws grabbing the tangle of silk. Others, seeing the way down full with their fellows, affixed their own webs to the branch and dangled toward her.

The nearest spider scrambled over her knees. She felt another coming down the back of her legs.

Hweilan swiped with the knife in front of her and her fist behind. The spiders stopped just out of her reach. The one she could see eyed the sharp steel of the knife as it swept past again and again. She half-considered bending up at the waist to extend her reach, but she feared that doing so would give the spider on the back of her legs the opening it needed.

The spider grasping her shins watched the knife go past twice, three times, and after the fourth it leaped, falling down, then grasping all eight of its claw-tipped legs around one breast and shoulder.

Hweilan screamed and instinctively pulled her head away as far as her neck would stretch. But against her will her eyes looked down and she saw the spider's fangs twitch once, then spread wide, each point filling with a shiny, clear droplet of venom.

A round knob of wood struck the spider's head. A sharp *crack* of shattering chitin, and the thing flew away. She heard another strike, and the weight across the back of her legs flew away.

"Get gone, you!" shouted a reedy voice, followed by *thwack-thwack*!

Hweilan twisted her head around, swiped her own hair from her face, and looked for her rescuer. There stood Gleed, swiping at the spiders with the staff that was taller than he was. For a creature that had probably been old when her grandfather was born, the goblin was surprisingly spry.

But there were too many. Hweilan had first numbered the spiders at dozens. Looking up, she saw that there had to be at least two score, perhaps more. They had seemed eager before, coming for her. Now, they were enraged. But they seemed to have forgotten her for the time being.

Those hanging from the web or clinging to her perch jumped to the forest floor and scrambled for Gleed. Those still in the branches leaped for him. The closest in the near branches overhead turned their swollen bodies and spat out lengths of web that caught in the slightest breeze.

But it was all in vain. The runes etched into Gleed's staff and burned into his leather robes flared with a green light. Fire sizzled from his open palm, and emerald flame flared along the length of his staff. The shards hit the spiders in a shower of sparks. The nearest took the full brunt of the attack and burst into smoking pieces, but some tried to dodge, and the missiles glanced off their thick shells. Still, it soon took the fight out of them, and they scurried into the underbrush, trailing acrid fumes behind them. Green fire caught in the strands of silk riding the air, and even as it burned them to ash the flames raced up the strand to catch on the spiders themselves.

It was over in mere moments. A rattling of leaves and underbrush as the spiders fled, and then there were only a few left. Even though the flames were dying, still all it took was a waggle of the staff in their direction, and they too joined their fellows for the deeper shadows of the forest.

Hweilan hung there dumbly, the knife dangling from one hand.

Gleed turned to her. "You survived Kesh Naan," he said. "I am most pleased. But I see you still have much to learn."

She glared at him. "Just get me down."

• • ◎ • •

"Drink this," said Gleed. He held out a brass goblet from which a thick steam rose.

Hweilan, sitting in front of the crackling hearth inside Gleed's tower, frowned at the proffered drink. "The last time I drank something you offered, I passed out then woke up naked in the woods."

The old goblin smiled, revealing sharp yellow teeth. "See, you *are* learning. Well done. But this is only mulled wine with a few special herbs. It will warm you up and help you to relax. Nothing more."

Hweilan took it and sniffed the steam. Her scowl turned to a grimace.

Seeing it, Gleed chuckled. "I didn't say it was good wine."

Despite the smell, holding the warm liquid in her hand made Hweilan realize how thirsty she really was. She took a quick drink and forced it down. She almost choked. "Gah! That is . . . foul."

But Gleed had already turned away to tend something in the fire, and he ignored the comment.

The wine seemed to settle in her stomach only a moment, then the warmth spread throughout her whole body. She felt her skin flush, and a pleasant tingling started at the crown of her head and worked its way slowly down the length of her body to her toes. She made sure Gleed wasn't watching, then finished the rest in two gulps.

"Want some more?" said Gleed, who still hunched over the fire. He hadn't even glanced behind him. Hweilan thought he must have the ears of a bat.

"Yes," she said.

He didn't laugh as he took the empty goblet from her, but she could see the amusement in his eyes. "Grows on you, does it not?" he said.

"It tastes like the bottom of a horse bucket, but the way it feels . . ." She shrugged. "I like it."

"You like it now," he said, handing her a full goblet, "but you'll learn to love it later." He gave her a conspiratorial wink. "Always a danger with such things."

She took the goblet and breathed in the steam.

"Take your time with that one," said Gleed. "I want you relaxed, not insensate."

The goblet stopped halfway to her lips. "For what?"

Gleed pursed his lips in thought, then said, "You know of the *uwethla*?"

She started to shake her head, then stopped. Hweilan of Highwatch had no idea what *uwethla* were. But she was more than that. The well of her memory, quiet and still since she'd woken in the woods, suddenly rippled, as if stirred by something swimming just below the surface. A hundred lifetimes of her people . . . she'd seen them, sometimes through their own eyes. She'd felt them, every pleasure and pain, and the words came to her unbidden.

"*Wethresta*," said Hweilan. "*Wethre unekwa lahena.*"

"He binds it," said Gleed, translating, his voice taking on the singsong chant of words spoken by rote. "He binds the words of power to the skin." He blinked once, very slowly and purposefully, then nodded. "You have the Lore. You passed the first test. You have earned your first *uwethla*."

Gleed turned back to the fire and removed a long rod of steel, wrapped in leather on one end, the other ending in a sharp point, which glowed red. He raised it, smiled, and Hweilan knew what was coming.

Seeing the red hot steel, she knew it would hurt like unholy hell. But after what she'd been through, after being the sole survivor of her family's slaughter, after enduring torture at the hands of Kunin Gatar, after being chased across half of creation, after having her mind ravished by Nendawen and spiders biting every inch of her skin and enduring all the sorrows of a hundred generations . . .

Well, a little pain in the skin seemed a small price to pay.

Her gaze hardened. "I didn't need the wine for this."

Gleed watched her a long moment, his eyes no more than slits. "Yes, I see that now," he said. Then he nodded at the door. "Outside."

• • ⊚ • •

They crossed the bridge and followed a path along the shore. At the end of the path, where water and light came together at the lakeside, Hweilan removed the cloak and kneeled near the water's edge, the water lapping less than a foot from her knees. Her wet hair lay heavy against her skin, but she felt hot, partly from the wine and partly in anticipation of what was to come.

Gleed stood behind her, moon- and starlight sparkling in the runes etched into his robes, almost as if they'd been sewn with diamond dust. In his left hand he held a wooden bowl, filled to the brim with a clear liquid that reflected no light at all. In his hand he held the pointed steel shaft, the end of which still held the heat of the fire.

"The Lore is to Know," said Gleed, his voice again toned to rote. "But to Know the Lore is a matter of the Heart. I will bind the Lore to your Heart. Do you wish it?"

Hweilan of Highwatch would have recoiled at the very thought of this, and her voice, now very small, did say, *What are you doing?* That voice would always be there—at least she hoped that some part of her would always be Hweilan of Highwatch—but she was something more now, and becoming more still. What . . . she wasn't sure yet. But she could feel the power coursing in her veins. And in her heart, she still remembered all that she had seen in her vision. She felt its absence, the loss like a hunger. And she knew there was only one way to fill it.

She stood and turned her back on the light rippling across the dark water. Looking up at her, Gleed saw that the sharp horn of the moon stood over her left shoulder, almost like the curve of a bow, and he had a momentary vision of what was to come. He shuddered and said again, his voice weaker this time, "Do you wish it?"

"*He nethke,*" said Hweilan, her voice clear and strong. "*Kethne kyerhewun.*"

She spoke the words perfectly, and she understood them—"I do wish it. Let it be done."

"So be it," Gleed said, and dipped the glowing tip of steel into the bowl. The liquid therein sizzled, but it did not steam, instead soaking into the hot metal like parched ground drinking in the first summer rain.

Hweilan kneeled again. She did not flinch or close her eyes as he approached with the hot steel. She forced herself to watch, to focus on the red hot point of metal.

"The Lore," Gleed said. "Upon your heart, I bind it."

He plunged the tip of the steel into her skin, beginning just above the swell of her left breast. Pain shot through her entire body. Her fists clenched involuntarily. Empowered by the sacred water, her skin did not burn or crisp, but took the fire into its very essence, even as her blood boiled and sizzled.

She did not scream.

• • ⓝ • •

Later, as Hweilan slept in her pallet beside one wall, Gleed sat up, staring into the glowing embers in his hearth.

Tonight by the lake, he had felt the very first tingle of fear. The first in a long, long time. When he plunged the hot metal into the girl's skin, tears filled her eyes, but the gaze that burned behind them showed only hunger and eagerness.

For the first time in all his years, Gleed thought perhaps the Master had bitten off more than he could swallow.

CHAPTER NINE

The time had come. Jatara woke.

The last thing she remembered was the sound of steel cutting the air. A heavy blade. Iron wrought not for beauty or craft, but purely for the purpose of killing. Honed to a razor's edge.

It had pierced her cloak, her coat, her shirt, and the shift beneath with the ease of hailstones shattering spider silk. Skin and flesh beneath had parted just as easily. The bones between shoulder and neck had offered some resistance, but the weight of the iron and the strong hand wielding it had proved superior, and the sword had gone all the way into her right lung. The darkness that filled her vision had been hot—the heat of drowning in her own blood.

Tasting it.

Savoring it.

Reveling in it.

And when she woke, the world was cold. Dark. The chill of winter stone and sunless soil. Jatara could feel it all around her. The mountains' height. Their roots, buried in cold ground. The weeping of a thousand winters burying all in cold. In dark. In emptiness.

So empty . . .

She woke to hunger, and that overwhelmed everything else.

The hobgoblins had made their camp only two days' march from their nearest shelter—a cave stashed with provisions made worryingly low by a long, hard winter. But after this day's work, their worries were no more. They feasted on horseflesh, and better yet, on manflesh. It was a good day's work.

An ambush on the thirteen out of Highwatch had not been without sacrifice. They'd lost nine of their own—five to the pale woman with the strange, half-shaved head and one eye. That one eye had made them hesitate at first, for the god Gruumsh One Eye was hated and feared by their people. Just when they'd been on the verge of letting her go out of pure superstitious dread, she had dropped her steel and fallen to her knees, as if in a daze. As if Maglubiyet himself had stripped her soul and given it to them, an offering.

They'd dragged the slain riders behind them—clothes and armor and all, back to their camp. The sun fell, and they stoked their fires, bold and full, to beat back the cold, but the clan knew the ancient way of the warrior. They took the horses' limbs and ate the flesh raw off the bone, giving thanks to Maglubiyet and slaking their thirst in new blood.

But the riders, the ten men and three women . . .

These they cast in a pile after stripping them of their weapons. The Damarans and their leader had fought well, had brought glory to their gods. The clan would feast on them with all due ceremony after the proper rites.

And so Jatara lay in the pile of corpses, amidst her slain companions. Because she had been the leader, because she had been the last to fall, because she had killed more than any other among her fellows . . .

Because of these things the clan laid her topmost on the pile of corpses. They whispered prayers to Maglubiyet and sprinkled the blood of their feast upon her as they made the sign of the slain on her face and covered over her one staring eye.

And just when their revel was at its height, when the warriors had slaked their thirst, filled their hunger, and settled into their self-satisfied celebration . . .

Jatara woke.

The thing inside her stirred, and with its stirring, her limbs twitched with life, and awareness returned to her, like the stoking of fire from dormant ashes.

She blinked once, saw the stars overhead, framed by the snowcapped peaks, the darkness between them made all the blacker by the shine of starlight on frost.

Jatara smiled.

She could feel the wound on her right side, breaking all the way through muscle and bone, rendering her right arm useless. But that would be easily healed, given proper nourishment.

Jatara blinked again and sat up, stirring the pile of corpses beneath her. She could hear the hobgoblins nearby reveling around their fires. She could feel the stamp of their feet as they danced their victory. The tremor their feet sent through the earth mirrored the beating of their hearts. . .

. . . that sent the blood racing through their veins . . .

. . . that filled the night with its song . . .

. . . that called to Jatara and the new power within her.

She tumbled off the pile of corpses, her pale feet striking the ground. Her killers had taken her boots. The leather would be flayed into strips, the strips braided to harness armor or perhaps a belt.

Better this way, she thought. She could feel the pulse of their celebration in the ground. Could feel the stamp of their feet, the beats of their hearts, and the heat of the life within.

Her stomach growled.

Her mouth watered.

She came forward out of the dark.

The leader of the hobgoblins stood before the greatest fire, Jatara's sword held high above his head. He had stripped down to a loincloth and gouged his flesh in honor of Maglubiyet.

He roared. He sang his song of victory into the dark. He waved the steel of his victim for all his followers to behold.

And then his victim stepped out of the darkness and into the heat of his fire. A blasphemy to the honor he did his god. She could feel the blood in his veins. So close. So hot. The life. The *nourishment*.

She ran from the darkness, left arm outstretched, fingers flexed to rend.

"Mine," she said, and fell upon him. It was the one thing that would not leave Jatara's mind. It set the rhythm of her heart. It sang in her blood. "Mine. Mine. Mine."

Killing the hobgoblin chief had been easy. Her fingers opened around his throat, closed, and pulled. His heart had still been beating when she'd ripped it from his chest. She'd done it so quickly that his people were too shocked to do anything but stand open-mouthed while their chief died. But it didn't last. Many had weapons in hand already, and in moments every empty hand had found steel or club. Then the slaughter began.

Jatara did not know how many blows she'd suffered. But the power was surging in her, the fire, burning and consuming and demanding ever more. Warm flesh and hot blood slaked her thirst, and her wounds healed. Broken bone fused. Torn flesh knit together. Even skin closed. And every strike upon her only fueled her fury. It did not take long for the hobgoblins to realize this foe was beyond any of them.

The clan shaman, an old crone of a goblin, fell on her knees before Jatara and closed her eyes. On the back of the old crone's eyelids, she had painted her skin so that they seemed to glow. "Blessed of Maglubiyet! Blessed of Maglubiyet!"

Jatara crushed the crone's neck beneath her left foot.

By then, most had already fled into the dark, but a few still in the blood ecstasy of their celebration fought on. They died with the rest. Even as Jatara let the last broken, lifeless body fall from her grasp, the final footfalls of the hobgoblins faded into the mountains.

So hot was the thing within her that she took no thought to find her boots or replace her torn clothes. She took only the sword that the hobgoblins had taken from her, then she was back on the hunt.

And that was when she noticed.

It had been many days since that wretched little wench had gouged out Jatara's eye. The physical pain had lasted for days. The blow to her pride had never healed. But now . . .

Jatara waved a palm in front of her face, just to be sure. Then, very carefully, like a baby bird taking its first step out of the nest, she closed her left eye. For the first time in days the world did not go black. She could see. The spirit inside her . . . the feast . . . it had not only brought her back from the verge of death. It had *improved* her. Not only could she see, she could see better than she ever had. Her vision could pierce the dark.

And still, she knew which way her brother had gone. Even though he was dead, still some cord connected them, past and present, and if she wanted to she could point to the paths he had taken, like a child with her eyes closed can still find the sun.

The trail was days old, but it had not faded to her new senses. Beyond sight or smell, she took the sense of the trail into her mind, like dry fleece soaking in a rich wine. The scent of her beloved and her quarry became one with her awareness. There was nothing but the hunt.

Two days after the slaughter of the hobgoblins, Jatara came to a hollow in the hills filled with the strangest standing stones she had ever seen. A casual glance might have mistaken them for ice, but Jatara's newfound senses knew they were crystal—albeit of no kind she had ever seen. Some stood almost straight up, many times her own height, but most leaned haphazardly at seemingly random angles.

Kadrigul had gone in there, she knew, and part of him had never come out again. Still, Jatara could sense something of him deeper in the mountains. There was no trail there. It was as if he had disappeared inside the standing stones and reappeared many miles away.

She didn't understand. But it was not understanding that drove her anymore. And so she continued on, deeper into the mountains.

CHAPTER TEN

After Hweilan took her first uwethla, Gleed's teachings filled every moment of every day, but Hweilan reveled in them. True, there were days when the rasping prattle of the old goblin's voice grated on every nerve, like the ceaseless *scritch-scratch-scratch*ing of a windblown branch scraping against her bedroom window. But mostly she gorged on the new knowledge.

Some days they sat huddled near his fire while rain pelted the lake and the wind set the entire tower and its covering bells to tinkling. She learned the names and natures of every tree and plant. She learned to make poultices and mix various herbs to speed the body's healing. And she learned their opposites: which roots, barks, leaves, and buds could be used to make poisons ranging from the deadly to those that would merely numb the senses. She learned which roots and berries could be crushed to make a paste that would mask her scent and even hide her from creatures whose eyes saw heat in the dark. But these were the easy lessons.

Gleed also taught her rites sacred to Nendawen and Dedunan—though part of Hweilan still thought of the latter as Silvanus. Of the nature of Jagun Ghen, she had seen much in her vision, but Gleed taught her the Lore—how generations of her people had learned to fight him. He taught her the words of power, and how to bind the words themselves with the *uwethla*. Etched into her skin, they would bind the Lore in her mind. But etched into arrows . . .

"They are deadly to the demons of Jagun Ghen."

Hweilan and Gleed were sitting just inside the woods near the lakeshore. Through the branches she could see the decrepit tower, its myriad bells and trinkets twinkling in the late afternoon sunshine. A small fire burned in its ring of stones between them, and next to it lay a pile of fresh sapling branches, which Gleed was teaching her to shape and harden into arrows.

"These demons can be killed then?" said Hweilan.

She remembered the first night she had seen Nendawen. Green light had wreathed the black iron of his spear, and looking back, had there not been symbols etched into the metal and along the shaft? Had the light not leaked from them, like water eking through the first cracks of the summer thaw? Perhaps. Although her mind had been so numbed by terror and exhaustion at the time that she thought her newer knowledge might be coloring her memory. But she remembered one thing for certain.

Seeing Nendawen and the spear in his hand, the thing—the demon—possessing Kadrigul's dead flesh had done something she had not seen it do even when facing Kunin Gatar. It had *feared*. It had beheld the Master and the weapon in his hand with abject terror and despair leaking from every pore. It had forsaken its shell and fled. Nendawen had thrown his spear, and here again the details were cloudy, but she thought it had consumed the fell spirit. Eaten it like a choice morsel.

Gleed pursed his lips as he considered her question. "Killed . . . ? Hm. Well, that depends on what you mean by death. They are spirits, and if by killed you mean 'cease to exist,' then no. That is not possible for *any* spirit. But they can be . . ." His brows knit together, making the deep wrinkles of his face deeper still. "Captured. Contained. Rendered powerless." Gleed shrugged. "Words fail here."

She looked down at the narrow shaft of wood in her lap. The arrow seemed a frail thing, but she had sensed the power in the words of their chant as they made it. A hint of that power leaked from the *uwethla* she had etched halfway up the shaft. It was almost like a scent, but this one did not hit the nose. It touched on something deeper, some lower part of the brain that was much more awake in beasts than men.

"This will capture them?" she asked.

Gleed smiled. "I am glad you asked."

She waited, and when he said no more, she said, "Well . . . ?"

"Tomorrow," he said.

"Tomorrow?"

"This is something that, to understand, you must *see*. You must experience for yourself. Tomorrow, we send this demon that hounded you back to the Abyss." He smiled, showing all his sharp, yellow teeth. "Sleep well."

• • ⊛ • •

Hweilan lay in her pallet that night, remembering the horror of the days after she fled Highwatch. There had been that brief moment of elation, seeing her Uncle Soran coming for her when she'd been told all her family was dead. But her first look at his empty eyes, and she had known. It wasn't her uncle. Something that knew only destruction and hunger looked at her through those empty eyes.

That thing had chased her through the mountains, through the realm of Kunin Gatar, until the queen herself—with a little help from Lendri—had finally destroyed Soran's body. But still the thing had come after her, filling Kadrigul's body. Looking back, she realized that in her heart she had known that at the time, though she hadn't stopped to consider it. When she did, she knew her instincts were true. Even after the body was destroyed, the demon found a new "home" and came after her. If it could do such things, move from dead flesh to dead flesh as if it were nothing more than changing clothes . . . then the real fight was against the spirit within. She had seen that in her visions and since gained understanding of it from Gleed's teachings.

But that did not make the thought of facing the demon again any easier. Had not Nendawen dealt with the thing already? Apparently not.

And here, Hweilan's visions were lacking. These most sacred rites were for the chosen few. The chosen one—the Hand of the Hunter.

When sleep finally took Hweilan, the last night she'd spent in the Giantspires haunted her dreams.

Emerald light sparking around barbed black iron.

A presence of flame and hunger screaming as it fled across the cold water.

A streak of black and green as the spear arced overhead.

A maelstrom of darkness and light of a thousand colors.

A scream that struck beyond hearing, searing itself into her bones.

After that, the Master, his eyes glowing from the mask, framed by crooked antlers. His right hand dripped blood.

Hweilan woke with a gasp.

Gleed was just stirring the fire in the hearth. "You're awake," he said. "Good. Get dressed."

• • ⊗ • •

They walked through the woods most of the morning. Always uphill, the stream that fed the waterfall ever on their right. Gleed said nothing the entire time. It was the quietest he had been in a tenday or more. Standing outside the tower, the morning still only a glow above the jagged horizon, he had said, "Think on all you have learned. Make the Lore fresh in your heart, ready in your mind. For what you are about to learn, you will need every lesson. Stay sharp."

After that, nothing but the sounds of their breathing and footsteps and the forest around them. Even the forest sounds grew quieter by the mile, as if they were entering a temple where silence reigned and the very air demanded whispers.

The land grew steeper, the trees thinned, and by midmorning they were climbing stone outcroppings as often as they walked deer trails. Despite his age and apparent frailty, Gleed scaled them, agile as a monkey.

They stepped onto the height just shy of midday. It was a flat area, completely treeless, the ground mostly windswept grass and lichen-encrusted stone. It was the first time Hweilan had seen so much sky since . . . how long? Since she'd come to this strange land.

The few clouds that marred the overhead blue seemed very close. The frayed gray hems of their skirts seemed almost close enough to touch. Beyond the rim of the height, the land fell away in hundreds of miles of forest, broken only by the silver sparkling of rivers and Gleed's lake, far below them.

Gleed kept walking, his staff thumping the ground in front of him. "Not much time now," he said. "Come. We must hurry."

Looking past him, Hweilan saw where he was headed. Land and sky, everything around her was the very picture of wilderness. Except for one thing. In the very center of the height, a black shaft, well over twice Hweilan's height, stood up from the ground. Her first glance at it made her heart skip a beat. She recognized it. Nendawen's spear.

When she had first seen it, the first arc of the moon breaking the horizon, it had seemed a fragment of night. Seeing it there under the light of the late morning sun didn't change her first impression. The smooth wood of the shaft and iron of the point, half-buried in the earth, reflected nothing. The small bit of shadow it cast in the short grass seemed more a part of this world than the weapon itself.

That was where Gleed pointed with his staff. "Inside is all that remains of the demon in this world. We must perform the rite when no darkness remains, when the sacred weapon stands fully in the light, surrounded by not even a hint of shadow. Only then can the spear be cleansed from the evil within. Here."

He tossed something and she caught it—a bag, slightly larger than her hand, made from the skin of some animal and tied shut with a cord of braided hair.

"What is it?" she asked, loosening the knot of the cord.

"Ashes from yesterday's fire," said Gleed. "Rowan ash, sacred to the Master. Scatter it in a circle around the spear. Leave no gaps. And say the Words with me. Bind them in your heart."

Hweilan did as she was told. The little goblin leaned upon his staff and began to chant in the language of the People.

"Great Nendawen, Hand of Dedunan, Child of Ao,
Our Master whom we serve, hear me now."

Hweilan repeated the words, her mind and tongue comfortable in the ancient tongue.

"Bless now our circle, bound in the ash of sacred flame.
Bless now our hands, whose blood flows in your name."

The last of the ash sifted out of the bag, completing the circle in a tiny mound of gray dust. Even as the last of it fell, Hweilan heard the thick flutter of feathers and looked up. Upon the haft of the spear sat a raven, its feathers as black as the weapon's shaft, but the bright midday sunlight reflected a deep blue off its crown and beak.

"Once," said Gleed, the cadence of his voice still locked in chant, "in the days of creation, Raven and his clan were all the colors of the rainbow, for of all the beasts who fly, they were the dearest to Dedunan, the Forest Father. But then came Jagun Ghen, the Unending Hunger. Destroyer. The Unslakable Fire. But Raven did not fear his fire, flying through flame and smoke in his hatred of our enemy. Still that hatred burns in them, and as a sign of the smoke through which they have passed, and the dark ones they hunt, their feathers are black, and shall be so until the Last Day."

Gleed looked up at the sun, then down at the small sliver of shadow that remained at the bottom of the spear. He turned to Hweilan and fixed his one good eye on her.

"What will *you* give to hunt Jagun Ghen?" he asked.

She remembered the words from her vision, from a hundred lifetimes, and she spoke them perfectly.

"*Iskwe gan nin,*" she said. My life's blood.

"*Kethne kyerhewun*," said Gleed. Let it be done.

Hweilan drew the knife from the sheath at her belt. The knife Lendri had given to her. The knife she'd regained after she'd woken from her vision. She held her left arm straight out, the knife's one sharp edge toward her. With her other hand she grasped the blade and slid her palm outward. The steel made a clean cut from the outer side of her palm to the soft flesh between finger and thumb.

The raven let out a rattling caw, and she could hear the inhuman words in its cry—*iskwe! iskwe! iskwe!* Blood! blood! blood!

"Do as I do," said Gleed, then kneeled and pressed his head onto the ground. Hweilan did the same. Together they sang—

"*O Master of the Hunt, Hand of Dedunan,*
Accept now our offering, in your name.
Bind that which was broken
Restore the Balance
That light might shine in our hearts again."

Hweilan felt a massive pulse ripple the ground under her, almost as if Nendawen's spear were a nail driven into stone and a giant's hammer had just struck it. She dared to look up.

The raven atop the spear stood with its wings outstretched to the noonday sun. Beyond him, gathered just outside the ring of ash, were hundreds of wolves. But she could see through them, as if they were made of morning mist. Only their eyes seemed solid and bright.

And standing in their midst was Scith, dressed in the finery of a Var warrior. Flames still danced in his hair and from his clothing, but they did not consume him. His visage was grim and proud. Just beyond him, wolves milling about her feet like puppies yipping at a mother hound, stood Merah, Hweilan's mother. But she was not wearing the gowns and robes of the Damaran court. She dressed as a Vil Adanrath warrior, and the blood pulsing from the wound at her head only made her look all the more fierce. Hweilan's father stood beside her, dressed in his finest armor, and even though he was insubstantial as the rest, the sunlight glinted off his steel, blinding and pure.

Hweilan could not look away, could not even force herself to blink.

"Behold!" Gleed whispered next to her.

She could not look away from her family, but from the corner of her eye she saw a green light flicker and pulse along the haft of the spear. The ground shook beneath her again, then once more, so strong that she felt her bones rattle, and her deepest senses—the ones beyond sight, hearing, smell, taste, and touch—felt something go out of the spear, screaming and clawing as it did so, but helpless against the greater power that thrust it down.

Gleed leaped to his feet and began to dance and caper around the spear, laughing and cackling as he did so.

"I won't do it, Hweilan," a rasping voice said from behind her.

Hweilan forced herself to sit up and turn around. Just outside the circle of ash, swaying in something between a crouch and lurch, was Lendri, just as ghostly as the rest. His chest was an open ruin, and he held his own heart in one hand. The heart was still beating, dripping blood down his arm and onto the ground, where it hit and sizzled to steam.

"You can call me," said Lendri, "but I will not return. Not even for you. Let my exile end. Please. Let me rest."

Hweilan squeezed her eyes shut and said, "No. You're dead."

She turned around again, opening her eyes. Gleed still danced around the spear. Raven and spear were gone. Beyond, the ghost wolves were fading, as was her family. Even as he faded, her father raised his hand and said, "In the midst of life, we are in death. Thin is the veil that separates us, and it can be lifted."

And then he was gone.

CHAPTER ELEVEN

AFTER THEY RETURNED TO THE TOWER, GLEED watched as Hweilan poulticed and bound the fresh wound in her hand, and they ate a good meal on the lakeshore as the sun set and the bats began to flutter around the lake, feeding on the night bugs.

Gleed built a small fire as the crickets' song began in full force. The old goblin leaned in close to the fire, stirring it far more than it needed, and Hweilan knew he was gathering his thoughts. The set of his brow and tightness of his jaw was not anger, so she didn't think she'd done anything wrong. But he seemed unusually solemn, even grim.

He jabbed at the fire, sending orange sparks to sparkle up amongst the silver and blue of the stars, then he said, "You saw something up there."

The question took Hweilan by surprise. "What?"

"Upon the height," said Gleed. "You saw the . . ." He squinted as he searched for the word, then shrugged and said, "The *Ebun Nakweth*."

"Witness Cloud?" said Hweilan, then it came to her. "You mean the ghost wolves?"

Gleed nodded, but his eyes had narrowed, reminding Hweilan very much of a frog in whose sight a tasty fly has just wandered.

"Yes, I saw them," said Hweilan.

"That is good. Blessed hunters. Sacred to the Master. That you saw them . . . you did well today, Hweilan."

"Thank you."

"You passed your first test with Kesh Naan, and you have learned much from me. You will still learn from me in the coming days. But soon—very soon—you will meet your next teacher. Lore you have. Making you are learning. Now, you must Hunt."

"Gleed, I've been a hunter most of my life."

The goblin reached around the fire and grabbed her arm, hard enough to hurt.

"Not like this, Hweilan." He looked up at her, eyes most serious. Then he licked his lips, looked around and said, almost in a whisper, "To hunt animals, to hunt men, even to hunt aberrations of dark magic . . . these are nothing like hunting the demons of Jagun Ghen. And even if your huntsmen were the hardest men in your land, they are nothing compared to Ashiin."

"Ashiin?" said Hweilan, trying the name. It meant "fox" in the language of the Vil Adanrath.

Gleed's eyes widened and he looked out into the dark. "Shht! Quiet, foolish girl."

Hweilan looked around, seeing nothing but the clear night sky, the bats fluttering over the lake, and the impenetrable dark of the woods beyond.

"Learn from her," said Gleed. "But do *not* trust her."

Hweilan stared at him. "What? I . . . I don't understand. Don't trust her? Why? If she is to teach me . . ."

"That one," Gleed whispered, "serves the Master. But for her own reasons. If she thinks you do not further those reasons . . ." He shuddered and looked around again, and his voice dropped even further. "Do *not* trust her. If you value your life, heed me, girl."

He stood and started to walk away, but she called out to him. "Gleed, I . . ."

He stopped and looked over his shoulder. "What?"

"The Witness Cloud . . . you saw them?"

"Yes. I have seen them many times."

"Did you see . . . anyone else?"

His brows crinkled into a deep wrinkle, his one good eye almost disappearing in the folds of skin. "One?" he said.

"What?"

"You said any*one* else? Not any*thing*. I saw wolves, ravens, owls, bears . . . hunters. All beasts sacred to the Master. Creatures I honor and respect. But I would not call them 'anyone.' So tell me: who did you see?"

Hweilan swallowed and looked away, uncomfortable under the intense gaze of that single eye. She didn't know if she could trust him. Growing up in Highwatch, hobgoblins and all their cousins had been nuisances at best—and more often than not a true menace. But Gleed was like no goblin she had heard of. She sensed a hardness in him, belied by his grizzled old frame. And no one would ever accuse him of being charming. But he had a weight of years about him that Hweilan could only find one word for—wisdom. And after all she had seen, she sorely needed counsel.

"Well?" he said.

"I saw my family," she said. "My mother, my father, and Scith—a Nar who helped raised me. My . . . my friend. He was like a second father to me, after my real father was killed. And . . ." Her breath caught in her throat.

"Yes? Spit it out, girl!"

"Lendri," she whispered.

Gleed shook his head.

"A Vil Adanrath," said Hweilan. "Of my mother's people. He told me he had sworn some sort of blood oath to one of my ancestors. After my family was killed, after Scith died, he helped me."

"And you saw this . . . Lendri in the Witness Cloud?"

"Yes. And . . . and once before."

Gleed's brows rose at this. "Do tell."

"My first night here, in your tower, when . . . when I ran. I saw him."

"Here? You saw this wolf-elf *here*?"

Hweilan realized the source of his dismay and shook her head. "No. Lendri's dead. He died the night the Master found me. Just moments before. Lendri died defending me."

"And you saw him in my tower?"

She nodded. "He had his heart in his hand. Still beating. And again, on the height, in the Witness Cloud. He told me . . ." She closed her eyes, hearing the words again so that she could get them exactly right. "He said, 'You can call me, but I will not return. Not even for you. Let my exile end. Please. Let me rest.' "

Gleed looked away into the dark, considering her words for a long time, then said, "You're sure. Those were his exact words?"

"Yes."

"Tell me of this Lendri. Tell me everything you know. Everything. Leave nothing out. No matter how inconsequential it seems."

Hweilan did. Beginning with their first meeting, and relating every detail Lendri had told her about their heritage.

When she finished, he stood a long time, leaning on his staff and staring into the dying flames of the fire. After a while, he nodded and said, "I will think on these things. We will speak of them again."

And with that, he turned and walked off, leaving Hweilan alone with her thoughts. But he was not gone long. He returned carrying two goblets.

"A little wine after dinner," he said as he handed her a goblet. "Good, yes?"

Hweilan took it and asked, "You think I really saw him? Saw Lendri and my family?"

Gleed took a drink of wine, sat, and nodded. "I do not doubt it. It is the *why* that puzzles me."

"What do you mean?"

"The Witness Cloud . . . servants of the Master. Those who have passed on into the next life. They watch us always, and sometimes they even come to our aid. But for family members to come, that is a rare thing indeed. For when the faithful leave this world in death, they join their god. They may watch, but for them to come back . . ." He took another drink, and said, "A matter of great import it must be. What was it this Lendri said again? About exile?"

" 'Let my exile end.' "

"Hmm." He shook his head again. "Much thought. I will give this much thought."

She waited a long time, watching the fire's flames grow ever smaller. After a while, she took a sip of the wine and asked the one question that had come to her. "My next teacher. You said I will meet her soon. How will I find her? This . . . Ashiin?"

Gleed looked up. "She will find you."

Hweilan shuddered. The darkness out there suddenly seemed very close, perhaps even watchful. She filled her mouth with the wine and forced it down.

• • • • •

She woke in the woods, gray-green dawnlight all around her, the morning birds in full song, the mist still thick under the trees. Sitting up, the thick blanket of dry leaves under which she'd lain fell away. Her head felt thick, and she knew—

"Gleed," she muttered. He'd done it again—drugged her wine, and she hadn't even seen it coming.

She combed the leaves and twigs out of her hair and tied it in a loose braid. At least she was wearing clothes this time. Standing and looking around, she realized she'd been here before. She recognized the irregular contortions of the trees, as if they'd been frozen in the midst of some ecstatic dance. Seeing them, with their odd cracked-and-wrinkled-bark faces, they reminded her very much of Gleed's capering around the Sacred Circle after he'd cleansed the Master's spear of the demon.

One of Gleed's lessons from days ago came to her—

The Balance, sacred to Dedunan, our Master's Master. Birth and death, light and dark, summer and winter, predator and prey, silence and song . . . all serve their purpose in the Balance. All work together. For one to gain mastery over the other would be only to sow the seeds of its own destruction.

Silence and song . . .

Alone in the forest, Hweilan thought she stood in the very midst of that balance. There was a stillness all around her, but through it all, the world beat a gentle rhythm. Closing her eyes, she almost thought she could feel the heartbeat of the land beneath her feet. So much of the time, all of Gleed's prattling seemed only that. But here, now, she sensed the truth of that lesson. It filled her with a sense of . . . not peace, but readiness. Come what may, she felt ready.

And then she saw it.

She hadn't really been looking at any one thing. She'd fallen into old habit, branded into her at a young age by Scith, letting her gaze relax, concentrating not on any one spot, but letting her eyes soak in the whole scene before her. Mist, trees, a hundred shades of shadow among them. But then one of the shadows moved. Just a little. Her eyes focused on that spot, and for just a moment she thought she saw two sparkles—eyes?—then they were gone.

She will find you. Gleed's words.

A heavy weight hit her back and shoulders, and she fell beneath it, her face and chest smashing into the soft carpet of leaves. Her lungs constricted as the full weight crushed her, and then it was gone.

Hweilan rolled instinctively, then forced herself into a crouch, both fists on guard in front of her.

A woman stood before Hweilan a few paces away, leaning upon a staff and watching. Hweilan recognized her. The clothes of stitched skins and leathers, the elflike features, dark skin covered in darker inks, and the thick pelt of hair. It was the woman who attacked her outside Kesh Naan's lair.

Seeing the woman in better light, her mind in a much better state than it had been during her first days there, Hweilan noticed that the sides and top of the woman's hair were pulled back and into a braid that fell off the back of her head and over one shoulder. Woven into and dangled from the braid were bits of bone, feathers, leaves, and even tiny flowers. But it was the woman's golden eyes that captured Hweilan's attention. They seemed to draw her in. Both were split with a vertical black slash. Fox's eyes.

"Ashiin," said Hweilan.

The woman straightened and bowed, almost formally, a gesture befitting any noble visitor Hweilan had ever seen in her grandfather's hall. It was a strange juxtaposition to the woman's savage image. She cast her staff aside and walked toward Hweilan.

Hweilan returned the bow and said, "Ashiin, I am——"

The woman backhanded Hweilan, the arm and fist only a blur before smashing into Hweilan's face. Ashiin's leg lashed out, swiping Hweilan's feet out from under her. Hweilan turned the fall into a roll and kept moving.

She leaped to her feet again, spraying leaves around her, and just had time to see Ashiin before the woman's fist struck her temple.

When Hweilan woke, the ceiling of leaves and branches seemed to waver behind a tinge of red. Her head was pounding, and her right eye and the skin around it felt full to bursting. She heard the rustle of footsteps through the leaves, and then Ashiin was standing over her.

"You survived Kesh Naan," she said. Her voice was surprisingly deep for a woman. "You listen to that old goblin ramble. The soft teachings are over, girl. Do better tomorrow, or I kill you. Now get up and I will teach you something."

CHAPTER TWELVE

Kadrigul's jaw came off in her hand. That was almost Jatara's undoing. As the last of the desiccated flesh and tendon gave way, the bottom half of the skull simply fell away, and in that moment, she almost let go. Almost . . .

She had found her brother's remains high in the mountains, near the edge of a frozen stream that ran at the foot of a forested height. Just looking at that hill had made her shrivel inside. Her newfound senses, so alive, had seemed to evaporate like droplets of water falling on hot iron when she neared that place. But she'd found her brother's corpse just the same. Scavengers had not touched it, but one look was all it took to confirm that flames had destroyed the body. Only dried remains of flesh and black, papery skin remained. All that she had left of her beloved brother.

Their people did not bury the dead. In the frozen wasteland of their home, the ground was hard as stone throughout the year. Those whose remains could be found—it was rare for one of the Frost Folk not to die a violent death; either given the gift of death in battle against their enemies or slain by one of the many beasts of their homeland—were given to the ice. But Kadrigul had died in fire.

Jatara took the skull and fled that place. She knew, as a fly trapped in a spider's web knows that the tremble of the silk is the oncoming spider, that to remain there with the moon growing fuller by the night would be her doom. She had to be far, far away before the moon rose full.

And so she went back to the one place where she'd last had a strong sense of her brother—the collection of crystal standing stones.

There, she waited and watched. For days and nights she waited, sustaining herself on whatever beasts and vermin she found. The stones were quiet in the daytime. They still had an awareness about them, but it was dulled, sleeping. Still, she kept a half-hearted watch, but mostly she spent days crouched in some deep shadow of rock, where she stared into the empty sockets of Kadrigul's skull. All she had left of her brother. Empty bone. It fueled her rage while the stones slept.

But at night, under the stars . . . Jatara the watcher felt watched. She could not determine who was watching or from where, but the stones seemed to draw her. Whether they had their own sort of cold, distant intelligence or were just a window through which some power looked, Jatara could not decide. But she knew that whatever they were, they would come to her eventually.

One moonless night when the stars shone bright as lamps over the peaks, a mist rose in the valley. Even had Jatara not seen that—it was far too cold for any natural mist—she would have known. She could feel the power building in the stones. Her natural sight saw nothing, for soon the entire field of stones was hidden in the murk. But Jatara had gained other senses, and her new eye could see things she had never imagined. And so she saw the power surge in the very center of standing stones, like the hot core of a live ember. It flashed, then died away. And then she heard them.

A band of hunters emerged from the tangle of giant crystals. Eladrin, all wearing enchantments like lords of the south wore their finest clothes to court. They led fierce little hunters, who rode on the backs of tundra tigers. Jatara had heard of such things, but never had she seen them with her own eyes.

The band headed into the high mountains. Jatara let them go, watching them long after lesser beings would have lost sight of them. She wasn't interested in them. But they had come out of the place where her brother had gone, very much alive. He'd emerged and been killed not long after. So these hunters . . . what might they be hunting? That interested her very much. And so she left her hiding place and found another one down in the valley. She would wait.

• • ◎ • •

Kovannon watched the last of the uldra hunters disappear into the crystals, dragging their captives on the snow behind them. Tonight's hunt had done for an evening's entertainment. They had found a particularly foul-tempered troll skulking about and had their fun before finishing him off. The local hobgoblin tribes were growing harder and harder to find. Foul brutes that they were, they weren't entirely stupid and had learned to give the area a wide berth. Kovannon would have to begin hunting out of the other portals soon. But they had managed to track down a few half-starved stragglers. They hadn't known anything—had, in fact, babbled on and on about things for which Kovannon had no interest—but perhaps the queen could glean something from their minds.

Still . . .

Something wasn't right. Something beyond the melancholy mood that a poor hunt always put him in. It nagged at the raw edge of his mind, patting and pawing like a cat playing with a wounded bird.

His two other eladrin companions lingered with him.

"You feel it?" said Ulender, his voice scarcely above a whisper.

"Yes," Kovannon said.

"It's like . . ." Ulender didn't finish.

"I know."

Durel looked around, shuddered, and said, "Should I recall the Ujaiyen?"

Kovannon was about to answer when he heard it. Footsteps crunching through the snow. The others heard it as well, for they all turned to stare in the direction from which the sounds came.

The figure had apparently been lying on the ground under the snow, for fine white crystals still lay in clumps on its shoulders and head, and frosted the entire figure, making the bright starlight sparkle off its frame. There was no grace in the thing's gait, but it came on with a terrible willfulness, as if the movement of every muscle were carefully considered. Even Kovannon's sharp eyes could make out no distinct features under the covering of frost, but the thing's eyes gave back a light that did not come from the stars but from some inner fire.

Seeing that, he knew what they faced. He could feel it in his bones. Everyone in Kunin Gatar's realm knew of the thing that had invaded, killing many of their people and even managing to hurt the queen before she killed it. What approached them . . . it could not be the same one. Kunin Gatar had killed that one. But Kovannon knew that where you found one fly, more were soon to follow. If one of these things had been killed by their queen, then it seemed that one of its kin had come looking for revenge.

Kovannon heard the steel of Durel's sword sliding out of its scabbard and the first syllables of an incantation upon Ulender's lips.

"What is it?" said Durel.

Kovannon sidestepped to give them room to fight. "Durel," Kovannon said in their native tongue. "Ulender and I will hold it off. You go for help."

"What?" said Durel. "Whom shall I bring?"

"Everyone," said Ulender, and by the tone of his voice, Kovannon knew that the wizard knew what they were up against. "Bring everyone."

"Stop!" Kovannon called out. "Name yourself."

The thing kept coming, neither slowing nor increasing its pace.

Kovannon tried the same phrase once more in Damaran and Nar. The thing stopped a dozen paces away, its breath sending up a cloud. The heat from its body had melted all but the thickest snow, and, close as it was, Kovannon saw that the figure was not an "it" at all. A woman. A hard woman, obviously used to long treks and hard living, but there was no mistaking the feminine curves. Yet there was nothing womanlike in the way she moved. In fact, there was very little human in her posture.

She shook her head, as if shooing a fly, then fixed her right eye on Kovannon. He took an involuntary step back as if an adder had just struck at him.

"Name yourself," Kovannon said in Damaran.

She cocked her head, birdlike, and said, "Why?"

Durel still had not moved. Kovannon waved at him. "Durel, get moving!"

Durel began to sidestep away, though he kept his sword raised and his eyes on the woman.

The woman cocked her head the other way. "Give me what I want, and I will go away."

"Go away?" said Kovannon. "I'm afraid that choice is beyond you now. You come to the queen's threshold uninvited . . . for that, there are consequences."

"Queen?"

"Enough," said Ulender. "Durel, go! *Now!*"

"Very well," said the woman.

She lunged—startlingly fast, taking to the air in a single leap. Durel had been moving away, but slowly and carefully, unwilling to take his eyes off the danger. That caution killed him.

Durel saw the attack in time, sidestepping and bringing his blade around in a graceful flourish so that the woman impaled herself on the yard of steel when she hit the ground. Kovannon heard the sharp snap of the point piercing through hard muscle, going in just under her ribs and coming out dark and wet from her back.

The weight of her landing forced Durel back a step, but he kept his grip on the sword. Later, looking back, Kovannon wondered if Durel might have lived had he let it go, letting the momentum of her leap carry her away. But he didn't.

The woman reached out with both hands, wrapped one hand around the side of Durel's head, and gripped the back of his neck with the other. He had time to open his mouth and draw breath to scream, but that was all. She yanked him forward, bringing his face into her open mouth.

One clear, high scream, and then the scream itself drowned as the woman ripped away his jaw.

Ulender's incantation rose to a final shout, and lightning split the clear night sky—a blinding blue arc that struck the steel protruding from the woman's back, filled her body, and shot outward in a hundred smaller tongues of blue wisps of light. Her back spasmed into an arch and she fell back into the snow, pulling a writhing Durel down on top of her. Hitting the ground forced the sword partway out of her.

Even as the thunder from Ulender's lightning faded and the final echo died off the mountainside, Kovannon heard the woman growling. Not in pain. Not even in fury like an animal. But in pleasure, like a starving mongrel worrying the first bite of flesh off the bone.

Ulender's magic had stunned Durel as much as the woman—Kovannon prayed it might have knocked him unconscious. They might be able to get him through the portal and to healing in time. But no, his wet screams resumed, louder than ever, and his hands and feet hammered at the ground as he struggled to get free.

Kovannon heard Ulender beginning another spell.

"No!" he shouted. "You'll kill Durel!"

"He's dead already!" Ulender said.

Or as good as, Kovannon realized. Moving forward, he drew his own weapon. An axe, crafted especially for chopping bones, not wood, and bound in many spells by the finest smiths of Ellestharn.

The woman pushed herself to her feet. In one hand, she held Durel up by his scalp. He was still trembling, but the fight had gone out of him. With her other hand, she reached forward, grabbed the sword's hilt, and pulled it out of her.

"Stand back!" Ulender called, and began the final words that would release the spell.

Kovannon shuffled sideways through the snow.

The woman brought the sword around, almost nonchalantly, and cut Durel's head from his shoulders. A gout of blood shot up from the gap between his shoulders, spraying the woman, then the body hit the ground.

Ulender was pronouncing the last word of the spell when the woman took one step forward and hurled Durel's head at him. It struck Ulender in the chest, knocking him back. The gathered power of his magic sparked and fizzled out of his fingers, falling on the snow where it steamed.

She threw the sword next. It tumbled end over end one full revolution before burying itself in Ulender's gut. His eyes went wide and he sat heavily in the snow. He looked down at the steel protruding from his body, opened his mouth, and a stream of dark blood ran out over his chin.

"Hurts, doesn't it?" said the woman, and she turned her gaze on Kovannon.

He raised his axe and stood his ground.

"Tell me of this . . . queen," she said.

Kovannon just stared back at her.

"No?" said the woman. "Why? Aren't you afraid of what I will do to you if you don't tell me?"

Kovannon swallowed and then spoke the wholehearted truth. "I am *more* afraid of what she'll do to me if I do. Death at your hands would seem a relief by comparison."

The woman cocked her head, again reminding Kovannon of some strange bird. And not in many, many years had he felt more like a helpless worm.

"I believe you," said the woman. "If she is the type of queen you say, then she will understand this. Tell your queen that nothing this side of Toril is safe. Her people come out, I kill them. She comes herself, I kill her. These lands are closed to her and all her people. Unless she gives me what I want."

Kovannon could scarcely believe it. *Tell your queen,* she said. That meant she was going to let him live.

"What is it you want?" he said.

"Give me the girl, and I'll go away."

CHAPTER THIRTEEN

Do better tomorrow, or I kill you.

And Hweilan had done better. She'd still taken a beating. In fact, on the second day of training Ashiin broke Hweilan's right arm. But Gleed had set the bone and given her the foulest-tasting concoctions to speed the healing.

"Let the right arm heal," Ashiin told her the next day. "Until it does, you fight with your left. You do as I tell you, or I break the left. Then you'll fight with your feet. Disappoint me there, and I break your neck."

Hweilan learned to fight with her left. At first with nothing more than her naked fist. Then a blade. Then with whatever came readily to hand.

She preferred the blade. By the time her right arm had healed, Hweilan knew a dozen ways to kill with the sharp edge, fifty with the point, and several with the pommel. Once, her determination and fury got the better of her, and she gave Ashiin a deep gash down her forearm. She was so shocked that she froze, eyes wide, and—

Ashiin might have punched her. But it could just as easily have been a kick or a swipe of the elbow. Hweilan could never remember. But she did remember waking to see Ashiin standing over her, completely undisturbed by the steady stream of blood running down her arm, and *drip-drip-dripping* off her middle finger and onto Hweilan's face.

"You never apologize for doing as I tell you," said Ashiin. "And you *never* let go your guard. Now get up."

Hweilan got up.

For the first time since Hweilan had known her, Ashiin smiled. "That was a good strike. You're learning. Well done."

And so it continued. Day after day. In the deep woods, learning to use tree trunks and boughs and the uncertain ground to her advantage. In the streams, learning to swim and fight despite the cold water, the constantly shifting rocks, and the current ever pushing at her.

Once Hweilan had learned to defend herself and learned to strike to kill, then she learned to hunt. Not like Scith had taught her. He had taught her to track, how the animals used the landscape to their advantage, and how to use it against them. He told her that in ancient days, men learned to hunt by watching wolves, by hunting as pack and exploiting their prey's weaknesses. Ashiin taught her to stalk, to use her enemies' fear against them, and to hunt as the fox, by choosing her prey, getting in close and quiet, and striking before the prey even knew she was there.

"Every enemy has a weakness," said Ashiin. "Find it. Use it. And the strongest foe will fall before you."

But no matter how strong she grew, how fast, how agile . . . still she was no match for Ashiin. The woman moved quick as an adder and hit harder than a bull.

One evening, after a particularly rough beating from her teacher, Hweilan's spirits were so low that she actually confided in Gleed.

The old goblin had already set a cold, clammy poultice on her swollen right eye. He was setting another concoction to simmer on the fire before he set about the work of pulling her right arm back into its socket.

"H-how?" said Hweilan. Her jaw was trembling so badly that she had to close her eyes a moment and gather the strength to speak. It wasn't pain. She had long since passed beyond the pain. But the very last threads of her body's strength were fraying and about to snap. "How c-can I ever pass her tests?"

Gleed stood behind her, set a gentle hand on her hanging shoulder, and placed the flat of his other palm on her back. "Ready?" he said.

She nodded.

He pulled.

She screamed.

But she did not pass out. That was something. Last time, she had passed out.

"Fighting," said Gleed, "killing . . . it's more than knowing how. It's about how far you are willing to go. And you, Hweilan, you are still holding back. When you hunt Jagun Ghen and his minions, you cannot hesitate. You must strike without pity, without remorse, no matter the face they wear."

Hweilan moved her arm tentatively. It sent a glass-edge of pain sliding down her spine, but it still wasn't as bad as last time.

"She's trying to make me into a beast," said Hweilan. She couldn't help the tone of petulance in her voice. She'd been raised in a household of knights, to whom honor was more precious than life. To them, battle was an art, could even be a sacred act of devotion. To Ashiin, killing seemed a primal instinct, a need, no different than hunger or fear. To Ashiin, being a killer was not a matter of doing, but being, and Hweilan feared that she could never become that.

"She is not." Gleed turned away from the iron cauldron he had been stirring. "A beast cannot be *made,* stupid girl. A beast is woken. No. Ashiin is not making you into a beast. She is trying to beat the scared, spoiled little girl out of you so that when the beast does come—and it will; it will—a little of the woman might survive."

• • ◉ • •

Three days later, when it was time for her lesson with Ashiin, Gleed followed her out of the tower, a bundle on his back. He saw the inquiring look she cast in his direction as she climbed out of the tower and into the gray morning.

"I go with you today," he said.

"But Ashiin said—"

"Today, you will learn from us both."

"Oh, this can't be good."

He summoned the bridge and they crossed into the woods. Mist still curled around their ankles as they walked, and the remnants of last night's rain dripped from the boughs. Hweilan watched every shadow, and her ears strained at every sound. Most days she walked to the woods Ashiin haunted, but on several occasions her teacher had ambushed her. It had been a while since that last happened, which made Hweilan think she was due for another.

Less than half a mile from Gleed's lake, the woods thinned around a scattering of lichen-covered boulders. They were taller than they were wide, and set deeply into the soil. Mostly featureless, there were still enough irregular curves and grooves to them that Hweilan suspected they might have once been sculptures. It was there that she usually followed the slope upward to the drier woods. But Gleed kept going straight ahead, keeping the heights to their right.

"Where are we going?" she asked him.

Gleed talked while they walked. "You remember when we spoke of the skin between worlds?"

Hweilan did. One of Gleed's lessons from many days ago. He'd told her that Toril and the Feywild were not the only worlds. There were many—some almost mirror-images of this one, with only the slightest variations. Some so different that the very air was poison, the light fire. And the barriers between them—Gleed used the word *dehwek,* meaning "skin"—ran thin in some places.

But the concept . . . it was not unlike what the shade of her father had said that day on the height. *Thin is the veil that separates us, and it can be lifted.*

"Portals you mean?" she'd asked.

Gleed had merely shrugged. He had his Lore, and when the names by which she knew things differed from his own, he simply ignored them.

"All things have their own song," he'd continued, explaining that every creature had its own rhythm—a unique voice, a heartbeat, breath. So it was with the worlds. Each sang to its own rhythm, and if one could learn their songs, one could pierce the "skin between worlds." But it was a very delicate matter, taking intense concentration and care. Fail at the song, and the skin would remain impenetrable. Make an error, and one could fall into the wrong world—and never live long enough to realize one's mistake.

"You remember the songs I taught you?" Gleed asked, pulling Hweilan from her reverie.

"I do."

"Good. You're going to need them."

• • ◉ • •

They walked most of the morning, coming to the stream where Gleed had first found Hweilan. They followed it until it spread out the width of a tourney field and fell over the lip of a cliff.

Ashiin was waiting for them there, crouched in the shadows of an ancient willow whose branches played in the river. She looked at the little goblin through narrow eyes, her face otherwise expressionless. "Gleed," she said.

"Ashiin." He did not bow—in fact lowered his staff and stood ramrod straight.

Hweilan eyed them both warily.

"She is ready?" said Ashiin.

"She can open the way," said Gleed. "For after . . ." He motioned to her.

"For that," said Ashiin, "she is ready."

Ashiin stood, her staff in one hand. Hweilan had once asked her about the skull on its top, and the tails and scalps dangling from its length—asked what they signified. *Others who have displeased me,* Ashiin had said. Ashiin reached behind her back with her free hand, and when she stepped into the sunlight, she brought her hand back around, and something flashed there. Hweilan immediately stepped back, ready to put up her guard.

Ashiin smiled and flipped the thing in her hand, causing the sunlight to ripple silver and gold along it. She caught it and held it out. "Recognize this?"

Hweilan did. The single-edged blade was as long as her forearm, the silver steel etched in curving designs that suggested eddying currents. It was the knife Menduarthis had given her.

"That's mine," she said.

"*Was* yours," said Ashiin. "A warrior who loses her weapon has no more claim to it—unless she can take it back."

Hweilan frowned. Not so much because the thing was precious to her. It was one of the loveliest knives she'd ever seen—and she'd grown up among dwarf craftsmen. But the fact that someone had taken it from her and was taunting her with it raised her hackles. Still . . . she knew she was no match for Ashiin. Not yet.

Ashiin smiled. "Look before you leap. Consider before you strike. Like the fox. A wise choice. Do well today, and the knife will be yours again."

Suspicious, Hweilan scowled. "You'll give it back?"

"Give? No. You're going to earn it."

• • • • •

The waterfall almost seemed to whisper, and even though it fell a good twenty feet or more, it scarcely caused a ripple in the pool into which it fell. The pool itself reflected the gray sky and surrounding trees before its far edge shattered into three streams that wound their way through a swampy lowland. As she and her teachers climbed down the slick rocks next to the waterfall, Hweilan could hear it. *Something about this place . . .*

Beat to its own rhythm . . . sang its own song . . . Gleed would have said, and she wouldn't have disagreed with him. She couldn't quite bring herself to think of it as sacred, not quite, but there was very definitely something . . . other in every sound, every scent, and the way the light rippled over the water. It was altogether different from the faith of Torm in which she'd been raised. But she'd also been raised by Scith, who, even though he honored and respected the faith of Vandalar and his family, was devoted mostly to Aumaunator, Keeper of the Sun. Moreover, being a master hunter and tracker, Scith had also given Silvanus great respect, and taught Hweilan of the Balance and the sacredness of all living things. What she was sensing . . . seemed much closer to that, and she took some comfort in the familiarity.

Once they reached the bottom, Gleed led them along a narrow path to the fall itself, where in one place—the only place as near as Hweilan could see—a notch of rock thrust out, causing the curtain of water to spray out in a perfect fan shape, about twice Hweilan's height but no more than a pace or two wide.

Gleed unshouldered the bundle, reached inside and produced a wide, flat drum. It was no more than a couple of inches deep and had a skin only along one side. The back was a webbing of taut cords, both binding the skin and serving as a handle. Sacred symbols had been burned all around the wooden rim and painted on the skin itself.

"You know the song," said Gleed, and handed the drum to Hweilan.

She took it. She'd done this several times—but in Gleed's chambers or sitting by the lakeshore in front of his tower. Never like this. Never for real.

She stepped toward the veil of water and beheld her own reflection. Just beyond it, only black rock. She curled her left hand into a fist, then extended her thumb and smallest finger as Gleed had taught her. Holding the webbing of the drum in the other hand, she began a rhythmic beat, first in time with her own heart, then varying as she found the rhythm of the fall. Once she had it, she began the chant.

Midmorning though it was, the sun had not yet peeked through the high curtain of cloud. But as her words found the inherent power in the veil before her, she began to see light rippling in the water—tiny threads of silver shooting up like minuscule arrows, and threads of gold and crimson sparking as they wound back and forth. Hweilan didn't allow her eye to catch on them; she looked beyond—and realized she could no longer see the black, dripping stone behind the water. No stone at all. She saw something she knew could not be coming from this side of the water—sunlight.

She gave the drum a final hard slap with her thumb and shouted the final word of the song. The veil of water responded with a flash of green light.

"Well done," said Gleed. He took the drum from her.

Hweilan turned to Ashiin and gave the silver knife a pointed look.

Ashiin smiled. "Oh, you aren't getting it that easy. Come."

She stepped through the veil of water, and Hweilan followed.

CHAPTER FOURTEEN

Warmth rushed over her like a wave. She had never in her life felt the very air she breathed so wonderfully warm and dry. Hweilan had grown up in Narfell, where in winter exposed skin would freeze in moments and the snows only melted in high summer. This was the complete opposite of that in every way. The air held no moisture at all. It was like being in a kitchen where the ovens had been stoked for days. The water from the fall dampening her skin evaporated at once, and she actually felt the pores in her scalp loosen and expand. Unused to such warmth, her body broke out in immediate sweat.

Scent hit her with such force that she actually stumbled back a step. Not because it was foul, but simply because it was so alien to anything she had ever experienced. The smell of dust and rock baked under the sun. Mixing through it all were the scents of plants who survived in a land that obviously went months at a time without rain.

The land around her was not desert, but close to it. The soil was sandy, and from it sprouted a scrublike grass the color of straw. It grew in clumps. Here and there were twisted bushes, their tiny leaves rattling in the slight breeze. And the . . .

She had no words for them. They weren't mountains,

though she could see a range of mountains along the near horizon. Most of the land before her seemed to be a rolling landscape broken by dry gullies, and amongst them were towers of rock that rose hundreds of feet in the air, their tops flat as watchtowers. Behind her, she saw that another one rose at their back, its side so sheer and its top so far away that she could not see how high it was.

"Where are we?" said Hweilan.

"Far, far away from your Highwatch," said Ashiin, "so don't harbor any unwise ideas."

Hweilan tore her eyes away from the height and looked at Ashiin. "You think I'd try to run?"

"You wouldn't be the first."

"I swore an oath. To Nendawen himself. I—"

"Do *not*!" Ashiin advanced on her, but Hweilan held her ground. The two women stared into each other's eyes, standing only inches apart. "Do not speak the Master's name lightly."

"Do not treat my word so lightly."

Ashiin took one quick step back and brought her fist around, the pommel of the silver dagger aimed for Hweilan's face.

But Hweilan was ready for it—had in fact been expecting it. She ducked under the blow, stepping back as she did so, hoping to get out of Ashiin's reach. But the staff was already coming around for her midsection. Too high to leap and too low for her to duck under in time. Instinct took over, and Hweilan caught the staff, absorbing the brunt of the blow with an open palm, using the momentum to tighten her grip.

Pain shot up her arm, but Hweilan forced her grip to hold. Ashiin yanked, pulling Hweilan toward her fist. But again, Hweilan had been expecting this, and she rolled under the blow, planting her shoulder in Ashiin's chest and using the force of the woman's pull against her.

They both went down. Hweilan had not forgotten that

Ashiin still held the knife, so as soon as they hit the ground, she released the staff and rolled away. She came up in a crouch. Dry soil crumbled under her hands.

The staff was already coming for her—straight down, so hard and fast that Hweilan heard it cutting the air. Hweilan twisted aside, pivoting on her hands as she did so. The staff grazed her shoulder, then slammed into the ground. But Hweilan kept the pivot moving, and brought the toe of her boot around, aiming for Ashiin's side.

Adder-quick? Had that been how Hweilan once thought of Ashiin? No. Adders were slow compared to her. Ashiin twisted away. Hweilan missed her ribs completely, but her foot connected with the staff. It sent pain radiating outward, down to her toes and all the way up to her hip.

The staff went flying.

Hweilan was moving too fast, her heart hammering too hard, to cry out her triumph. But in her mind, she screamed—she exulted. It was the first time she had ever disarmed her teacher.

Ashiin swiped out with the other hand, and bright sunlight flashing off bright steel blinded Hweilan for just a moment. But a moment was all it took. The blade struck her in the throat, and she went down.

Hweilan's chest constricted, and she forced herself not to gasp, for she knew she'd only fill her lungs with blood. But then the realization set in. Her throat hurt, but the knife had not cut.

"Flat of the blade," said Ashiin, standing over her. "Had I used the edge, I'd be watching you die now."

Hweilan's fist closed on the ground. It was sun-baked and hard, but still, a fair amount crumbled in her palm. Before her good sense could overcome her rage, she screamed and threw the dirt in Ashiin's face.

Her teacher shrieked—more out of surprise than fear, Hweilan would decide later, remembering this moment. But that instant of surprise was all she needed. She brought her leg around with all the strength she could muster and swept Ashiin's feet out from under her.

Hweilan swiped her own knife—the one Lendri had given her—out of her boot, and then she leaped. There was no grace or elegance to it, but she came down upon Ashiin, one knee driving into the woman's gut. She brought her own knife around and jammed it onto Ashiin's throat—the back, dull edge of the blade.

Her face was only inches from Ashiin's. Sweat poured off her and bled tracks down the dust on Ashiin's skin. "Had I used the edge, I'd be watching *you* die now."

Ashiin grinned—smiled through the tears washing the dirt from her eyes. "You're learning, girl," she said. "Much better today. But you still have a lot to learn."

She motioned downward with her chin. Hweilan looked down and saw the point of the silver blade resting just under her left breast.

"No good to kill your enemy if you die trying," said Ashiin.

"Depends on the enemy," said Hweilan.

Ashiin laughed and pushed her off.

"I'm starting to like you, girl."

• • • • •

Hweilan and Ashiin crouched amongst the broken rocks a hundred feet or so up the broken side of the stone tower. It was not the same rock formation where they'd first come to this place. It had taken them all the morning to walk there. Both women had stripped down to loincloths and their boots. Hweilan still wore a thin strip of cloth tied around her neck, wrapping around front to cover her breasts, and tied behind her back. But Ashiin was naked from the waist up, covered only in the dozens of braids of her thick hair. In the tiny cave where they'd left their other clothes, Ashiin had a cache, and from it she'd produced a clay urn. Inside was a black paste that smelled much like the tiny blue flowers that grew in the shadows near Gleed's lake.

"To protect us from the sun," Ashiin had explained, and they smeared it over every inch of exposed skin. "And from prying eyes."

The paste spread slick on their skin, and over it they spread liberal amounts of dirt, which stuck to the paste. Hweilan knew that if they chose their cover well and did not move, even a hawk would have a hard time seeing them.

Less than half a mile from where they hid, tents lay in a tight grouping. At first, Hweilan thought it was for the most obvious reason—the camp would lay in the shade of the rock during the hottest part of the day. But on closer inspection she saw the real reason. In the center of the camp was a ring of stones, no more than three feet across.

"A well," said Hweilan.

"The only water for ten miles," Ashiin said, confirming Hweilan's sight of the stone ring. "Out there"—she pointed to the miles of scrubland—"if you know what you're doing, you can dig and bring up enough water to survive. But not enough to keep your horses alive."

The camp seemed mostly empty. Hweilan assumed most of the people were inside the tents, escaping the heat of the day. But a few men, long spears in hand, sat under lean-tos, watching over the band's score of horses.

"Why are we here?" said Hweilan.

"Those folk down there," said Ashiin. "They survive by scavenging, raiding and hunting. A tough breed."

"Hunters? They serve the Master?"

"They honor the Hunt, which means they please the Master. Life in these lands has always been hard, but in recent years it has become harder still."

Ashiin looked down at the camp to be sure no one was looking up their way, then she pointed to the far horizon.

Hweilan followed her gaze. On the horizon, Hweilan saw something.

"Dust," said Hweilan. "Something out there is stirring up dust. Coming this way." She glanced down at the camp.

"They won't see it before it's too late."

"Haerul," said Ashiin.

"What?" The name tugged at Hweilan's memory. Something she'd seen in the Lore of Kesh Naan. Something . . ..

"The father of your grandfather's grandfather," Ashiin explained. "He lived in lands far to the east of here. Hard lands, populated by people born to war, who would rather die than suffer an insult. Their khans were men of great renown. Great warriors, feared even as far as Cormyr. But Haerul . . . the mere mention of his name would make the proudest khan's bowels turn to water. If they knew Haerul's band was in their land, the fiercest warriors would huddle close to their fires and pray to all their gods and ancestors."

"Why are you telling me this?"

"Because tonight, you're going to find out how strong his blood runs in you. That cloud of dust you see on the horizon? Agents of the new lords of Vaasa. Too arrogant to believe they need fear the dark. Tonight, you are going to show them they are wrong."

• • ◉ • •

It took the dust cloud a long time to cross the open plain. Hweilan and Ashiin sat in the shade, sipping water and watching the riders draw closer. The sky was beginning to take on the purple and orange shades of evening before the cloud was close enough for the guards down below to see it and raise the alarm. The result was like watching the stirring of an anthill. People ran around, hiding possessions in shallow ditches, covering them with blankets, and spreading dirt on the blankets. As near as Hweilan could tell, there were no more than a half-dozen men in the camp, a few oldsters, and twenty or so women and children. A few older girls led a band of children up toward the rocks below where Hweilan and Ashiin hid, where they soon disappeared.

"What could they possibly have worth taking?" Hweilan asked.

"The current rulers of this land are building an army," said Ashiin. "Locals are not particularly eager to join, so these agents . . . force the issue. They ride in and take any fit to bear arms—or serve in other ways. Young men and women are their favorite, though lately they've been taking older children as well."

"How do you know all this?"

Ashiin smiled. In the lavender evening light, her yellow eyes gleamed and her pointed teeth shone. "The tyrants here are not the only ones with agents." She looked over her shoulder, up at the dark crevice in the rock face above. "*Rusheh, tekaneh!*"

There was the slightest rustle from the dark, and a shape emerged on silent wings, gliding over them before taking to the higher air. Its feathers were the mottled color of the surrounding lands, but its eyes were round and orange as a desert moon. Large as a man's torso, it was the biggest owl Hweilan had ever seen. She soon lost sight of it in the dusk light.

Hweilan heard the gallop of the newcomers long before she could get a good look at them. Sounds traveled far in this open and empty land, and it was almost full dark. On the eastern horizon, which they faced, she watched as the arc of a full moon, fat and blood red, rose in the dust raised by the riders.

The world seemed to shift around Hweilan, and deep in the dark places of her mind she heard a *BOOM,* as if a distant mountain had fallen. She had only felt this once before. On the night Lendri died. The night she had first seen . . .

"Nendawen," she said, speaking aloud before she realized.

"Yes," said Ashiin. "The Master has come. Time to go to work."

In the distance, a wolf howled.

• • ◉ • •

The old women had the fires stoked, stirred, and burning high. What food and drink they could offer, they laid out in readiness. They could have run, forsaking their tents, grabbing what they could carry, and riding away. But they had done that before, and they remembered what it had cost them. Besides, the nearest well was over ten miles away, and if they rode there only to find it occupied by a superior force, their horses would likely die before they could reach the next well.

The riders did not ride in at full gallop. No need. These were thugs coming to take what they felt was their due. Only the leader wore full armor—steel plate that looked black in the night. Covered in the dust of a long ride, it reflected little of the firelight.

He and his two guards rode into the middle of the camp, where the elders and men stood in a row. Ten riders fanned out behind the leader while two more wound their way through the camp, sneering down at any who dared to look up at them and trampling piles of belongings. One of them lowered the point of his halberd so that its blade sliced through a tent's support rope, causing half of it to collapse.

The leader took off his helmet, handed it to the man on his left, and made quite a show of wiping the dust and sweat from his eyes.

"How many?" he said.

The old man a pace from his horse's nose looked up and said, "My lord?"

"How many did you hide up in the rocks?"

"We hid nothing, my lord."

The leader smiled indulgently. "It's better that you tell me. And tell me true. I am guessing a few young girls we'll want, hiding with the children. Those we'll probably leave. For now. *If* you tell me the truth."

The old man looked to the old woman beside him. She looked away.

"My men are tired from a long day's ride. If they can sit by the fire and rest their bones, they will be most grateful. Most pleasant. If they have to spend half the night up in those damned rocks, rooting out your whelps . . . well, they might be less than pleasant. So I'll ask you once more: how many and where are they?"

The old man looked to the old woman again, then back up at the leader, his jaw flapping. He almost told, but then he clamped his mouth shut.

The leader held out an open hand to the man on his right. The rider slapped a spear into the hand, and the leader brought the shaft down on the old man's shoulder. Hard. Bone cracked, and the old man went down.

The men in the row of villagers cried out in anger and reached for their weapons.

"Now! Now!" The leader put the point of the spear on the old woman's throat, and his guard to his left did the same to another woman. "You men don't want this to go any further, do you?"

Several of the other riders dismounted and relieved the villagers of their blades.

"What were you planning on doing with this?" said one of the riders as he wrenched a short sword from the grip of a middle-aged man. The rider clenched his fist around the pommel and punched the man in the gut hard enough to knock him to the ground.

The leader counted off five of his men. "Get up in those rocks and find any lost kittens."

The men nodded and kicked their mounts into motion.

"Stop!" the leader called. They did. "Idiots," he said. "You'll break your horses' legs up in those rocks. You've been in the saddle all day. I'm sure your legs could use a stretch."

The men grumbled but did as they were told, handing the reins of their horses to other riders.

The leader dismounted, clapped, and said, "Now! What's for dinner?"

• • • • •

After seeing to their horses, the newcomers settled around the fires and proceeded to eat most of what little food the villagers had. The village had nothing but water to drink, but the raiders had brought their own, stronger stuff, and before they were halfway through their meals, bottles and skins were being passed around, and the men's voices were growing louder by the moment.

"Must've hid the kittens particularly well this time," said the man on the leader's left. He laughed and passed the bottle. "They're getting craftier."

The leader smiled, took the bottle, and was about to say something when a shape the color of new flame bounded into the camp. Sleek and graceful, it leaped soundlessly into their midst, stopped not ten feet away, and stared right at the leader. All red fur, golden eyes that shot the fire back at him, and two triangular ears. A fox. And not the small foxes of this land, which seemed all ears covered by scraggly brown or black fur. This one was almost large as a brush wolf and red as blood, save for its paws, nose, and the last handspan of its tail, all of which were black as cold malice.

The villagers stared at the alien creature, and the newcomers all turned to see what had captured their leader's attention.

"Have you ever seen its like?" said the leader. "It's beautiful."

"It's mine!" said his second, and leaped to his feet, spear already in hand. He bounded over the fire, weapon raised.

The fox seemed to smile at him, then yipped and trotted off, almost prancing.

Three men ran after it, spears raised.

Laughing, the leader watched them. Two were half drunk and one far more than half. But the beast seemed in no hurry to lose them.

One spear flew, its aim true despite the man's drunkenness. But the fox leaped aside at the last moment and the spear struck dirt.

"Quick! We'll lose it in the da—"

A shadow rose from behind a bush, and there was a flash as steel caught the firelight and streaked toward the man's throat. Before he hit the ground the shadow bounded two steps to the next man, plunged the knife into and out of his throat, then kicked him away. Both men were down, their feet hammering the ground, the second man trying to scream but only producing a choking, gurgling sound.

The third men yelled as he struck with his spear, but the shadow slid out of the way and snatched it from his hands. A blur as the spear whipped around, knocking the man's feet out from under him. The point came down, a loud *crack* as it shattered a rib going through him, pinning him to the ground.

"To arms!" the leader shouted. His men found their feet—more than a few swaying—and drew blade or grasped spear. Villagers scattered in every direction.

The shadow walked into camp, almost casually, and by the graceful walk and the curve of hip, the leader knew—

"A woman!"

Nearly naked but seemingly covered in the dust from which she'd sprung. Her long, dark hair pulled back. The only color the firelight rippling in her eyes and the blood dripping from the dagger she held in one hand. She seemed altogether undisturbed by the four spearmen surrounding her.

She walked until the nearest man's spear touched the flesh just above her navel. She looked at the leader, cocked her head, and blinked once.

He couldn't help but chuckle. "*Who* are you?"

"My name is Hweilan."

No fear in her voice. No deference. Not even challenge. Flat. Emotionless.

The leader shook his head, utterly perplexed. "My name is—"

"Your name doesn't matter," she said in the same disinterested tone.

"You'll show some respect!" said the man to her left, and raised the butt of his spear to strike.

The woman twisted sideways around the spear at her gut, grabbed it with her free hand, and kicked its wielder so hard that he went backward with enough force to flip his feet over his head. The woman kept turning and brought the spear around to block the next man's strike. She swiped his spear aside, then backswiped with the point of her own. The leader actually saw the iron point rip the man's jaw from his face.

Another man screamed and threw his spear, but she simply knocked it out of the air.

"Stop this!" the leader screamed. "You men, fall back!"

His men retreated, their spears and blades held on guard. The leader stepped forward, his own sword held before him.

The first two men she'd struck had stopped their kicking. The one she'd impaled still had both hands gripped around the spear, but the leader was quite sure the man was dead. The one she'd kicked and robbed of his spear was on his feet again, but still doubled over and obviously having trouble breathing. The last man was on his knees, making a terrible mewling sound as he used his blood-soaked hands to try to reattach his jaw.

"The way you took out my spearmen," said the leader, "impressive, I must admit. But they're both half-wits and quite drunk. You stand no chance against the rest of us."

The woman tossed the spear on the ground.

The leader smiled and opened his mouth, intending to say, *Very wise. Now get down on the ground.*

But the woman flipped the knife in one hand, caught with the other, then motioned for him to come for her.

"I have five more hardened warriors up that slope," said the leader, motioning with his sword. "Elgren! Morn! You men, get down here!"

"Those five are dead," said the woman. "Nine down. Five to go."

The leader put on his bravest face, but he still had to

swallow before he could find his voice. "You cannot count. There are six of us."

The woman smiled, teasingly. "Oh, you I'm not going to kill."

"Enough of this," said the leader. "Kendremis, deal with her."

He stepped back, and the man to his left stepped forward. He wore no armor, and only a light cloak over fine linen clothes. He extended both hands, his fingers already weaving intricate patterns.

Kendremis smiled as he began his incantation. "*Uth duremmen ta—*"

The point of a spear burst out from his chest, his back arched, and a gout of blood ran down his chin.

Eyes wide, the leader whirled to see one of the villagers holding the spear. He heard the snap of bowstrings, and the *flifft* sound of arrows cutting the air. Like that, and it was over in seconds. He stood alone. The only one of his men still making a sound was the poor fellow trying to hold his face together. But one of the old women stepped forward with a club and put an end to that.

The villagers turned their eyes on the leader.

"No!" said Hweilan.

The leader looked to her. "What—?"

"Run," she said.

His sword dipped. The point was trembling, and the blade suddenly felt very heavy. "You're letting me live?"

"That depends on you."

He opened his mouth, but a great howling cut him off. Wolves. Dozens of them at least, howling from every direction. The leader swallowed and looked around. Eyes from the darkness sparkled in the light cast by the fires.

"What is this?" And even he heard the rising panic in his voice. He whirled, looking for a way of escape. And that's when he saw it. The moon had risen high enough out of the dust to lose its bloody pallor, and it shone down like new ivory. Standing on the nearest height, framed by the moon, was a man. Or something like a man. Taller than any man he had ever seen. Crooked antlers sprouted from his brow, and even from the distance of a hundred yards or more, he could see eyes shining with green fire.

Hweilan said, "You should start running now."

CHAPTER FIFTEEN

Hweilan sat atop Gleed's tower, her legs over the edge, her heels drumming an irregular rhythm against the ivy-covered stone. Heavy clouds, thick with rain, hung low in the sky. With evening coming on, the light growing grayer by the moment, the woods across the lake were impenetrable gloom. When she and Ashiin had returned to the Feywild, the cool had been most welcome, and they had both bathed in the falls, washing away the blood and dirt. The shock had felt good. Welcome. After the warmth of where they'd been, she'd even welcomed the shivering. But, hours later, she was still shivering.

After coming back, after what they'd done, she'd had to seek a high place. She'd grown up in a fortress on the edge of the mountains. Her bedroom window overlooked a garden, but beyond the garden wall she'd been able to see to the horizon, and she had spent many nights watching the moon rise over the snowfields. She'd grown used to the confines of the Feywild woods, but she couldn't bring herself to love them. To clear her head, she needed to see distance. Gleed's tower was a poor substitute, but it was the best she had.

Today had not been Hweilan's first blood. She'd killed before. Hunting, she'd killed more animals than she could remember. And she'd killed two people—but both times, those people had been intent on killing her. It had been kill or be killed. Today had been different. She'd gone looking for a fight. True, those she and Ashiin had killed would be no great loss to the world. After what she'd seen them doing, she knew every last one of them had it coming.

Still . . .

Hweilan couldn't quite decide what she was feeling. Not guilt. Not over those men. Regret? Perhaps. Part of her missed the Hweilan that had been. The girl who always had someone to watch out for her, to take care of her.

But that only brought the anger back. She used to have people who cared for her and took care of her. But they had been taken from her. Killed. And those who had done it were still breathing. And that planted a cold shard of ice in her gut.

And so, round and round, back and forth, these thoughts went through Hweilan's mind. No conclusion. Just a wrestling of conflicting emotions.

All the doors to the stairways and upper levels of Gleed's tower had been locked or blocked with rubble, so Hweilan had simply used the vines to climb up the outside. Behind her, she could hear someone doing the same. The rustling vines stopped, and she heard bare feet rustling through the leaves and vines that covered the tower's top. Gleed, then. She didn't turn when she heard her teacher walk up behind her and stop.

"You're thinking about what happened," said Gleed.

Hweilan shrugged.

"This wasn't the first time you've killed."

"No."

A long silence, then Gleed asked, "Then why are you up here? Something is troubling you."

"I miss the high places," said Hweilan. "I miss—"

Gleed waited. But when Hweilan didn't finish he said, "You miss what?"

"The way I used to be."

"You're better than you used to be," said Gleed, an edge

entering his voice. "You think you could have dealt with those dogs without Ashiin's training?"

"No."

"Then why—"

Hweilan whirled to her feet. "Because I—"

Gleed stood his ground. He looked up at her, scowling. "Yes, well? Spit it out."

"I enjoyed it."

"Good." Gleed turned away, chuckling. "You're learning. That old fox is good for something after all."

"You don't understand."

"No, it is you who do not understand. You come from a line of warriors, girl. You think they did not enjoy the heat of battle? Of killing their enemies?"

"My father never enjoyed killing."

"Then your father was a fool."

Hweilan snarled and drew the knife from her belt as she lunged.

Green light washed over her and she found herself caught fast. The vines and branches had come alive, cracking the air like tiny whips as they writhed and twisted around her legs, then encased her torso, and finally her arms. Hweilan shrieked and thrashed and fought, but the vines only pulled tighter, constricting, pulling her arms close. In moments, she could barely move. She found herself staring at the old goblin, green light sparkling off his upraised staff, his free hand weaving an intricate pattern in the air.

"You really think you can take me?" said Gleed. "Even Ashiin knows better than to challenge me on my own ground."

He was only inches away. Hweilan gathered her strength and tried once more to break free, but the vines were strong as steel wire, and she could feel the power running through them.

"You ever disrespect my family again," said Hweilan, "and I'll kill you."

"You really think you could?"

"Even *you* sleep."

He held her gaze. Neither looked away. The green fire of his magic sparkled in his one good eye. The other dead eye was flat and gray as a stone.

He smiled. "But would you *enjoy* it?"

Hweilan spat in his face. "Curse your mother."

Gleed through back his head and cackled, then wiped the spittle from his face. "Oh, I did. Believe me. And long before the shriveled old monster deserved it. Still, I guess this exchange of sentiments makes us even. Does it not?"

Hweilan tried again to move. Still nothing. She might have been encased in stone. "I meant what I said."

"I don't doubt you. But you've got a lot to learn before you can take me."

His gaze shifted and locked on the blade held in her hand. The light from his staff seemed to catch there and glow like an emerald brand.

"She *did* give it to you then," he said.

It was the blade Menduarthis had given Hweilan. More than a foot of sharp steel, etched with waves and whorls. Ashiin had been true to her word and returned the knife to her.

"Ashiin was the second one to give it to me," said Hweilan.

"Then I shall be the second to take it away," said Gleed, and he reached for it.

Hweilan tightened her grip.

"Let go," Gleed said.

"No."

Gleed twitched his fingers, and the vines around her right arm and wrist tightened even further. Hweilan felt her skin press into the muscle beneath, and the whole pressing almost flat against the bone. She gritted her teeth and forced her fingers to hold the fist around the hilt of the knife.

I will not *scream,* she told herself. *I will* not—

Skin tore, and the vines bit into the flesh beneath. She held the grip a moment longer, but when the vine began to worm its way through flesh and into bone, her body betrayed her. Her fingers went limp.

Gleed snatched the blade. "Thank you," he said and turned away, holding the blade close to the light emanating from his staff.

The vines loosened, but not enough for her to break free. Warmth began to spread down her forearm, a dark stain spreading down her sleeve.

"Ahh," said Gleed, studying the blade. "Now this is a wonder. A real beauty."

He waved the blade before her face.

"Can you read the steel's riddle?" said Gleed.

Hweilan tried to move, but the vines only bit into her again.

"This particular knife," said Gleed, "has quite a history. A lineage rivaling even your own—and that is saying something. Not ancient, no, but quite special. This particular tooth was forged in the depths of Ellestharn. Do you know of this place?"

"The palace of Kunin Gatar," said Hweilan through teeth clenched in pain and anger.

"Very good, girl. Very, very good. Not a nice place. But one of great power. And powerful indeed were the hands that crafted this blade. Wise in the ways of wind and waves."

"I didn't care for the place much."

Gleed laughed, low in his throat, croaking almost like a toad. "No, I don't suppose you would. But then, the queen has always had a taste for pretty girls. Still . . . the power she wields is not without its uses."

With that, he began an incantation. Not the usual spells in the speech that Hweilan knew—the tongue of her Vil Adanrath ancestors. This was something altogether different—long vowels and harsh consonants that rasped in the back of the throat. A speech of cold wind cutting over sharp rocks.

Her eyes were drawn to the steel that Gleed still held, only a handspan or so from her eyes. The green light from Gleed's staff dimmed. But the etchings in the blade caught even that weak light, and Hweilan felt a breeze play over her skin.

Hweilan inhaled through her nose. Her head filled with the scent of everything around her—

—the green and all-too-alive scent of the vines and leaves around her—

—the coppery tang of blood leaking from her arm—

—the wet slate of the stone tower, so strong she could taste it in the back of her throat—

—the loamy, fish-tinged, muddy reek of the lake—

—the hundredfold, layer upon layer, smell of leaves, pines, and flowers—

—the rotting, years upon years stench of the bats and their droppings in the rooms of the tower below her—

—and nearest of all the underground, bordering-on-foul, yet tinged with spice scent of the old goblin—

Hweilan had always had a good sense of smell. More than anyone she knew, in fact. Scith himself for a while had taken to calling her his "little hound." But this . . .

It was as if some sweet, spicy feastday cake had been sifted down to its individual ingredients, and each one presented to her senses for scrutiny. She could identify every one.

Gleed hummed, then mused aloud. "The things one with your . . . gifts can do. Eh?"

His words brought her attention back to the moment. Back to her captivity and the little toad lording it over her. She scowled down at him.

"Gifts . . ." Gleed said, almost to himself, as if tasting the word. "Gifts, gifts, gifts. Oh, that a lowly little bug such as I were to be blessed as you . . . eh?"

He brought the knife around in a wide, theatrical arc, worthy of the finest tavern bard, and stopped it with the point resting in the soft flesh underneath Hweilan's chin. He pressed, trying to force her to raise her head.

She refused, instead clenching her jaw tight. She felt the cold steel pierce skin, then flesh. Felt the warm trickle of blood slide down the razor-sharp edge.

Many in this world are stronger than you, and those stronger may try to take from you. They may try to take your life, and they may succeed. But you must never give it to them. Make them pay, Hweilan. Make them pay.

Her mother's words. Given to her on the day she took Hweilan to see her father's dead body.

Hweilan clinched her jaw and forced her head down, driving the steel deeper so that she could look Gleed in the eye.

The slight widening of his eyes brought her great pleasure, despite the increased pain.

"You are a spiteful little nit, aren't you?" said Gleed. "You'd walk barefoot over red hot coals just for half a chance to vex me. Wouldn't you?"

Despite the almost half inch of steel lodged in her skin, Hweilan forced her lips to smile. In truth, she'd grown to respect the little goblin, if not to like him. But after what he'd said about her father, she'd gladly seize the opportunity to throw him off his own tower and feel guilty about it later.

Gleed pulled the knife out—one swift motion that sent a thin gout of blood splattering on her vine-wrapped feet.

"Fool," said Gleed, and again he held the knife in front of her. Her blood, a thick, dark rivulet, ran down the blade. But a thin trickle, splintered as a lightning bolt, ran down the flat of the steel, caught in etched swirls, and ran down their path. "How long did you carry this, completely ignorant of its power? This little trick I've just showed you . . . I can teach you to do that. Anytime you want. And more. So much more. Would you like that?"

"Let me free."

"If you were half as strong as you think you are, you could free yourself."

Hweilan scowled, at a loss for words.

Gleed's eyebrows shot up. "No? Well, then, perhaps you'd like to listen. Yes? Hm?"

She bared her teeth at him, but her gaze was pure malice. "Teach me, Master," she said.

The old goblin smiled. "I sense a sincere lack of sincerity in your words."

"Let me free."

"You remember the first night we met?" The malicious glee melted from his countenance, and he took on the lecturing tone she knew all too well.

She did. He'd tried to call her Meyla, some demeaning name meant to put in her place. She'd defied him.

"You are not the first I've trained," said Gleed. "I have instructed many in the Master's service over the years. But you are the first to know who she is. To remember. And yet . . . you don't *really* know, do you?"

"What?"

"Who you are. Only not so much who as *what* you are."

"I don't know what you're talking about."

"Liar," said Gleed. "You may not *know,* little girl, but I think you at least suspect. Don't you?"

Hweilan looked away before her eyes could betray her. Gleed was not the first to suggest such things to her. Menduarthis and Kunin Gatar had said something similar.

You're Damaran, to be sure. If you say you're kin to Lendri there . . . well, I have no reason to doubt you. But make no mistake. You're something else, too. Something . . . more.

The queen had ravaged Hweilan's mind, trying to find that something. But that something—whatever it was—had struck back, surprising and even hurting Kunin Gatar.

And the night she had first seen Nendawen, he had done something similar—and suffered much the same fate.

And even Kesh Naan, tasting her blood, saying—*What are you?*

That was the question. And yes, as Gleed said, she had suspected, had at the very least wondered. But to speak the truth—

"I don't know," she said.

Gleed lowered his staff. The vines around her did not loosen their grip, but the last of the light around Gleed's staff faded, and the evening darkness closed in. Hweilan felt as if a shroud were closing in around them.

"You were called," Gleed whispered. "You were chosen. By Nendawen himself. But you, dear girl . . . there's something about you that even the Master had not planned on."

He looked around, glancing quickly over each shoulder, and when he returned his gaze to her she saw the last thing she'd expected—sympathy. A softness that even bordered on . . . kindness.

Nothing he could have said or done could have caught her more by surprise.

Gleed came in close, the desperation in his gaze stilling her words. No. Not desperation. Fear. "The night has ears."

"But . . . but I saw . . . Jagun Ghen. What he'll do. What he is. What he could become. If he isn't stopped . . . if I don't stop him—"

"And then?"

All at once, the vines slackened, and Hweilan fell to the stone rooftop.

Gleed crouched in front of her and leaned close, so that his whispered words were still loud in her ears.

"And then what, girl? When Jagun Ghen is beaten and his sickness purged from the worlds . . . what then? You think the Master will free you? Nendawen is the Hunter. He has always been the Hunter. He will always be the Hunter. It is his nature. His only . . . *beingness*. The Hunter does not free his prey. I should know."

She looked up at him. "Why are you telling me this?"

"I can help you get away."

CHAPTER SIXTEEN

Foxes have ears.

Like many sayings, this one made its point by stating the obvious. An old saying in the Feywild, to understand it one needed to hear the whole thing: *Bears have strength, wolves have the pack, and foxes have ears.* The fox hunts by cunning, by studying its prey and using its surroundings.

One particular fox, the most cunning in this part of the Feywild, heard the words of the girl and the old goblin atop the tower. After listening, the hunter crept soundlessly away into the night-darkened woods. Before the girl and goblin had come down from their roost, the fox was already far away.

Well into the night, the fox came to the door between worlds and passed through, coming to a place of high, cold mountains. These lands had never been safe, but of late they had become particularly deadly as a new horror haunted them.

The fox could track this particular horror with senses that had long gone to sleep in the more "civilized" peoples of the world. The creature's very presence was an affront to this world, and it radiated a wrongness into the fabric of existence. It set a vibration through the hunter. First, no more than a mild irritation. An itch on the lower part of her brain. But as she drew closer to her prey the itch spread to a tingle, then a pulse that began in her head and shot through her whole body. By the time she reached her destination, she could almost feel her teeth rattling in her skull.

The fox found the pile of bones and gore. So fresh that it was still steaming in the cold, and the thicker pools of blood had not yet had time to freeze. The fox shook off its form, becoming the hunter on two legs.

"I felt you coming," said a voice from behind her.

The hunter turned. There in a well of darkness formed by a crack in the mountainside, she could just make out the dim, red glow of two eyes. The voice spoke in the ancient speech, but it sounded as if two voices were trying to speak through one mouth. The hunter could hear a great deal of ferocity in the more dominant tone, but it was weakening. The other sounded slightly off key, almost as if words themselves were not suited to a human tongue.

"The question," said the voice from the dark, "is why."

A shape emerged from the darkness and into the starlight. The hunter gasped.

The thing had probably been human once. The lean features and pale skin reminded her of the Frost Folk, who dwelled in the far northern regions of the world. She had hunted them before and knew their ways. But if that was indeed what the creature had once been, it had grown beyond that. The hunter knew that the true power was inside the creature, a being of insatiable hunger and fire, and that the body she saw was nothing more than a covering, like a gauntlet over a fist.

The monster had been hunting her own quarry for many, many days. She had taken to eating whatever she could kill in order to feed the thing inside her, and the body had begun to take on the traits of her food. Hair had become coarse and full, more like an animal's than a human's. Her hands ended in yellow claws. There were the beginnings of feathers sprouting along her limbs. Cracked and broken lips could no longer entirely cover the thick, pointed teeth filling her jaws.

"You are no match for me," said the creature, stepping forward. "Here, in this world, I am the wolf, and you are the little lamb. Were the moon full and your Master beside you . . . then you might stand a chance. But the moon is only a sliver, and not yet risen."

The hunter walked backward, matching the creature step for step. "Wolf that you are, you have not found the one lamb you seek. The one you *need* more than any other." She let the thing dwell on that a moment only, then said, "Have you?"

The thing snarled, and in it there was nothing of the woman it had once been. Only the hunger within.

"I know what you're looking for," said the hunter, and she even managed to put a little tremble in her voice. "I know *who* you're looking for."

"And . . . ?"

"And I can bring her to you."

The creature stopped its advance. Its claws flexed, raking into the stone. "And what do you want in return?" it said.

Ashiin smiled. "I want you to kill her."

CHAPTER SEVENTEEN

Y̶OU WERE CHOSEN. BY NENDAWEN HIMSELF. BUT *you, dear girl . . . there's something about you that even the Master had not planned on.*

Hweilan rolled Gleed's words over in her mind, again and again. She had come to the High Place where the old goblin had taught her to remove Jagun Ghen's demons from a blessed weapon. Yesterday, when she had so needed to see distance, she'd thought Gleed's tower was the best she could do. But she'd been too caught up in her own welling emotions to think clearly. There was a better place. This place.

The wind in her hair felt good. Soothing. Of all the places she'd been in the Feywild, this was the one place that most reminded her of home. A completely treeless height, covered in grass and lichen-encrusted rock. She could see sky all around. The seemingly impenetrable forest lay beneath her, and even Gleed's lake was no more than a blue shard occasionally sparkling under the sun.

She had woken long before dawn, Gleed still snoring in his nest of blankets beside the hearth. Hweilan had no idea what lessons he had planned for her that day. But after what he'd told her, she didn't much care. She'd dressed quietly and fled to this place. The ring where Gleed had sent Jagun Ghen's minion back to . . . wherever, was no more than a windswept bit of ground. She sat on the edge of the height, looking down on the miles on miles of forest, though her eyes didn't really see them.

In her blood . . . something other.

This voice came to her with such strength that she flinched. Not Gleed's words. Spoken with a laugh. By Menduarthis.

How long had it been since she thought of him? Yet he'd risked his own life to save hers. Was he even still alive? The last time she'd seen him, he'd been unconscious on the ground, blood gushing from his scalp. But he had been the first to tell her—

Something other. What . . . ?

. . . you're one of us. Menduarthis's voice again. *A mortal nature? Yes. But also . . . something else. Something* magical. *The blood runs thin in you, perhaps, but it runs true. Someone from . . . well,* somewhere else *planted a seed in your family garden. You're something else too. Something . . . more.*

At first, she'd thought he simply meant her Vil Adanrath heritage. That was her connection to Nendawen, after all. But no. She'd been a fool, and she should have known all along he meant something else, something more, if she'd only taken the time to think.

That night, when she'd very first seen the Master, when Nendawen had saved her from Jagun Ghen's minion, he had invaded her mind.

Hweilan chuckled at that, but there was no humor in it. Only bitterness.

Scith had once told Hweilan that if wolfpacks became too bold and dangerous in an area, some Nar tribes would leave a swiftstag corpse out for them to find. Only they would imbed razor-sharp steel in the corpse. A hungry pack who found the frozen carcass would lick at the frozen flesh, the heat from their own body thawing it, but at the same time making their tongues numb. So numb that they didn't feel the sharp steel slicing into them until it was too late.

But what Nendawen had found . . . it had been far worse than biting down full force upon sharp steel. How he had . . .

Howled did not describe it. No word she knew described it. His pain had shattered their connection.

What had Nendawen found? Found inside her?

. . . there's something about you that even the Master had not planned on.

What?

Did it matter? Did it really? What it all came down to was—

I can help you get away.

"Get away," she said the words aloud, only half-aware she did so.

To where?

Her family was dead. Her friends. Everyone she had ever loved. And the one responsible was sitting in her home.

And that, more than anything, made all her confusion, all her questions, burn away. Wealth, power, prestige, honor . . . none of it meant anything without family. And Jagun Ghen had taken hers away. Had taken away everything from her. That left her with only one thing—

Vengeance. Cloak it in "justice" if you like. Paint it with concepts like honor or even saving the world. True or not—didn't matter. It all came down to one bare, burning truth: That thing had killed her family. She was going to kill him or die trying.

And then what, girl? Gleed had said. *When Jagun Ghen is beaten and his sickness purged from the world . . . what then? You think the Master will free you? Nendawen is the Hunter. He has always been the Hunter. He will always be the Hunter. It is his nature. His only . . . beingness. The Hunter does not free his prey. I should know.*

And then what . . . ?

And then what . . . ?

"Doesn't matter," said Hweilan. It didn't. After that . . . she didn't much care. Nendawen could finish the job and swallow her whole. Hweilan no longer cared. If he demanded years of service from her, if she was doomed to train other servants for eternity . . . well, she'd cross that bridge when she came to it.

Until then, only one thing mattered: killing Jagun Ghen.

Hweilan stood. She wasn't yet ready to return to Gleed and listen to him prattle, but she was done moping. She turned her back on Gleed's lake—

And there, no more than five paces away, stood Ashiin, leaning upon her staff.

"Going somewhere?" said Ashiin.

Hweilan opened her mouth to say, *I was going that way,* but thought better of it, and instead asked, "What do you want?"

Ashiin blinked. Had Hweilan ever spoken to Scith with such an insolent tone, he would have told her he had no time for ungrateful little girls and left her to spend the day on her own. Her mother would have given her a tongue-lashing to make her ears bleed.

"Defiance," said Ashiin. "It can be a good thing. When you are in the right and your opponent in the wrong. When death is preferable to your opponent letting you live. Which are you now, girl?"

"You won't kill me," said Hweilan. "I am the Hand of the Hunter. Chosen of Nendawen. He needs me."

"If I can kill you, then you are not the Hand he needs."

"The day is not over," said Hweilan. It was one of Ashiin's favorite sayings. It meant that just because you couldn't do something, it didn't mean that you couldn't learn how to do it.

Ashiin stood there a moment, impassive. Then a grin broke her face. And finally she threw back her head and laughed.

"Defiance can also be a bad thing," she said, "because little girls use it simply for spite, to no good reason. That is you, O Hand of the Hunter." A hardness, ever so slight, entered her eyes, though the smile stayed on her lips. "There is still much of that in you: the little girl who wants her own way and damn the consequences."

Hweilan scowled. "Is that why you came to find me? To lecture?"

"You want a lecture, go back to the old goblin."

"Then why—?"

"Your father's bow."

For a moment, the world spun around Hweilan. Even though she could not string the bow—could barely even bend it—she had carried it with her out of Highwatch and through the days of horror that followed. She had risked her life to retrieve it and convinced Menduarthis to risk his. It was the last thing she had of her father.

And she had not seen it since coming here.

"What about my father's bow?" said Hweilan, and all the defiance and then some was back in her voice.

"You want it back."

It was not a question, but still Hweilan said, "Yes."

"Such a fine weapon—a master's work for a master's hand—is not a relic. It is a weapon, meant to be used."

Hweilan took in a breath to speak, but Ashiin cut her off.

"Time you learned to use it."

Hweilan's jaw snapped shut, and for a moment she couldn't breathe. "Wh-what?"

The smile melted from Ashiin's face, but the hardness stayed in her eyes. Hardened even further. She turned, stepped away a few paces, then turned to face Hweilan again. She sat crosslegged, almost on the very spot where Nendawen's spear had once rested, her staff across her lap.

"Sit," said Ashiin.

Hweilan's feet were moving before she knew it. She sat across from Ashiin.

"The old goblin has taught you the *uwethla*," said Ashiin. "Has taught you how to craft them into your weapons to capture the demons of Jagun Ghen."

"He has."

"The *uwethla* the old goblin has taught you are of two kinds." Ashiin reached across the distance between them and traced Hweilan's *uwethla* that began with the spider just over her left breast, then continued with the webbing and sacred words over her shoulder and onto a portion of her neck until it ended just below her jaw. "*Tunaheth,* the *uwethla* that sleeps, like memory, waiting to be woken. And there are *hrayeh,* the *uwethla* that bind, that capture, like those etched into your arrows. But there is the third kind, rarest and most powerful of all. The *shesteh.*"

Hweilan knew the word. "Home," she said.

"Yes. Like the *hrayeh,* they contain a spirit, but where the *hrayeh* contain a spirit against its will, the *shesteh* invites a willing servant, an ally. And your father's people, Hweilan, these knights on their flying beasts, even they knew of this, though they had their own words and rituals for them. Those symbols etched into your father's bow?"

"*Shesteh,*" said Hweilan. She had always wondered at them. They so resembled the runes on the robes of the priests of Torm and on the knights' armor that she had always assumed they were merely part of the faith. And no knight would ever speak of them, not even Ardan to his daughter.

"Yes," said Ashiin. "You think your grandfather's knights could plant an arrow in an enemy's eye from three hundred feet away simply because their weapons were well made? No. They had help."

"But . . . but the Knights of Ondrahar knew nothing of Nendawen, of *uwethla,* of—"

"Truth is truth, girl. What the servants of Nendawen can know and use, so can the servants of Torm. Words may change, but Truth is immutable."

"You mean my father's bow is—"

"No," said Ashiin. "No longer. Remember: I said that the spirit the *shesteh* contains is an ally. I'll go further: It is a friend. A sister. I do not know the sacred rites of your father's people, but I do know that somehow their bows contained a sacred spirit. Some lesser spirit servant of their Torm?" Ashiin shrugged. "Perhaps. But I do know that its connection to the wielder was . . . intimate. When your father died, the spirit in his bow joined him with his god. The bow is now an empty vessel. But an empty vessel can be filled again."

Hweilan looked down, and her gaze turned inward. "But . . ."

She could not find the words. If the runes were sacred to Torm . . . well, she had been raised in her father's faith. She had never been what even the most magnanimous would call devout, but she had honored the faith. But with her oaths and service to Nendawen . . . where did that leave her? She had not consciously forsaken Torm. Had he forsaken her?

"You will craft new *uwethla* into the bow," said Ashiin, as if reading her thoughts. "*Shesteh* into which Nendawen will send one of his own spirits."

Hweilan did not understand. But again words came to her out of the past, words spoken to her in a dream—

You do not need understanding. You need to choose. Understanding will come later . . . if you survive.

"What must I do?" she said.

Ashiin smiled. Not one of good humor or kindness. This one showed every pointed tooth in her jaw.

"So glad you asked," she said. She reached behind her back and produced a stake—a shaft of white wood no more than a foot long, sharpened to a lethal point on one end. "Into this you will craft *hrayeh*. To call forth your ally, to waken the bow, Nendawen requires sacrifice."

"Sacrifice?"

"We're going hunting."

CHAPTER EIGHTEEN

THIDREK WAS NOT THE SAME MAN WHO HAD RIDDEN out of Helgabal some tendays ago. His family had been noble for only three generations, but unlike many young aristocrats, Thidrek had never grown soft. He knew power came to those who seized it, and once attained, he could never let his guard down. In the conflict that brought Yarin to the throne, Thidrek's father had backed the usurper. That gamble had paid off, and Thidrek had become one of the king's most favored advisors.

And so when word arrived that Highwatch had fallen, that the High Warden, who had never loved Yarin nor received any love in return, lay dead, the king wasted no time. Thidrek led a delegation out of Helgabal two days later. He rode with forty warriors—a healthy mix of men loyal to the king and mercenaries loyal to the king's gold.

Thidrek had almost felt a king himself. He carried power and authority, and every man and woman in his company answered to him. Thidrek bore the king's good will and offer of friendship to the new rulers of Highwatch. Securing that relationship would help to solidify Yarin's precarious power. But more importantly, securing this alliance would forge Thidrek's own future in the Damaran court.

The Gap had been the first sign of trouble. Its reputation

was grim even in the best of years, and it was the first time Thidrek had been more than a few miles in. But with forty armed horsemen around him and the authority of the king in his hands, he had not feared any real trouble. Yarin had given them plenty for the "tax"—silver coins and the cast-off weapons no longer fit for Damaran knights. Four days inside the Gap they had seen their first hobgoblins—scouts watching them, bold as you please, from distant heights. On the sixth morning, they had woken to find their night watch in the hands of hobgoblins.

Thidrek had not been particularly worried. Concerned, yes. But such was not atypical behavior for the more aggressive mountain tribes. And so he came forward and addressed the foremost hobgoblin, offering the usual tax.

The goblin grabbed the hand of the watchman being held between two of his fellows. As the Damarans watched, the goblin cut off one of the man's fingers, tossed it to Thidrek, and said, "He loses one each time you insult me."

In the end, the goblins left after taking four times the usual tax and two of their pack horses. For just a moment, Thidrek considered fighting—it galled him to give in to such foul creatures—but a quick count showed a score of hobgoblins, all armed. And if he could see twenty, there were probably fifty. He knew his seasoned fighters would probably make short work of the rabble, but they still had many miles of hard country to cross, and he didn't want to fend off attacks the whole way. So he'd paid.

There had been three more such incidents—each one costing more. Thidrek knew that if Highwatch did not resupply them, they would not have enough food to make it back to Damara. His advisors sensed his worry, and one day one of them did something one rarely did in Yarin's court: he spoke the truth.

"The mountain tribes always feared Highwatch more than they feared anyone in Damara," he said. "Yarin negotiated the tax, but it was Highwatch that kept the goblins in line.

If the knights in Highwatch are truly gone . . . we might do well to choose another way home, my lord."

When they left the Gap, Thidrek hoped the worst of their troubles were behind them. But then they met the first Creel.

The Nar barbarians did not attack or attempt to "tax" them, but they greeted the Damaran delegation with an attitude just shy of disdain. Thidrek could not understand their uncouth tongue, but he still knew an insult when he heard one, and his face flushed when he heard the Creel snickering at him and his men.

Their leader looked down his nose at Thidrek and said, "Ride to Nar-sek Qu'istrade. Leave the road at your peril."

And then they'd ridden away, leaving the Damarans to ride through their dust.

"They aren't going to escort us?" said Almar, who was Thidrek's second.

"You really want their stench the whole way?" said Thidrek. But he shared Almar's offense. To greet a royal delegation with nothing more than an order to watch their step . . .

They saw more Nar at a distance as they rode for Nar-sek Qu'istrade, but none approached. The half-dozen guards who kept the gate at the entrance to the valley, the so-called Shadowed Path, let them pass without incident. But Thidrek could feel their eyes on his back, and when the gates shut and locked behind the last of his men . . . that was when the first true fear hit Thidrek.

His initial excitement in Damara had given way to unease in his first days in the Gap. Their encounters with the hobgoblins had filled him with confusion and—truth be told—a fair amount of shame. The Creel had shamed him further. But hearing the tall iron-shod doors clang shut and the crossbars being dragged into place . . .

Thidrek was afraid. The grassy valley through which they rode was miles wide, but he still felt as if the door to his cell had been slammed behind him.

Hundreds—perhaps thousands—of Creel held the valley, lounging around in filthy camps or riding around and sparring. A few stopped and watched the Damarans ride past, but none spoke a word, and there was not a hint of deference even in the gazes of warriors who were scarcely more than boys.

The mountain height on which Highwatch rested rose before them. It was not elegant, but it did have a functional beauty to it. Perched on the heights, turrets jutting out from cliffs hundreds of feet high, it looked like a castle out of a bard's tale. Still, Thidrek felt repulsed by it. He could put no name to it, could see nothing particularly repellant about the castle, but he could *feel* it. The sight of it pushed at him. It was like walking against the current of a river.

About halfway across the valley, the horses began to feel it too. At first it was merely a few mounts tossing their heads. But soon there was not a rider among them who wasn't struggling to keep his or her horse under control. The beasts' eyes rolled in their heads, and Thidrek even saw one horse do its best to wrench its head around far enough to bite its rider.

"My lord, this is pointless!" Almar said. Then his horse kicked up its rear legs, and the man had to fight to keep his saddle.

"Withdraw!" Thidrek called out. "Withdraw!"

He wrenched his own horse around. Once turned away from Highwatch, the beast set off in a gallop. Thidrek gave the horse its head for a hundred yards or so, then wrenched back the reins. The rest of the company soon gathered around him.

"What's gotten into them?" Almar said.

One of the men whom Thidrek didn't know answered, "Could be some enchantment to keep horses back. Gods know if I lived among all these damned Nar, I'd want just such a thing."

Thidrek forced a smile that he in no way felt. "Almar, choose twenty men to stay here with the horses. Order them to make camp. The rest of us will walk."

• • • • •

"What is this place?" one of the men said as they passed the first of the buildings.

"Kistrad," Almar answered.

It was a ghost town. Most of the buildings still stood, though here and there they passed the scorched skeleton of a house's frame still standing amidst the ashes. Some of the stone buildings bore marks of fire, and no one had bothered to repair any of the season's storm damage. Thidrek thought he could hear rats scuttling in the late afternoon shadows, but he saw not a soul.

"Not even a stray dog."

"My lord?" said Almar, and it wasn't until then that Thidrek realized he had spoken aloud.

"Nothing."

"Nar don't keep dogs," said one of the other men.

"Yes," said Thidrek. "That must be it."

They walked on, staying to the main thoroughfare—the widest path through the village, and the only one paved. The sun sank behind the mountains before them, and the shadows grew thick and cold.

The road led to Highwatch's main gate—though it was hardly a gate as Thidrek understood them. Castles had walls, and castle walls had gates. Highwatch's main defenses were the heights themselves, and her main gate was twice the size of any Thidrek had ever seen. But it was not a passage through a bailey wall. It was an entrance into the mountain itself. One gate was open wide. Its timbers scorched, all but two of the massive hinges broken, it hung loose, resting against the stones of the road. All that was left of its mate were shards of blackened wood and twisted metal littering the ground around the arch. Thidrek could see a half-dozen paces or so into the tunnel, but beyond that all was darkness.

"Well," said Almar, "what do we—"

"Quiet," said Thidrek, who was staring into the darkness. "Something's coming."

Every man's hand went to the hilt of his sword, and Almar drew his half out of the scabbard.

Shapes that were slightly less darkness than the blackness beyond moved toward them. Thidrek could hear their feet shuffling over the dust and grit on the ground, and with each step, the shapes grew more distinct.

Four men. All obviously Damarans by the cuts of their hair and their clothes. But their clothes were filthy, fraying at the seams, and hung loose on their frames. In the last moment before the nearest of them stepped fully into the light, Thidrek thought he saw red fire, like sunset through stained glass, glint deep in their eyes. Thidrek gasped and took a step back.

"Did we startle you, my lord?" said the nearest of them, and then all four men bowed. "Forgive me. You are Lord Thidrek of Goliad, are you not?"

Thidrek swallowed hard. Something in the man's voice set Thidrek's teeth on edge. But he managed to say, "I am. And you are . . . ?"

"Morev," said the man. "We have come to welcome you in the name of Lord Guric of Highwatch. And to bring you to him."

Almar slammed his blade back into its scabbard. "You are our escort?"

Morev kept his eyes fixed on Thidrek. "We are."

"Lords of Damara are more accustomed to being escorted through their host's gate," said Almar. "And *not* having to walk through a dusty ruin before being greeted."

"My most profound apologies, Almar of Brotha. Our forces are, sadly, much reduced of late. I trust our Nar servants did not offend you."

Almar opened his mouth to retort, but Thidrek cut him off.

"How do you know our names?"

Morev smiled, and Thidrek shivered at the sight. There was no mirth in it. Not even the feigned obsequiousness one might expect from a high-minded servant. Thidrek had once seen a jackal, brought by some southern trader to his father's court. He remembered that jackal and how it had seemed to grin just before it pounced on the hare that was its dinner.

"Your reputations precede you, my lords," said Morev. "Come. You are most welcome."

Highwatch proved to be even more of a ghost town that Kistrad. Although something deep in Thidrek's brain thought perhaps the ghosts might be real in the fortress. They saw not a soul in the halls. No guards posted at any of the dozens of gates and doors through which they passed. No servants sweeping halls or courtyards that were in desperate need of it. No one lighting the evening lamps, for there were no lamps, and their escorts carried no torches. They walked in darkness, ever upward into the heart of Highwatch. Even when they passed through courtyards or avenues open to the sky, there was not so much as a raven or a sparrow. Highwatch was barren.

Despite the seeming emptiness, Thidrek could feel eyes on him, watching from heights above that he could only guess at, or staring from the shadows that faded to absolute black as evening gave way to night.

"I hope you will forgive our lack of lamps, my lords," said Morev. "Since the recent . . . unpleasantness, I fear our supply of oil and pitch has grown thin."

"With summer, trade should resume, yes?" said Thidrek.

"We hope."

"We saw fires in the Nar camps we passed," said Almar.

"Indeed," Morev replied. "The Nar burn grass and horse dung that they cache throughout the year to dry. Here in the fortress, we do not care for the stench."

"You mean they cook their food on . . . on shit?" said one of Thidrek's men.

"Yes," said Morev. "And for warmth and light. Narfell is not a place known for its abundant forests. What few there are hug the mountains here, but the Nar—and especially the Creel whom you saw—are creatures of unbreakable habit."

"Remind me not to dine with the Nar."

"Oh, not to worry. We have a most special meal prepared for you, my lords."

Standing outside the main hall, for a moment Thidrek dared to hope that he might have been wrong, that every sense in his body and mind were raw from lack of sleep and good food. The receiving chamber was long overdue for a good sweep and scrub. Even the cobwebs overhead looked stale and abandoned. But there was blessed, blessed light. A brazier wider than a paladin's shield burned a healthy bed of coals next to the far wall, and Thidrek could smell incense there as well. A dozen torches burned in sconces along the wall, their smoke pooling thick overhead before it finally leaked out through vents in the roof. More Damarans stood as guards, their backs as straight as the spears they held. They did not look at Thidrek and his company, and their clothes were just as dirty and worn as that of Morev and his fellows, but after occupying a sacked fortress cut off from trade with everyone except a bunch of dung-burning barbarians, what could one expect? Even the four Nar standing guard farther down the hall were dressed in their finest and looked at Thidrek and his men with proper deference.

One of the doors opened, and a huge Nar stepped out. He was dressed as the rest of his countrymen in various bits of wool, fur, and horse leather, and he wore the sides and crown of his hair in the traditional topknot, but when he spoke, his Damaran was flawless.

"I am Vazhad," he said. "I serve Argalath, Lord Guric's chief counselor. I have come to take you to my lords."

The man showed nothing. No deference or respect. No contempt. No amusement. No emotion whatsoever.

"Very well," said Thidrek. "Do your men hold our weapons while we are in the hall?"

"That is not necessary."

"Then proceed."

Vazhad nodded and pulled the door wide. Almar scowled when the man simply stared at them without a bow.

"I will announce you," said Vazhad.

Thidrek led them inside. As the last man passed, Vazhad called out, "Thidrek of Goliad and company!"

More torches burned inside the main hall, but there was no brazier, and the hearths held only cold ash in their beds. Orange torchlight and dancing shadows filled the hall but gave no warmth. Full night had fallen, the upper windows stood dark, and Thidrek could see steam as he breathed.

He led his men across the hall where an impressive Damaran sat in a simple oak chair upon the dais. A smaller man, swathed completely in thick robes and a cowl, stood behind his right shoulder.

Thidrek had heard of Guric, of course, long before Yarin had told him the full story. He'd been sent by his father to Highwatch to strengthen relations between the two houses, but he'd been besotted by some lordling's daughter whose father had chosen the wrong side during Yarin's ascension. He'd chosen love over his inheritance and been taken into High Warden Vandalar's household. But then his wife died. He'd given up everything for an empty bed and no heirs. However, Guric had not accepted his fate. He'd seized what he wanted and sat as the new lord of Highwatch. Thidrek couldn't help but admire that. Should things continue to worsen for Yarin in Damara, Thidrek could do far worse than look to Guric as an ally.

Thidrek stopped at the foot of the dais and kneeled. He heard his men do the same behind him.

"Lord Guric, High Warden of Highwatch," said Thidrek, "I bring you the good will and congratulations of Yarin Frostmantle, rightful ruler of Damara."

"Please stand, Thidrek," said Guric. "We have no suppliants here. Though I hope you'll forgive me keeping my seat. I'm afraid my duties have kept me so busy of late that I am quite famished."

"Of course, my lord," said Thidrek, and he put on his most ingratiating smile as he rose. But he felt it falter when he looked up. There it was again. For just a moment, he'd seen a red, hungry fire burning in Guric's eyes. Surely it was just a trick of the torchlight. . . .

"Why are you here?" said the robed one behind Guric.

Thidrek scowled. No *my lord* or *why have you honored us with your presence?* It had been spoken like one might speak to a chambermaid knocking on the door after her duties were done.

But looking into the depths of that cowl where the torchlight did not penetrate, Thidrek felt his offense and resolve waver, and the fear that had dogged him since entering the valley came back full force.

Thidrek swallowed and, in a near panic, fell back on the rote he had turned over in his mind a hundred times since leaving Damara.

"A-as I said, we have come to bring you the good will of King Yarin—and to offer his congratulations and sincere gratitude in successfully bringing the king's justice to the traitor Vandalar."

"And . . . ?"

"And we have come to invite you to renew your vows of fealty and friendship to Yarin, the rightful King of Damara."

"There," said Guric, "we come to it."

"Highwatch is not in Damara," said the robed man.

"Nevertheless—"

"Enough!" said Guric, and he pushed himself to his feet. Thidrek flinched, but Guric had not spoken in anger or offense. In fact, he was smiling down on Thidrek. But the smile lined Thidrek's veins with frost. "There are new lords in Highwatch now. Are you hungry?"

"A-am I—?"

"Hungry," said Guric.

"Y-yes," said Thidrek.

"I am *starving*," said Guric.

The lord of Highwatch moved so quickly that Thidrek only had time to draw in a breath to scream.

But Guric swept past Thidrek, knocking him to the cold stone floor.

Almar shrieked—a high-pitched wail so loud that Thidrek actually heard the man's throat tear. The other men yelled and tried to run, but Guric's guards caught them.

Thidrek scrambled to his feet and gaped at the scene before him. Every one of his men caught in the arms of a Damaran or Nar—except for Almar. It had not been the scream that tore the man's throat. Guric had one arm wrapped around Almar's waist, the other tangled in his hair, and was bending the man over backward. For one absurd instant it looked like some horrific dance. Then he saw the blood. So much blood. Guric had his face buried under Almar's jaw, and by the movement of his head, Thidrek knew he was biting, rending, chewing . . .

Wide-eyed, hand trembling as he reached for his sword, Thidrek forced himself to look away.

And wished he hadn't. He looked right into the eyes of a Damaran holding one of his men. There was no mistaking it. They glowed, red like fire, but with no warmth. Only hunger. And then Thidrek noticed something that had escaped him before. He and his men were breathing great clouds of steam in their panic. But not a wisp of breath escaped any of the Damarans of Highwatch. They weren't breathing.

Thidrek felt warmth as his bladder released. His hand refused to grip the hilt of his sword. As a knight, he knew that in the thick of battle, the body's natural reaction was to fight or flee. His mind screamed, *Flee!* But his body had not the strength. It was all he could do to keep his feet.

Guric straightened, and the sound of flesh and tendons ripping and tearing made Thidrek's gorge rise. Had he anything in his stomach he would have spewed it out, but he only filled his mouth with bile. The lord of Highwatch threw his head back and swallowed. Then he looked down at Thidrek.

"That took the edge off," he said.

"Whuh . . . whuh . . ." was the only thing Thidrek could manage.

"What are we going to do with you?" said the robed man. "Fear not. A man of your . . . stature is worth more to us than a meal. We have something very special for you in mind. A bit of lore I have been most eager to try—and one in which we find ourselves of sore need."

"Wh-*what*?" said Thidrek.

Thidrek felt strong arms seize and lift him. He didn't struggle.

"Sarkhrun . . ." said the robed man.

Thidrek heard the man before he saw him, shuffling out of the deeper shadows behind the dais. A dead man . . . a *dead* man was coming at him. Some small part of Thidrek's brain that still clung to rational thought reminded him that he seemed to be surrounded by dead men, but there was no mistaking the thing that approached him for anything but a shambling corpse. Skin hung off stiffening muscles in tatters, all but a few lanks of matted hair had fallen out. The eyes had either sunken all the way into the skull or fallen out altogether, for suddenly, the only gaze there was red hunger.

"Our brother Sarkhrun," said the robed man, "one of the first to join us. But as you see, his spirit seems to have outworn his body's welcome. If the hunger grows too strong without being sated, the effects are as you see—irreversible. We cannot have that. Our brother deserves better."

The corpse stopped in front of Thidrek and reached out one emaciated hand. The stench coming off the thing . . .

Thidrek screamed. All reason had left him, and the most bestial instincts of his body took over, and at the moment every fiber of his being fought to survive.

It was a useless fight.

The thing holding him held his head steady while the corpse used his fingernail to gouge deep into the skin of

Thidrek's forehead. The thing carved a pattern there, a rune all of sharp angles and hanging arms, like a broken holy symbol.

Hot blood ran into Thidrek's face. He blinked it away and saw the corpse before him fall to the ground. The light in its eyes died and it was then truly a corpse.

Thidrek's forehead was a mass of pain. That pain suddenly flared, like fire, and although he could not hear it over the sounds of his own screams, he could feel the skin there sizzling and popping.

But it was a backward burning. Whereas normal fires blaze and send light and warmth outward, the symbol on Thidrek's forehead blazed, and a hideous, cackling, rending fire came *inside* him. Thidrek felt—actually *felt*—veins in his brain swell and burst, felt minuscule sections of the spongy mass inside his head crisp and burn as the new life inside him took over, pushing the Thidrek down, binding and sealing him inside the tomb of his own mind.

The man holding him let him go, and Thidrek's body stood on its own strength. Sarkhrun looked out from his new eyes, forced his new lips to pull back in a grin, and said, "It worked."

CHAPTER NINTEEN

ASHIIN HAD OPENED THE PORTAL FOR THEM, MAKING slight variations to the rhythm of the drum. And instantly, Hweilan saw why. They had not stepped through the veil of water into the near-desert land of towerlike mountains. No. She *knew* these mountains.

"The Giantspires," she said.

She didn't know this particular valley, no. But that peak off in the distance . . . she knew those ragged edges. She'd seen them out her bedroom window her entire life. She was seeing them from the other side, which meant that she was many miles north of Highwatch.

"Yes," said Ashiin. "The Giantspires."

Hweilan waited for the warning to come—*Don't think of running home, girl*—or some such. But it never did.

"Close your eyes," said Ashiin.

She did.

"Can you feel it?"

She could. That grating on her nerve endings, as if tiny shards of ice filled her blood, and every pulse of her heart sent their jagged edges into her flesh. And the pulse, the steady drumbeat at the back of her skull. She had first felt it during her flight from Highwatch, and she had first realized what it was in the realm of Kunin Gatar.

"Jagun Ghen," said Hweilan, and opened her eyes.

"One of his minions, yes," said Ashiin. "You can sense it."

"Yes," Hweilan said, "ever since . . ."

She searched her memory. She had first noticed this new sense in the foothills with Lendri, after the fall of Highwatch. But in her visions in Kesh Naan's cave, she had seen Jagun Ghen break into Toril, possessing a young Argalath. And she had been around Argalath many times in her life. The man had always made her skin crawl, but nothing like this. This had begun . . .

"When Jagun Ghen began hunting you," said Ashiin. "This . . . sense, this pulse on your brain, bordering on pain, that is not from the Master, nor from you."

"You mean," said Hweilan, "Jagun Ghen is . . . is in my head?"

The thought horrified her, made her feel sick.

Ashiin shrugged. "Not like that, I think. He and his minions can sense you, but you can sense him. This connection goes both ways. If he could read your thoughts, I think you could read his. Can you?"

"No."

"Have you tried?"

"No!"

"Try now."

"What? Are you mad?"

"*Think*, you stupid girl. If he can sense your thoughts, do you think he'd balk at it? No. He would use every weapon at his disposal. Would you do less?"

Hweilan gritted her teeth. Ashiin had a point, and she knew it. As much as the thought repulsed her, if she could gain an edge . . .

She took a deep breath, released it, then closed her eyes. The pain was still there, the nagging pulse, and concentrating on it made it seem worse. She did her best to relax, to concentrate on that sense, growing stronger by the moment. But that's all it was—a sense of danger drawing nearer.

"Nothing." She opened her eyes and looked at Ashiin. "I can feel it coming, but nothing more."

"It is close?"

Hweilan looked around. The sun rode high in the sky, but it only made the shadows under boulders and in the cracks of the cliffside seem all the darker. Pines and underbrush grew in the valley floor. They swayed in the wind, and the shadows under them twisted and shifted constantly. Anything could be hiding in the valley. Hweilan shivered, and only part of it was from the cold.

"Getting closer," she said.

"You feel ready for this?" said Ashiin.

"No," said Hweilan. She remembered looking into the eyes of what she'd thought was her Uncle Soran, and then at Kadrigul. The former had gone toe to toe with Kunin Gatar, and the latter had ripped Lendri's heart from his chest.

"Good," said Ashiin. "If you felt ready, I'd know you're still a fool. The more important question: are you willing?"

Hweilan looked down at the stake in her hand. She'd carved the *uwethla* herself. They were rough, and she could still smell the charcoal scent of the burned wood. But she could feel the power in them. Dormant, yes, but still there.

"Yes," she said.

"You're going to need everything I've ever taught you to survive this," said Ashiin.

Hweilan closed her eyes again. She had learned much since she had last faced one of these monstrosities. The familiar pounding was much the same—still bordering on pain—but after so many tendays of training with Ashiin, she knew how to use the pain, not to deny it but embrace it and use it to fuel her will. Every drumbeat in her skull was a little stronger than the last. But rather than resist them, she opened herself, let her muscles relax, let the pounding send her blood and breath racing through her body.

"I'm ready," she said. But when she opened her eyes, Ashiin was gone.

Hweilan considered her options. She remembered how these things had tracked her before. No matter how far and fast she and Lendri had run, those things had always managed to find her again. She could sense them, and she had every reason to believe that connection ran both ways.

"No sense in hiding," she told herself. That left only one option: choose the battleground.

She had the knife Lendri had given her. Fine steel and razor sharp, but not much more. Then there was Menduarthis's blade. After their conversation, Gleed had taught her a few of its tricks, which might prove useful. But ultimately, all that was just decoration. If Kunin Gatar hadn't been able to stop one of these things, no amount of weaponry and magic would help. It all came down to the pointed shaft in her hand. Somehow she had to get that inside the thing.

Hweilan looked down at the bottom of the valley a few hundred yards below. What trees there were grew down there—tall pines with thick scrub at their feet. She could use them. Not to hide—she'd already decided there was no use in that—but she could use them to her advantage.

If she hurried. The drumbeat in her skull had taken on a sharper edge, each pulse piercing. The thing was close. Hweilan ran.

She made it to the woods and had passed the first trees when she saw her mistake. The thing was already there. Hweilan stopped and took a defensive crouch, Menduarthis's knife in one hand, the *uwethla*-covered stake in the other.

A dozen or so paces in front of her, crouching on a log, was a horror from her nightmares. Still vaguely human, the emaciated features and pale skin were being overrun by more bestial features—thick, coarse hair that stood on end off the back of her head; twisted sprigs that looked like half-formed feathers sprouted up the back of her arms and shoulders; thick fangs protruded from bloodied lips. The hand that had struck the log raked upward, dislodging more pieces of wood and ice, and Hweilan noticed that both hands and feet ended in claws. Still, there was enough left to suggest the woman that the thing had once been. It was the eyes that finally gave her away. One teary blue orb looked at Hweilan with nothing but a sad, pathetic madness. But the other . . . a blazing, fleshy jewel. A new eye—one birthed from some foul power. Still, Hweilan remembered all too well the day she had gouged it out.

"Jatara," she said.

The thing on the log cocked its head, and the blue eye blinked, as if with confusion or wonder, and then it said, "Ja-Ja-Ja*t*a*r*a. Yes. Bits of her are still here. Little bits and bits. Very tasty. Not as tasty as you, I'd bet, I'd bet, I'd *bite*."

Jatara leaped. Not up into the air, but straight at Hweilan, like the loosing of an arrow.

Hweilan rolled to the left and came up again, swiping out with the silver steel of her knife as she did. But it cut only air.

The Jatara-thing had slid through the carpet of old pine needles and come to a stop against the bole of a tree. She crouched there, panting, both eyes locked on Hweilan.

The reek hit Hweilan and almost caused her knees to buckle. It was a stench that hit the mind more than the nose—the smell of a thousand years of burning rot.

"You killed muh-m-my brother," said the Jatara-thing, and in the words Hweilan heard both voices—Jatara's, drowning in darkness and fire, and the *other*.

"No," said Hweilan, and it was the truth.

"Saw him die," said the thing. "*Watched* him die."

"Yes," said Hweilan, "I did," and she brandished the stake in front of her. The *uwethla* carved into it flared, like slumbering embers fanned by a breeze.

The Jatara-thing hissed and its eyes closed to razor-thin slits.

"Going to stick that in me, are you?"

"Yes," said Hweilan, and took two steps forward.

"You can try," said the thing—and leaped again.

Hweilan tried to turn the spike of the stake into her foe, but Jatara was *so fast*—a blur of shadow in the air, and then the force of a battering ram hit her.

The stake flew from Hweilan's hand, and it was only a reflex brought on by pain that caused her other hand to tighten around the knife and keep it in her grip. All breath left her body in one pained gasp, and she felt muscles grind and tear against her bones at the force that hit them. Hweilan flew back—skidded against the rough bark of a tree, shredding the shirt off her back—then hit the ground and tumbled end over end.

She forced herself to move—again acting more by instinct than conscious thought—rolling away and pushing herself to her feet. The world rocked and shivered around her, and she had to force breath back into her battered body. Lights danced before her eyes, and she clenched her jaw so tight that she felt the roots of her teeth stabbing into her jaw and she tasted blood.

"I've been waiting," said a voice, and Hweilan realized it was coming from above her. The Jatara-thing had taken to the boughs. "Scouring these hard lands. Eating vermin. H-hunting for you."

Hweilan's eyes scoured the ground around her. *Where was the stake?*

"Searching," the voice continued, "sniffing every trail. But they all went cold. Where did you go, m-my little morsel?"

There! The stake was lying half-covered in pine needles just beyond a tree to Hweilan's right. She ran for it.

On the ground only a pace from the stake, Jatara hit the ground, landing in a crouch. "Wherever you were . . . you should've stayed there."

Hweilan dodged to the right, putting a thick tree trunk between them. She waved Menduarthis's knife in front of her and chanted, *"Bi viekka okhadit! Bi viekka okhadal!"*

The symbols in the knife flickered and then blazed, for a moment only, and as the light faded a wind whipped through the valley, making the boughs wave and causing the carpet of needles to erupt into the air.

Hweilan knew they would cause no real harm to the Jatara-thing, but it might prove enough of a distraction for her to be able to reach the—

Claws raked through the front of her shirt, shredding skin and flesh beneath.

A hundred combat lessons ingrained into her mind and body took over, and Hweilan reacted on a level deeper than conscious thought, back-stepping, counter-striking, side stepping, and lashing out with steel and fist. She felt her enemy's blows deflecting off her fist and forearm as Ashiin had taught her, and she felt her knife cut and pierce flesh. But the thing inside Jatara was relentless. For every blow that Hweilan landed, she avoided two and blocked another.

The wind summoned by the blade died away, and tiny shards of bark and wood and millions of pine needles settled to the ground like a dry rain. Hweilan jumped back and away from Jatara, and for once her enemy did not follow, but stood her ground, watching.

Hweilan's chest heaved. Her body ached. Blood ran down her shoulder and chest where claws had torn away her skin and bit deep into the muscle beneath. Her free hand that she had used to divert her enemy's claws and teeth throbbed with pain. She could feel hundreds of blood vessels in her skin and the flesh beneath that had burst and were turning her entire forearm into one massive bruise. She flexed the hand, and by the pain that shot all the way into her teeth, she knew that part of the bone had cracked.

"Gooood," said the Jatara-thing, and for a moment it closed its eyes and breathed deeply through its nose. "Fighting . . . fear . . . makes your blood run w-w-with . . . *heat*. Makes you taste so much m-more . . . *sweet*."

She charged again, her clawed feet raking through the ground, her talons outstretched before her.

Hweilan just had time to swipe the other knife from the sheath and pivot her body to one side.

The ivory-yellow claws almost missed her entirely.

Jatara's right hand missed, but the left gouged a thick divot of skin and flesh out of her left arm. But Hweilan's steel struck as well—Lendri's knife in her right hand slicing up and into the tendons under Jatara's left arm, her left burying Menduarthis's knife between two of Jatara's ribs, then letting go, leaving it there, while Hweilan rolled and tumbled away.

Jatara shrieked, but it was half-laughter as she turned again to face Hweilan. Her left arm hung loose at her side and only gave a feeble twitch as she tried to move it.

"You think your steel can hurt me?" she said. "Hurt me really?"

Hweilan crouched and picked up the sharpened shaft of wood from the forest floor. "No," she said. "Not *really*. But this will. Really."

Jatara's eyes narrowed with suspicion. She watched Hweilan a moment, then looked down at the steel dagger protruding from her chest. No blood leaked from it. She reached for it with her right hand.

Hweilan whispered the incantation—"*Dalvi batunik. Dalvi batunik dal!*"

Although she couldn't see them, she knew the runes etched into the blade flared—this time not summoning winds, but calling upon the forces of winter itself, of cold and frost and—

The Jatara-thing shrieked as the flesh around the knife—her dead heart, the muscles of her chest and arm, and the fist grasping the knife's hilt—froze solid.

Hweilan charged, the stake raised high. The Jatara-thing struggled—Hweilan could feel the power of fire stirring inside it, counter attacking the knife's magic, thawing the muscle and bone—but it was not quick enough.

Hweilan brought her fist down and buried the sharp point of the stake deep into the Jatara-thing's neck.

She stepped back, wide-eyed with triumph—

But nothing happened. No sudden green flame catching in the *uwethla*. No nothingness suffusing into Jatara's gaze.

Jatara lurched forward—one quick step—and caught Hweilan with her one good arm, wrapping her in a crushing embrace around her lower back. She felt her body pressed in close to the dead flesh, and no matter how hard she struggled, she could not break free.

"Surprised?" said the Jatara-thing, and the charnel reek of her breath washed over Hweilan, and she had to choke back bile. Jatara leaned in close, like a lover sharing an intimate secret. "Oh, I searched for you so long . . . so long. Every trail ran cold. I'd be searching still, if not for . . . for what, hmm?"

Hweilan beat at the creature with her bruised arms and both legs, but she might as well have been trying to push over one of the nearby pines.

"What would you call it?" said Jatara, and she squeezed.

Hweilan shrieked. She heard her spine *snap* like a branch broken over against a knee, but she didn't feel it—couldn't feel it, couldn't feel anything below her waist. And then the arm was gone.

Hweilan fell to the ground. She had to force breath into her body. Panic was setting in—a primal reaction, for she could feel nothing below the new pain in the middle of her back. Her back. Her back! That monster had broken her back, like a child tired of an old plaything.

The Jatara-thing paced around her. A predator toying with its defenseless prey.

"You would call it treachery, I think," said Jatara. She pulled the stake out of her neck and brandished at Hweilan. "This, I mean. See it? See!"

Against her will, Hweilan looked at it, and despair and horror settled in over her. It wasn't the stake she had made. The engravings were there, burned into the wood, but there were subtle differences. Not true *uwethla,* but close imitations. And there was no power in them. She could feel their absence, just as surely as she could no longer feel her legs.

"Never never would I have found you," said the Jatara-thing, "without help. Your . . . friend? Brought me to you.

Though I wouldn't call such a one friend. Would you?"

Hweilan's mind reeled, and she fought to remain conscious. Gleed's words—spoken to her so long ago—came to her again. Spoken about Ashiin—

. . . do not trust her. That one serves the Master. But for her own reasons. If she thinks you do not further those reasons . . .

"The end," said the Jatara-thing. "The end. You were the last. Oh not the last that your Master will try to send against my master. But the last who had a chance. By the time the next Hand is ready, it will be too late. This world suits us. All the hungers and lust and wanting . . . we will fit in quite nicely here. By the time your lord sends another, it will be too late. Finished. The end. And this?" She waved the counterfeit stake over Hweilan, then tossed it aside with contempt. "A fake. Yes?"

"That one is," said a new voice—

—and the air behind Jatara shimmered—

And a hand lashed out, the symbols etched in the wood in its grip already flaring, and plunged into Jatara's back.

Jatara's jaw stretched, but it was the thing inside her that screamed—a sound of cracking mountains that filled Hweilan's soul as the being of hunger and fire was bound and trapped. Green fire spewed out of Jatara's eyes and mouth, and an inky, viscous fume leaked out of her ears. A final spasm shook the body, and then it fell, lifeless and free.

Ashiin stood behind it. She cocked her head and looked down at Hweilan. "I am thinking you have questions. Yes?"

CHAPTER TWENTY

It was the most horrifying feeling Hweilan had ever known. Below her waist, she could feel nothing. Her loins, her legs, her feet no longer existed to her. But radiating above that point in her back . . . pain. It was as if that break in her spine was a seed of agony, newly hatched and sending shoots of fire into every fiber of her body. Every beat of her heart seemed to spread the pain farther.

She couldn't even muster the strength to weep. It was all she could do to keep her body breathing.

Ashiin crouched beside Jatara. Taking her time, she wriggled her fingers into a glove, then yanked the stake out of the corpse. A final spark shot out of the *uwethla* along the stake's surface, followed by a faint smell of brimstone.

"Have you figured it out yet?" said Ashiin.

Hweilan clenched her jaw against the pain and took three careful breaths through her nose, then forced the words out. "Gleed was right. About you."

Ashiin, still kneeling beside the corpse, looked at her and smiled. "Sometimes I despair of you, girl." She stood and slipped the stake into an empty pouch at her belt. "I switched the stakes. That much, at least, I hope you have realized by now. You seem to think I tried to kill you—and you're remembering the bitter words of that old toad to fuel your conclusion." She shook her head. "That makes you an idiot, dear girl."

With that, Ashiin grabbed Hweilan's right wrist and began dragging her out of the woods. The pain was unbearable, and Hweilan screamed so loud that she heard the echo off the nearby mountain.

"What I have to tell you," Ashiin said, her own voice calm and utterly relaxed, "is best said in the light. Besides, we should get away from the stench of that thing."

Ashiin dragged Hweilan out from under the cover of the trees. The dead weight of her legs made a despair grow in Hweilan that was worse than anything she had ever felt. Worse even than the day she'd seen her father's dead body. Worse than the day Scith had told her that her family was dead. Worse than the day Scith himself had been killed and Hweilan had helped to burn his body. All of that had brought fury and sadness and grief. But at least there had been the hope of something else—even if it was only revenge. Now . . . what did she have? Her hope for vengeance, her calling as the Hand of the Hunter . . . all over. She'd failed.

Sunlight washed over Hweilan as they left the woods. Ashiin dragged her around a fallen tree, walked just beyond it, then dropped her.

"I switched the stakes," Ashiin said, and she crouched beside Hweilan. "But not so that thing could kill you. If I wanted you dead, I'd have killed you myself long ago."

"You . . ." Hweilan forced the words out. "Brought me . . . here. She . . . it . . . *knew*."

"Yes," said Ashiin, and she cocked her head in that odd way that always reminded Hweilan, more than anything else, how truly inhuman Ashiin was. It was a movement that was altogether bestial. "I came here. I told that thing you'd be coming, and I brought you here. But this was a lesson, Hweilan. For you. Now what have you learned?"

"You said . . . this was . . . sacrifice. To use . . . the bow."

"No," said Ashiin. "I said that to wake the bow, to make

it your ally, Nendawen requires sacrifice. I never said *this* was the sacrifice. You really think that filth was sacrifice? That was justice. To waken your father's bow . . . you have yet to make that sacrifice."

Hweilan tried to lash out, but her strength was failing her, and the woman was just out of reach.

Ashiin laughed. "Your back is broken, and still you fight. I like that."

"I . . . hate you."

"That hardly matters. Those bandits you killed, they were meant to show me you could kill when the need arose—and to show *you*. Success in battle is not only about skill. Many skilled warriors have died under a peasant's axe. Success in battle is about will—the willingness to kill another. To hesitate, even for a moment, means death. That's what the bandits taught you.

"Today's lesson was far more important: You are no match for Jagun Ghen and his minions. No matter how strong you become, how adept a fighter, no matter whose blood runs in your veins . . . you're no match for them, Hweilan. And you never will be."

That was it then. She'd failed. Nendawen could find a new Hand. All the effort and agony of the past months . . . all for nothing. She might as well have gone back to Highwatch that day after running from Jatara. At least then, perhaps she and Scith could have died together and she might have taken a few of her enemies with her.

Several of the tendrils of pain originating from her back had wormed their way into her chest, and even as Hweilan struggled to breathe, the tendrils seemed to constrict. Every breath cost her more than the last. Her entire torso seemed to have turned to some cold, immovable metal.

"My . . . back!" said Hweilan, and in the cough that followed, she tasted blood. More than her back then. Other things were broken inside her. That was some relief, at least. She no longer had to worry about the rest of her life. That would be over soon. Hweilan closed her eyes, and despite the pain she managed a smile.

Ashiin laughed. "Little fool."

She felt Ashiin cradle her head in one palm and lift. Hweilan thrashed out with both hands, pummeling Ashiin with her fists.

"Stop that," said Ashiin.

Hweilan struck harder—hard as she could—though that was scarcely more than the force a small child could muster.

Ashiin reached inside her vest with her free hand and said, "Open your mouth."

The world was beginning to go fuzzy—light and darkness bleeding together—and Hweilan couldn't feel if her mouth was open or not.

Ashiin's hand moved to her face, and Hweilan thought she saw something cradled in the woman's fingers. Then the smell hit her—acrid and earthy, but with the sharp fumes of strong spirits. Hweilan's throat closed instinctively and she tried to jerk her head away. But Ashiin had a handful of her hair in a tight grip.

"Open," said Ashiin.

She must have done so, for in the next moment liquid fire filled her mouth and ran down her throat. Hweilan screamed, what little of the liquid was left in her mouth spewing onto Ashiin. She thrashed, breaking Ashiin's grip, and new strength filled her limbs. The heat from the liquid caught. It didn't spread. It went down her throat and *exploded,* sending waves of heat through her whole body. The tendrils and shoots of pain that had been growing inside her withered and evaporated, like dry petals thrown on fire.

Hweilan's eyes flew open and she froze, afraid to move. Her whole body was in agony. Her *whole* body.

She could feel her legs again. Feel her feet. Even her toes, which felt as if ten-score hot needles were burrowing inside. In that moment of paralysis—brought on by shock and the fear that if she moved, the feelings would go away—Hweilan actually felt hundreds of tiny strands inside her backbone writhing and twisting and burrowing as they knit back together.

Hweilan sat up and took in a great draft of air—so much so fast that it was like a scream in reverse, filling her lungs with much-needed air.

"Hurts, doesn't it?" said Ashiin. She was still crouching beside Hweilan, a mischievous grin on her face, her yellow fox eyes glowing in the sunlight. "Most things worth anything bring a certain amount of pain."

Wide-eyed, Hweilan looked down at her feet, and just to be sure, she tried to wiggle first the right one and then the left. They moved—and better, she *felt* them move, felt the rough fiber of her stockings moving between her skin and boot. So plain. So mundane. Yet at that moment it was the most wonderful feeling in the world, better even than the clean air filling her.

She looked down. Through the rents in her shirt, her skin was still coated in blood, but it was drying, and the wounds themselves—which she knew had cut to the bone—were gone, the skin beneath smooth and almost glistening. All of her *uwethla,* the puckered scar where Gleed had stabbed her to drive in the silver spike, even the kan brand upon her palm—all still there. But of the newer wounds there was no sign.

Ashiin helped Hweilan to her feet. "Now, as I was saying: you are the Hand." As if to demonstrate, she raised her own, waving the fingers. "That . . . concept—for what you are—was chosen for a reason. A hand is made of the palm and many fingers. Many parts. And the hand itself is only an extension of the arm, and the arm is part of the body. And the body itself is nothing without the head and heart."

Hweilan could only stare at her. The woman had just led her into an ambush, watched while that . . . that *thing* had snapped her back like an old branch, and she was crouched there, lecturing, calm as you please.

"You'll never defeat Jagun Ghen on your own. You are the Hand. And the Hand does not strike alone." A slight pause, then, "When I first met you, this was what you were."

Ashiin lowered all her fingers except one, and this one she kept loose. She wiggled it over Hweilan's bare arm, scratching slightly with the nail.

"A minor irritant," said Ashiin, "an annoyance. That's all you were. But you learned. You learned from Kesh Naan—"

—the finger stiffened, and another joined it, and Ashiin poked her, not hard enough to break the skin, but close. Hweilan winced—

"—you learned from Gleed—"

—three fingers, and Ashiin poked again—

"—getting stronger, yes. But still no stronger than a nagging pain. And then you came to me—"

—all fingers open, the thumb held straight and close beside the palm, and Ashiin brought it around, striking Hweilan hard in the fleshy part of her arm. She staggered a little but did not fall over.

Hweilan said, "Stop th—"

"Now you are strong. Strong enough to deal with many enemies. But Jagun Ghen is not just any enemy. He is ancient and cunning, and he does not know mercy or pity or remorse. Strike him all you like, and you are only going to rile him."

Ashiin gave her three quick strikes with the edge of her hand—upper arm, forearm, and a hit on her thigh hard enough to bruise.

Hweilan tried to back away, but Ashiin caught her wrist with her other hand, stopping her.

"Now," she said, "you must learn to use it all—and more. The hand is only an extension of the greater body—of the greater mind. You must have the *whole*."

With that, Ashiin clenched the upheld hand into a fist and punched.

But Hweilan had been expecting it, and she batted the fist aside with her forearm.

"Stop hitting me!"

"*Make* me stop." Ashiin lashed out again, first one fist, then an open hand—the fingers out and stiff, aimed for Hweilan's gut.

Hweilan blocked both and kicked. Ashiin pushed the strike aside.

And then they were at it—master and pupil, punching, kicking, blocking, striking and counter striking, rolling, sliding, jumping. Hweilan connected now and then, but for every one punch or kick she managed to land, Ashiin landed three.

But whatever had been in the concoction Ashiin had given her, it was still at work. Hweilan could feel its fire coursing through her system. She had to drop to avoid a kick, and on the frosty ground her feet slid from under her. The sharp stones beneath cut deep, raking a wide swath of skin from her arm, but by the time she was on her feet again, she could feel the skin closing.

"You see?" said Ashiin, circling her. "After all you've learned . . . still, you're no match for me. And you think you can hunt Jagun Ghen? I've taught you only a fraction of what I know—and time is running out."

"So . . . ?"

Ashiin charged, one fist coming around. But it was a feint. Hweilan blocked the strike with her forearm and Ashiin grabbed her. The next thing she knew she was flying through the air—her sight registered the peak, the treetops, a bit of blue sky between, and then she hit the ground. All the breath left her body, and for a moment the world went black.

When her vision cleared again, she saw that she had skidded to a stop next to the fallen tree. Ashiin was crouched atop it, her forearms resting on her knees, both hands outstretched, palms open—a long curved shaft of wood resting across them.

Her father's bow.

Ashiin said, "Time you learned to use this."

Hweilan stared up at the bow a long time. Seeing it in Ashiin's hands stoked her rage again. That had been her father's, and she had carried it through death and worse. To see Ashiin holding it, that smug look on her face . . .

Hweilan reached for it. Ashiin smiled and pulled it back.

Growling, Hweilan lunged, but Ashiin leaped into the air, backflipped, and landed on her feet on the far side of the log.

Hweilan crouched atop the log and stopped, gauging the distance. She knew she could leap that far and more, but she knew Ashiin would no longer be there when she landed. The woman was too quick.

"Why do you want this?" said Ashiin. "It's just a pretty shaft of wood. No use to you. Might as well burn it."

"No," Hweilan said, though it came out more of a growl, and she had to force herself not to leap. Her rage was getting the best of her. She didn't bury it, but she channeled it. Had to *think*. Coming at Ashiin in berserk fury would be folly. Hweilan knew she had to think, to plan.

"Reminds you of your father, yes?" said Ashiin. "That's all it is, then. Like a baby's favorite blanket. It fuels your childishness."

Hweilan felt something touch her left hand, and she looked down. Though her wounds had healed, much of her skin was still coated in blood, and the scent had drawn something out of the rotted crevices of the log on which she crouched. She had no idea what it was. Almost as large as her hand, it was not a spider, but its chitinous, segmented body walked on spiderlike legs, each of which ended in a tiny, sharp claw. A half-dozen fangs under the thing's staring eyes opened, and tendrils emerged from the mouth and ran along her skin. It tickled.

Ashiin mistook Hweilan's glance down. "Touched a nerve, did I, girl? You want your father? Shame on you. Your father and mother were warriors. What would they think of you now? Had he lived, what would your father do with this bow? What would he do to Jagun Ghen's minions who killed him?"

Hweilan looked up at her teacher and let the tears gathering in her eyes run down her cheeks. They were tears of rage, but if Ashiin believed otherwise . . . good. She needed a moment's distraction. She held Ashiin's gaze. She *needed* her eyes up here.

"My father was killed by a dragon," she said. Ever so slowly, Hweilan turned her left hand so that it was palm upward. She heard the thing down in the log rattle a moment, surprised by the movement, then the tendrils tickled her fingertips, searching upward. Her palms and wrists had as much blood, and the sweat of the fight had kept them moist. The tendrils searched upward, and Hweilan felt the sharp claws on her fingers as the thing climbed onto her hand, searching for the wet blood and sweat inside her sleeve.

Ashiin scowled at Hweilan's words. She hadn't known how Hweilan's father had died, and Hweilan knew Ashiin hated *nothing* more than being wrong about something.

"That does not change my point," said Ashiin. "Were your father still alive, how would he use this weapon? Would he run through the hills looking for help? Or would he rain death on those who killed his family?"

"Rain?" said Hweilan and looked up.

It worked. Ashiin glanced up, just for a moment, and Hweilan brought her left hand around, hurling the thing of claws and fangs right at Ashiin. Surprised and enraged, the insect flailed and snapped its legs as it flew through the air. Ashiin looked back down, and her eyes widened at the sight of the claws and fangs headed for her face.

Ashiin swiped with the bow, batting the insect away. The yew struck the thing with a *crunch* of shattering chitin.

Hweilan hit Ashiin full force an instant later. They tumbled down in a cloud of dead pine needles and dirt, and when they separated, each of them coming to their feet in a defensive crouch, facing each other, Hweilan held the bow.

They stared at each other, master and student weighing each other, waiting for the other to strike. At last Ashiin stood straight, relaxing, and smiled. "Well done, Hweilan. You are ready."

CHAPTER TWENTY-ONE

Hweilan cradled the bow in her arms as they walked back. Ashiin opened the portal, taking them through the falls into the Feywild, and led the way back to Gleed's lake.

But Hweilan's mind barely registered any of that. After so long without it, she had her father's bow back. Holding its familiar weight in her hands, it seemed that she stood on a knife's edge between her past and present. The arc of pale wood inscribed with sacred runes—she could not look at it without seeing her father, dressed in his full armor, holding it in one hand as his squire fitted the quiver to his back. But mostly she saw the smile he'd always given her before leaving. This bow summed up her childhood: the comfort of her father's love, mixed with the grief of his leaving. With that leaving came both pride and dread. She knew her father was going out to keep their lands safe, to help those unable to help themselves. When she was very small, he'd seemed almost a demigod to her. But with that was the knowledge that he might not come home again. Every parting held the chance of his death. And one day that time had finally come.

Remembering all those things, Hweilan realized they proved Ashiin's words true—*like a baby's favorite blanket, it fuels your childishness.* But she would not let the feelings go.

She was the Hand of the Hunter, Chosen of Nendawen, but that could never erase where she'd come from.

But Ashiin's other words were true as well. It was a weapon, meant to be used. More than memories of the past, the bow held for her the promise of a future. Despite the grief and regret tempering her emotions, Hweilan felt one thing above everything—an eager anger. That thing, Jagun Ghen, had slaughtered everyone she'd ever loved. As she'd learned from Kesh Naan, he had done that countless times over generations to her people. Time for that to end.

Hweilan had just detected the first scent of the lake when Ashiin stopped. Most days after training they parted ways there, but usually Ashiin just melted into the shadows and was gone, sometimes with a farewell, sometimes not. It was the first time Hweilan could remember her teacher stopping.

"What?" said Hweilan.

Ashiin looked away a moment, glancing toward Gleed's tower, then back at her. "Remember what I told you. When the time comes, you must not hesitate. To kill. A great deal depends on this."

Hweilan looked at her, puzzled by the sudden emphasis. She'd passed every test Ashiin had laid before her. Why this reassurance now? So she simply said, "I know."

Ashiin gripped both Hweilan's arms and squeezed, hard enough to hurt. "Do you really, girl? You swear it?"

Taken aback, Hweilan stared into Ashiin's eyes. They were deadly serious. Even desperate. Why . . . she didn't know, but there was no mistaking Ashiin's urgency.

"I swear it," she said.

Ashiin held her gaze a moment longer, then let go. A moment later, she was gone, leaving nothing but a rustle in the undergrowth.

• • • • •

When Hweilan stepped back onto the island, she saw Gleed climbing down the outside of the tower. She stood at its base and watched. It never ceased to amaze her that a creature who relied so heavily on his staff while walking the ground could be agile as a squirrel in the trees and rocks.

He stopped about halfway and looked down at her. "Your father's bow? Ashiin gave it back, I see."

"I wouldn't say she *gave* it back exactly."

"Ha! I don't doubt it." He looked around, staring into the swiftly falling twilight. The bats were not yet out, but the shadows under the trees were thick already, and the first stars would be out soon. "Come up," he said. "Quickly."

She didn't understand, but didn't argue. Holding the bow in one hand, she worked her way up the vines and branches. She could hear Gleed muttering above her, and as she came near, she saw a particularly tight knot of vines and leaves writhe and part, like the opening of a huge vertical eyelid. Beyond was a crumbling window, leading into the tower.

Gleed climbed into it and she heard him call, "Quickly, girl!"

She wedged the bow in first, then pulled herself in after.

The old goblin muttered again, and the vines and leaves closed behind her, plunging them both into darkness.

"Half a moment," said Gleed, and he spoke an incantation, quiet but clear. His staff lit first, suffusing the chamber with a green light. It caught in hundreds of symbols and runes and scratchings around the chamber. Some seemed to have been painted with some sort of metallic ink, some carved into the stone itself, and a few were even shoots and roots that had been braided and twisted into unnatural shapes. But every one of them caught the arcane light and seemed to kindle lights of their own—a hundred variations of green, blue, red, gold, and silver.

"What is this place?" said Hweilan. She could see no other way in or out. The window through which they'd come had been completely sealed by the vines, and if there had ever been another door in wall or floor, she could find no trace of it.

"A place safe from prying ears and eyes," said Gleed. He shuffled to the middle of the floor, then turned and sat. "We must speak. Please, sit."

She sat cross-legged in front of him, the bow across her lap. Gleed's one good eye had closed to little more than a slit, buried in the wrinkles of his brow, but his other—usually a milky white—stared wide, and caught every glow and sparkle in the room. Hweilan wondered how blind that eye really was, or if it merely saw things the other could not.

"We spoke once before," said Gleed, "of your friend Lendri, of his ghost coming to you—and your family in the Witness Cloud. Have you seen them since?"

"No," said Hweilan.

"Tell me again what he said—as exactly as you can remember."

"The first time—the night you brought me to the tower and I tried to run away—he seemed angry, accusing, blaming me for his death—and my family's. But the day in the Witness Cloud, he seemed . . ." She searched for the right word in any of the languages she knew, could not find one, so simply chose those closest. "Sad. And desperate. He said he would not return, no matter who called him."

"You're certain? Those were his words?"

"Yes."

"This Lendri . . . he was an exile?"

"So he said."

"Do you know why?"

"No," said Hweilan. "He never told me."

"Hm. Well, whatever it was, until that sin is atoned, his ghost cannot rest, I think. Why he comes to you, now . . ." Gleed shrugged. "I can only guess. I am not Vil Adanrath and I am no priest, but I will tell you this. The Witnesses are always here." He waved her hand and looked around to emphasize her point. "The ancestors watch, even now. The veil separating us from them is thin. At times of need or great import, that veil is lifted so their presence might encourage us and their wisdom guide us. Why you see Lendri, why Dedunan has not allowed him rest . . . it seems that this Lendri is not done with you."

"I don't understand."

"I'm not sure I do either. But I do believe that your friend cannot rest, and his one hope of rest seems to lie in you."

Hweilan considered this, but the more she thought, the more baffled she felt. The only thing she knew of Lendri's exile was that it had something to do with the oaths he had sworn to one of her forefathers—one he held so sacred that he had sought her and helped her at the cost of his own life.

"You cared for him?" Gleed asked.

Hweilan needed little time to consider before answering this honestly. "I barely knew him. But when I needed him, he was there—even if the reasons were his own. And he died trying to save me. I am indebted to him."

Gleed nodded. She thought he seemed pleased, but also that he was still holding something. "Remember that in the days ahead," he said.

"What do you mean?"

"You remember what we discussed last night?"

For a moment Hweilan was annoyed that he had disregarded her question, but then his question sank in. Fighting the demon, having her back broken, healed, and then regaining her father's bow . . . it had driven last night's conversation from her mind. *I can help you get away,* Gleed had said.

"That's why we're in here," she said, looking around at the glowing symbols. "A place safe from prying ears and eyes."

"Yes," said Gleed. "What I am about to tell you, you must tell *no one* else. Not the Master—*especially* not Ashiin—and if you so much as mutter it in your sleep, you'll kill us both. You—"

"Gleed, stop." Hweilan was surprised at the vehemence in her voice, but she pressed on despite the old goblin's angry scowl. "I know what you said. But I don't care. I don't want to get away. I am the Hand. I'm going to kill Jagun Ghen."

Gleed snorted. "Stupid girl. You couldn't 'kill' him if you tried. Not even the Master—"

"Send him to the Abyss, then," she said. "Bind him, banish him . . . I don't care what name you put on it. I'm going to deal with him, once and for all, or die trying. I don't *want* to get away."

"I know. You think I'd have gone to the pain of teaching you if I didn't want Jagun Ghen gone? But what about after?"

She looked down at the bow, and again her father's face came to mind. "After that . . . well, I'll decide then."

Gleed gave her a sharp poke with the end of his staff. "No, you won't! Stupid girl. Wait till then, and it'll be too late! Have you learned nothing from Ashiin? If you want to win, you must plan. You must plot. You must *prepare*."

"Why do you care?" The question came out before she had really considered it. But hearing it, she knew it cut to the heart of the matter. What Gleed was telling her . . . it walked a bit too close to treachery.

The old goblin looked away. Both eyes closed, and for a moment all sense of power left him, and he just seemed very, very old.

"I have served the Master for . . ." He sighed and opened his eyes. The mantle of power seemed to settle back over him, but his voice still seemed more tired than anything. "Years on years on years. I am devoted to him, in my own way, and I do not regret my choice. But those years . . . I feel them. And I know what they have cost me. I know what they will cost you. You don't. All you can see is your rage and your mission. Good. You'll need that in the coming days. You'll need that and more to defeat Jagun Ghen. But after . . . you have something I never had, girl. A chance. There's something in you, something I suspect has made even the Master wary. He hadn't expected it. But he knows it's there now. Make no mistake of that. He will try to conquer it. Or tame it. But if he can't, once you've proved your usefulness to him . . . well, he is the Hunter. Once his favorite prey is gone, he'll need another."

Hweilan let that sink in. She'd been afraid a long time. But her chief fear had been of failure, that all the horrors that had killed her family and ruined her life would win. All her efforts these past days had been directed at *never* allowing that to happen. Nendawen and the power he offered her gave her the one thing she needed more than anything else. Hope. But Gleed's words chipped away at that. Could Nendawen be both her hope and her doom?

"You're saying once Jagun Ghen is gone, Nendawen will kill me?"

"I'm saying there are worse things than death, and if you don't want to discover them firsthand, you had best plan." Gleed fixed his empty eye on her, and again she was convinced that it wasn't blind at all. "In the venom dream of Kesh Naan, you saw your ancestors, yes?"

"Yes."

"Your Vil Adanrath ancestors."

Hweilan knew where he was going with this. Kunin Gatar and Menduarthis had come to much the same conclusion. That one of her ancestors was . . . other.

"You know something," she said. "You know what it is—that, whatever it is, inside me. You know. 'I can help you get away,' you said. You wouldn't have said that if you hadn't figured it out. How did you figure it out?"

Gleed smiled. It was the look he gave when he was entering the role of teacher, very pleased with himself at knowing things others didn't.

"You would do well to remember that I did not always live in this crumbling old tower, that my lore is deep, and that I know others beyond this place. Your mother left her people. She seldom spoke of them to you, did she?"

"A little. She told me stories, taught me some of the traditions."

"But nothing intimate. In fact, I'd wager she never once spoke of her own parents, and that if you ever asked, she seemed less than pleased at the question. Would I win that wager?"

"Yes," Hweilan said, and her memories of those times suddenly seemed very fresh. Merah's life in Highwatch had not been unhappy, but neither had it been easy. Her father's mother had never been able to see beyond the "half-elf barbarian" with whom her favorite son fell in love. Hweilan had always assumed that her mother had left her people and their traditions to bring some peace in the household and to try to fit in to her new life. It had never once occurred to her that Merah might have had reason to leave the Vil Adanrath.

"Your mother's mother," said Gleed, "was Thewari of the Vil Adanrath. That much I have learned. But your mother's father . . . I have searched and asked everyone I know in all the former lands of the Vil Adanrath—I even went to their new home and asked enough questions to make me leave with their arrows at my back—and I cannot find the name of Merah's father. In all the world, I can think of only two people who might be able to tell you."

Hweilan tried to think of who that might be. She couldn't think of a single person, so she finally said, "Who?"

"Your mother."

That brought a flare of pain and anger to Hweilan, and she almost shouted that her mother was dead. But then she realized that for one such as Gleed, death might not be an insurmountable barrier. So she said, "And the other?"

"Lendri."

She let that sink in, but still it made no sense. "You think Lendri's ghost has to tell me of my grandfather, and that might . . . what? Help me escape from Nendawen when the time comes?"

Gleed pursed his lips and took his time before answering. "Why Lendri has come to you . . . I don't think he is being driven to tell you of your grandfather, no. I think this Lendri has a different fate. But I do think that finding the name of your mother's father—and Lendri might well know—could be a key to a great box of secrets. I cannot give you those answers. But I will counsel you this: We all serve someone, Hweilan. You, me, Ashiin . . . we serve Nendawen. And Nendawen serves a greater one above him. His master may well serve someone above him. In this world and all the others, there is no such thing as complete freedom. We all serve. If the time comes when our Master's leash no longer fits you . . . well, you would do well to find one that does."

"And you think my grandfather—"

"I think this old goblin has given you a place to look," he said, his voice harsh and solemn. "One you should keep to yourself. And right now, that's all I think." But then his voice softened. "Sometimes the teacher can hold your hand, and sometimes the teacher can only point the way. In this, I am only pointing."

They sat in silence awhile, Gleed staring at Hweilan and Hweilan staring but seeing more inside than out.

When Gleed finally spoke again, Hweilan knew by the tone in his voice that the conversation was over. He laid a most reverent hand on the bow in her lap, and said, "You are ready to use this?"

Hweilan held his gaze. "More than ready. But Ashiin said it first needs sacrifice."

Gleed closed both eyes slowly and nodded. "Yes. And that comes tomorrow."

CHAPTER TWENTY-TWO

The Feywild

That night, Hweilan was afraid to close her eyes. Not because of the thought of sacrifice and awakening the bow—there was trepidation there, yes, but that was tinged with more eagerness than anything. The simple fact was that, given her past experiences with Gleed, she was half afraid that she'd close her eyes and wake up naked in the woods. She promised herself that no matter what Gleed offered her to drink, she would refuse it.

But as it turned out, Gleed would allow her nothing.

"You will eat or drink nothing till dawn. Let your strength be my teachings, the visions of Kesh Naan, and the wiles of Ashiin."

She lay awake that night as long as she could, eyes half-closed, watching Gleed as he fed sweet grass and oak leaves into the fire and waved the smoke over his face, muttering as he meditated. But no matter how hard she tried to stay awake, her body was exhausted. The strength from Ashiin's potion had long since worn away, and Hweilan seemed weaker than ever. Long before midnight, she slept.

Gleed woke her, prodding her with his staff. The chamber lay in darkness, lit only by a somber glow of embers from the hearth.

"Up," said Gleed. "It's time. Bring your weapons."

He led her outside. Stars still sparkled overhead, but a thick mist lay over the lake, hiding the far shore and woods. Dawn was only a glow in the east. But something was alight on the far shore, a flicker of red through the fog.

They crossed the bridge, and Hweilan saw that the glow was a large fire burning in a ring of black stones.

"It begins at dawn. One drink from the stream," said Gleed, "then we prepare. And bring some water back with you." He handed her an empty skin.

"What begins?" said Hweilan.

"Your final test. The hunt."

"What am I hunting?"

Gleed looked away, staring into the fire. "You are being hunted, girl. By the Master. After, you will begin your hunt of Jagun Ghen. If you survive."

Those words brought others back to her mind. Words from a dream long ago that she realized had been more than just a dream—*You do not need understanding. You need to choose. Understanding will come later . . . if you survive.*

That time had come. Fear welled out of Hweilan's gut, making each breath an effort. She remembered her last encounter with Nendawen, how he had completely overwhelmed her. But, Hweilan reminded herself, she was stronger now—not only in body, but in heart and mind as well. She was ready. She didn't know if she could survive Nendawen, but she knew she was ready to begin her own hunt. If she died, so be it. Today, the uncertainty would be over, one way or another.

Hweilan walked to the stream, splashed water on her face to banish the last vestiges of sleep, filled the skin, and then took a long drink. As she came up out of the water, she saw a reflection rippling on its surface—a dark shape, its head framed by antlers.

She gasped and sat up. But it was only the branches of a nearby tree. Still, she could not shake the feeling of being watched. She glanced back at Gleed, but he had his back to her and was busily preparing something near the fire.

It took all her courage to turn her back on the stream and keep her pace at a leisurely walk as she went back to the fire.

"Sit," said Gleed.

She sat beside him.

"First, you must prepare the bow," Gleed said. "Then, you must prepare yourself."

As the eastern sky slowly grew brighter and the stars dimmed overhead, Gleed instructed her on the proper symbols to cut into the bow. She used the same enchanted spike that Gleed had used to give Hweilan her first *uwethla*. Praying and speaking the sacred words, she heated it in the fire till the tip glowed red, then carved the *shesteh* into the bow, Gleed telling her exactly which ones to use.

The last one surprised her. It was *ashiin*, the symbol for "fox."

She started to ask about it, but then the answer occurred to her. Ashiin had been her teacher in the hunt, had instructed her to stalk and kill as the fox. What symbol could be more fitting?

Gleed took a white leather bag out of the folds of his vest, untied it, and upended it over the fire. A heavy silver powder spilled out. No more than a handful, but it utterly doused the fire and filled the air with an earthy, bitter scent.

"Water," he said, and Hweilan handed him the skin. He splashed a generous amount on the coals and ashes, then stirred them with a stick, muttering an incantation as he did so.

He picked a cooled coal out of the fire pit and said, "Lean close."

She did. He used the coal to paint sacred symbols on her forehead, both cheeks, then down her nose and chin. While he did so, she twisted her hair into a tight braid. Holding the finished rope of hair in her hands, she noticed for the first time how long it was. Her last days in Highwatch, her hair had been just past her shoulders. Now, the tip of her braid touched her waist. Had she really been here that long? She looked down at her arm. She'd never had the palms of a proper court lady, but now they looked exactly like what they were—the hands of someone who spent most days in the wild, using tools of the hunt and killing. Her arms were a mass of scratches and scars, and the muscles under her skin were hard and tight. If there was anything left of the soft castle girl who had come to the Feywild, it was buried deep inside her.

"In life we walk to death," Gleed said, "but death is no end for those who walk in faith and courage. Look now through the ghost of fire—and do not fear death if it finds you today."

He lowered his hands, and the familiar sigh he gave told her that the formalities were over. It was almost time.

"You may take any weapon you wish," he said, "except for the bow. I will guard it. If you survive this day, it will be returned to you, strong once again."

Gleed reached around the fire, then handed her a large wooden bowl, filled with *samil,* the dark green paste that would mask her scent.

"Don't be shy with that," he said.

She took it, dipped three fingers in, then stopped. "No."

"No?"

Hweilan looked at the sky. The last of the stars were fading and the last of the bats had gone home. "How long do I have?"

"Not long," said Gleed.

"The Master will have his wolves?"

"Undoubtedly. You need the *samil.*"

"I have a better idea," said Hweilan, and she ran for the tower.

• • ◉ • •

When she emerged, the last of the stars were gone, and the sky in the east was truly a pale blue. As she stepped off the bridge and onto the lakeshore, a series of howls wafted out of the east.

Gleed's eyes went wide. "He's coming, girl. Coming now. What are you doing?"

Hweilan was trembling too much to be careful, so she threw the large satchel on the ground and tore open the flap. When Gleed saw what she was after, he let out a shriek.

"Are you mad? They'll smell that a mile off!"

"I'm counting on it," said Hweilan as she pulled the stopper out of the green glass bottle. It was filled with a viscous liquid. *Maaguath*. Hweilan had made it herself. Spread on a blade, it would burn an open wound like fire and prevent the blood from clotting. But it smelled like something that had died in the bottom of a wine cask.

She spread a thin line of it on the back of each of her boots, stoppered the bottle, put it in her pocket, then gathered the other things she needed. She stood, made sure both her knives were secure in their sheaths, then managed to give Gleed what she hoped was a brave smile.

"See you soon," she said, then ran into the woods.

More howls broke the morning silence. They were much closer.

• • © • •

Head bowed, staff across his lap, Gleed waited by the ashes of his fire. The howls had stopped, and that told Gleed they were close. When wolves truly began the hunt, they moved silent as ghosts. Much smarter than their yammering domesticated cousins.

Gleed did not hear the Master approach, but he sensed his presence. The power of Nendawen resonated far beyond mere sight, and all of Gleed's senses knew beyond doubt that he was no longer alone.

Keeping his gaze down, he stood, turned, and kneeled.

He heard a growl, so low and strong that it made the ground tremble beneath his knees. He looked up and saw Nendawen before him, spear in one hand, fresh blood dripping from the other. His eyes blazed green from the mask of bone, and four of his wolves stood around him. The nearest was the one growling. A huge monster, all black fur, even standing straight up Gleed would not have been able to look it eye to eye.

"My Master," said Gleed, and prostrated himself.

"Master of Making," said Nendawen. "My disciple is ready?"

Eagerness came off Nendawen like a musk. Gleed knew that Hweilan's life hung by a spider's thread. She was the Chosen of Nendawen, but the Master would accept only the most worthy and would show her no mercy. The girl had to earn her place. But Gleed also knew that there was something in the girl that even the Master had not planned on, had not even seen.

"Hweilan inle Merah stands ready," said Gleed, his face still in the dirt.

The wolves started snuffling, exhaling through their noses into the dirt, then inhaling in quick puffs of air. Gleed looked up and saw that Nendawen himself closed his eyes and took in a deep draft of air.

"She did this?" said Nendawen.

"I tried to make her wear the *samil*," said Gleed. "She refused."

Nendawen opened his eyes. They blazed with pleasure. "She *wants* me to find her."

Gleed swallowed and said, "She does."

"So be it."

Nendawen raised his blood-drenched hand, pointed in the direction Hweilan had gone, and his four wolves bolted, leaving a spray of dirt and leaves in their wake.

The Master looked down on Gleed, said, "Be ready," then ran after his wolves.

Gleed closed his eyes and prayed, "Grant her your aid, Forest Father."

• • • • •

The largest of the wolves took the lead. He had sharp senses, but their prey's scent was so strong that it took little effort. Wolves were not by nature forest hunters, preferring open plains or treeless hills. But these were no ordinary wolves. They had hunted prey in every environment in every world. His packmates tore through the brush behind him, their thick fur heedless of thorns and sharp branches.

The reek was getting stronger. So thick that the leader knew if he stopped to breathe it in fully it would fill his head, drowning out all other scents. He was used to following tiny streams or rivulets of scent. This was like wading through a summer swollen stream.

And then it split.

The leader stopped so abruptly that the two wolves behind actually passed him before stopping, their muzzles low to the ground as they searched through the confusion of scents.

Their prey was alone. On two legs. Her scent was overwhelming. She was alone. They knew this. But her scent had suddenly split in two different directions.

The Master joined them. He kneeled, his weaponless hand brushing the forest floor as he searched the trail. He raised his head and inhaled, sensing their divided trail.

He pointed after one trail. The pack leader followed it, another wolf at his heels. The master and the other wolves would follow the other trail.

The scent was still thick, but not nearly as thick as it had been. Their prey was running now, quickly as she could.

The wolves ran faster.

The trail kept them to the low ground for a while, following the foot of the hill. But in a valley choked with thornbushes, the scent turned uphill, heading for higher ground where the brush and trees would thin out. Stupid of her, the leader knew. Down here in the thick woods, she might have stood a chance. Up on the heights, the wolves would be in their element.

The leader slowed his pace, not out of weariness, but to allow his prey to gain some ground. He hoped to find her near the top, where there would be only a few trees.

But halfway up the hill, the trail turned again, running along the lee of the hill, then plunging down again, back into the thick woods of the valley. The leader growled in anger and anticipation, then increased his pace, his companion following him stride for stride.

Their prey's scent grew thicker with every step, and by the time they were in the valley again, breaking through brush and weaving through the tree shadow, the smell was almost overwhelming. They were close. Almost upon her.

The leader stopped and raised his head, his ears pivoting forward to take in every sound. His companion did the same. They kept their heads still as the trees around them, but their eyes flicked back and forth, searching the scene before them for the slightest hint of movement. The leader knew by the scent—now tinged with the unmistakable aroma of fear—that their prey was close. And their prey knew it too. She had stopped and gone to ground. She was probably watching them even now, her heart fearful and hammering like a rabbit's.

His companion let out a small bark and surged forward. The leader followed, his gaze raking through the forest ahead.

There!

Movement in the thick shadows in the hollow ground under a tree root.

Even though his companion had seen it and moved first, so great was the leader's eagerness that he passed the other wolf. Approaching the tree, he slowed just enough to gather strength in his hind legs, then sprang. His front paws hit the soft soil, sending an explosion of soil and leaves as his open jaws plunged into the hollow.

The shape in the darkness before him sprang aside—too fast and *far* too small for a human. The smell was so overpowering in the close quarters that the leader's eyes filled with tears, so he saw his prey before him in a blur as it bounded past him—

—and into the jaws of his companion.

One swift shake of the wolf's head, and the prey's back snapped.

But it was only a rabbit. Its gray fur had been smeared with some thick liquid.

The leader understood at last how the girl's trail had split. He threw back his head and howled, the sound of their defeat filling the morning air. He knew the Master would hear and understand.

CHAPTER TWENTY-THREE

HWEILAN HEARD THE HOWL AND KNEW HER FIRST ruse had been found out. No matter. It had separated her hunters, giving her a slight advantage, but more importantly it had bought her time, and that's what she needed. She had to make it to the falls in time to prepare her trap. She could hear the roar of the falls before her as she ran down the trail, but she couldn't yet smell the water spray. A ways to go still. She ran faster.

Hweilan had taken every one of Ashiin's lessons to heart. The woman was the most skilled hunter and remorseless killer Hweilan had ever known. But her ways were not the only ways of the hunt, and in her childhood Hweilan had been taught the battle skills of Damaran knights, Nar warriors, and every way of the hunt Scith had known. One method in particular had been favored by members of the Var tribe to kill large numbers of swiftstags with only a few warriors. Ashiin had never taught Hweilan anything close to it, which meant that there was a very good chance that the Master and his wolves would know nothing of it. But swiftstags were prey, prone to a herd mentality, and never the smartest of beasts. Wolves were the most cunning hunters of any animal. For her plan to work, she had to change one vital element. She would not be able to frighten the wolves into her trap. She doubted if Nendawen's hunters felt fear. But the urge to kill? That was the rhythm of their heart. If she couldn't drive them, she could lure them.

Which meant she needed bait.

Hweilan had taken a length of rope from her supplies in the tower. She prayed it would be enough.

• • ⊚ • •

The prey's scent was close. It mingled with the moist air of the forest so near the falls, but the water scent did nothing to lessen the reek of whatever the girl had spread on herself.

The Master ran with them most of the way down the valley, but as the mist from the falls filled the tree air, making it seem as if they ran through a forested cloud, the Master slowed, allowing his wolves to outpace him.

The wolves had not heard the howls of their pack leader since his signal of his defeat, but they knew he and his mate would be coming to rejoin the hunt. And so the wolves ran faster, eager to prove their prowess by finding their prey first.

Footing became more uncertain with every step, the thick carpet of leaves slick with dew, the ground beneath muddy. But the ground had leveled out somewhat. Still not flat, but no longer on the steep incline that it had been. The wolves ran faster.

They heard her before they saw her.

It was no wolf's howl, but a most impressive imitation. It had none of the beauty of true wolfsong, but what the girl lacked in splendor she made up for in fury. A true warrior's challenge.

Through the mist they saw her, a dark shape, crouched and ready, steel in one hand, a branch in the other.

Bloodlust overpowering them, the wolves charged, black lips pulled back over their teeth.

Almost there—

The girl threw the branch. A good aim, but the lead wolf dodged aside, and the wood clattered harmlessly into the sodden ground. It slowed him just enough that his companion gained on him, and they ran for their prey side by side, so close that they brushed each other's fur.

They leaped for her together.

The girl did not leap to the side or fall to the ground as the lead wolf thought she might. Had she done so, her steel raised, she might have drawn first blood as they passed over.

Instead, she leaped back.

In the air, jaws opening to strike, the wolf couldn't help but be impressed. The girl was light on her feet and amazingly strong for a human. Her jump backward took her a long way. But he knew it would be her death. She would come down, and the wolves would come down on top of her.

But then something stopped her in midair, for just an instant. Her backward motion stopped, and she went down, straight as a stone. In that last moment before she disappeared into the mist, the lead wolf saw the rope around her waist, the other end pulled taut before her, secured to the cliff wall—

Which was now behind them.

The wolves fell into the mist. They just had time to realize what was happening and take a breath before they struck the river.

• • ⊚ • •

Leaping backward off the cliff, Hweilan's right boot had slipped, just slightly, on the wet rocks. Not enough to spoil her leap, but enough that she turned in the air, and when the rope pulled taut and swung her back toward the rocks, she was just a bit too far sideways. Rather than hitting the rocks with both feet flat, knees bent to absorb the force, her feet struck sideways, slipping on the mossy wet rocks. Both boots slid out from under her, and her body slammed into the rocks. It was all she could do to keep her grip on the knife in her hand.

The loop of rope around her waist slipped up under her arms, and she felt skin rubbed off her back.

Hweilan put the blade between her teeth, biting the steel against the pain, as she used both hands to climb. Her boots tore through the thick moss and slipped on the rocks, forcing her to take three times as many steps as she should have, but her desperation spurred her on. The other end of the rope was bound in a tight knot around the bole of an old oak whose iron-hard roots had burrowed through the rocks. But one slight pass of sharp steel, or even a good bite with sharp teeth, and Hweilan knew she'd be joining the two wolves who were probably going over the falls about now.

Her right hand gripped the lip of the cliff while her left kept hold of the rope, and she pulled herself up. Hweilan thought she must have leaped farther to one side than she'd thought, because a tree stood before her. Too late she realized—

Nendawen stood before her, spear planted on the ground beside him.

The moment's hesitation defeated her. In that brief instant of realization that the Master stood before her, Hweilan did not know whether to strike, roll to one side, or leap back off the cliff. The indecision cost her.

Nendawen's bloody hand shot out, gripped the rope around Hweilan's waist, and pulled her into the air. He brought the spear around so quickly that she never saw it, only heard it and felt the wind of its passage as the sharp iron head sliced through the length of rope binding her to the tree. And then he threw her over his head and high into the air. She crashed through branches, and that told her she was not headed for the cliff. Which meant she had a hard landing—

She came down in the soft, muddy ground. Of all the trunks and roots surrounding her, she missed every one, which told her that Nendawen had not meant to injure her. She slid a long ways and used the momentum to come to her feet. When she looked up at Nendawen, the burning emerald gaze told her he had not spared her out of any mercy or kindness. He was a predator toying with his prey.

Hweilan grabbed the knife from her mouth and cut the rope off her waist. She considered drawing Menduarthis's knife as well, but she wanted at least one free hand if she had to grab at something—like a spear headed for her throat.

Nendawen glanced over his shoulder where his wolves had leaped over the cliff.

You did not learn that from the Fox, he said.

"No," she said. "I learned it from a Var warrior. And that wasn't the only thing he taught me."

Nendawen laughed, a sound not unlike the thunder of the nearby falls, then said, *Show me.*

Hweilan was taken aback at such a simple challenge. She had a knife in hand and another at her waist. In truth, Scith had taught her very little of knife fighting. It was not the Nar way. The knights had taught her basic skills, but in knife fighting Ashiin was her true master.

No? said Nendawen. *Then I will show you.*

He drove his spear into the ground—so hard that Hweilan felt the ground shake under her feet—then he came for her, moving with a purposeful stride. The sheer presence of the Master almost overwhelmed Hweilan. He stood at least eight feet tall, every inch of him scarred muscle. But that was not what was so intimidating. Nendawen exuded an aura, like the heat of a forge fire, but one that hit the mind and hidden senses.

Hweilan almost ran. Every primal sense of her being knew that death was coming for her.

But no. This was the day. If she fled, she *knew* the Master of the Hunt would kill her. Without pity. Without remorse. And she would deserve it. After all she had lost—after so many who had died so that she might live—to run now would be to spit on their pyres. If she was to die today, then she wanted to be able to face her parents in the next in the afterlife—her grandfather, Scith, and even Lendri—and she wanted to stand before them without shame.

Ashiin's teachings came to her.

An advancing foe has one disadvantage: You know he's coming. Choose your ground, and prepare. When he strikes, make him strike on your terms.

Hweilan crouched and planted one foot well behind the other. She had one chance at this.

Both hands outstretched, claws dripping blood, Nendawen lunged.

Hweilan leaped, throwing her feet and lower body first, sending her body in a slide. She had hoped Nendawen's legs might be far enough apart for her to slide between, but there was no room. So she slid to one side, one of Nendawen's hands brushing the top of her head. As she passed, she struck with the sharp steel in her hand, aiming for the soft flesh behind his knee, hoping to sever the tendons there. If she could cripple him, she might have a chance to finish him before the other wolves arrived.

But the muscles there were as strong as old tree roots. Hweilan had honed the knife's edge till it was as sharp as a razor. It cut through the skin, but despite all her strength behind it, the blade only nicked a shallow wound in the tendons and muscle.

Hweilan scrambled away before Nendawen could turn and strike. She whirled, coming up in a defensive crouch, knife held before her.

Nendawen stood several paces away. He looked down at the blood dripping down the back of his leg. Hweilan thought she heard it sizzle as it struck the sodden leaves.

He looked up, his gaze locking on hers. *You drew first blood*, he said. *The Fox has taught you well.*

A scent struck Hweilan, so sudden it filled her head and so strong she could taste it—the salty iron taste of raw meat combined with the sweetness of flower buds. Her eyes were drawn down, following the scent, and she saw that her knife blade was steaming. Nendawen's blood on the edge soaked into the steel, and even as she watched, it spread, turning the entire blade the color of heart's blood.

She had scarcely had time to wonder what this might mean when something else broke through her senses— the sounds of something approaching through the forest, crashing through branches and tearing up the forest floor. No, not something, but two somethings. The other two wolves had arrived.

Even as Hweilan looked back up at Nendawen, the two massive wolves joined him, one on either side. The leader looked down at the Master's wounded leg, let out a plaintive whine, then licked it, cleaning the wound. When all the blood was gone and no more had joined it, Hweilan knew the wound had healed. The wolf returned its gaze to Hweilan, its eyes golden as a summer moonrise, and growled.

Hweilan knew she could never take all three of them at the same time. Not with only her knives.

"You won't face me alone, then?" she said, forcing a defiance into her voice that she didn't feel.

No, said Nendawen. He reached out his right hand, and something struck Hweilan a glancing blow on the back of her shoulder, knocking her to the ground.

She scrambled back to her feet, but Nendawen and the wolves had come no closer. In fact, a tangled mass of roots, branches, and thorns had come up out of the ground, forming a sort of throne for the Master, and he sat with his spear across his knees. Hweilan understood what had struck her. The spear had flown through the air and returned to its master's hand.

The wolves sat on their haunches to either side of the throne, still watching Hweilan, none of the threat gone from their eyes, but otherwise showing no sign of coming for her. Two shapes—one black, the other a shade lighter than the mists themselves—flew out of the trees and landed on Nendawen, one on each shoulder. A horned owl on his right, and a raven on his left. No sooner had they settled in than a snake, striped with every color of the rainbow, slithered out of the tangled throne and coiled around Nendawen's leg.

"I . . ." Hweilan searched for the right words, searched every teaching and memory of the venom vision she had, but came up with nothing. So she simply said, "I don't understand."

The Fox has taught you well, said Nendawen. *Now, we shall see if you believe that—and if she believes it.*

"Wha—?"

Something heavy landed behind Hweilan and she whirled. Ashiin stood several paces away, just close enough to be distinct in the mist, her staff in one hand.

"Ashiin?" said Hweilan.

"A good trick with the wolves," said Ashiin. "I will remember that one." Her voice softened, she said, "Remember your vow," then charged.

Hweilan tried to sidestep away, but her teacher was far too quick. The staff came for her head. She ducked under it, then blocked the kick that had been coming for her midsection. Hweilan tried to drive her fist into Ashiin's ribs, but the woman twisted away—and then the staff was coming for her again, straight down this time. Hweilan slid out of the way, but on the wet ground her feet slipped. She used the fall, turning it into a roll, and tumbled away.

"Why?" she screamed, even as Ashiin came after her again. It took all her efforts to avoid or block strike after kick after strike.

At last, Ashiin snarled in frustration, sidestepped away, and said, "You're holding back. Use that knife!"

"I don't understand. Why—?"

"Only one of us leaves here alive today, girl," said Ashiin.

And then she charged again, jabbing and swinging with her staff, kicking, punching, again and again, giving Hweilan no time to do anything but evade and block.

"Hweilan," said Ashiin, though she did not let up on her attack. "If you hold back, I will kill you. I have no choice."

Hweilan screamed, blocked a punch, then returned one of her own. "No," she said through clenched teeth. "I won't kill you."

"You swore," said Ashiin, and she jabbed with her staff.

Hweilan twisted to the side, let the staff pass her, and grabbed it with her free hand.

"Enemies!" she said, and delivered a kick to Ashiin's midsection that sent her back. Hweilan tried to keep her grip on the staff, but Ashiin was too strong and ripped it out of her hand. "I swore to kill *enemies* without hesi—"

Ashiin screamed and came at her again, striking so fast with the staff that Hweilan was forced to backstep. But Ashiin followed, and rather than her fist, her free hand swiped out with claws, barely missing Hweilan's left eye and raking down her cheek.

She stepped back, out of Hweilan's range, and licked the blood from her fingers. "Today, I am your enemy," she said. "I am your death."

Hweilan had one trick left, one little surprise she had brought from the tower. She reached inside her shirt pocket with her free hand, thanked her ancestors and all the benevolent gods that the pouch was still there, and pulled it out.

She had no time to undo the thick knot, for Ashiin came at her again. Hweilan blocked and counterstruck with her fist and even landed one good hit with the pommel of her knife across Ashiin's temple. Not enough to break bone, but Ashiin's head snapped to the side and she tumbled away.

Ashiin came to her feet, a feral smile on her face. "That's the spirit! Had you the heart to use the blade, I'd be dead."

Hweilan seized the moment and drove the point of her knife into the pouch and twisted, tearing open the small bag.

"I didn't mean for you to use the knife on yourself, stupid girl," said Ashiin, then charged again.

Hweilan threw the bag. It lost half its contents or more in the air, but there was still enough inside that when it struck Ashiin right between the eyes, a fine red cloud erupted into her face.

Ashiin screamed, and Hweilan couldn't help but smile.

The pouch held nothing more than the ground yellow *tranta* leaves that Gleed liked to sprinkle on venison. "Gives it bite," he'd say, and he was right. It was the strongest spice Hweilan had ever tasted, even a little sprinkle making her eyes water. She could only imagine what it would do in a person's eyes.

Ashiin struck out blindly with her staff, tears streaming down her cheeks as she rubbed at her eyes with her free hand.

Hweilan seized the moment. She turned the knife in her hand and gripped it, just like Ashiin had taught her—

And charged Nendawen.

He sat no more than ten or fifteen paces away. Too far for surprise, she knew, but she had to try. She had sworn. Ashiin was right. Sworn to strike her enemy without hesitation. But Ashiin was not her enemy. She couldn't believe that. Her teacher had to have been forced into this. Forced by Nendawen. And in Hweilan's mind, that qualified him as the enemy of the moment. Her rational mind knew she had no chance against the Master, but where her reason failed, something more primal took over. It was the need to survive that made a trapped wolf gnaw off its own foot rather than die in the trap, the defiance that made a dying man spit in his torturer's face. It was pure, unbridled fury.

Nendawen stood. At the sudden movement, the birds on his shoulders flew into the mists, the wolves at his feet fled, and the serpent on his leg slithered back into the thorns. He planted the butt of his spear on the ground beside him and held out his bloodied hand to her. Hweilan could hardly believe it. She'd thought surely the wolves would have come for her, eager to tear her apart.

Hweilan put all of her rage and defiance and fear into her scream, holding on to just enough reason to aim, and planted the knife into the Master's chest. Ashiin had indeed taught her well, and the point of the steel slide between Nendawen's ribs and pierced his heart.

So stunned was Hweilan that she let go the knife and stepped back, afraid to believe that it had worked.

Nendawen looked down at the knife buried in his chest. The light in his eyes had not dimmed in the slightest.

Well done, he said. *You are ready.*

Nendawen, still holding the spear in his other hand, grabbed the knife with his other. But he did not remove it. He *twisted,* tearing open his own chest, slicing away muscle and skin, breaking the ribs.

Hweilan could not move. The presence coming off Nendawen washed over her, paralyzing her. His eyes seemed to gaze down on her from mountain heights. Nendawen raised his bloody hand until it was just over Hweilan's face. It was dripping. Hweilan's nose identified the source before her eyes. Blood. Nendawen held some wet, fleshy mass in his hand, black in the dim light, and it was dripping blood. It was a heart, his heart, and it was still beating.

Eat.

The word settled in her mind, and for a moment Hweilan revolted. But after the notion settled, it spread, like a river overflowing its banks to soak the parched earth. Hweilan the castle girl turned away at such savagery, but Hweilan the hunter exulted in it. This was not a new Hweilan. This was something far older, something that had been sleeping within her all her life. She didn't just accept the idea of eating the living heart. She *wanted* it.

Hweilan seized the heart and pulled it into her open mouth. She bit down, and her mouth filled with blood. It seared like fire. Her throat convulsed, swallowing it, and she bit down harder, breaking through the tough flesh. The *snap* of her teeth breaking through the living muscle reverberated through her head and sent a shudder through her body. Flesh tore free, and she swallowed.

The world pulsed around her—sight, sound, scent, taste, thought, all beating the same rhythm. Light and shadow ceased their separation and bled together. Hweilan could feel the flesh and blood inside her, its power radiating outward through her whole body, filling her mind.

She had once watched a snake shed its skin. When she was seven years old, travelers from the far south had come, and besides a bard who shared tales and songs from those lands, they had brought an assortment of strange creatures—long-necked birds, turtles, a family of monkeys, a horse no larger than a spring lamb, and a serpent the color of spring grass. The beast master had apologized profusely, for the snake could do little more than huddle in its crate, scratching against the branch and stones there as it struggled out of its skin. Hweilan had watched it for hours. The feeling in her now, she imagined it was like that, only in reverse—not struggling out of old, dead skin, but every fiber and fluid of her body growing into a new one from the inside out. Her veins seemed too full. Every beat of her heart threatened to burst them.

Hweilan fell forward, catching herself on her forearms. Her braid had come loose in the fight with Ashiin, and her hair spread over Nendawen's feet. She could feel hot wetness leaking from her eyes, falling in thick drops. They dripped onto the Master's feet. Through the haze she saw they were not tears. She was weeping blood.

Rise, my Hand.

And suddenly she felt she could—the weakness, the struggle melted away—felt she *must*.

Hweilan pushed herself to her feet and found herself staring at the dozens of tiny leaves and flowers that hung from the Master's neck and draped his torso like a priest's stole. Her senses came alive as never before. She could feel every touch of air upon her skin, wafting through her hair, cooling and slowly drying the blood from her face.

Taste and smell hit with such force that they almost became one. Scent of bone filled her mind—salty, rich tang of marrow. *Red.* She could actually *taste* the color red in Nendawen's bones, in Ashiin's, and in her own. The perfume of the flowers around Nendawen's neck filled her head, and Hweilan knew that they still lived and grew, fed by the life-force of the Master.

But around all that, Hweilan could sense the world itself—the forest, the river, the ground beneath her, the misty air. The world, or at least this part of it, was more than just alive. It was aware. Its mind reached into the sky and burrowed deep into the ground itself, its spirit linking earth with heaven, taking nourishment from both. The trees' topmost branches ran fingers through clouds, and their tiniest, deepest roots tickled the fire at the heart of the world. Every creature in the forest—from the tiniest spiders making their webs in the topmost branches to the great serpent coiled around the roots in the underground lake miles below—warranted a fragment of the awareness, and a tiny part of Hweilan's mind connected with them as well, like the first droplets of water seeping through the cracks in a dam. Hweilan knew that if she took the time to pry at those cracks, eventually they would burst, but she also knew that doing so might cause them to flood her own mind, and there was the very real danger of drowning in that awareness. Was this the mind of Dedunan? Is this what the Balance actually *felt* like?

All this passed through Hweilan's mind in the time it took for a small droplet of blood to fall from her chin and strike the toe of her boot. She felt its impact all the way up her leg, and in the profound silence the sound of liquid on leather seemed as loud as thunder.

Take your weapon, my Hand, said Nendawen, and he held the knife out to her.

It was still the color of heart's blood, but with her new heightened senses, Hweilan could see the blood swirling and flowing inside the steel, filled with the life of the Master. She took it and could feel the life inside it.

With this in your hand, said Nendawen, *part of me will be with you. Always.*

Hweilan bowed her head. It had all been a test then. Tempting her to kill her teacher. A test of character? Whatever the case, she had passed. She was ready. She was the Hand at last.

The Hand does not stand alone, said Nendawen, and he forced her to turn.

Ashiin stood there, her staff held crossways behind her shoulders, her hands outstretched to hold it. Tears still ran down both cheeks, but she stood straight and proud. Still . . . something in her eyes . . . Hweilan felt a sudden pang of fear in her gut.

"Ashiin . . . ?"

"Quiet," said Ashiin, then smiled, "stupid girl."

You stand ready? said Nendawen.

"I stand ready," said Ashiin. "And your Hand stands ready."

So be it.

Hweilan felt the spear's passage over her right shoulder, saw the blur of black and green fire, and the spear struck Ashiin, pinning her to the earth.

Hweilan screamed.

Chapter Twenty-Four

The Master was gone. His spear, his wolves, the raven, the owl, and serpent . . . all gone. Hweilan was alone, kneeling in the wet leaves over the dead body of her friend. She was too stunned to weep.

How long she kneeled there, staring down at the bloody corpse, she could not remember. The river rolled on, the thunder of the falls unending. The mist gathered on Hweilan, and on Ashiin's corpse, soaking them. Late in the morning, thick clouds gathered overhead, and a heavy rain pelted the forest, washing Hweilan's tears into the mud.

Hweilan heard footsteps slushing through the muck behind her, but she did not turn to look. They stopped just behind her.

"Stupid girl."

Gleed's voice, words spoken with equal parts sympathy and exasperation.

"Go away," said Hweilan.

"You have no reason to cry."

"Everyone I've ever cared about is dead."

"Well, thank you," said Gleed, all sarcasm.

"You know what I meant."

"I know that, yet again, if you'd stop to *think*"—he whacked her across the back with his staff—"you'd have no reason to feel sorry for yourself. We are not murderers,

Hweilan. You passed that test today, girl. Please tell me you understood what you did."

Hweilan whirled on Gleed, fury in her eyes. "She's dead, Gleed! The Master killed her right in front of me!"

Gleed smacked her with the staff again. "Ashiin *gave* her body. For you. She told you that to awaken the bow, to call your ally, would require sacrifice. Did she not?"

Hweilan's fury and grief faded, as if washed away by the rain. "You mean . . . ?"

"I mean you need to get off your knees and be the Hand," said Gleed. "For yourself, for Ashiin, and for your world."

• • • • •

Gleed led her to the height where she had first seen the Witness Cloud. He summoned one of the creatures of mud and vines that had first carried Hweilan to his tower, and the thing bore Ashiin's lifeless body behind them.

At the summit, in the midst of a circle of ash, lay Hweilan's bow. The rain had not slackened, still coming down in a torrent, and there were no trees for shelter, but the ground inside the circle was dry as old bones, and the pale wood of the bow seemed to sparkle under the light of an invisible sun.

Gleed stopped and turned to face Hweilan. "I will instruct you in what to do," he said, "but *you* must do it. You are the Hand, and you owe your friend the work of your hands."

He spoke a string of arcane words and waved his free hand in an intricate gesture. The vaguely human-shaped mass of vines and mud holding Ashiin melted back into the earth, leaving the corpse of Hweilan's friend lying on the ground.

"Gather wood," said Gleed. "Enough for a pyre. Pile it in the circle on top of the bow."

Hweilan's jaw opened and her eyes went wide. After all she'd lost—

"Don't worry," said Gleed. "Inside the sacred circle, not even a dragon's fire could harm that bow. Now do as I say."

Hweilan obeyed, returning to the nearby woods to gather dead wood by the armload. She piled them atop the bow, then returned for more. After at least a dozen trips, she had a large pile, filling the circle.

"Now green," said Gleed. "Cut fresh branches for her bier."

Hweilan did so, using her knife to cut large pine branches and smaller, softer shoots off the oaks. She didn't know if this was proper for the rite, but it felt like the right thing to do. Returning to the circle, she made a thick bed of the pines, then lay the softer oak sprigs on top.

"Well done," said Gleed. "Now, take your steel and cut nine strands from Ashiin's hair. No more. No less. *Nine* strands."

Hweilan knelt beside Ashiin's corpse. Her eyes were still open, and the rain had pooled there, overflowing down the sides of her face. There was no illusion of tears. Tears came from the living. Seeing those dead eyes . . .

Hweilan clenched her jaw, took a deep breath, and gently closed Ashiin's eyes. The dead flesh under her fingertips . . .

She withdrew her hand, and found it was shaking.

She took the longest of Ashiin's braids, cut the bands of leather and thread binding them, and began to gently comb out the hair with her fingers. It was wet and heavy, and the scent of Ashiin that wafted up from it made Hweilan choke back a sob. She chose nine of the longest strands and sliced them off.

"Let me hold them," said Gleed, "while you place her on the pyre."

Hweilan did so. She could feel the heavy, dead weight of her friend, but she had no trouble lifting the corpse. Whatever strength Nendawen had given her, it was still there. Hweilan crossed one of Ashiin's ankles over the other, put both hands over the bloody gaping hole in her middle, then spread her braids over the bier. By the time Hweilan was finished, her shirt and both hands were coated in her friend's cold blood.

"Step back," said Gleed.

She did, and he began a long prayer. Much of it was similar to the prayers Lendri had said when they had burned Scith's body, but Gleed also recounted Ashiin's deeds, her lineage, and her sacrifice. He spoke many other words besides, in his own language, and although Hweilan could not understand them, she was surprised to hear the affection in their tone. Gleed and Ashiin had never had a kind word to say about each other, although Hweilan had often sensed a grudging respect between them. Perhaps that was what she heard in his tone.

Finished, Gleed raised his staff, green fire already gathered there, and spoke a word of command. Flames roared to life in the wood. Not green, but scarlet red—the color of the Fox. So intense was the heat that Hweilan was forced to step back farther. Rain evaporated before it could strike the pyre, and soon the entire hilltop was enveloped in a cloud of steam.

"Now," said Gleed, turning back to Hweilan, "weave three braids with the nine strands of Ashiin's hair. Blessed, these shall be your bowstrings. Weave them with devotion and love. Honor her memory, and these strings will never fail you."

By the time she'd finished and bound the final hoop in the third bowstring, Hweilan could feel the power in the three strands. Ashiin's hair, still just a shade above black, now had a crimson cast to it, as if the blood coating Hweilan's hands had worked its way into the strings as she wove them.

Together, she and Gleed stood, watching the flames consume Ashiin. Hweilan remembered her teacher, and remembered all her other teachers and friends. This was only the second pyre she'd watched burn, but the list of her beloved dead seemed to be growing all the time. The pyre collapsed with a crack and roar, sending thousands of orange sparks dancing into the sky. If she counted all of her ancestors who had been killed by Jagun Ghen, there might not be enough sparks for each to have one. And as the flames burned lower, Hweilan felt her rage growing again.

The rain and flames stopped at almost the same time. A wind came out of the west, setting the trees to dancing and blowing away the cloud cover. The sun was already low in the sky, and it bathed the hilltop in orange dusklight.

They waited, watching the smoldering ashes. When the first stars made their appearance in the east, Gleed motioned at the remains of the pyre with his staff.

"Retrieve your bow—and what is left of your friend."

Hweilan looked down at him. "Left?"

"You will see."

Hweilan stepped into the sacred circle. The ashes were still warm, but not hot enough to burn as she pawed through them. She saw something pale, and her first thought was—*bone*—but that was foolish. Fresh bone was not so pale and would've burned in the fire. It was her bow, and as she pulled it from the ashes, she saw that Gleed had spoken truly. It was completely unharmed. Not a scorch mark. Even the ashes fell away from its surface.

And there, lying in the open area from which she'd taken the bow, lay a skull. Much darker than the wood of her bow, it was equally unscathed by the fire, but it still had the dark tone of fresh bone. It was not human, nor was it a fox, but seemed something in between, as if the sacred flames had blended Ashiin's two natures into one. It felt warm under her touch, but not from the fire. With her new senses, Hweilan could feel the life in the skull.

"Ashiin?" Hweilan whispered.

"Bring them, Hweilan," Gleed called.

She walked out of the ashes, carrying her bow in one hand and her friend's skull in the other. Gleed sat inside another, smaller circle nearby, his staff across his lap. She sat opposite him inside the circle.

"*Shesteh* you have made," said Gleed, pointing at the bow. Then he pointed at the skull. "Now, finish them."

Gleed instructed her as she used the tip of the red knife to carve matching *shesteh* into the surface of the skull. With every etching, some of the living blood inside the knife seeped into the bone, mingling the life of Nendawen with the life of Ashiin.

When she had finished, Gleed said, "Now stand and string your bow, Hand of the Hunter."

He took the skull from her and held it reverently in both his hands. She looped one of the strings on the bottom of the bow, then planted it behind one ankle and in front of the other, just as her father had taught her. She grabbed the top of the bow and pulled. It bent in her hand. Not with ease. She had to put effort into it, but the bow bent to her will, and she fitted the other loop over the bow. Releasing it, the bow bent under its own strength, pulling the string taut, and Hweilan felt a tremor pass through it.

She held it in one hand, and in that moment all she could think of was her father and mother.

Gleed held up the skull to her, and she saw that he had fitted a series of woven bands across the back and bottom, so that it formed a mask.

"Don your helm, Hand of the Hunter," he said.

She did. It fit her head perfectly, almost like a second skin, and as its warmth settled onto her, she felt the presence inside it settle into her mind.

Hweilan sent out her own thought—*Ashiin . . . ?*

But whatever was left of Ashiin had no voice. Only the cunning of the Fox remained. Through the mask's eyes, Hweilan's sight seemed more focused, as if Ashiin herself pointed out the stir of leaves, the sound of Gleed's breath, the last cracklings of the fire were all distractions. When something small and furred leaped from one pine tree to the next, Hweilan's eyes were already on it, expecting its movement.

Thank you, Hweilan thought, her heart aching.

"I'm ready," said Hweilan, surprised.

"Not yet," said Gleed. "There is one more thing you need."

CHAPTER TWENTY-FIVE

"Why have you brought me here?" said Hweilan.

Gleed had taken her back in the direction of his tower, but when they made it to the lake, rather than summoning the bridge, he led her along the shore to where the stream tumbled into the lake. These were the falls she had heard on her very first night in the Feywild. They had seemed to shun her then, warning her to go away, and she had avoided them ever since. Even now, standing with her bow in hand, filled with new power, she wanted nothing more than to leave. The constant susurrus of the water in the dark sent a shiver down her spine.

The old goblin smiled at her discomfort. "A minor enchantment only," he said. "I keep it here to ward off . . . undesirables."

That didn't change Hweilan's question, which he still hadn't answered, so she asked again, "Why are we here?"

Gleed scowled at her lack of good humor. "Ashiin taught you of the meaning of the Hand. It is an extension of the heart and mind, made up of many parts."

"Yes."

"You have all that you need," said Gleed. "Almost."

She raised an eyebrow, but she was still wearing the bone mask, so he did not see it.

"Where you are from, hunters have hounds, do they not? And even the Master hunts with his wolves."

"So?"

"So I am thinking the Hand could use a wolf."

He turned to face the falls, raised his staff, and shouted something in his native tongue.

Beside the stream, a huge tree, gnarled and twisted with age . . . moved. Hweilan gasped and took a step back. Two knots about halfway up the tree's trunk parted, one moving up, the other down, and Hweilan realized they were more than just knots. They were eyelids. Two shining eyes—one amber as hardened sap in sunlight, the other a rich brown not unlike the color of Gleed's favorite tea—looked down on them.

"Gergalgellem," Gleed said to it, "if you would be so kind."

The tree twisted further, lowering one massive branch into the water, parting it like a torn curtain. Beyond lay a cave.

"Follow me," said Gleed, and he stepped into the stream, skipping over rocks just below the surface, stepping in to the deeper water that rose well above his knees, then climbing onto the lip of rock and into the cave.

Hweilan followed, soaking her boots in the crossing, then having to bend low to fit inside. No sooner had she passed inside the cave than the tree outside moved, and the water fell back over the entrance.

Whether it was Ashiin's spirit, Nendawen's blessing, or just Hweilan's intuition, something about this errand seemed wrong, as if they shouldn't be here.

Green light from Gleed's staff lit their way as he took them deeper and deeper into the earth, through dripping tunnels that twisted and turned, sometimes even seeming to spiral back around. Hweilan could sense an immense weight overhead, and her brain knew for certain—

We're under the lake, Hweilan thought.

"Where *are* we going, Gleed? I've never heard of a wolf living under a lake."

Gleed kept walking as he talked. "I've kept him down here, safe from prying eyes."

"Him?"

"It was a near thing. When I went back for him, something else was nearby, looking for bones of its own. Some *thing* of Jagun Ghen, I think. I risked my shriveled old neck to retrieve these things, you know."

"No, I *don't* know," she said. " 'A wolf' and 'him' and 'bones.' What are you going on about?"

Gleed stopped, turned to face her, and the light of his staff flared. The green glow spread out, and Hweilan saw that they had stopped in a large chamber. Arcane and holy symbols glimmered on the stone walls and from the dozens of stalactites and stalagmites throughout the chamber.

She had never seen the old goblin look more pleased with himself. "Come. Look."

He motioned with his hand to a mound of stone behind him. It might have been a massive stalagmite once, but it had been flattened and hollowed out, forming a stone basin, filled with water that *drip-drip-dripped* continually from above. Rivulets of overflow ran off one side, forming a small stream that ran off into the darkness.

Gleed held the light of his staff over the water, and as Hweilan looked down, she saw that the basin was no more than a couple of feet deep, the water clear as finest crystal. The scent of it—she had never smelled water so clean and pure—defied all reason when she saw what was at the bottom of it.

A pile of bones, the round, grinning skull resting on top.

"That's . . . ?"

"Lendri," said Gleed.

Hweilan was more confused than ever. What did this have to do with—?

"You remember what we spoke about before," said Gleed. "That Lendri might know things. About you. Things that you could . . . put to use when the time comes. Well, every hunter needs a wolf. You are Vil Adanrath. The way of the wolf is the way of your people. Call him. Call Lendri. Bring him back to fight at your side and redeem himself."

Hweilan let that settle in. If Lendri would come, he would be a powerful ally. But he'd told her that wouldn't happen.

"He saw this coming," said Hweilan, though it was more to herself.

"What?" said Gleed.

"Lendri saw this coming somehow," she said. "It's why he told me what he did: 'You can call me, but I will not return. Not even for you.' "

Gleed nodded and finished for her, " 'Let my exile end. Let me rest.' Heed my counsel, Hweilan. Do this, and you may both get what you want. You need an ally. For now and for later. If this Lendri helps you, perhaps he will earn his rest at last."

Hweilan looked down at the bones for a long time.

At last she tore her gaze away from Lendri's bones, looked at Gleed, and said, "Tell me what I must do."

The old goblin smiled, the old mischief back, and said, "Take off the mask."

Hweilan reached for the strap and took off the helmet, severing her link with Ashiin's spirit.

Gleed gave the bone mask in her hand a pointed look. "She is a good friend to you, but she is the Master's, heart and soul. After you've sent Jagun Ghen and his ilk back to the Abyss, if you choose to set your sights elsewhere . . ."

He didn't finish the thought. Didn't need to.

She said, "I'll deal with that when the time comes. Now what do I do?"

Gleed's mirth faded. His one good eye closed to little more than a slit, and he fixed the other on her. "Tonight, Hweilan, we walk the ghost path. You must not falter, and you must not fear. I can get you there. I can bring you back. But only you can call your friend."

"I understand."

The old goblin prepared the rite. He prayed to Dedunan, his voice bold and clear, as he sprinkled a fine powder of ground oak leaves around the rim of the basin. Where the trickle of water spilled over the basin, he poured even more, then kissed the rim. He then took holly berries, crushed them one at a time between his fingers, and painted a stripe down the back of both his and Hweilan's eyelids, then a long stripe from forehead, down the nose, across the lips, and finally ending at the chin.

"So that all we see and all we speak may have the Blessing of the Forest Father," he said.

When he was finished, he sprinkled more things into the water. Their scent told Hweilan what some of them were—dried rose petals, blue pine, moss, and lichen—but many were strange to her, smelling sweet, foul, and everything in between.

"*Drakthna* will stop our hearts," he said, "and the roots of the sweet white *iruil* will wake them again."

Hweilan swallowed hard and said, "You mean . . . ?"

"We walk the ghost path, girl. The living do not go there. Only the dead."

He put both hands into the basin, formed a cup with his palms, then lifted them out. He drank the water, though much of it spilled down his face and neck.

Hweilan stepped forward. She had a bad history with drinking Gleed's concoctions. She swore to herself that if she woke naked in the woods after this, her first order of business would be drowning the little goblin in his own lake. But surely if he was drinking the same thing, had even gone first . . .

"Hurry, girl," said Gleed, and she heard the strain in his voice.

She put both her hands into the water. It was cold, but in a way that was more soothing than painful. Blood still smeared her hands in places. Too late for it now. Hweilan brought her full palms to her face and drank.

The water had an earthy taste, and it seemed to go to work inside her at once.

Her body began trembling so badly that she had to sit down. Other than the rite in which she'd eaten part of Nendawen's heart, she hadn't had a thing to eat since the day before, and her body seemed light and fragile as a hollow eggshell.

Only a few feet away, Gleed shuddered, his breath caught in his throat, and he fell over. His head actually bounced off the stone floor as it hit.

Hweilan's heart had taken on an irregular beat, each more painful than the last, and she just had time to set her bow aside and lower herself to the ground when the darkness closed in around her.

• • • • •

Sight did not return first, but sound. She could hear a wind blowing, and from somewhere far off the raucous song of a murder of crows. There was no sensation of opening her eyes, but suddenly she could see. No sense of smell or taste, or even feeling. Hweilan had the senses found only in unremembered dreams.

What she saw did nothing to dispel her feeling of dreaming. A featureless plain, gray as ancient dust, stretched in every direction. Something on the plain swirled, but she could not tell if it was dead grass or swirls of dust. Her vision wouldn't focus.

Wolves howled in the distance, and she heard the ravens again.

"Gleed?" she called, though she couldn't even be sure that she had a mouth. But she heard the words, and she heard the response—

"Here . . . here . . ."

She went toward the sound, wading through the grayness. She found him, though he seemed little more than a slightly darker, slightly more solid bit of grayness amidst the gloom.

"What is this place?" she said.

"Where the dead wait," said Gleed. "Quickly. Find your friend."

"How?"

"He is your blood, and sworn by oaths to your family. You are bound. Follow that binding."

She had no idea what he meant by that, but just thinking about it, she became aware of . . . *something*. Some sense pulling her in one direction. She followed it.

The howls of the wolves faded behind them, but the sounds of ravens grew closer. And then Hweilan saw them—a black cloud of hundreds of ravens, swirling over the gray plain, one or more of them diving down again and again.

And then she saw at what the birds were diving. Lendri walked the plain beneath them. Or shuffled more like. He moved like an injured man, in a sort of dragging limp, one hand clutched to his body. As she drew closer, she saw why. Just as she had seen him before, he held his own heart in his hand, and the gaping wound in his midsection that had killed him was still a bloody mess. Blood drenched his naked body. Only his almost-white hair seemed clean, which struck her as strange.

"Lendri," she called.

He didn't stop. Didn't even look up.

A raven dived down, gouged a large bit of flesh out of Lendri's back, then flew off again.

"Go to him," said Gleed.

She did, stopping in front of him.

One of the ravens shrieked and dived for Hweilan, but one look from her and it exploded in a mass of burning feathers. The others cawed their displeasure and flew away.

"I will not come," said Lendri, not even looking up.

She said, "Why?"

"Let me rest," said Lendri. "Just let me rest."

Hweilan heard the ravens again. They had flown off, but not far.

"As soon as I leave, they'll come back. Is that the rest you want?"

He looked up at her then. His eyes were empty sockets, and tears of blood leaked from them. "Why can't I rest? So long . . . I have been apart from my people. Even in death, I cannot join them. Why?"

"Because your work is not done," said Gleed.

"What more can I give? I died trying to protect the girl."

"What did you do?" said Hweilan.

"I tried to stop that monster, and he ripped my heart out."

"No. Not that. What did you do that earned your exile?"

Lendri actually laughed at that, though it was all bitterness. "I chose my friend over my clan. When my sister chose to love a man rather than one of her own people, my father sent me to kill him and bring her back. But she was already carrying his child. And he was my friend. So I chose to stand by them."

"That's it?" Hweilan couldn't believe it.

Or could she? Her mother was only part Vil Adanrath, but Hweilan had run up against that unyielding hardness on many occasions. Her father had often said that her mother's will could crack stone and make the mountains bleed.

"I broke my oaths," said Lendri.

That hit Hweilan hard. Was what Gleed was suggesting to her—fulfill her mission as Nendawen's Hand, then run on her own—anything less? No. She knew it was far worse. Betraying oaths to family and clan was one thing. Betraying an oath to a being like Nendawen . . .

"Did you know my mother's father?" said Hweilan.

Lendri recoiled at that, so strongly that for a moment he was no longer a bloody, broken elf, but looked like a wolf, caught in a trap.

"You did, didn't you?" said Hweilan. "Why does the question frighten you? Tell me his name!"

"I knew him," said Lendri, "and I know his name. But I will not speak it before a goblin sorcerer."

Hweilan tried to look at Gleed, to see his reaction, but he was still only a blur. No matter. She'd deal with that later. She was here for a different reason.

"Lendri, Nendawen came to you. Sent you to find me. You remember?"

He turned away at that, trying to get away, but she stopped him.

"I told you before—on the mountain that day with Menduarthis—and I tell you now: I want this. I *want* to serve Nendawen and hunt those who killed our family."

He turned back to her then and looked up at her through those empty, bloody sockets. "Then why do you ask your father's name?"

Hweilan ignored the question. "Will you come back with me? I need your help."

Lendri closed his empty eyes and turned away. "Let me rest."

"You have no rest, you fool!" said Gleed. "You have only an endless existence of ravens pecking at your flesh while you feel sorry for yourself. You want to rejoin your people? Regain your honor? Die in peace? Then redeem yourself! Help the girl!"

"I am the last," Hweilan told Lendri. "The last of our people. Your oaths to my ancestor bind me to you. As long as I need you, you will never rest. Come with me, Lendri. I beg you. Help me."

"She speaks the truth," said Gleed. "And consider this: She may be your last chance. Help her, redeem yourself, and then you may die in peace. But if you stay here, sniveling under hungry ravens when you could have helped her, and she dies out there fighting Jagun Ghen, who do you think will come for you then? It will not be Dedunan, come to take you to rest. If Nendawen comes, it will only be to drag away your cowardly soul to make sport for a High Hunt."

"Be silent, Gleed," said Hweilan, then she returned her attention to Lendri. "He will not help me to save his own skin—or his own soul. He will not help me for his own reward. He will help me because it is the right thing to do. *That* is honor."

The featureless plain suddenly shook around her, and Hweilan heard a huge thunder that she instinctively knew was only in her mind. Ravens cawed again, but they seemed faint, and Lendri was fading away.

"The *iruil*!" Gleed shouted. "It's working. It's—"

Hweilan and Gleed both sat up at the same time, drawing in such a great draft of air that it sounded like a scream in reverse.

"—bringing us back!" Gleed finished.

Hweilan was still trembling and felt weaker than ever. Gleed fumbled for his staff, and its meager glow flared again, but Hweilan couldn't make her eyes focus. Everything seemed to waver before her.

"Did it work?" she said. It came out a raw croak.

"It is in Dedunan's hands now."

Hweilan heard it first. A bubbling like a heated cauldron. The sound drew her gaze to the basin. Still shaking, she forced herself to her feet. Gleed did the same beside her, leaning heavily on his staff. Together, they looked at the basin. The sprinkling of oak leaves around its rim was sparkling, and the water within was no longer clear or calm. It had gone cloudy as milk. It bubbled. Steam rose from the water, and a thousand lights of as many colors danced within.

Gleed rasped, "I think we should stand ba—"

The basin erupted in a spray of water, steam, and light. A wolf leaped out of the water. It landed on the ground, its legs shaking, then fell over. Hweilan noticed at once that its sides weren't moving. The wolf wasn't breathing.

She said, "Is that . . . ?"

"Lendri," said Gleed.

At the sound of his name, the wolf's head lifted off the floor and looked at them.

"He's—" the words caught in her raw throat.

"A wolf," said Gleed.

"Dead," said Hweilan. "Look, Gleed! He isn't breathing."

The old goblin studied the wolf a long time, then said something she didn't understand.

"What was that?" she asked.

Gleed spoke louder this time. "*Ren kucheh.*"

Vil Adanrath words. They meant *living dead*.

CHAPTER TWENTY-SIX

THE NEXT DAY, HWEILAN STOOD BEFORE THE FALLS. She had scrubbed the previous day's dirt and blood from her body, bound her hair in a tight braid with long strips of leather, and dressed in new clothes that Gleed told her Kesh Naan had made with her own hands. The clothes fitted close enough that Hweilan wouldn't snag them on branches and thorns, but they flowed over her skin, smooth as silk, so that she didn't feel in any way constrained. The red blade of Nendawen rested in a plain leather sheath at her hip, and Menduarthis's knife was tucked into one of the boots she had worn throughout her stay in the Feywild. The bone mask in which Ashiin's spirit rested rode on her other hip, in a special harness Gleed had made. She had a few supplies in the pouches on her belt and a pack on her back, nestled next to a quiver stuffed with new arrows. The bow she held in her hand.

Gleed stood beside her. "You still lack one thing, I am thinking," he said, "and I must confess I'm most surprised you haven't asked for it in all this time."

Hweilan looked down at the old goblin, and now that the time had come for farewells, she was surprised at the sudden affection she felt for him.

"What do you mean?" she asked.

Gleed reached into his robes and pulled out a curved bit of antler bound to a leather thong.

"My *kishkoman*," she said. Seeing it, memories flooded her mind—of her mother mostly—and Hweilan found herself fighting back tears as she took the whistle knife from Gleed.

"You have become something great," said Gleed, "but that doesn't mean you should forget where you came from."

"Thank you," she said, and surprised them both by kneeling and giving the old goblin a hug.

Gleed's ruddy skin took on a rich brown tone, and Hweilan realized the old toad was blushing. "You know the way out," he said, and pointed to the falls. "The portal works both ways. If you ever need a rest from hunting demons, come see your old teacher. We'll share a special drink beside my fire."

She laughed. "Your special drinks tend to end with me waking naked in the woods."

He smiled up at her, trying for mischief, but still looking sad.

"I will come back," she said. "If I can."

Gleed swatted in her direction, as if shooing a fly. "Get gone, you. You have work to do."

Hweilan turned and shouted, "Uncle! Come!"

"Why in the Nine Hells are you calling him Uncle?" said Gleed.

"He is my uncle, of a sorts," said Hweilan. "Brother of a distant grandmother, and blood brother to my distant grandfather."

"His name is Lendri."

Hweilan knew from the venom visions of the nature of the Vil Adanrath, and she knew that Lendri, like all his people, could take on the form of a wolf. Why he had returned from the dead as one, neither she nor Gleed were sure. But Hweilan suspected it was by choice. And until he decided to walk on two legs again and talk to her, she would not call him by his rightful name.

"He can't tell you the name, you know," said Gleed. "Not while he's . . . like that."

"True." Still no sign of him, so she called again, louder this time, then turned back to Gleed. "Why do you think he wouldn't tell my grandfather's name?"

Gleed shrugged. "Elves and goblins don't exactly have a loving history. He doesn't know me. He has no reason to trust me. Can't say I blame him."

She looked down at her old teacher. "You really think my mother's father can help me, when . . . *if* the time comes?"

"I think the same thing I thought the last time you asked me: There's something in you from somewhere else. Something the Master had not even suspected. *If* the time comes when you need to find out about that something else, your mother's father seems the most reasonable place to start, yes?"

Hweilan looked away, searching the nearby woods for any sign of the wolf. "If he'll tell me."

"I see no reason why he shouldn't tell you."

"When I asked him, he looked frightened."

Gleed thought on this awhile, then said, "We were walking the ghost path, Hweilan. Things there are not always what they seem."

Hweilan shrugged, conceding the point, but she was not so certain in her own mind. At the mention of her mother's father, Lendri had looked truly terrified, and she didn't think there was any mistaking that emotion in any world.

"Uncle!" she called again, loud as she could. Still nothing. She put the *kishkoman* to her lips. It had been so long since she'd last done this. It felt good to be doing it again. Even after all that had happened and after all she had become, this filled her with simple, honest pleasure.

She blew the whistle as hard as she could—so hard that a sharp pain filled her own ears. Gleed didn't even wince, she noticed.

From the woods came a howl. Less than half a mile away, she guessed.

"He's coming," she said.

Gleed actually bowed to her then, and there was no mockery in it. "The Blessing of the Forest Father, the Master of the Hunt, and all your ancestors be upon you, Hand of the Hunter."

Hweilan took out the drum and beat the rhythm to open the portal between worlds. It glimmered to life just as the wolf rejoined her, fresh blood staining his muzzle. Together, they stepped through the falls and left the Feywild.

Part Three

The Giantspires

CHAPTER TWENTY-SEVEN

"Darric of Soravia," said the woman, and she looked around at the others, "and company, meet Uncle."

Darric could take no more, so he said, "Hweilan, what in the Hells happened to you?"

Hweilan looked at him a long moment but gave no answer. Mandan was eyeing the wolf more warily than the woman standing over him with a knife in hand.

And so it was Jaden who brought the main point home. He wiped the back of his sleeve across his mouth, looked to Darric, and said, "So what now?"

Darric opened his mouth to reply, and only then realized he had no idea. Most of their company lay dead, their horses fled, and they were a day away from—

"Highwatch," Valsun said to the woman. "It is fallen then?"

"Yes," said Hweilan, and the acid was plain in her voice. She said something to the wolf in a language Darric didn't recognize. The beast gave her a look that he found unnervingly human, then bounded back into the dark. She stepped over Mandan and went after the last Nar corpse holding one of her arrows. "Gather what you want," she said. "The Creel scattered. Doubtful they'll come back, but there are worse things in these mountains than Creel, and your idiot wizard lit a beacon for anything within ten miles."

Hureleth . . .

Darric had to close his eyes and swallow very carefully to keep his emotions in check. Too much was happening too fast for him to think clearly. But remembering the wizard's fate brought one practical concern to the forefront of his mind.

"We must tend the dead."

Hweilan crouched at the very edge of the torchlight, her back to him. Darric could not see what she was doing, but the sound of tearing cloth was quickly followed by the sound of steel cutting through flesh and bone.

"How?" she said without turning. "You plan to dig graves into the rock? It'll take you a day to gather enough wood for pyres. You could spend the rest of the night gathering stones for cairns, but if you do that, gather enough for yourselves as well. You'll have company long before dawn."

"You suggest we leave our comrades for wolves and ravens?" said Valsun, who had finally found his feet again.

The woman shrugged as she came back to them. "Wolves and ravens have to eat too. Better that than— Do *not* touch that!"

Darric's hand froze less than an inch from the arrow that protruded from the chest of the body next to him. The body lay as lifeless as the stones beside it, but something about the arrow had caught his attention and refused to let it go. Although it appeared only as black wood when he looked at it directly, when he looked away he thought he could see tiny flickers of green flame trickling along its sides. It was a lovely thing, and Darric had long admired a well-crafted weapon. The whorls and sharp thorns of the runes . . . they had an odd look to them. Almost like claws. Still, they had an alluring beauty to them, and before he knew what he was doing he'd pulled off his glove with his teeth and was reaching out, his skin needing to feel the smooth shaft of wood.

But Hweilan's words broke the spell. Startled and feeling strangely ashamed, like a boy caught at some mischief, he looked up at her. "What?"

She kneeled beside Darric and grabbed his arm, which he suddenly realized he still hadn't lowered. She pulled it away. "Touch that with naked skin and I'll be putting an arrow in you next."

"I don't understand."

"Move back," she said.

He did, and she settled in next to the corpse. She studied it—no, she was studying the arrow, he saw, almost like a scribe struggling over some difficult passage in an old tome.

Valsun walked over, Mandan looming behind him.

"What's she doing?" Jaden called, who was still standing well back.

"Be silent," Hweilan said. "All of you."

She reached behind her head and pulled off the bone mask. There, in the dying light of the torches, Darric got his first good look at the woman he had risked his life to find. Although he hadn't seen her in almost ten years, he recognized the features. The fine cheekbones and slight cant to the eyes made him believe those who said her mother had elf blood. But she had the strong nose and chin of her father's family. A dark paint stained her eyelids, and she had symbols on her cheeks and forehead very much like those on the arrow. A young woman's face, but the look in her eyes held no more youth. They had seen too much. There was pain and hurt there, but something else as well. Anger and determination, yes, but beyond all that was a look that Darric had only seen in triumphant predators and religious zealots.

She drew a knife from her belt, and in the light of the fires, Darric could have sworn the blade was red. Using it ever so carefully so as not to damage her arrow, Hweilan dug into the chest of the corpse.

Unable to hold it any longer, Darric turned to the side and became very noisily sick.

• • • • •

The hobgoblins were already busily looting the dead when their leader came into the camp. Even though he stood a head taller than any of the others, his movements alone showed he wasn't one of them. His form was too lithe, his movements too graceful.

Whoever had done the killing hadn't been gone long. The fire in the tree had burned itself out, but the thicker branches were still glowing with heat in the breeze, and its acrid smoke filled the little valley. It definitely had not been another goblin clan though. He knew that for certain. Goblins would have never left so many weapons, armor, clothes, and fresh meat.

"Here!" his second called.

They had seen the blazing tree from miles off, and they'd come in ready, in full armor, weapons drawn. But they were too late.

"What have you found?"

The leader used the common speech because, of all the languages he knew, he could not wrap his tongue around the foul goblin speech. Still, he had to admit the creatures had their uses. He'd seldom met fiercer fighters, and they knew this country better than he did.

His second pointed at the corpse at his feet. It wore no armor, but layers upon layers of clothes. Well-made boots that had obviously seen long use. The pale hands—bare, despite the cold—made the leader suspect this fellow had been a wizard of some sort. He'd needed the bare hands to work his spells—and those scars and missing digits showed he'd had more than his fair share of mishaps.

"The Ujaiyen?" his second asked.

"No," he answered. "Ujaiyen wouldn't have needed two arrows to take him down. And they certainly wouldn't have hacked at him afterward. This looks like locals."

"Out of Highwatch then."

"So it would seem."

The leader kneeled beside his second for a closer look. "I see now why this one has so many clothes," he said. "He needs them to hold all his pockets."

The man had dozens, all filled. Some with typical oddments—needles and thread, bits of food, a small pouch of very pungent tea, some coin. But the others revealed what, if not who, this fellow had been. An oilskin pouch filled with pasty pellets that smelled as if they'd come out of the north end of a southbound bat. Various powders and herbs. Tiny jewels of various cut. And at least a dozen tiny scrolls bound in assorted colors of thread.

"Wizard?" said the hobgoblin.

"Either that or he just robbed one."

His second chuckled. Another thing he liked about hobgoblins. They had a sense of humor. A pleasant change from where he'd come from.

He rolled the corpse over but didn't find anything else. He stood and began scanning the nearby ground.

"What?" said his second.

"This!" he said and kneeled beside a boulder. The object he'd seen had rolled into the dust and grit where it still lay. "Foolish for them to leave this lying about."

The wizard's orb. Dull as the dust in which it lay. But it flickered, just a little, deep in its heart, when the leader picked it up and stashed it inside his coat.

His second stood and watched the rest of the troop work. They were almost done. He looked to his leader and said, "By their clothes, most of the dead came from west of the mountains. But there's a few dead Nar." His voice took on a brittle tone—"And the other."

"Ah, yes," he said. "To that."

He walked over and looked down at the corpse. Unlike many of the others, it had not been savaged by weapons or the jaws of some large animal. One gaping wound in the chest. It was obvious what had killed him. A very well-aimed arrow, which the archer had then used a knife to retrieve.

"The same as the others, yes?" said his second.

"The third in two tendays." He scratched at his cheek, considering. "We've been trying to find a way to kill these damned things for months, our only reward many dead hobgoblins."

His second grunted his agreement, then said, "Something is hunting Highwatch's monsters."

"And doing a damned fine job," he said. "So far at least."

"Who?"

"That is the question of the hour, is it not?"

He left the corpse and walked around. Not far away, two hobgoblins were looting the corpse of a Nar. Another one of the damned Creel that he had come to hate so much. He'd learned enough in the past months to recognize the distinctive cut of their clothes and the unique stitch of their boots.

"Another arrow kill?" he asked.

"Yuh," said one of the hobgoblins, and pointed at the wound. "And bless my bones, I hope I never run into the archer. Thing went all the way through a rib and out the back again. Whatever bow loosed that arrow . . ."

"Stop! Do *not* move!"

The hobgoblins froze and those nearby did as well, turning to see what the matter was.

The leader kneeled beside the nearest hobgoblin. Only a few inches from his right foot, in the muck of frozen blood and dirt . . .

He picked it up.

"What is it?" his second asked.

"Feathers," he said. He turned it in his fingers, examining it. "Fletching from an arrow. Our archer retrieved his arrow but couldn't save the fletching."

He twirled the fingers of his free hand, and a slight current of air wafted through the feathers and brought the scent to his nostrils. Closing his eyes, he inhaled deeply.

There.

Mostly it was what he'd expected. Dirt. Blood. The scent of the bird itself—a raven most likely. The glue that had been used to fix it to the arrow shaft. But *there*! Ever so faint—so faint that even he almost missed it. But there was no mistaking it.

It brought him such delight that he laughed aloud.

"What?" his second asked. "What is it?"

Menduarthis stood. "I misspoke. Our archer retrieved *her* arrow."

"Her?"

"My little flower. She's back."

Chapter Twenty-Eight

"Get up." The words came to Darric from a great distance. Whispered words, but spoken close and with great urgency. Mandan's voice. He ignored them and tried to grab on to the departing dream. "Darric, get up. You need to see this."

Darric forced his eyes to open. Mandan loomed over him, only inches away. Seeing his brother's eyes open at last, Mandan moved away.

"It's light," said Darric, sitting up.

Darric got his first good look at their campsite. Hweilan had led them there the night before, dawn only a pale promise in the east. She'd taken them ever higher into the mountains by paths that would've made a goat's nerves raw. In the dark, their only light that of the stars and the waning moon, Darric didn't know how they'd made it. Jaden had actually begun sobbing and refused to go on at one point, but Hweilan told the man that if he fell behind he was on his own. And she'd moved on. Jaden's sobs hadn't stopped after that, but he'd kept up.

She led them to a small valley formed in times past when snow actually thawed in summer, the runoff carving a shallow crevice in the side of the mountain. Snow hadn't melted there in almost a hundred years, but still the valley was choked with scraggly pines whose roots burrowed through the stone. One ancient giant had fallen over, the main body of the trunk long since gone to rot, but its iron-hard roots had formed a sort of canopy over the crater left by its fall. Years of other branches falling had formed a roof of sorts. It kept the worst of the wind off them and would shield most of the light from the small fire Hweilan had allowed them.

Every man among them had collapsed from exhaustion. Valsun and Jaden had been snoring even before Hweilan had the fire going, and they were still sleeping. As for Hweilan . . . no sign of her or the wolf.

"How long did I sleep?" Darric asked Mandan.

"All the night and most of the morning."

"Midday already?"

"Just past." Mandan's voice was strangely flat. Not angry exactly, but it had a solemnity to it that Darric recognized. Something was bothering Mandan. Something serious.

"What is it?" Darric asked.

Mandan growled deep in his throat. "Follow me."

With that he rose to a crouch—the deadfall ceiling was far too low for him to stand to his full height—and crawled out of the pit. Darric secured his cloak and followed.

Cold hit his face and bit into his lungs, waking him instantly. Damara had bitterly cold winters, but *nothing* like this. Since entering the Giantspires, he'd slowly acclimated to the cold. But they'd been for the most part in valleys or the fissures between the mountains where their guides had led them. They were much higher now. Thin as the air was, it seemed to make it only all the easier for the cold to pierce. Down in the passes, morning cold cut like a knife. Up here, Darric felt like he was breathing in a fume of needles.

"Where is . . . she?" Darric couldn't bring himself to say her name.

"Shh," Mandan said. "That's what you need to see."

He led Darric to the edge of the valley where the trees hugged the broken wall of the mountainside. And then they climbed again, over boulders and through fissures in the mountain formed by eons of ice and wind. They were almost at the height of the pines when the ground leveled out somewhat, and Darric saw that it was not really mountainside at all, but a sort of saddle of rock that dropped away again on the other side.

Behind a boulder near the far edge Mandan crouched, turned to Darric, and put a single finger to his lips. Darric kneeled beside him, and they peeked over the rock into the next valley. It was much shallower and wider than the one in which they'd camped. It had once held trees, but every one had been laid flat—probably by an avalanche. Most still lay there, like a fallen army of statues. The dead trees filled the entire valley for miles down the mountainside—except for one spot, right below them. There, a great wedge of rock, large as a farmhouse, thrust upward, and it was easy to see how the river of snow and ice had passed around it, leaving a little island of bare earth, open to the sky. In the very midst of that bare patch, Darric could just make out a circle, drawn in some dark soil, or perhaps a scattering of ash.

"I'm so glad you woke me for this," said Darric. "Truly I have never seen such a circle." He put a smile on his face as he said it, trying to soften the sarcasm and stir Mandan's sense of humor.

But Mandan only scowled. "She was here! I swear it. Her and the wolf, and she—"

A raven cawed, so loud and so close that both Darric and Mandan jumped. The bird—without a doubt the largest raven Darric had ever seen—sat on the nearest boulder to their right, just upslope. It glared at them, completely without fear, then flapped its wings and let out a long croak.

Had it been there the whole time? Darric couldn't remember. Surely they would have heard such a large creature landing. But how could they have missed—?

And then Darric saw beyond the bird. The saddle of the mountain continued upward until it hit the mountainside proper, no more than twenty feet from where they hid. But there at the foot of the cliff the rock split in a fissure. Not huge, but big enough for someone to fit in. And someone had.

Darric saw the eyes first, bright and fierce, then the glow of skin, and Hweilan emerged a moment later.

Her bone mask was gone, but paint still adorned much of her face and the rest of her skin. So much skin—*far* more than modesty allowed even in the most decadent Damaran court. She still wore the same close-fitting trousers and high boots from the night before, but above that was only a strip of cloth tied around her neck, covering her breasts, and then bound around her back. It left her entire midriff and arms exposed. Darric saw that more of the strange symbols adorned her—most with blue ink, but he saw that some were scars—and she was drenched in sweat. So much so that it steamed off her in the cold. How—?

She walked toward them. The raven hopped halfway around, gave her a baleful look, then flew off.

Hweilan almost made it to them before her knees gave out, and she leaned heavily against the rock before sliding to the ground. Darric saw that she had a fresh bandage around her right hand. Blood and some greener substance had soaked through on her palm.

"Are you hurt?" said Darric.

She took a moment to catch her breath, then glared at them both. "I've never liked spies."

Darric and Mandan exchanged a glance.

"We—"

"Have all the stealth of a swiftstag herd. I heard your friend up here awhile ago. Now here you both are. Why?"

Darric opened his mouth to speak, but Mandan beat him to it.

"Something woke me. The others were still asleep—except you. No sign of you. I thought . . . well, I went to look, and I saw . . ." His voice had had an apologetic tone to it, but suddenly it hardened. "I saw what you were doing. What you did."

Hweilan said nothing, but her gaze did not soften.

"She was dancing in the circle," Mandan continued. "Dancing around something—an arrow, I think—and chanting. Like some damned witch." He pointed at her hand. "I *saw* her slice open her own hand, making some cursed bloodpact with who knows what. And then . . . in all those fallen trees, under all the branches and shadows, I . . . I thought I saw . . ."

"What?" Darric asked.

"Yes," said Hweilan. Her eyes had narrowed. There was still ferocity there, but something else as well. Curiosity. "Tell us what you saw."

"*Thought* I saw," said Mandan. "Shapes. But I . . . I don't know. But then she"—he pointed at Hweilan—"fell on her knees in front of the arrow and I *know* I saw a flash of light—*green,* damn it all!—and I thought I heard . . ." He swallowed hard and clutched at his chest. Darric knew what lay there under all his layers of clothes—a silver medallion in the form of a gauntlet, holy symbol of Torm the Loyal Fury. "No. I *know* I heard a scream. But not from her, and not from the direction of our camp. And . . . by the True Resurrection not by anything I've ever heard in this world. It . . ."

A shudder shook him, so violently that Darric heard the mail rattle under his coat.

Darric looked to Hweilan. She'd caught her breath and managed to sit up without leaning against the stone. But she still sat watching Mandan warily, like a hound who has happened upon a strange, new scent.

"Do you deny this?" Darric asked her.

Her eyes shifted to him, but she didn't otherwise move. "I don't know what he did or didn't see or what he did or didn't hear." No hint of apology in her tone.

"You know what he asks," said Mandan. "The circle, the black arrow, the chanting, all those etchings on your skin, and that . . . that scream. What witchcraft is this?"

But Hweilan chuckled. "Witchcraft?"

"Answer me," said Mandan.

"I don't answer to you."

Darric could see his brother getting very riled. His thick hair was beginning to stand on end, and even in the cold his skin was flushed. He put a hand on Mandan's shoulder, "Brother, we—"

"No!" Mandan turned his gaze on Darric, who flinched back. "No I *will* have an answer from her. You told us we were coming to aid any who survived from Highwatch and to find out what happened. But I've known all along it was her you were really after. And damn it all, *Brother,* we find her as some sort of savage demonbinder calling upon gods-know-what foul powers. It's her soul needs saving!"

Darric held Mandan's gaze a long time, searching for a retort. But he had none. So he looked to Hweilan. "Do you deny his words?"

She sighed and her shoulders slumped. Darric could see she was trembling. Had she slept at all during the night?

"We'll talk," she said. "But back by the fire. The rite always makes my blood run hot, but now . . ." She shivered. "And besides, I'm famished."

• • ⊛ • •

When they returned to the camp, they met a grisly sight. A dead ram lay near the entrance, its throat a ravaged mess.

"Uncle has brought us breakfast," said Hweilan.

"The wolf?" Mandan looked about, and Darric could see him bristling again. "Where is it?"

Hweilan shrugged and said, "*He* is not far. I'll gut breakfast if you two would rouse the fire."

Mandan scowled at them both, then ducked back inside the shelter. Darric did not follow. He turned and watched as Hweilan crouched beside a pile of gray branches. With one hand she lifted them, then reached under them with the other and retrieved her pack. When she stood and turned back, she held a long knife in one hand.

Darric took a step back and cursed himself. He sensed no threat, but she was so . . . *not* what he had expected. Expected? No. Darric had to be honest with himself—and felt his face flush at the thought—what he had *hoped*.

She stood there, studying him. At last she said, "Brother?"

Darric blinked twice. "What?"

"You call him 'brother.' But you are Damaran, through and through. And he is . . . not."

"He is as Damaran as I am."

"And something more besides."

She turned away, kneeling beside the dead ram, and set to work with her knife. Darric caught himself watching. Not the gruesome work of the carcass. The strap of skin she wore across her chest was indeed tied around her neck and back, but by thin strings only. It left her back almost entirely bare. He saw more inks there, more scars, but beneath the skin her muscles rippled as they worked.

"Darric, is it?" she said, not turning from her work. She reached inside the open carcass and began digging out the offal. "I think I remember you now. As a child, I never traveled west of the mountains—except once. When I was seven. My family traveled to Soravia. I don't remember why. But I remember some of the other nobles' children. There was one—a boy a year or two older than I was, I think. His father's oldest and heir, but still younger than most of the other nobles' sons. Very eager to prove himself. But the other nobles' sons were older, bigger, and they didn't seem to like him much. One of the games—a game I was not allowed in, being a little girl—turned rough. No, more than rough. With no adults around, it turned into a brawl, and several of the bigger boys decided they would show the younger one their dislike once and for all. Shame him. And so—"

"And so they beat me," said Darric. He was still looking at her, though he was seeing the distant memory. "Bloodied my nose, loosened a tooth, and knocked me to the ground. I was in the process of getting up—my father always told me it was no shame to be beaten, but there was no greater shame than *letting* yourself be beaten—when this little hellcat of a girl—half the size of the smallest boy there—stood over me, brandishing some sort of horn or antler in one fist. She cursed them all for cowards, waved her weapon at them, and dared the biggest one to step forward if he wanted a real fight. They laughed. The biggest boy did step forward, reached to take the little upstart's weapon away, and—"

"And I stabbed his hand," said Hweilan. She stopped her work and looked over her shoulder at him.

Darric nodded and swallowed. In the years since, he'd told that story two-score times, and thought about it hundreds more, usually laughing but at the very least with a smile. But he couldn't smile now. Could barely even move. Seeing her here now, the memory was too fresh.

"Not badly," she said. "But the little whoreson jerked away so fast that he opened a gash. And then my mother happened on the scene, and the real fury began."

Darric remembered. Hweilan's mother had dressed as a Damaran, but there was no mistaking her for one. Even without the slight cant to her eyes and the sharp ears, there was something altogether *other* about her. He'd heard, as had all the noble Houses, how Vandalar's son and heir had married some eastern barbarian. They hadn't known the half of it. The look in her eyes—the gaze she had cast on the gang of youths—had sent them running, and Darric knew that most of them had been fighting tears.

"That little boy's name was Darric," said Hweilan.

"I'm not a little boy anymore."

Her voice went hard again. "And I'm not that girl. Now either help me or join your friend. The sooner this is done, the sooner we eat."

• • • • •

They sat around the fire. The four Damarans and Hweilan. The fleeing horses had taken the Damarans' supplies, so they had to content themselves with water from their skins for drink. But everyone chewed greedily on the roast ram. They could hear crows feeding on the offal and bones outside.

Once the worst of their hunger had been satisfied, Hweilan looked to Darric and said, "Why are you here?"

Darric gave Mandan a pointed look. His brother returned it but kept his mouth shut.

"Not everyone in Damara has forsaken Highwatch," said Darric. "Many try to curry favor with the usurper. Others are too weak to oppose him and so fear any association with Vandalar, who never supported Yarin. My father remembers the friendship of your House, but even he cannot openly oppose the king."

"Tell the whole truth, Brother," said Mandan, his voice hard. "Because we are going to get the whole truth out of her. I promise you."

If Hweilan was bothered by the angry look in Mandan's eyes, she gave no sign of it. She merely took another bite of meat and looked to Darric.

He could not meet her gaze, so he looked into the fire and said, "My father was saddened to hear of Highwatch, but he would send no aid beyond a few search parties in the western Gap, hoping to find survivors. I . . . grew angry."

Valsun snorted. "You cursed Duke Vittamar for—what was it?—being a craven dotard. Darric told the duke if he was too timid to stand beside a sworn ally, then Darric would go himself. And so he did."

Darric shrugged and continued, "Valsun and Mandan came with me. We hired what swords we could, and . . . well, here we are."

"About that," said Hweilan. She chewed a moment, then swallowed. "Explain the 'brother.'"

Mandan said, "Why is it any of your—?"

"If you are 'going to get the whole truth' out of me," said Hweilan, "then I'll have it from you. I saved your lives last night. You can answer me out of gratitude if nothing else."

A tense silence followed, broken only by the sound of the flames.

"Well *I'm* grateful," said Jaden. "I could've done without the mountain goat walk in the middle of the night, but this particular goat makes up for that."

Mandan growled, and Jaden flinched back, his eyes widening.

"Easy, Mandan," said Darric, then looked to Hweilan. "Forgive my brother. You've cut a sore vein there."

"I don't give a half-damn," said Hweilan. "Brother here has accused me of witchcraft."

Mandan's jaw tightened and he took a deep breath through his nose, and for a moment Darric feared things were about to move beyond his control.

"But that isn't what's *really* bothering you, is it?" said Hweilan, completely unconcerned. She took another bite of roast ram, swallowed, then continued, "Brother there speaks well and dresses like a proper knight, so I'm guessing our good Duke Vittamar raised him in his own household. An orphan then? Because if he's blood to you, Darric, it's only half-blood, and the other half isn't human."

Mandan sat up and was half into a lunge over the fire when the growl *hit* them. For the briefest instant only, Darric feared it was Mandan himself and that the rage was upon him. But Mandan had frozen still as a dead branch. The growl filled their little branch-covered dell, and it hit the gut like a drumbeat, low and strong.

And then Darric saw the wolf. He'd come down into the hollow by another entrance and stood just behind Jaden's left shoulder. His black lips were pulled back over his fangs, his ears lay flat against his head, and every bit of fur around his head and neck stood on end. Jaden's eyes were wider and brighter than new-minted coins, and his chin was trembling.

"You should sit down," said Hweilan, her voice utterly calm, even relaxed.

"Aye," said Jaden, just daring the slightest nod. "Do sit down. Good idea."

Mandan gave the wolf a long, careful look, then scowled at Hweilan and sat.

The ground-shaking growl stopped, and the wolf covered its fangs. His ears rose, twitched, and he settled on his haunches to watch Mandan through narrowed eyes.

Jaden and Valsun let out a sigh, and Darric realized that he too had been holding his breath.

Hweilan took a long swallow from her waterskin, tied it shut, then looked right at Mandan. There was no apology or sympathy in her gaze, but no anger either. Darric felt very, very grateful for that.

Before the mood could sour again, Darric started talking. "Northern Soravia borders on the Great Glacier. A wild country. But still there are people who eke out a living there. Hunters, herdsmen, woodcutters . . . rugged folk. Some years ago, something began slaughtering their herds. And then woodsmen disappeared. A monster of some sort, said the locals. My father sent men to hunt down the beast. They heard tales of a great bear, a huge savage man, or something in between. They followed the trail of rumors into the villages near the mountains. There, they found a young woman, whom locals said had been ravished by the beast. She bore a child. She and the villagers were about to kill it—cast it on a pyre—but my father would not permit it. He said that no matter the crimes of the father, innocent blood would not be spilled in his land. In the tendays that followed, his men found a half-mad savage in the mountains, whom they said could turn into a great bear. They killed him. But my family raised the child. Mandan. His fury burns as hot as his joy, and he sometimes speaks before he thinks, but I have never known a finer man."

"True words," said Valsun.

In other realms, Darric knew such a thing would never have happened. Madness they would call it. But Damarans honored deeds more than heritage, and Darric's father—despite his faults—was Damaran to the core. He had raised Mandan in the faith and never once blamed the boy for his father's sins. And Mandan had never disappointed them.

Hweilan said, "For a craven dotard, your father sounds like a good man."

Darric blushed. "I do not regret my actions—coming here—but my words to my father are a shame to me. Do not make light of them."

"Your turn," said Mandan, his voice tight with barely controlled fury.

Hweilan nodded, considered a moment, then said, "Even fleas have fleas."

Mandan blinked, completely taken aback. "What?"

"You accused me of witchcraft. I can see why someone who has never known the world beyond the faith of Torm might think that. But you are wrong. I am no witch and no demonbinder."

"And what in the Nine Hells do fleas have to do with that?" said Mandan.

"Aye, good question," said Jaden, then shrank back at the look Mandan gave him.

"Swiftstags feed on the grass," said Hweilan. "Wolves feed on the swiftstags. Fleas feed on the wolves. But there are things smaller still that feed on the fleas. And probably even smaller things that feed on the smaller things. And when the wolves die, they feed the grass. Such is the way of all things. To live is to feed on life and, in time, to die and pass that life on to another. Life, death . . . the Balance."

"You've gone over to Silvanus then?" said Mandan. "That's what this is? I've met a druid or two in my time, and you're—"

"No," said Hweilan. "Fleas on fleas."

"*What?*"

"Calm yourself and listen. The world is a bigger place than your simple answers, because you have never asked the big questions."

Mandan shook his head in frustration.

"Please," said Darric, "explain."

And so Hweilan told them of her mother's people, of their exile in this world from a war in another. And as midday began to turn to afternoon, she told of the beings they served. Not gods, for they themselves served the gods.

"Exarchs," said Valsun, his voice fallen to a fascinated whisper. He had always loved theology and philosophy—so much so that Darric had often thought the man would've made a fine priest. "Or primordials perhaps."

Hweilan shrugged. "Neither. More and less. They are . . . primal. They served the gods—especially the one you call Silvanus—in their own way. And here"—she gave Mandan a pointed looked—"you will understand what fleas on fleas has to do with this. As I said, to live, to eat, to die and in turn feed others . . . that is the way of all things. That is the way of Silvanus. But what happens if one eats and eats and eats, and then refuses to die? When one lives only to consume? When one eats too much, grows too much . . ."

"Disease," said Valsun.

"Yes. To eat, to consume and devour only for the sake of devouring . . . it is disease and death. Any creature that does that only brings about its own doom—but perhaps not before killing everything around it. That is Jagun Ghen."

And as afternoon turned toward evening, Hweilan told them the history of her people and their war against Jagun Ghen. Much of it she told very much as Lendri had once told it to her, sitting in that cave with Menduarthis. But she had learned—and seen and lived—so much more since then, and she put it into her own words. After a while, even Mandan's deep scowl softened, and he listened with rapt attention.

She told them that Jagun Ghen had escaped into this world, and she told them what would happen unless he was stopped. And then as the darkness began to fold over their little camp, pressed back only by the light of their little fire, her story turned more personal. There was much she kept to herself, but she gave them the essentials—how a spellscarred Nar demonbinder had been trying to call forth some dark power and ended up opening the door for something far worse than he could have ever prepared for. Jagun Ghen had possessed him and used him to bring forth others of his kind.

"These demons are not of this world," she told them. "So bringing them here is no easy task. It would be like dragging an eagle to the bottom of the sea—and having to find a way to keep the eagle alive. It took Jagun Ghen and his new host years to prepare, to find the proper Lore, and to put his plans in motion. But once he had everything he needed . . ."

Firelight danced on all their faces. Hweilan set more wood on the fire and stirred it.

Darric broke the silence. "Highwatch. Your people, your family . . . they—"

"They were the sacrifice, yes. Their blood brought Jagun Ghen into the world more fully—and allowed him to begin to bring forth others like him. You met one of them last night. You saw what only one of them can do, while its power is not yet fully grown."

"I'm sorry, Hweilan," said Darric. Valsun and Jaden echoed his sentiments.

The anger had gone out of Mandan but he still looked solemn. "I grieve for your people," he said. "I never met your grandfather or family, but all spoke of them with honor. I pray to bring justice to their killers. But that still does not explain what I saw today, or how you learned to kill that thing last night. And your scars—"

Darric broke in, "Mandan—"

"No, Darric! Highwatch fell less than four months ago. But look at her scars. Look! None but the one on her hand are new. And as for your friend here"—Mandan did not turn but pointed with his thumb at the wolf behind him—"explain *that*."

"The wolf?" said Valsun.

"Just a wolf?" said Mandan, still staring at Hweilan. "Then tell us: why doesn't he breathe?"

Darric blinked and sat up straight. And he saw it too. Hweilan and the men—their breath steamed in the evening cold. But not the wolf. And now that Darric watched, he saw that its sides did not move.

" 'Uncle' is not alive," said Mandan. "And I for one have never heard of any servant of Silvanus who makes a companion of the undead."

Jaden, who had finally relaxed in the wolf's presence during Hweilan's tale, paled, and he very carefully scooted away from the wolf, closer to Valsun.

"The wolf *is* undead then?" said Valsun. He had his own medallion in his hand and was looking sidelong at the wolf.

"Not like you're thinking," said Hweilan.

"What does that mean?" said Mandan.

"It means as I said before: You aren't asking the big questions. Uncle is no longer alive as you and me, but he and I are not evil. Had we wanted to kill you, I could have left you for dead last night—or killed you in your sleep. Or I could kill you all right now."

Darric heard the absolute assurance in her voice. She had no weapon close by other than the knife she had used to prepare their food. But she had no doubt of her own words.

"And the rest?" Darric asked. His voice was gentle but firm. "Forgive me, Hweilan, but Mandan's questions are just. How did you learn so much in so little time? And the scars . . ."

She told them of her escape from Highwatch and how she came to the realm of Nendawen, how he had chosen her as his Hand to hunt and purge Jagun Ghen and his servants from this world. Much she left out, partly because she knew they would not understand, but mostly because many of the wounds—those in her heart—were still too fresh to speak of, and she would not share such intimacies with strangers.

"Time . . ." She shrugged. "It passes differently there, I think. I don't know how long I was there. Months . . . years perhaps? I don't know. I learned. I learned how to deal with Jagun Ghen and his ilk. And now I'm back. And I'm going to hunt down every last one of them."

A heavy silence settled over them. Mandan was staring into the fire, and Darric recognized the look on his brother's face. He was wrestling with some inner conundrum, turning it over and over in his mind, worrying over it. Valsun was looking upward, almost wistfully, and Darric knew the man well enough to gauge his thoughts. All this talk of Silvanus and Nendawen, the Feywild and a generations-long war with some sort of evil demigod—Valsun was figuring a way to work it into his own understanding of the world. And Jaden was simply looking from face to face, reminding Darric of nothing so much as a henhouse rooster wondering which grub to peck.

"You'll never make it back to Damara," Hweilan said at last. "Four men headed west through the Gap, with nothing to pay your tribute to the local tribes. Some of the kinder tribes might make you fight one another to the death and invite the survivor to join them. How'd you like life as a hobgoblin, Mandan?" She gave them a wicked smile.

"We aren't going west," said Darric. "We came here to help survivors of Highwatch."

"And who'll help us?" said Jaden.

No one answered.

Hweilan's eyes had locked on Darric. "That's your decision then?"

Darric looked to his men. Mandan just scowled and shook his head.

"I swore my sword to you, my lord," said Valsun. "Nothing's changed that."

They looked to Jaden. "Well, sure as the Hells are hot I'm not walking back west through the Gap by myself, am I?"

CHAPTER TWENTY-NINE

DARRIC WOKE TO THE SOUND OF RAVENS CAWING. He opened his eyes. It was still full dark. The embers of their fire cast the faintest glow into their little hovel. Mandan was already sitting up, the other two men stirring . . . and Hweilan nowhere in sight. After talking most of the afternoon and well into the evening, she had stoked the fire, wrapped herself in her cloak, and been the first to sleep. But she and all her belongings were gone.

"What's that racket?" said Valsun, sitting up and blinking.

Jaden stretched but stayed in his blankets. "Sounds like the ravens who shared our supper."

"Ravens aren't night birds," said Mandan. "Something's riled them."

The branches around the nearest entrance rattled, but before any of them could so much as reach for a weapon, Hweilan came back inside.

"We're leaving," she said. She was wearing a full pack, a knife sheathed at her belt, another tucked into one boot, and her bow in hand.

"What's wrong?" Jaden asked.

"Company on the way," she said. "Stoke the fire and throw on the rest of the wood, then get moving." With that, she turned and was gone.

"Why burn the wood?" Jaden asked as he climbed into his cloak and began gathering his few possessions.

"The fire," said Darric as he threw on the wood and stirred the coals back to life. "It might distract whoever is coming long enough for us to get away."

"Who is coming?" said Jaden.

"You're in the Giantspires, son," said Valsun as he followed Hweilan. "Whoever it is, it can't be good."

Darric and the others followed.

• • ⊚ • •

Hweilan led them up the same saddle of the mountain to where Darric and Mandan had found her that afternoon. Only they went in the dark, no light but that of the stars and moon, and a hard wind coming down off the mountain that made the already frigid air deadly. They had just made the level height where Hweilan had found Darric and Mandan when Jaden fell and did not get up again.

Hweilan kept going, headed for the crevice in the cliff.

Darric tried to pull Jaden to his feet, but to no avail. The man sat there, huddled inside his cloak and shivering.

"Up, Jaden. Now."

"Let me die here," he said. "I'll go back to the fire. Better a quick death in battle than freezing to death."

"He's right, my lord," said Valsun, who had turned back to help. He too was huddled in his cloak and shivering. "We need a defensible shelter. No use running if the cold kills us."

Darric could no longer feel his face, and his feet and hands felt hard and brittle. His layers of clothing had kept out the worst of the cold so far, but he could feel it seeping in already, and they'd only been outdoors a short while. He knew his men were right.

Jaden looked up to where Hweilan was already disappearing inside the crack in the cliff. "I miss the wizard," he said. "Could always count on him for a fire."

Mandan looked to Darric. "What do we do?"

Darric thought only a moment, then called out, "Hweilan! Hweilan, stop!"

She rushed back to them, her movements stiff, the whites of her eyes shining with fury, even in the dark.

"Are you mad? Why not just blow a horn if you want to tell everyone within a mile where we are?"

Darric held her gaze. How could she not be freezing?

"This won't work. We need a defensible shelter out of the wind—and a small fire at the least."

"You want to die?" she said. "You go back to the fire and—"

"And if we don't, the cold will kill us anyway."

She cursed under her breath, turned—and stopped. Darric knew she was giving serious consideration to leaving them. Then she shook herself, tucked the bow under one arm, and began rummaging inside the large pouch on her hip.

"What's she doing?" said Jaden.

Hweilan tossed something into his lap. "Don't eat it," she said. "Just chew and swallow the juice."

She gave each of the others a small dark lump, longer than it was wide and slightly pliable.

"What is it?" said Valsun.

"*Kanishta* root," she said. "Start chewing, then keep up. You fall behind and you're on your own."

Jaden was the first to plop the root in his mouth and start chewing. His jaw worked a few times, he froze a moment, then began coughing.

"Agh! That's foul beyond . . . beyond . . ." Another chew, a swallow, then very eager chewing. "Oh, that's heavenly. I take it back. Stuff and stiff the wizard, *this* is magical."

He hopped to his feet as the others began chewing. Darric almost gagged. It tasted like roasted garden soil. No, worse. It—

And then the warmth hit him. His entire head flushed, filling with heat, as if someone had emptied a bucket of steaming water over his head, for it spread all the way down, making even the tips of his toes and fingers tingle.

"Better?" said Hweilan. "Then move. Now."

The men hurried off after Hweilan, who had already disappeared through the crack in the cliffside.

It proved to be more than a cave entrance. Beyond was a tunnel, leading up through the rock, albeit not very far. Through a very tight squeeze—Mandan barely managed it—they emerged on a higher level of the mountain saddle. The wind hit them full force, but with the *kanishta* root's juices flowing through them, the cold no longer had much bite. Still, on the ice-slick path, it made for very treacherous going, and the men often slipped, slid, and fell as they rushed to keep up with Hweilan. But keep up they did. Darric discovered that the *kanishta* root not only filled his body with warmth, but with vigor—at first with such a rush that his hands shook. But Hweilan set a brutal pace, leading them ever higher into the mountains, and Darric found himself using every bit of energy the root gave him.

The eastern sky was lightening when their path finally leveled out somewhat. It was still hard going, but Darric no longer felt as if they were climbing more than walking. The mountain's peak rose on their left, its snow-covered heights gleaming in the moonlight. But Darric soon lost sight of it as their path plunged into a tree-choked ravine.

Hweilan slowed, and by the way she constantly looked around, Darric could see she was agitated.

He caught up to her and whispered, "What is it?"

"Listen."

Everyone stopped. At first Darric could hear nothing beyond the sound of the men's labored breathing. Then he caught it, just on the very edge of his hearing—a plaintive *yip-yip*.

Darric could tell by the way Mandan's posture had stiffened and he looked at the woods with widened eyes that he had heard it too—probably better than any of them.

"What?" said Jaden.

"The wolf," said Mandan.

"Uncle," said Hweilan.

"The wolf?" said Valsun. "What . . . ?"

Hweilan unhitched the bone mask from where it rode on her belt. She fitted it to her face, and for just an instant, Darric thought he saw a tiny sparkle of green play along the edges of the runes burned into it. Hweilan's eyes, seen through the bone, seemed suddenly feral.

"What?" said Darric, at the same time he heard Jaden mutter, "Oh, this can't be good."

She took the bow off her back, strung it, and fitted an arrow to the string. "Your men know how to use those weapons?" she said.

Darric nodded. "Yes."

"Then look like it."

"You mean—?"

"I mean," she said, raising her voice just enough for everyone to hear, "get a weapon in your hand. And stay by me. This place is no good."

With that, she turned and set off at a jog.

"No good?" said Jaden, taking off after her. "No good for what?"

Mandan hefted his club and slapped it into his other hand. "What do you think?"

• • ⊛ • •

What started as a jog soon fell into a run, and despite the invigorating *kanishta* root, the men in their heavy clothes and mail struggled to keep up. The sky was growing brighter all the time, but gloom still ruled under the trees, and Darric often lost sight of Hweilan. But he kept his men on the path and urged them on until catching sight of her again.

The path ran into a cliff face, its bottom strewn with house-sized boulders and choked with thick brush. The pines ran right up against it, standing amidst the boulders, their branches tickling the cliffside. To their right, brush clogged a steep slope for a few dozen paces before falling away to nothingness, and on their left, the forest continued up the slope of the mountain. Darric caught sight of the peak between the boughs.

Darric stopped and looked around as the others gathered behind him. There was no sign of Hweilan.

Jaden bent over, hands on knees. He was breathing so hard that he accidentally spat out the gobby mess of *kanishta* root. He cursed, picked it up, and after wiping off the worst of the dirt and grit, plopped it back into his mouth.

"Where's . . . our lady . . . friend . . . got off . . . to?" he said between gasps.

Mandan was breathing heavily as well, but he stood straight, his head held back, his nostrils flaring as he took deep drafts of the breeze off the mountain. "We have bigger problems."

Jaden said, "What?"

"I smell—"

And then a gale hit them. Darric heard the howl of it coming down the mountain an instant before it struck, snapping branches from trees and raising a wave of pine needles off the ground that swept over them, stinging exposed skin and forcing Darric to close his eyes. His cloak caught the wind like a sail, and he had to fight to keep his feet. That's when he heard them.

Voices in the wind—hoots and cries, and mixed with it all a gleeful cackling. Shielding his eyes with one hand, Darric squinted against the cloud of pine needles and grit. A dozen or more figures were charging up the path behind them. Ugly scraps of black-iron armor covered clothes made of hide and pelts. The bits of hair that protruded from their helmets was so coarse and thick that it seemed more like fur, and their narrow eyes drank in every bit of dim dawnlight and cast it back, like a dog's eyes. Most of the figures held iron-shod spears more than twice the height of their wielders. Hobgoblins. Bigger and meaner than their goblin cousins, Darric knew that even with Mandan in full rage they'd stand no chance against so many.

"Run!" Mandan roared, and pushed Darric up the path.

"Move-move-move!" Darric said, and got the men moving, Mandan bringing up the rear. If they could make it to the cliff, at least they could keep their backs against the rock and fight only on one front.

The wind came back around again, slapping Darric's cloak against his legs. He stumbled, but Mandan caught him and kept him going.

Valsun, several paces ahead, was passing between two boulders when Darric saw it—something moving up from the ground. His first thought was it was a snake, but then he saw—

"Valsun!"

But it was too late. Running full speed, Valsun's shins struck the tight cord, and he went down. From behind the boulders, two hobgoblins leaped over the path, crossing in midair and pulling the rope in a tight loop. Valsun managed to shake one leg free before the cord tightened, but his right boot caught. The hobgoblins didn't even spare the others a glance. They turned and ran, dragging Valsun behind them.

Enemies behind and before, Jaden stood dumbstruck.

"Move, you fool!" Darric said as he passed Jaden. He rounded the largest of the boulders where Valsun had disappeared, then he too skidded to a stop.

Valsun lay on his back against another boulder, his sword on the ground well out of reach, his two captors standing over him, the points of their swords at his throat. But in front of Darric was the biggest goblin he had ever seen—had ever heard of. He had all the typical goblin features—coarse, bristly hair, pointed ears that stood out from its head, a scarce bump of a nose between two slit eyes; he wore only rudimentary clothing—but he was easily eight feet tall, most of it muscle. Arms wide, the monster lunged.

Darric ducked and swiped with his sword. He didn't put full force into the blow, fearing Jaden or Mandan might be coming up behind him, and the blade only sliced a narrow gash along the back of the creature's helmet-sized hand.

And then the hobgoblins were all around—rising from behind boulders, jumping down from thick boughs where they'd been hiding. Those charging up the path hadn't been attacking. They'd been driving Darric and his men into the real attack, and it had worked perfectly.

The giant goblin grinned and made another quick swipe at Darric. Again Darric struck, but the monster was ready for it this time and pulled away laughing.

Behind him, Mandan roared and Darric could hear his club cutting through the air. Jaden was screaming. Darric kept the point of his blade raised at the monster as he turned sideways and risked a quick glance. Mandan stood between the two boulders where Valsun tripped. Swinging his club, he was holding back a half-dozen goblins. One of them lunged with a spear and the club struck, shattering the shaft and sending its wielder reeling back.

Beyond Mandan, Jaden lay on his belly, a cackling hobgoblin straddling his legs and beating him with a cudgel while two others tried to pry the cleaverlike sword from his grip.

That quick glance cost Darric his advantage. He felt something strike his knee hard, then pull. Turning back around, Darric planted both feet and looked down. One of the hobgoblins had come in with a long pole, a wide, blunt crook on one end, and he had Darric's leg quite nicely hooked.

The hobgoblin pulled, and Darric stumbled. He struck at the pole with his sword, but the shaft was thick ash wood. He put a good nick in it, but nothing more. He used his free hand to grab the loop of the hook and pull. With such poor leverage, he knew he'd never pull it off, but if he could just hold it steady long enough to step out—

A tight grip closed over his sword arm. The huge goblin had his sword arm in one bony fist. The monster grinned and yanked. Darric lost his footing and went down. The hook of the pole slid up his waist and caught in his belt. But he kept the grip on his sword. Screaming, Darric thrashed and kicked, but the monster's grip only tightened.

"Hoy!" a voice called, and Darric looked up into the face of a hobgoblin, who had stepped forward. He held a curved sword but seemed in no rush to use it. "Drop that steel or Grunter here'll snap your arm like twig."

The huge goblin grunted as if to confirm his name, then gave a tug and a twist as if to drive the point home.

Darric thrashed harder. He managed to bring one foot around and drive the toe of his boot into Grunter's knee. It was like kicking an oak.

Grunter smiled, revealing tusk-yellow teeth. "Tickles," he said, and grunted again.

The hobgoblin with the sword shrugged and said, "Break it."

Grunter grabbed Darric's arm with his other fist, both tightened—

"Well done! That will be *quite* enough!"

The voice spoke elegantly accented Damaran, and the wind twisting through the field of boulders seemed to carry it. It was firm, confident, but no shout, though it carried to every ear.

The wind died, and a strange silence settled on the scene. Grunter's grip on Darric's arm did not lessen, but neither did it move. Darric had no doubt the brute could do just what the other had claimed—snap his arm like a twig. He risked another glance at his comrades. Valsun's position had not improved. Jaden was weaponless, had two grinning hobgoblins on his back and one standing on each arm. Mandan still held his club in one hand. The shattered remains of one of the hookpoles dangled from his waist, and two cords of braided leather were tangled around his left arm—the other ends held tight by four hobgoblins. Darric could see their wide yellow eyes through the slits in their helmets. They were obviously torn between trying to pull Mandan over and the thought of pulling him *too* close. Just behind them, another hobgoblin leaned against a rock, moaning and cradling his shattered forearm.

"Everyone just *calm down*."

A figure emerged from the forest—taller than every person gathered except for Mandan and Grunter, but he moved with the grace of a dancer. A long cloak and deep cowl hid his features. He stopped just behind the nearest goblin.

The cowl faced Darric. The voice had a mocking tone that seemed altogether at odds with the present situation. "Quite enough excitement for so early in the morning, don't you think?"

Darric goggled, no idea what to say. But he did take the opportunity to regain his feet and wrench the hookpole away. Grunter's grip tightened slightly, causing Darric to wince. He still held his sword, but he could no longer feel the hand gripping it.

"Easy there, Grunter," said the cloaked man. "We're just talking. For the moment."

"Who are you and what is the meaning of this?" Darric asked him.

"Where is she?"

Darric blinked, taken aback by the question, then said, "Where is who?"

A tense silence followed, and Darric could feel a heavy gaze from inside the cowl weighing him. "Her pet has been trailing my friends for miles," the man said. "I know she is nearby."

"Then you know more than I," said Darric. "On my father's name, I do not know where she is."

"Seeing as how I don't know your father, that oath holds little weight for me."

Mandan growled and yanked on the cords tangling his left arm. Those holding it stumbled but kept their feet. Standing atop the boulder in front of Mandan, a hobgoblin loosed his bowstring, and an instant later Mandan's club sprouted an arrow.

"Calm yourself," said the man.

Mandan kept his place, but Darric saw his hair bristling and the muscles in his face had tensed so much that his skin looked like a tightly bound drum. If this went much further, there'd be no controlling him. Keeping Mandan in check when he was afraid was hard enough. But when he went beyond fear and into a true rage . . .

The cloaked man chuckled, then said, "If I wanted to kill you, you'd be dead already. Truth be told, I have no interest in any of you. But I am most eager to speak to the lady."

"And who are you?"

"I'll ask only once more," the man said. "Then I'm going to tell Grunter there to snap your arm. Urdu and Oluk over there will start poking holes in the old man. The little one who makes so much noise they'll save for later fun. Your big and bristly friend will start sprouting arrows, and then . . . well, and after that, do you really care?" All mockery left the man's tone. His voice went hard and solemn, and he said, "Where is she?"

"I told you I don't know."

A long silence. Darric and Mandan exchanged a glance.

"Would you tell me if you did?" said the cloaked man.

Darric told the truth. "No."

"Very well," the man said, his voice all false regret. Then he raised it to a shout. "Razor Heart! Have your—"

"*Stop!*"

Everyone looked up.

The cliff was not an unbroken face. Ledges and cracks riddled its side where years of ice and tenacious roots had broken through the rock. A few dozen feet over them, two figures emerged on the ledge, one moving very stiffly.

The foremost was a hobgoblin, his helmet gone, blood leaking from his mouth, his left eye swollen shut. His hands were unbound, empty, and he held both out. Even from the distance, Darric could see they were trembling. Standing behind him, another figure held a fistful of the hobgoblin's hair in one hand and a naked blade under his throat. As she stepped into the growing light, Darric recognized the fearsome bone mask.

She called down to the cloaked man, "This fellow says he's your second, and war chief of the Razor Heart clan. If your war chief is this easy, the rest of you shouldn't be much of a problem. Let these four idiots go. I'll release your chief and you can all skulk off."

The cloaked man was staring up at her, obviously considering. He shrugged and said, "I don't skulk. You kill the chief and your friends will join him."

"They aren't my friends," said Hweilan.

And then Darric heard the growling. Everyone else did too, for every eye turned to look behind the cloaked man. The wolf stood only a few paces beyond the hem of his cloak, its hackles raised and trembling, its black lips pulled back over fangs longer than arrowheads.

"You'll join them as well," Hweilan told the cloaked man. "You can all sit on the rim of the Abyss and argue over whose fault it is while I go off to breakfast."

The man looked back up at Hweilan, then faced his men. "Oh bells of the Hells, this isn't going how I planned at all. Let them go."

The hobgoblins cried out in protest.

"Oh, calm down the lot of you. They aren't going anywhere. Hweilan would never leave an old friend behind. Besides, she's deep in debt to me."

"And who are you?" she called down.

The man lowered his cowl and pushed his cloak back over his shoulders. He held no weapon that Darric could see. His armor was very fine—finer than any Darric had ever seen, in fact—a breastplate, spaulders, and tassets made of many layers of fitted metal, that still managed a silvery sheen despite the layer of dust. He wore no gloves against the cold, and even his clothes seemed fitted more for elegance than warmth. He wore no helmet, and his long black hair was an unkempt mess.

His features would have had an almost feminine beauty if not for his strong chin, but there was something disconcerting in the gaze. And then Darric saw it. His eyes had no pupils. An eladrin. Why in the unholy Hells was an eladrin running with a band of mountain goblins?

"My name is Menduarthis," he said for all to hear. Then he pointed up at Hweilan. "And you still owe me a kiss."

CHAPTER THIRTY

"Menduarthis," said Hweilan, followed by something in a language Darric could not understand. But he knew a curse when he heard one, and this one sounded impressively foul. The wolf snapped and growled even louder.

"Is that any way to greet an old friend?" said Menduarthis.

Most of the tension had one out of Hweilan's stance, but she still hadn't released the hobgoblin chief. "How . . . how . . . ?"

"Articulate as always, my little flower," said Menduarthis. "Why don't you come down?"

Hweilan glanced at Darric and each of his men. Menduarthis caught it.

"As long as they behave themselves, they have nothing to fear from us." Menduarthis looked to Darric. "You and your men *will* behave, won't you?"

Darric glared at him.

"Come now," said Menduarthis. "Things are finally calming down. You don't want to get everyone all riled up again, do you?"

"I have no idea what's going on," said Darric.

"That much is obvious," said Menduarthis. "I have your word?"

Darric looked to Valsun, who looked down at the steel tickling his throat. He nodded very carefully.

"Jaden?" Darric called.

"Tell me how I'm *not* behaving now?" Jaden called. His voice was muffled because his face was smashed into the dirt, a hobgoblin's hand pressing down on the back of his head. "I behave any more and I'll be digging with my teeth!"

"Mandan?"

Mandan didn't even look at Darric. He snarled at Menduarthis.

"Aren't you quite finished with this nonsense?" said Menduarthis. His lips curled in a smile, but his gaze had gone cold.

Mandan roared and gave a sudden, hard yank on the ropes tangling his left arm. Caught off guard, the hobgoblins holding the ropes flew off their feet. One at least had the good sense to let go. But the other two held on. Mandan turned his club. The knobby end of it connected with the face of a goblin's helmet with a loud *clunk* and he drove his boot into the chest of the other, sending him flying backward. Both went down, the former moaning and clutching his head, the latter kicking and struggling to breathe.

But Mandan merely stood straight and wriggled his left arm until the ropes fell away.

"*Now* I'm finished," he said.

A few of the hobgoblins laughed at that.

Menduarthis spread his arms. "See? All friends now?"

Hweilan released her grip on the chief, who fell to his hands and knees and sighed with relief.

Menduarthis turned to the wolf, causing it to growl anew. "Oh, I know who you are," said Menduarthis. "Don't make me twirl my fingers."

• • ◉ • •

Hweilan and the chief came down together. Blood still stained his chin and cheek, but he had regained his composure, and the blood only served to give him a more savage look. Hweilan had bow in hand, but her arrows still rode in her quiver. Watching her . . . Darric stared. She moved with the grace of a panther. Of the fiery little castle girl Darric remembered, nothing remained. Here they were surrounded by mountain hobgoblins, not a one of them without a weapon, led by some sort of eladrin sorcerer, and she showed not a hint of fear.

She stopped several paces from Menduarthis, then said, "What are you doing here?"

Menduarthis raised on eyebrow. "How good to see you again, Menduarthis. Thank you so much for saving my life, Menduarthis. So sorry for leaving you for dead, Menduarthis. How have you been, Menduarthis?" Both eyebrows went up. "No?"

"You and your new friends have been following us for miles. Why?"

"Well, I *did* risk my life for you. Gave up quite a prominent position in a powerful queen's court. For you. Even risked my life fighting that whatever it was. For you. You owe me."

"I *owe* you?"

"Most certainly, little flower."

She watched him a moment. Though she was at least two heads shorter than him, she still managed somehow to look down on him. "And what do I owe you?"

Menduarthis smiled. "I told you already. A kiss."

She watched him, saying nothing. Several of the hobgoblins chuckled.

" 'Get me to Lendri,' you said, 'then help us to get out again, and afterward, I will kiss you.' Your words. And I seem to remember stipulating not one of those how-good-to-see-you-big-brother pecks on the cheek. A *real* kiss. Right here. Right now."

"And then . . . ?"

Menduarthis shrugged. "I held up my end of the bargain. Time for you to pay up. And then we're even."

"Very well."

"*What?*" The word escaped Darric before he could stop it. All eyes turned to him.

She took off the bone mask and hitched it to her belt. But her face was no less a mask, completely devoid of any emotion. "What's the harm in it?"

"Oh, sod it!" Jaden called. "If it'll get these brutes off me, *I'll* kiss him!"

Menduarthis turned to look where the hobgoblins still held Jaden facedown in the dirt. "Get off the loud fellow. He's spoiling my moment." Then he looked to Darric. "And you keep quiet. This doesn't concern you."

One of the hobgoblins tousled Jaden's hair, then he and his companion got off. Jaden pushed up and brushed the worst of the dirt off his clothes and wiped it from his lips.

"Hweilan," said Darric, "you can't be serious."

"Urdu," Menduarthis called, "if that one speaks again, poke a hole in the old man's cheek."

The wolf, still crouched a few paces behind Menduarthis, growled.

"Oh, stop this," said Hweilan, "the lot of you."

She stepped forward and grabbed the back of Menduarthis's head with her free hand, pulled him down to her, and kissed him, long and hard. The man was so caught by surprise that for a moment he simply stood there, wide-eyed and stiff-lipped. But then he closed his eyes and returned the kiss.

The hobgoblins cheered, and Darric felt his face grow hot.

Hweilan pulled away, took one step back, and said in a husky voice, "How was that."

Menduarthis swallowed and blinked. "That was . . . quite nice."

"We're even?"

"We are."

Hweilan punched him. She moved so fast that her arm was only a blur of motion. Her gloved fist struck Menduarthis's face with a *crack* that spun him halfway around before he hit the ground.

The hobgoblins cheered even louder, a few of them even hopping up and down like apes and banging sword or spear on shields.

Menduarthis sat up, rubbing his cheek, and glared up at Hweilan.

"Oh, Menduarthis," said the war chief, "I like this one!"

• • ◉ • •

The hobgoblins led them farther up into the mountains. After returning weapons to Valsun and Jaden, the hobgoblins mostly ignored them, sparing them only an occasional glance just shy of contempt, like tolerating two stray dogs whom they have decided to feed dinner scraps.

Grunter patted Darric's arm with surprising gentleness and smiled. His yellow teeth were as big as teacups. "Not broken," he said. "You good."

But Mandan the hobgoblins treated like a long-lost relative finally come to visit, clapping him on the back, laughing, and pushing a sloshing skin into his hands.

He scowled in return. "I don't understand."

"You fought well," Menduarthis said. He had stopped rubbing his cheek, but his jaw and the left side of his face were already puffy and beginning to bruise. "You held your own and did not surrender. A true warrior. They like you."

Mandan's scowl deepened.

Menduarthis looked at the skin. "You'll insult them if you refuse."

The hobgoblins watched expectantly. Mandan looked to Hweilan, who merely shrugged.

"Oh, Hells, I'll take a drink if he won't," said Jaden, and stepped forward.

But the point of a hobgoblin's dagger at his stomach stopped him. "You get your own drink, *Klarsuf*."

Jaden backed away from the steel. "Klar what?"

"*Klarsuf*," said Hweilan. "He's naming you in Goblin. Means 'dirt mouth.'"

"He's saying I have a dirty mouth? What's he? My mother?"

Menduarthis answered, "He's saying in the fight that you ended up on your face in the dirt. You can get your own drink."

All eyes returned to Mandan. He looked down at the skin in his hand. "So this is their way of apologizing?"

The hobgoblins laughed.

"More of a salute," said Menduarthis. "They aren't sorry for the fight. They *enjoyed* the fight. It's more their way of saying, 'Well done.' "

Mandan looked down on the nearest hobgoblin. "Even you?"

The hobgoblin had taken off his helmet. He smiled up at Mandan, even as he rubbed his chest. "Aye," he said. "Good kick." He nodded at the skin. "Drink."

Mandan handed his club to the hobgoblin so that he could untie the knot in the skin. He spat the *kanishta* root into one palm then upended the skin into his mouth. Lowering it, he winced and swallowed.

"Gah! That's . . . gah!"

The hobgoblins roared with laughter. The one whom Mandan had kicked in the chest took the skin and gulped from it. "Puts hair on your ears," he said.

And with that, they set off, going back the way they had come for a quarter mile or so, then taking a smaller side trail up into the heights.

"So tell me," Menduarthis said to Hweilan. "That was your first kiss, wasn't it?"

She scowled. "No."

Menduarthis spared Darric a glance, then gave Hweilan a beaming smile. "I mean your first *real* kiss, with a real man. Not some boy behind the tapestries after the feast?"

Hweilan's scowl deepened, and a blush crawled up her neck and into her face. "Go away, Menduarthis."

He laughed, gave Darric a cruel wink, then strode ahead to confer with his hobgoblin war chief.

• • • • •

Walking through the woods, Darric managed to stay next to Hweilan, whom the hobgoblins seemed to be giving a wide berth. Menduarthis was the only one of their company who spoke with her, but he had not come back, and Darric couldn't see him at all.

Darric looked around at the hobgoblins and asked Hweilan, "I'm a little confused. Are we captives or guests?"

A hobgoblin winding through the trees to their left said, "For Maaqua to decide."

Hweilan looked sideways at Darric. "Hobgoblins have sharp ears."

Darric knew of Maaqua. Reputed to be a sorceress of some repute, she led the Razor Heart clan, who had negotiated with King Yarin and been granted the right to "tax" the Gap. Never mind the fact that Yarin didn't exactly control the Gap, so he didn't really have the right to grant anything. The treaty meant, essentially, that Damarans could pass the Gap as long as they paid the Razor Heart. And if the Razor Heart happened upon any of Yarin's enemies . . . well, then it most likely became a matter of how much they could pay. The fact that Darric and his men were Damarans might work in their favor.

But if this Maaqua knew enough, she might know that Darric's House was not exactly high in Yarin's esteem.

"For Maaqua to decide?" said Darric. "What does that mean?"

"It means you should have stayed home," said Hweilan.

• • ⓝ • •

Highwatch

Argalath was still trembling when he entered the chamber. Vazhad supported him on one side, one of his acolytes on the other. The stone chamber, deep in the mountain beneath Highwatch, had been darkened to accommodate their master. Only one guttering candle in the middle of the floor shed its flickering glow through the room.

Lord Guric stood along the wall, staring at nothing. But when Argalath entered the room, a tiny tremor passed through him, a slight ripple of the skin, and his gaze fixed on his master.

"Zadraelek?" he said.

"She found him," said Argalath, his voice barely above a whisper. His mind had still been linked with Zadraelek when the arrow hit him. It had taken all of Jagun Ghen's will to sever that link before he was trapped along with his brother.

"He is . . . ?"

"Yes."

Vazhad released his master long enough to unfold the small camp chair he'd been carrying, then set his master in it.

When Argalath was settled, he sighed with weariness, then looked up at his acolyte and said, "Bring her."

The acolyte bowed and ran back the way they had come.

"What are you planning to do?" said Guric.

"The girl is in Maaqua's territory," said Argalath. "We will send the surprise I have prepared for her."

"And what makes you think the old crone will help?"

"We don't need her help," said Argalath. "She just needs to stay out of the way."

He looked down at the chamber floor. The dim light of the candle caught in the symbols and circle painted on the floor.

"The portal is ready," said Guric.

Chapter Thirty-One

The Razor Heart led them all the rest of that day and well into the night until they came to the hobgoblin's fortress. Much like Highwatch, most of it had not been built so much as carved out of the mountain itself. From a distance, Hweilan suspected one would not even know there was a fortress there at all, mistaking the watchtowers for crags and caves. Maaqua met them in what passed for a courtyard before the fortress's main gate.

As the granddaughter of the High Warden of Highwatch, part of Hweilan's education had been learning every tribe, faction, and leader of the mountain clans. Maaqua was both less and more than Hweilan expected. She didn't look old. She looked *ancient*. "Older than old dust's grandmother," Scith would've said. Even her wrinkles had wrinkles. She was small for a hobgoblin, and made smaller still by her hunched posture. She leaned heavily upon a gnarled staff, and Hweilan recognized at once her people's kinship with Gleed. Her reddish skin hung loose off her bones, and what little hair remained wafted like stray cobwebs on the breeze.

But the old crone watched them with bright, alert eyes, and Hweilan could feel power radiating off Maaqua like waves of heat from an open oven. Her very bones seemed to thrum with it.

Her clothes and robes were mostly of hide and wool. Hweilan had seen finer on peasants in Kistrad. But Maaqua wore a gold circlet on her brow. Three thornlike barbs rose from it, and two clasped around each temple. Three rubies, only slightly dimmer than Maaqua's eyes, sat in the crown underneath the middle barb.

Maaqua had supposedly once been a disciple of some half-demon whose own ambitions had caused her to get sucked into some dark level of the Abyss. Or so the tales said. True or not, Maaqua led one of the most powerful tribes of the Giantspires, and both the lords of Damara and chieftains of Narfell treated her with respect—or avoided her altogether.

Behind her stood the largest hobgoblin Hweilan had ever seen. Not a bugbear like the one they called Grunter, but a true hobgoblin. He could have easily stared Mandan eye-to-eye. Hard muscle wrapped his frame. He wore no armor—Hweilan suspected he didn't need any, for he had the cold, hard look of a seasoned warrior. During some of her first combat lessons as a child, the weapons master at Highwatch had told her, "If your enemy has the chance to hit back, you're doing something wrong." Advice Ashiin would've appreciated. This goblin looked as if he wore no armor because no enemy ever survived long enough to get close to him. The weapon on which he leaned only deepened this impression. His hands rested on the pommel of a black-iron sword, the blade of which was easily four feet long. Much like her own blades, the sword was decorated with many etchings, but instead of runes, they were in the form of dead or dying demons, and the pommel and guard of the sword itself had been crafted to look as if some demon champion lay impaled upon the blade.

The hobgoblins who had escorted them fanned out into a ring, surrounding them, leaving Hweilan, the wolf, the Damarans, Menduarthis, and the war chief at the center, just before Maaqua and her champion.

Menduarthis stepped forward and bowed. "Queen Maaqua, I present Hweilan of Highwatch... and companions."

"Of Highwatch?" said Maaqua. Her voice struck Hweilan. She'd expected a gravelly croak, something like a more feminine version of Gleed. Or perhaps the broken rasp of any old woman. But Maaqua's voice was clear and strong, and her words flawless Damaran, with scarcely an accent at all. "How recently of Highwatch?"

"I was born there," said Hweilan.

"Ahh," said Maaqua. Her voice sounded pleased, but her eyes narrowed as she studied Hweilan. "Then truly 'of Highwatch.' Perhaps one of the last living able to make that claim. The last scion of a mighty House in our presence. We are honored."

Maaqua leaned lower on her staff in a sort of bow. The champion behind her didn't move in the slightest.

"And your companions?" said Maaqua.

"Men of Damara," said Hweilan. "They came to rescue me."

"And you rescued them, eh?" Maaqua threw back her head and laughed. "Usual behavior of men. Think we need their help, but in the end, all men need a woman to undo their tangles."

Hweilan looked sidelong at Darric, who was doing his best not to scowl.

"And Menduarthis?" said Maaqua.

"We've met," said Hweilan.

Menduarthis made no attempt to conceal his pleased smile.

"Hweilan of Highwatch," said Maaqua, raising her voice for all to hear. "That is a name much spoken in the mountains of late. Word is spreading."

"Is that so?"

"It is," said Maaqua. "Those now *in* Highwatch are most eager to know of the last one *of* Highwatch."

He knows I'm back, thought Hweilan. In the Feywild, she had been protected from Jagun Ghen's attention. Hweilan could sense the presence of Jagun Ghen's minions when they were nearby, and she knew that sense ran both ways. She could sense nothing now, meaning there were none nearby. But Jagun Ghen was an ancient being, beyond her understanding. Could he sense her whereabouts over the long miles?

"An emissary came to me not three tendays ago," said Maaqua. "A Creel." She spat, and Hweilan heard many other of the surrounding hobgoblins doing the same. "At least in form. But this one slew our sentries with no more difficulty than wrenching the head off a sparrow. He stood before me, no heart beating in his chest, no blood flowing in his veins, taking in breath only to speak, and told me that the new Lord of Highwatch desires only peace with his mountain neighbors. Desires nothing more. Nothing except one thing."

"Me," said Hweilan.

"She is a smart one, Menduarthis," said Maaqua, "though not nearly so lovely as you said."

"And what did this emissary promise you in return?" said Hweilan.

"In return? Nothing. Masters like this one . . . reward is not in their nature. I should know. But he did promise that anyone who aided you in any way could expect future visits from the Lord of Highwatch. How did he put it?"

"A feast without niceties," said Menduarthis.

"Yes. Considering that he'd eaten an impressive amount of one our sentries and healed the wounds we'd given him, his words held a certain weight."

Darric stepped in front of Hweilan. "Surely one as powerful as Maaqua does not fear such threats."

Maaqua laughed. "See. There he goes again. Getting himself in a tangle. Stand back and shut your mouth, little boy. Your betters are talking."

Darric's face flushed and he opened his mouth to retort, but Valsun stepped forward and urged him back. "Easy, my lord," he whispered. "We must tread carefully here."

"Then why bring me here?" said Hweilan. "If you mean to turn me over to them, why not drag me straight to Highwatch?"

"See!" said Maaqua. "This one understands. She gets right to the point without all the false flattery."

Darric's flush deepened.

"You ask a good question," said Maaqua. "I have two reasons. First—and very much the lesser of the two—Menduarthis here speaks most highly of you. And even though the bastard is a constant itch on my rump, he has proved himself useful of late. His words to me are not without weight. Secondly—and here we get to the main point—Highwatch has become . . . a problem."

Hweilan snorted. "For you? Highwatch has been a problem for three generations."

The champion behind Maaqua scowled, but the goblin queen herself laughed. "True! Your people have often reminded mine not to reach beyond our grasp. And in turn we have allowed them the skies and steppe, so long as they remembered who owns the mountains. It was a . . . relationship of mutual benefit. Yes?"

Hweilan shrugged.

"But this new Lord of Highwatch . . . I hear things. Creel swarm the foothills like maggots on a nine-day corpse. They make for good sport. But other things now haunt the lands around Highwatch—and of late some of those things have begun creeping into the mountains. *My* mountains!"

"And—thus far," said Menduarthis, "we have been unable to—shall we say?—deal with the problem."

"Much as it pains me to admit it," said Maaqua, "your friend here speaks the truth. These . . . things have been preying on my people. Wiping out entire hunting parties. Rhan here"—Maaqua used her chin to point at the massive hobgoblin behind her—"managed to kill one of them. But we only have one Rhan."

"He didn't kill it," said Hweilan.

"Eh?"

"Your champion might have killed the body the thing wore, but the demon inside him, the true threat, *that* survived. And it will remember you."

Rhan pulled his lips back, revealing his tusks and yellow teeth, and snarled.

"I'd listen to her if I were you," said Menduarthis. "She knows more than her pretty face suggests. Just because you're the biggest hulk with the pointiest stick in the village doesn't mean you're immortal."

Rhan swept his black sword up in one swift motion and stepped toward Menduarthis.

"Rhan!" Maaqua said, and the champion stopped.

Menduarthis wiggled his fingers at Rhan, and a sudden breeze swept through the valley, spraying the hobgoblin champion in a cloud of dust. Another puff of wind swept it away. Menduarthis blew the champion a kiss, followed by a much less polite hand gesture.

"*Boys*!" Maaqua said. "You will *both* be silent. You can fiddle your own foolishness later when you aren't wasting my time."

Rhan growled and stepped back into his place.

"Now," said Maaqua, resuming her normal voice, "as I was saying, we have not yet—*yet*!—found an effective way to deal with these . . . things. I can't lose forty warriors for every one we take down—especially if you are right and the thing isn't truly dead."

"I am right," said Hweilan.

Maaqua gripped her staff in both hands and leaned forward, studying Hweilan through narrowed eyes. She stared a long time, then closed her eyes and inhaled.

She opened her eyes and smiled, "The Hunter has marked you."

"I am his Hand."

A murmur went through the onlooking hobgoblins. Even Rhan tore his gaze away from Menduarthis to stare at Hweilan, and he looked on her with something almost approaching admiration. The Damarans only looked confused.

"This explains much," said Maaqua. "Twelve days past, our scouts heard rumor of one of these things in our territory. Rhan led our strongest warriors to hunt and kill it. But all they found were corpses. On the way back, they found more. Five days ago . . . more rumor, followed by more corpses. It seems that something—or some*one*—is hunting the hunters."

"And doing a damned fine job of it," said Menduarthis.

"You know what these things are," Maaqua said to Hweilan, "and you know how to kill them."

"Yes."

"And how is that?"

"You let me go."

Maaqua started at that. "Eh?"

"You heard me."

"You misunderstood me," said Maaqua, a cold edge of steel in her voice. "I was asking how *we* might kill these things."

"*You* can't," said Hweilan. "*I* can. You want them dead? Then get out of my way."

Maaqua scowled, then went very still. "And then?"

"And then when I'm done, I'll tell Nendawen what a helpful little goblin you were."

Every hobgoblin in the valley drew a weapon. Rhan roared and raised his sword again. Uncle stepped forward next to Hweilan, black lips pulled back over his fangs and every hair on his body standing on end. The Damarans put their hands to weapons and stepped away from each other to give themselves room to draw and swing. Menduarthis stepped between Hweilan and Maaqua, hands raised between them, his mouth opening to say something he shouldn't. All this happened in an instant. In all the valley, Hweilan and Maaqua were the only two who didn't move.

"*Be! STILL!*" Maaqua roared, her voice echoing like thunder off the surrounding cliffs. She stood straight, no longer the wizened crone. Everyone obeyed. "The next one who so much as coughs without my leave will earn my most serious displeasure!"

The hobgoblins lowered their weapons, though they did not put them away. Jaden let out a very loud sigh, and Menduarthis lowered his hands and stepped back beside Hweilan.

Maaqua leaned on her staff again, then said, "Tell me. How is Gleed?"

Hweilan blinked and took an involuntary step back. "What?"

Maaqua chuckled. "See? Not half as smart as you think you are, girl."

"You know Gleed?"

Behind her, Hweilan heard Jaden whisper, "Who in the unholy Hells is Gleed?"

"It might surprise you to know," said Maaqua, "that I was not always the wise old husk you see before you. Nor was Gleed always content to putter around his little lake. There was a time—more than a few times, truth be told—that Gleed made Maaqua's toes tingle and beg for more."

Menduarthis gasped and his eyes went wide. He leaned in slightly to Hweilan and muttered, "That image is going to cause a few sleepless nights."

"I hold the Master of the Hunt in the highest respect," said Maaqua. "But don't think for a moment that means I'll tolerate rudeness from one such as you."

Hweilan took a careful breath to regain her composure, then said, "My apologies. Gleed is . . . well as ever."

"I feared as much," said Maaqua. "Ah, well. Now, back to—"

Maaqua flinched, as if something had stung her. And then Hweilan felt it too—that familiar pounding at the base of her skull. It didn't begin with a slow pulse and build as it usually did. It hit so fast that Hweilan thought she felt her back teeth pulsing.

The air a few paces to one side of Maaqua swirled in a miniature cyclone, gathering dust and grit—and something else, something darker—as it spun, taking shape. The wind burst outward like a wave. At its source stood a figure dressed in once-fine clothes gone ragged and caked with filth. It lunged, fast and hard as a tundra tiger, knocking both Rhan and Maaqua to the ground and then tackling Menduarthis.

Hweilan took three loping steps back, her hand already grasping an arrow and laying it across the bow. She fitted nock to string, raised the bow, and pulled the feathers to the corner of her eye. The runes in her bow blazed with green fire.

The figure stood, holding one arm across Menduarthis's chest, the other wrapped around his face.

Hweilan spoke the words of power, and aimed the point of her arrow. Looking beyond it, she got her first good look at the thing's face.

The arrowhead shook and faltered, and Hweilan gasped.

"Mother?"

CHAPTER THIRTY-TWO

EVERY HOBGOBLIN WARRIOR IN THE VALLEY SURGED forward, Rhan the closest of them all, but again, Maaqua's voice stopped them.

"Be still!" the goblin queen said as she regained her feet and stood on guard behind her raised staff. The gold crown hung slightly askew on her head, but a hot fire blazed in the rubies there. "Be still, all of you, I say!"

Merah looked at Hweilan from over Menduarthis's shoulder. "Well met, girl," it said, its voice rough and guttural. "We didn't expect you here so soon. Most fortunate for us both. Half a moment. You need to see something."

Hweilan's hand steadied. The voice had done it. Despite the body it wore, this was not her mother. She fixed the point of her arrow on the thing's right eye.

"I can put this arrow right through him and still get you," Hweilan said.

"I'd rather you didn't, please!" said Menduarthis.

"Silence!" the thing said, and tightened its hand over Menduarthis's jaw to force the point. But then it lowered him a little, and again Merah's face peeked over his shoulder. All the hardness, the muscles tight and taut as harp strings, was gone. The hunger was gone from the eyes, and Merah simply looked tired. No, she looked bone weary.

"H-Hweilan? Is . . . that you? I can't . . . can't see. I've been in the dark so long, Hweilan."

Hweilan forced her left hand to grip the bow and the three fingers of her right hand to maintain the tension on the bowstring. Her left arm suddenly felt as heavy as an anvil, and the effort of keeping it up made a small mewling sound escape her throat.

"Is that you, Hweilan?" Her mother looked at her and blinked, again and again, as if trying to clear dust from her eyes. "Say something. Please . . ."

Hweilan took a deep breath, swallowed, and said, "Let him go."

"Let . . . ?" She glanced down at the eladrin in her arms, and her entire body trembled. "Help! Help me, Hweilan! It's still in here with m—!" And then every muscle in Merah's body tightened, hard as old oak, her skin seemed to tighten over her frame, and her hair stood on end. The hands tightened around Menduarthis, and he breathed in a hiss of pain.

"Stop!" said Hweilan.

The thing's voice answered, "She's still in here with me, girl. Your mother. She's screaming now. Screaming for you."

"Stop it!"

"Put that bow down and we'll talk."

Behind Merah, Rhan took a careful step forward. At first, Hweilan thought the images carved into his sword had come to life, but then she saw that tiny flecks of lightning, each spark black as onyx, were playing up and down the blade.

"Your new friend moves another step," the thing said, "and I'll kill this one."

"Rhan, stop!" Maaqua said. "Let this play out."

"Kill him and I'll kill you," Hweilan said.

"You'd kill your own mother?"

"My mother is already dead," Hweilan said, and saying the words gave strength to her faltering conviction. "Defending her maidservants."

"Is that what they told you?" the thing said. "Her body was quite hurt. Death . . . a near thing. But my master is skilled. Most skilled. Her body has made quite a pleasant home for me. Though she does scream so. And cry. She cries for forgiveness from Ardan. *Begs* for it. Who was Ardan, girl?"

The world seemed to tilt around Hweilan, and she almost dropped the bow. Her right hand could no longer hold the full tension, and she slackened the tension in the string. The point of the arrow dipped, aiming at the ground.

"Much better," the thing said.

"He told me she died," said Hweilan, more to herself, remembering the words.

The last words she'd ever spoken to her mother had been in anger. She'd never seen her again after that. Someone had *told* her that her mother was dead. Scith had told her. *She died defending her maidservants.*

"I told you, girl," the thing said, raising its voice, "there's something you'll want to see. Now . . . watch."

The arm holding Menduarthis tightened further. Hweilan thought she heard something inside him crack, and he screamed. The thing's other hand, the one gripping his face, loosened its grip slightly and moved upward. Hweilan watched in horror as one finger dug a deep gouge into Menduarthis's forehead. He screamed louder and began to thrash. Wind swept down off the mountain, swirling through the valley and raising a great cloud of dust and grit. Hweilan could no longer see the hobgoblins, and Merah and Menduarthis were only a blur in the murk.

Hweilan raised the bow again and advanced. "Stop! Stop this now!"

Two things happened at once. The thing still held Menduarthis, but his entire face was a mass of blood. All the dirt in the air was sticking to it, forming a sickly black mess. As her gaze took this in, the darkest and wettest of the blood on his forehead flared with a red light, like a smith blowing fresh life onto hot embers. At the same moment a huge form materialized out of the dust cloud behind them. It was Rhan, sword high and ready to strike.

Hweilan opened her mouth to scream for him to stop, realized the blow would fall before the words escaped her lips, and so she turned her arrow on the hobgoblin champion and loosed.

The runes blazing along the arrow's shaft lost their light, perhaps sensing they were no longer headed for their sworn enemy. The arrow was just over half the distance, headed for the thick flesh of Rhan's shoulder, when a blazing shard of light struck it in midair. The arrow absorbed the force and did not shatter, but it flew end over end, disappearing into the dust cloud.

Rhan's sword came around.

"*NO!*" Hweilan screamed.

But it was too late.

A lesser warrior might have cut both Merah and Menduarthis in half. But even in the midst of the wind, Rhan's aim was expert and true. The black sword cut through Merah's neck, barely slowing as it passed through skin, flesh, and bone. Because there was no heart beating in Merah's chest, there was no spray of blood. The body simply went limp, hitting the ground an instant before the head. Even in death, the grip held, and the headless corpse pulled Menduarthis down with it.

The wind died away at once, and the dirt in the air was already beginning to settle when Hweilan rushed forward. Rhan was standing over the bodies, neither of which were moving.

"Bastard!" Hweilan screamed, and launched herself at him. The brute was at least three times her weight and two feet taller, but Ashiin had taught her well. She knew right where to hit him, planting her heel directly beneath the spot where his ribs joined his chest. He folded in half and went down.

Although he was fighting for breath, he still made it to his feet the same time Hweilan did.

"Stop this! Stop this right *now*!"

Maaqua stepped between them, her staff raised, sparks still leaking from its length. Hweilan noted the sparks were the same color as the shaft of light that had struck her arrow.

"You stopped my arrow, y—!"

From the corner of her eye, she saw Menduarthis sit up and raise one arm. Air swirled around him, fanning his hair outward and coalescing around his outstretched hand. It formed into a concentrated mass of force that shot out and struck the hobgoblin queen, sending her tumbling through the dirt.

Hweilan sidestepped and turned to face him.

One glance, and she knew it wasn't Menduarthis. The tendons of his neck stood out taut, and his skin stretched over the tight muscles of his face. The ever-mischievous glint in his eyes had gone out, replaced by an empty hunger. And the familiar pounding in Hweilan's mind was strong as ever. The demon was still here.

She reached for an arrow at the same time that Rhan roared and charged, black sword held high.

Another funnel of concentrated air struck the hobgoblin champion. It didn't send him flying as it had Maaqua, but it did knock him off his feet and backward.

Hweilan pulled the fletching to her cheek and aimed. The runes on her bow flared, and she realized she had to kill Menduarthis. She had to—

She loosed, but another wave of air struck the arrow, and it hit the dirt a yard to Menduarthis's left. Hweilan knew she'd have to get closer.

"Listen, Maaqua!" the thing said, turning its attention to her. "We know where you are. Bring us the girl, and we'll let you live."

Hweilan charged, fitting another arrow to her bow.

The thing raised a hand and spoke a word of power. Wind and dust funneled upward in a thunderous roar, and there was an ear-shattering *clap* as air rushed in to fill empty space.

The dirt was settling, showing dozens of hobgoblin warriors approaching and confirming what Hweilan's mind already knew: Menduarthis—and the demon inside him—was gone.

• • ⊙ • •

Hweilan stood over her mother's severed head. It had landed so that the open eyes stared up at the sky. Her mother was dead.

Moreover, she had been dead for a very long time. Had Hweilan taken just a moment to think, she would have realized that. She'd seen her mother's spirit, with her father, a golden light around them. That thing might have stolen Merah's body for a time, but the heart and mind of her mother had long since joined her loved ones.

Tears fell down Hweilan's cheeks and she let loose a string of curses in every language she knew. She'd faltered. She'd failed.

"Hweilan?"

She looked up. Darric stood a few paces away, looking at her like a little boy who'd just stumbled upon a hungry wolf in the woods. Mandan stood just behind him, club in hand, doing his best to keep one eye on Hweilan and the other on the dozens of warriors watching the situation unfold.

"I should have killed it when I had the chance," she said. "If I'd loosed at it instead of Rhan . . ."

"But . . . it had your mother," said Darric. "Anyone would've—"

"That wasn't my mother."

Saying it aloud drove the point home. Killing her family . . . Hweilan had thought that was the worst thing her enemies could do to her. She'd been wrong. This was worse. This was desecration, sacrilege, blasphemy . . . no word fit. She had no word for it in any language she knew. But what it made her feel, that was easy. Rage. Fury.

What she'd been doing these past days—hunting Jagun Ghen's minions—it had been stupid. If you want to kill ten thousand ants, you kill the queen. You kill the one laying the eggs, not the ones gathering the food. She had to take care of Jagun Ghen. After that . . . the rest would be easy.

"Hweilan," said Darric, "anyone here would have done the same."

"Stop talking," said Hweilan.

"Enough of this!"

It was Maaqua, approaching them, limping and leaning heavily on her staff, one hand clutched to her chest. She looked as if she'd just had the worst day of her life, but she was very much alive, and the glint in her eye made it seem as if she was ready to skin a tiger with her bare hands.

"What are you fools waiting for?" she said. "My mind is made up. Seize them."

About the Author

Mark Sehestedt used to live in New Mexico, but he doesn't anymore. He moved to Washington State, but he doesn't live there any more either. He now lives in Midcoast Maine and has no plans to leave. He has never lived in Delaware.

RICHARD LEE BYERS

BROTHERHOOD OF THE GRIFFON

NOBODY DARED TO CROSS CHESSENTA...

BOOK I
THE CAPTIVE FLAME

BOOK II
WHISPER OF VENOM
NOVEMBER 2010

BOOK III
THE SPECTRAL BLAZE
JUNE 2011

...WHEN THE RED DRAGON WAS KING.

"This is Thay as it's never been shown before... Dark, sinister, foreboding and downright disturbing!"
—Alaundo, Candlekeep.com on Richard Byers's *Unclean*

ALSO AVAILABLE AS E-BOOKS!

Follow us on Twitter @WotC_Novels

FORGOTTEN REALMS, DUNGEONS & DRAGONS, WIZARDS OF THE COAST, and their respective logos are trademarks of Wizards of the Coast LLC in the U.S.A. and other countries. Other trademarks are property of their respective owners.
©2010 Wizards.

DUNGEONS & DRAGONS

FROM THE RUINS OF FALLEN EMPIRES, A NEW AGE OF HEROES ARISES

It is a time of magic and monsters, a time when the world struggles against a rising tide of shadow. Only a few scattered points of light glow with stubborn determination in the deepening darkness.

It is a time where everything is new in an ancient and mysterious world.

BE THERE AS THE FIRST ADVENTURES UNFOLD.

THE MARK OF NERATH
Bill Slavicsek
August 2010

THE SEAL OF KARGA KUL
Alex Irvine
December 2010

The first two novels in a new line set in the evolving world of the DUNGEONS & DRAGONS® game setting. If you haven't played . . . or read D&D® in a while, your reintroduction starts in August!

ALSO AVAILABLE AS E-BOOKS!
Follow us on Twitter @WotC_Novels

DUNGEONS & DRAGONS, D&D, WIZARDS OF THE COAST, and their respective logos are trademarks of Wizards of the Coast LLC in the U.S.A. and other countries. Other trademarks are property of their respective owners. ©2010 Wizards.

WELCOME TO THE DESERT WORLD
OF ATHAS, A LAND RULED BY A HARSH
AND UNFORGIVING CLIMATE, A LAND
GOVERNED BY THE ANCIENT AND
TYRANNICAL SORCERER KINGS.
THIS IS THE LAND OF

CITY UNDER THE SAND
Jeff Mariotte
OCTOBER 2010

*Sometimes lost knowledge is
knowledge best left unknown.*

FIND OUT WHAT YOU'RE MISSING IN THIS
BRAND NEW DARK SUN® ADVENTURE BY
THE AUTHOR OF *COLD BLACK HEARTS*.

ALSO AVAILABLE AS AN E-BOOK!
THE PRISM PENTAD
Troy Denning's classic DARK SUN
series revisited! Check out the great new editions of
*The Verdant Passage, The Crimson Legion,
The Amber Enchantress, The Obsidian Oracle,*
and *The Cerulean Storm.*

Follow us on Twitter @WotC_Novels

DARK SUN, DUNGEONS & DRAGONS, WIZARDS OF THE COAST, and their respective logos are trademarks of Wizards of the Coast LLC in the U.S.A. and other countries. Other trademarks are property of their respective owners. ©2010 Wizards.

RETURN TO A WORLD OF PERIL, DECEIT, AND INTRIGUE, A WORLD REBORN IN THE WAKE OF A GLOBAL WAR.

TIM WAGGONER'S
LADY RUIN

She dedicated her life to the nation of Karrnath. With the war ended, and the army asleep—waiting—in their crypts, Karrnath assigned her to a new project: find a way to harness the dark powers of the Plane of Madness.

REVEL IN THE RUIN
DECEMBER 2010

ALSO AVAILABLE AS AN E-BOOK!

Follow us on Twitter @WotC_Novels

EBERRON, DUNGEONS & DRAGONS, WIZARDS OF THE COAST, and their respective logos are trademarks of Wizards of the Coast LLC in the U.S.A. and other countries. Other trademarks are property of their respective owners. ©2010 Wizards.

"Now, when I hear FORGOTTEN REALMS, I think Paul S. Kemp."
— fantasy book spot.

From *The New York Times* Best-Selling Author

PAUL S. KEMP

He never knew his father, a dark figure that history remembers only as the Shadowman. But as a young paladin, he'll have to confront the shadows within him, a birthright that leads all the way back to a lost and forgotten god.

CYCLE OF NIGHT

BOOK I
GODBORN
SUMMER 2012

BOOK II
GODBOUND
FALL 2012

BOOK III
GODSLAYER
SPRING 2013

"Paul S. Kemp has . . . barreled into dark fantasy with a quick wit, incomparable style, and an unabashed desire to portray the human psyche in all of its horrific and uplifting glory."
— Pat Ferrara, Mania.com

ALSO AVAILABLE AS E-BOOKS!
Follow us on Twitter @WotC_Novels

FORGOTTEN REALMS, DUNGEONS & DRAGONS, WIZARDS OF THE COAST, and their respective logos are trademarks of Wizards of the Coast LLC in the U.S.A. and other countries. Other trademarks are property of their respective owners.
©2010 Wizards.

Want to Know Everything About Dragons?
Immerse yourself in these stories inspired by
The New York Times best-selling

A Practical Guide to
Dragons

Red Dragon Codex
978-0-7869-4925-0

Bronze Dragon Codex
978-0-7869-4930-4

Black Dragon Codex
978-0-7869-4972-4

Brass Dragon Codex
978-0-7869-5108-6

Green Dragon Codex
978-0-7869-5145-1

Silver Dragon Codex
978-0-7869-5253-3

Gold Dragon Codex
978-0-7869-5348-6

Experience the power and magic of dragonkind!

Follow us on Twitter @WotC_Novels

A Dungeons & Dragons Novel

DUNGEONS & DRAGONS, WIZARDS OF THE COAST, and their respective logos are trademarks of Wizards of the Coast LLC in the U.S.A. and other countries. Other trademarks are property of their respective owners ©2010 Wizards.

Books for Young Readers

Enjoy these fantasy adventures inspired by *The New York Times* best-selling Practical Guide series!

M⚔NSTER SLAYERS

A Companion Novel to *A Practical Guide to Monsters*
Lukas Ritter
978-0-7869-5484-1
Battle one menacing monster after another!

NOCTURNE

A Companion Novel to *A Practical Guide to Vampires*
L.D. Harkrader
978-0-7869-5502-2
Join a vampire hunter on a heart-stopping quest!

Aldwyns Academy

A Companion Novel to *A Practical Guide to Wizardry*
Nathan Meyer
978-0-7869-5504-6
Enter a school for magic where even the first day can be (un)deadly!

Follow us on Twitter @WotC_Novels

DUNGEONS & DRAGONS, WIZARDS OF THE COAST, and their respective logos are trademarks of Wizards of the Coast LLC in the U.S.A. and other countries. Other trademarks are property of their respective owners ©2010 Wizards.

Books for Young Readers

Don't wait until you're accepted into wizardry school to begin your career of adventure.

This go-to guide is filled with essential activities for wannabe wizards who want to start

RIGHT NOW!

Ever wonder how to:

Make a monster-catching net?
Improvise a wand?
Capture a werewolf?
Escape a griffon?
Check a room for traps?

Find step-by-step answers to these questions and many more in:

Young Wizards Handbook:

HOW TO TRAP A ZOMBIE, TRACK A VAMPIRE,
AND OTHER HANDS-ON ACTIVITIES FOR MONSTER HUNTERS

by A.R. Rotruck

Follow us on Twitter @WotC_Novels

DUNGEONS & DRAGONS, WIZARDS OF THE COAST, and their respective logos are trademarks of Wizards of the Coast LLC in the U.S.A. and other countries. Other trademarks are property of their respective owners. ©2010 Wizards.

Books for Young Readers

R.A. SALVATORE & GENO

STONE OF TYMORA TRILOGY

Sail the treacherous seas of the Forgotten Realms® world with Maimun, a boy who couldn't imagine how unlucky it would be to be blessed by the goddess of luck. Chased by a demon, hunted by pirates, Maimun must discover the secret of the Stone of Tymora, before his luck runs out!

Book 1 THE STOWAWAY
Hardcover: 978-0-7869-5094-2
Paperback: 978-0-7869-5257-1

Book 2 THE SHADOWMASK
Hardcover: 978-0-7869-5147-5
Paperback: available June 2010: 978-0-7869-5501-5

Book 3 THE SENTINELS
Hardcover: available September 2010: 978-0-7869-5505-3
Paperback: available in Fall 2011

"An exciting new tale from R.A. Salvatore, complete with his famously pulse-quickening action scenes and, of course, lots and lots of swordplay. If you're a fan of fantasy fiction, this book is not to be missed!"
—Kidzworld on *The Stowaway*

Follow us on Twitter @WotC_Novels

FORGOTTEN REALMS, DUNGEONS & DRAGONS, WIZARDS OF THE COAST, and their respective logos are trademarks of Wizards of the Coast LLC in the U.S.A. and other countries. Other trademarks are property of their respective owners ©2010 Wizards.

Books for Young Readers